Praise for Lexi Bl
Merc

"I can always trust Lexi Blake's Dominants to leave me breathless...and in love. If you want sensual, exciting BDSM wrapped in an awesome love story, then look for a Lexi Blake book."

~Cherise Sinclair USA Today Bestselling author

"Lexi Blake's MASTERS AND MERCENARIES series is beautifully written and deliciously hot. She's got a real way with both action and sex. I also love the way Blake writes her gorgeous Dom heroes--they make me want to do bad, bad things. Her heroines are intelligent and gutsy ladies whose taste for submission definitely does not make them dish rags. Can't wait for the next book!"

~Angela Knight, New York Times Bestselling author

"A Dom is Forever is action packed, both in the bedroom and out. Expect agents, spies, guns, killing and lots of kink as Liam goes after the mysterious Mr. Black and finds his past and his future… The action and espionage keep this story moving along quickly while the sex and kink provides a totally different type of interest. Everything is very well balanced and flows together wonderfully."

~A Night Owl "Top Pick", Terri, Night Owl Erotica

"A Dom Is Forever is everything that is good in erotic romance. The story was fast-paced and suspenseful, the characters were flawed but made me root for them every step of the way, and the hotness factor was off the charts mostly due to a bad boy Dom with a penchant for dirty talk."

~Rho, The Romance Reviews

"A good read that kept me on my toes, guessing until the big reveal, and thinking survival skills should be a must for all men."

~Chris, Night Owl Reviews

The Man from Sanctum

Other Books by Lexi Blake

ROMANTIC SUSPENSE

Masters and Mercenaries
The Dom Who Loved Me
The Men With The Golden Cuffs
A Dom is Forever
On Her Master's Secret Service
Sanctum: A Masters and Mercenaries Novella
Love and Let Die
Unconditional: A Masters and Mercenaries Novella
Dungeon Royale
Dungeon Games: A Masters and Mercenaries Novella
A View to a Thrill
Cherished: A Masters and Mercenaries Novella
You Only Love Twice
Luscious: Masters and Mercenaries~Topped
Adored: A Masters and Mercenaries Novella
Master No
Just One Taste: Masters and Mercenaries~Topped 2
From Sanctum with Love
Devoted: A Masters and Mercenaries Novella
Dominance Never Dies
Submission is Not Enough
Master Bits and Mercenary Bites~The Secret Recipes of Topped
Perfectly Paired: Masters and Mercenaries~Topped 3
For His Eyes Only
Arranged: A Masters and Mercenaries Novella
Love Another Day
At Your Service: Masters and Mercenaries~Topped 4
Master Bits and Mercenary Bites~Girls Night
Nobody Does It Better
Close Cover
Protected: A Masters and Mercenaries Novella
Enchanted: A Masters and Mercenaries Novella
Charmed: A Masters and Mercenaries Novella
Taggart Family Values
Treasured: A Masters and Mercenaries Novella
Delighted: A Masters and Mercenaries Novella, Coming June 7, 2022

Masters and Mercenaries: The Forgotten
Lost Hearts (Memento Mori)
Lost and Found
Lost in You
Long Lost
No Love Lost

Masters and Mercenaries: Reloaded
Submission Impossible
The Dom Identity
The Man from Sanctum
No Time to Lie, Coming September 13, 2022

Butterfly Bayou
Butterfly Bayou
Bayou Baby
Bayou Dreaming
Bayou Beauty
Bayou Sweetheart, Coming July 26, 2022

Lawless
Ruthless
Satisfaction
Revenge

Courting Justice
Order of Protection
Evidence of Desire

Masters Of Ménage (by Shayla Black and Lexi Blake)
Their Virgin Captive
Their Virgin's Secret
Their Virgin Concubine
Their Virgin Princess
Their Virgin Hostage
Their Virgin Secretary
Their Virgin Mistress

The Perfect Gentlemen (by Shayla Black and Lexi Blake)
Scandal Never Sleeps
Seduction in Session

Big Easy Temptation
Smoke and Sin
At the Pleasure of the President

URBAN FANTASY

Thieves
Steal the Light
Steal the Day
Steal the Moon
Steal the Sun
Steal the Night
Ripper
Addict
Sleeper
Outcast
Stealing Summer
The Rebel Queen

LEXI BLAKE WRITING AS SOPHIE OAK

Texas Sirens
Small Town Siren
Siren in the City
Siren Enslaved
Siren Beloved
Siren in Waiting
Siren in Bloom
Siren Unleashed
Siren Reborn

Nights in Bliss, Colorado
Three to Ride
Two to Love
One to Keep
Lost in Bliss
Found in Bliss
Pure Bliss
Chasing Bliss
Once Upon a Time in Bliss

Back in Bliss
Sirens in Bliss
Happily Ever After in Bliss
Far from Bliss
Unexpected Bliss, Coming 2022

A Faery Story
Bound
Beast
Beauty

Standalone
Away From Me
Snowed In

The Man from Sanctum

Masters and Mercenaries: Reloaded, Book 3

Lexi Blake

The Man from Sanctum
Masters and Mercenaries: Reloaded, Book 3
Lexi Blake

Published by DLZ Entertainment LLC at Smashwords
Copyright 2022 DLZ Entertainment LLC
Edited by Chloe Vale
ISBN: 978-1-942297-60-4

Sign up for Lexi Blake's newsletter
and be entered to win a $25 gift certificate
to the bookseller of your choice.

Join us for news, fun, and exclusive content
including free Thieves short stories.

There's a new contest every month!

Go to www.LexiBlake.net to subscribe.

Acknowledgments

I started writing the Reloaded series as the pandemic we're currently in was ramping up, and the world felt infinitely more dangerous than it had before. And more boring since we were stuck inside and confused and everything seemed upside down. I'd spent the years before traveling and seeing the world, and now I was home constantly. Looking back on those days now I realize I found something in those seemingly endless hours when the doors were closed and it was only me, my husband, our three kids, and all those dogs. I found a version of us I wouldn't have without those days. A version where we held together, relied on each other, entertained each other. I cherish these times even as I'm excited they get to be out in the world again. But mostly I found myself truly understanding why I have loved one man for the vast majority of my life. My marriage became more precious to me during this time. We discovered that when we aren't constantly moving, we like to lie in bed and cuddle and talk and simply be together. Not bad as we approach thirty years of marriage. I thought a lot about my husband and our own romance and how it could have gone the way Deke and Maddie's did. We've known each other since we were twelve, and there were plenty of times we almost lost our way. Coincidence seemed to keep throwing us together until we finally figured out it was fate all along. So this one is for my husband and the three amazing souls we were gifted.

For my family

Prologue

Madeline Hill walked toward the rec center wearing her absolute sexiest dress. It was off the rack but had a designer label, and she'd had it tailored to fit her perfectly. She planned to tell everyone she met that it was just something she had in her closet. No big deal, really. This dress was simply what she wore now that she was in Los Angeles and had a dream job in big tech.

She'd spent half a month's salary on the dress, shoes, and handbag because she needed armor. After all, she was walking into her own personal war zone, and there was an enemy combatant to deal with.

Deke Murphy was back in town on leave, and she was going to let the man know exactly what he'd missed when he'd walked away from her. When he'd dumped her and made the biggest error of his life.

I think it would be a mistake, Maddie. I love you, but I can't be the reason you give up a scholarship to Yale. You have to go.

That day had come back to her in vivid detail. Not that she couldn't remember the worst day of her life, but being here in town brought a certain sharpness to every memory. She couldn't forget that they'd been sitting on her front porch when the man she'd expected to marry had told her college was more important than their little high school romance. She'd explained that she could defer and they would find a school for him to go to, but he'd been firm. He'd stood up and walked away, and they'd barely spoken all summer long.

It had been an awful way to break up. He'd enforced his will and proven he'd never truly loved her.

Now he would see that he'd walked away from a slot machine before it paid off. Big time.

"How do you walk in those shoes?" her mother asked as they strode along the walkway between the gravel parking lot and the prefab building that hadn't been updated in what had to be twenty years.

"It's easy." It wasn't. Those shoes hurt. Human toes weren't meant to form a perfect triangle, nor were they meant to arch the way these five-inchers did. But they had that sexy red sole that would let everyone know she was successful.

She was important and she'd escaped Calhoun, California. Deke Murphy had been right when he'd said she was far too smart to stay in their rural town where any party of size had to be held in a park or the rec center because that was how small they were.

"Well, it doesn't look easy." Her mom stopped before the double doors and gave her a once-over. "You're overdressed for this, you know that, right? You're dressed for some red-carpet premiere, not an eighty-year-old woman's birthday party."

Her mother obviously didn't know how Hollywood stars dressed. "It's barely a cocktail dress, Mom. And I told you it's all I have."

It wasn't, but she would get the lecture of a lifetime if her mom knew why she was wearing it. She would talk about humility and forgiveness and how it would set her free and shit. Of course if she'd seen the price tag, that would be an entirely different lecture. It didn't matter that she made an insane amount of money for her age. One still shouldn't ever pay more than $89.99 for any piece of clothing. The very specific price was due to the amount her mom had paid for her beloved winter coat with faux fur lining.

"Well, it makes me feel dowdy, but I probably am dowdy." Her mom reached up and brushed something off her shoulder. "You look stunning, Maddie. I'm being a prickly old broad, and I promised I wouldn't be. Of course I promised myself because my mother was a prickly old broad, and now I realize why she was. Menopause is hell, baby. Don't do it."

Her mom didn't look so bad. She looked damn good for Calhoun, but there weren't many places to shop out here.

Not that Maddie generally spent her time shopping. The dress was a lie, but a necessary one. She didn't want Deke Murphy to know that most of the time she wore jeans and T-shirts because no one cared what she looked like, only that her calculations were correct. The team she was on generally lived in pop culture T-shirts, track pants, and sneakers. She was one of two women, and if she'd shown up in a dress like this the men on her team would ask who she was and where she'd taken Maddie. Jerky Joe with the 180 IQ and no social manners would stare at her boobs trying to figure out which one was bigger and would have an equation to show why one breast was obviously better than the other.

The super-intelligent were weird.

But Deke didn't need to know that. All he needed to know was that her life was fucking fabulous, and she had everything she'd ever dreamed of.

And he was still in the Army digging latrines or something. Whatever girlfriend he'd found might be pretty, but she wouldn't be winning a Nobel anytime soon, and she definitely wouldn't be able to afford her own condo.

She hated that she now considered money a way to rank the world, but he was the one who'd shoved her into it. He had to deal with the consequences.

But her mom didn't. Her mom had merely wanted what was best for her.

"Did I say thank you for coming with me?" Her mom settled her purse over her shoulder. "I can't get your father off the couch during football season. I tried to tell him that one of the men will have made sure there's a TV with the game on, but he likes his comfort."

Her father worked forty plus hours a week as a warehouse supervisor for one of the agricultural collectives in the area. He'd started at eighteen, working an entry-level position in the field, and made his way up the ladder.

He'd been so proud to send his daughter to an Ivy League school. Way happier that she had a full scholarship.

She often wondered what he would have said if she'd told him she wasn't going because she was in love with a boy. She hadn't gotten that far because once she'd told Deke what she wanted, he'd shut down all those plans.

"No problem. It's been years since I've actually gone to one of these parties," Maddie replied, butterflies starting to stir in her stomach. She didn't want to think about why. She was merely excited that she got to show the boy who'd dumped her how okay she was without him.

The last party she'd gone to had been the one the town had for the graduating class. She'd been the valedictorian and the guest of honor. They'd served lemonade and lasagna roll-ups the women from the town had made.

Deke hadn't even shown up.

Maybe he wouldn't show up today either. Maybe he was at home watching the football game, too. The idea that he wasn't in that building caused a spark of panic.

"Madeline Hill! It's been an age."

She turned and Angie Dennings was striding up the walk carrying a car seat in one hand and balancing a covered casserole dish in the other. She was dressed somewhat like Maddie's mom in a skirt and breezy blouse, though there was no doubt she was younger. But it was also obvious both women were on the same road.

Husbands, babies, casseroles.

Her mom immediately went to the younger woman's side. "Angela, you shouldn't be carrying all that weight, honey. Let me help you."

"Thank you so much, Mrs. Hill. Randy's already in there. He helped with the setup, but this sucker needed another twenty minutes in the oven. Don't burn your..." She'd started to hand her mom the casserole, but Mom picked the baby right out of her hands.

Then her mom only had eyes for the baby in the carrier who kicked fat little legs and made adorable sounds. "Come on, angel. Let's get you inside. Your great grandma will be so happy to see you. Yes, she will. Yes, she will."

Her mother started inside the rec center.

"Did your mother steal my baby?" Angie frowned at the closing doors.

"Oh, yes. I don't know if the rumor has gone around, but Evelyn Hill wants to be a grandma, and her egghead daughter is married to her career, and by this time in her life she'd already had me and don't I want that, too?" Her mom could be a handful, but she loved her. And she really liked Angie. After all, Angie's last name had once been Murphy, and Maddie had forever been fascinated by the Murphy family. "You look amazing."

Angie blushed. "For a woman who recently had a baby."

"For a woman." She would leave it at that. She walked over and hugged Deke's sister. She'd been friendly with all the Murphy sisters, but Angie was particularly easy to like. She'd only been a year ahead of her and Deke in school. She and Deke had actually double dated a couple of times with Angie and the man who would eventually become her husband.

"She should have stolen these enchiladas because they are fabulous," Angie said, stepping back and looking her over. "Speaking of fabulous. Holy crap. What happened to the cute little nerd girl? You look like you could be a Hollywood star."

That was what she was going for. Sure it was mostly makeup and a whole lot of shapewear, but she was going for glam. "This old thing? Well, I'm actually here because I had a conference in San Francisco, and I thought I should drop in for a couple of days since it's not too far out of the way. When Mom mentioned the party for your grandma, I realized this was all I had to wear. Besides boring business suits. How's everything in your world?"

How's Deke? Does he have a girlfriend? Is he happy?

Is he miserable because he knows he gave up the best thing that ever happened to him?

Angie's face went blank for a second and then she smiled. A smile that didn't hold an ounce of joy. "It's all good. Everything's good. We're kind of surrounded by babies now, and Mom and Dad are great." She paused as though considering her next words carefully. "Have you seen Deke yet?"

Thank god they were going to talk about Deke. She shrugged nonchalantly. "No. Gosh. I'm trying to remember the last time I saw Deke. I guess I haven't seen him since graduation. How's he doing?"

Like she hadn't thought about him almost every day since the day he left.

"He's... I don't know if I should do this." Angie's hands held that casserole tight.

That had not been the reaction she'd been expecting. Something was wrong. Very wrong. Her mom had only told her that she'd heard Deke was back. Now that she thought about it, she hadn't mentioned she'd seen him around town. She hadn't told her he'd come over for a visit, which he usually did. Even after they'd broken up, Deke had checked on her mom and dad while she'd been in college. "What's going on?"

Angie bit her bottom lip but finally answered. "I'm going to ask you to be nice to him. You remember that night when I picked you up and didn't tell your mom that you had been drinking out at the lake?"

It had been right after Deke had broken up with her, and she'd stupidly gone out with another guy who'd left her at a lake party when she wouldn't make out with him. Angie had been the one to save her that night. "Yes."

What the hell had put that look on Angie's face? All the butterflies fluttering around her belly suddenly turned into a knot.

"I'm calling that in, Maddie." She sniffled and seemed to be trying to hold it together. "I'm not saying you would be mean to him. I know that's not who you are, but he's fragile, and I want to make sure…"

"Fragile?" Deke was anything but fragile. He was larger than life. He always had a joke and the quirkiest view of the world. It was what attracted her to him in the first place. Yes, he was gorgeous, but that openness he had to every possibility had been what really drew her in. He was a joy to be around, and part of that was his inherent strength. She'd always felt safe with him.

"He's not home on regular leave, Madeline," Angie explained. "He's home for six weeks to see if he's even going to be fit to go back. I personally hope he doesn't, but you know how stubborn he can be. I know it's his career, but they damn near killed him, and if that means he comes home to a farm job then so be it."

Her heart threatened to stop. "Killed him? My mom didn't mention he'd been hurt."

"We're not talking about it," Angie admitted. "He did most of his healing at an Army hospital, so if he doesn't take off his clothes you can't see the scars. I don't know why but they didn't touch his face. We're not covering it up, but he doesn't want a bunch of questions. All we're saying at this point is that he was injured in an accident and he should be back on his feet soon. But it's what they did to his soul that has me worried."

"Who? Who hurt him?" She could barely breathe at the thought of him being hurt. Had she spent the whole morning making herself as pretty as she could so she could find some revenge on him? Or because she'd hoped he might want to talk, might want to reconnect.

She'd been fooling herself because this panic wasn't about not getting revenge. It was about him possibly not being okay.

He was supposed to be okay.

"Maddie, Deke was captured by jihadists and held prisoner. He was freed by his unit but…he won't talk about what happened. Mom says he wakes up screaming and she doesn't know what to do. So I'm asking you not to do this." She gestured up and down. "All of this. He doesn't need you to show him how much better off you are. He knows."

"I'm not…" Damn it. She couldn't force the rest of the lie from her lips.

"Of course you are." Angie brushed away a tear. "I probably would, too, if I was in your position. I know how hurt you were. Or I wouldn't because I'm smarter than you in this way. I know damn well my brother didn't break up with you because he was bored or whatever excuse your big brain makes. He did it because he couldn't stand the thought of being in your way."

Hadn't she heard this a million times? "He wasn't in my way. I was going to defer. I was going to give us time to find a better way than him going into the Army. A year wouldn't have made a difference."

"It would have," Angie insisted. "You wouldn't have made it to Yale. You would have found another excuse and another until you were stuck here and you married him and had babies and didn't use those extraordinary talents you were given. And one day you would have resented him for it. You would have resented all of us. Do you love what you do, Madeline? Would you change places with me? I love my life, but it's mine. It's right for me. I don't think it would have been right for you. Tell me something, and you be brutally honest with me. Would you give up your job to be home with a couple of kids in rural California? Would you change places with me?"

Maddie felt a tear slip onto her cheek. She wanted to argue, to tell Angie that she had no idea what her life was like and what it would have been, but all she could think about was the fact that Deke screamed in the night and she'd wanted him to be miserable. So honesty took over. "No, I wouldn't. I want a family but not now. I don't hate this town. I have fond memories of it, but it's not my home anymore. I don't want a husband or kids right now. It would be very difficult to balance that life against my career. Now I want to see how far I can go. I want this chance."

She was on the cusp of an exciting life, of a life she'd dreamed about.

The one she'd wanted to share with Deke, but now she had to consider the fact that it wouldn't have been possible if she'd stayed here.

"Then don't do this to him."

Her heart ached. Maybe it always had. Maybe it hadn't stopped aching since the day he'd left her, but she'd buried the hurt under layers of arrogance. She felt it now, felt the keening hurt that had become a part of her. "He wouldn't want to see me?"

Angie's gaze softened. "I think he wouldn't want you to see him like this."

He was a proud man, and it would hurt him to have her see him so low. If she was in his life, she could insist on it, but they weren't together. They were miles and miles apart despite the fact that he was right behind those doors. "Is he talking to someone?"

"Who is he going to talk to out here?" Angie asked with a sigh. "He sits. Sometimes he watches TV with Dad, but mostly he just sits, and we try our hardest to take care of him but nothing seems to make a difference."

Shame washed through her. Deke was going through something horrible and she couldn't be around him, couldn't try to help because she'd shunned him for years. Once he'd broken up with her, she'd cut off their friendship, and now that seemed like such a terrible thing to do.

Oddly, even over the years she'd felt close to him. She'd made him the bad guy in her world, and that had been a way to keep him in her life without giving up an ounce of her pride.

But she remembered who he was. "He has trouble asking for help. Do you remember how he was when he broke his leg junior year? He was the biggest bear. He hated feeling helpless."

23

Angie nodded. "He gave my mom such hell because he wouldn't stay down. That's what scares me now. He's here but he's not here. I think he's back there, and I don't know how to reach him. And these stupid enchiladas are his favorite, and he's not going to eat them. He barely eats at all. But I don't know what to do so I bake enchiladas and muffins."

Deke was a man who needed to do something. He needed to feel like he was contributing.

He was a man who needed to be needed in order to feel centered.

"You can't treat him like an invalid. I know you want to take care of him, but that might mean something different with Deke. You need to give him something to do. Make him responsible for something," Maddie said. "Even if it's dumb. He needs a task to focus on, the more important the better."

"He's recovering from a couple of injuries. He needs rest," Angie replied.

And then it hit her. Deke loved kids. He'd been the teenaged boy who genuinely didn't mind watching younger kids. He would have them playing football or having tea parties with teddy bears. They lived in a small, working-class town. The older kids were always watching the younger ones, and Deke never resented it. "Make him feed the baby. Babies. Didn't Sharon have one six months ago?"

Angie nodded. "Yes, and Laurie had one two months before me. Mom calls us a baby factory, but that's what happens when you have five girls in eight years. You think that would help? He seems so distant."

"So bring him back." She wanted to walk into that rec center and wrap her arms around him, but she believed Angie that her presence could cause him distress.

They'd made their choices. He'd chosen to walk away rather than be the reason she stayed, and she'd chosen to be angry with the boy she'd loved since she'd first laid eyes on him.

They could have found a friendship, reconnected, but she'd been hurt and now she couldn't help him.

"Show him life didn't stop." Maddie was absolutely sure of this path. "Make him look down at his nephews and nieces and realize he still matters, that no matter how broken he feels, he can put himself back together. If he gives you trouble tell him how much you have to do and that you could use his help. Make him feel a little bad so he can find a way to feel good again."

"That could work." Angie sounded hopeful. "Cover him in babies. I can do that."

Maddie gave her a smile that wouldn't camouflage the fact that she was crying. "Good. Tell my mom work called and there's a problem I need to deal with. I'll come pick her up when she's ready."

"Maddie, I..." Angie began.

But she'd made her point, and there was nothing to do about it now. Maddie fished the keys to her overly expensive car out of her bag. "No, it's okay. I don't want to make this about me. I've already done that enough. And this is absolutely the first time I've worn this dress and these shoes, and I will probably never wear them again because they are uncomfortable."

She started for her car.

"I'll tell your mom," Angie promised. "And, Maddie, thank you."

She nodded and forced herself to walk away. It was time to move on. She thought she had, but if there was one thing she was absolutely certain of it was the fact that she'd never gotten over Deke Murphy.

Not even a little bit.

* * * *

He was surrounded by people he loved and he couldn't feel a thing. He felt numb, like someone had hollowed out his insides and he was walking around empty.

All in all, it wasn't how he'd thought his big homecoming would go.

Deke sat at one of the folding tables the ladies of his family had decorated with the same tablecloths they'd probably used at the party to celebrate his parents' marriage thirty plus years ago. That was how little things changed in Calhoun. Once he'd found the familiarity comforting. Now it was jarring because he knew he should recognize his childhood hometown as soothing, but his world was colored with blood and violence and anger.

He knew how small he was.

He knew how fragile he was.

The comforts of family and home could be stripped away so easily.

The doors came open and he watched as Evelyn Hill walked in carrying a familiar looking car seat. He was sure one of his nieces or nephews was in it. His sisters were breeding like rabbits.

He watched to see if Maddie walked in behind her mom. She was in town. His father had mentioned that casually this morning over the eggs and toast his mom had made. He'd barely touched it before, and after the news that the only woman he'd ever loved was not two miles away, he hadn't eaten at all.

He wasn't hungry anymore. Not for food or drinks or drugs. It was weird but he kind of wished he wanted drugs. It would mean he wanted something. Instead, he simply wanted to sleep, but even there he was tormented by dreams that seemed more real than his waking life.

What would Maddie think when she saw him? She would probably get down on her knees and thank the heavens he'd made the choice he'd made. He knew damn well she still resented him for leaving her. That would go away if she knew how easily he'd broken. She would be happy he'd spared her the horrors of being chained to him.

He'd played the encounter out in his head a thousand times. She would be gorgeous and happy. She would smile at him, but this time it would be the kind of smile someone gave a suffering creature to show solidarity and sympathy. She would ask him how he was doing and he would say what he always said. As good as can be.

And then she would walk away and go back to changing the

world. He would sit here and watch the world pass him by.

"Anything I can get you, son?" His mother had a red plastic cup in her hand, likely filled with lemonade or whatever punch she'd made. "Aunt Betty brought her seven-layer dip and deviled eggs, though she and Bobbie are arguing over whether to call them spiced eggs. I swear that new church Bobbie's going to takes things way too seriously. She brought an angel food cake to balance out Marian's devil's food cupcakes."

"I'm fine." The words were said with a calculated uptick of his lips. He'd practiced it in the mirror, a necessary mask to help him get through the next few weeks until he could get back to his real life.

His real life was Special Forces and whatever dangerous assignment he could get. A man had visited him while he was in the hospital. A man who hadn't introduced himself, merely asked him the same questions his superiors had and then gone deeper.

At the end of the interview the man had promised if he came back, there would be a job for him on his team.

His CIA team.

It felt like a good way to bury all the pain. It might be a good way to bury himself entirely.

His mother sniffled, but obviously tried to cover her frustration with him. "All right, then. You should know that Angie's made your favorite enchiladas. I hope you can eat some. Oh, there's Evelyn. I should go say hello."

He didn't want enchiladas. He wanted to see Maddie, wanted to know exactly how far out of reach she was now. When he'd been in high school he'd known she was too smart, too talented to end up saddled with him for life. Oh, it hadn't stopped him from falling crazy in love with her or from having two great years with her. But when she'd gotten into Yale…

He wanted to see how happy she was so he could know he'd done one good thing.

The door came open again but it was only the youngest of his sisters.

27

He had five. His parents had kept trying until they'd had the son they'd wanted so desperately. Not that they didn't love all their kids, but they'd wanted a son, too.

How disappointed would they be when they realized he wasn't good enough to carry on the family name?

He didn't think he would live long enough to carry on anything at all.

Angie's face was flushed, and he hoped she hadn't been crying. Everyone seemed to be crying these days. Not in front of him, of course. They did it behind closed doors and pretended everything was fine and great, and hey, did he need anything?

"Did you remember to take your meds?" His father was standing there with a bottle of pills in his hand. "The doc was hoping you would start on them this week, but I didn't see you take them this morning."

He reached out and grabbed the pills from his dad's hand. "I'll take them when I'm ready."

"They take a while to work." His father adjusted his glasses. "I've been reading up on them. It might take a while to adjust, and they might have to play around to get to the right dose. I was hoping you could make sure the dose is right before you think about going back."

"Dad, I really need some space."

He'd learned those were the magic words. He said them and his family backed off.

"All right. Just know we're here for you." His father stepped away.

Deke stared down at the antidepressants the doctor had prescribed. He wasn't that guy, right? He didn't need a pill. He needed to man up and get through it.

Or get back to work and let the inevitable play out.

He pocketed the pills. Why his father thought he should bring them to a birthday party he had no idea. They were perfectly happy sitting in the bathroom completely unused.

He sat back, listening to the conversations going on around him. They talked about soccer practices and whether the 49ers had what it would take to get to the playoffs. They complained about health conditions he didn't recognize but was probably going to know too much about if he kept listening in because his elderly relatives could really overshare.

None of it touched him. Once he would have thrown himself into tales of Uncle Earnest's battle with gout and offered to walk Clementine's service dog who needed way more actual service than Clem. He would have seen the surreal humor in all of it.

Now he felt nothing.

"Hey, Deke. I need you to feed Nicholas." Angie set the baby carrier on the table along with a bottle. She quickly had his nephew out of the car seat, and the little thing was already wriggling.

She wanted him to what?

He mentally corrected his previous thoughts. Panic. He could feel some panic. It pushed through the numbness and made him remember bad things could still happen to him. "Ang, go ask Mom. I haven't fed a baby before."

"Mom is trying to deal with cousin Christine, who is crying because someone criticized her meatballs and now she's sure she'll never find a husband," Angie countered. "You know how these things go. It's chaos."

It was, but chaos could be fun. If he was the man he'd been before, he would be playing his devil's food cupcake aunt off the angel food one to see how much he could eat before they realized what he was doing. But he wasn't that man anymore. He was the man who had no idea how to feed a kid he couldn't toss a sandwich at. "I don't know what to do."

"It's easy. You shove the nipple end into his mouth. I know you know what a nipple looks like. I remember your high school years," she said with a no-nonsense practicality he remembered but hadn't seen from her since he'd gotten home. Angie had been his closest sister and the one who always let him know when he was being a moron. Now she was one of the ones who cried a lot because she didn't know what to do with him. "Honestly, get it anywhere close and he'll take care of things."

She passed him over so quickly he had no choice but to hold the kid. Or he would drop him, and he couldn't do that. Damn. She pressed the bottle into his hand and stepped back.

He couldn't do this. What the hell? "Angie, I need some space."

He used his magic, get-out-of-jail-free-card words.

His sister put her hands on her hips and looked so much like their mom he almost laughed. "And I need to get Grandma's cake fixed because some dumbass didn't keep the box flat and now I've got icing roses that look like they exploded. Do you want to fix that? Or sit there and feed a hungry baby? I will warn you that Janine took a class at the hobby store and thinks she knows how to fix things. She won't touch the cake herself because she doesn't want to take the blame. But she has no problem bossing me around. Which one, Deke? Which one sounds like more fun?"

They both sounded terrible, and since when did he have to make choices? He thought the whole got-tortured-by-jihadist thing would have bought him more time, but his sister looked serious.

"Baby." Dealing with Janine when she thought she knew how to do something was awful. She used to tell him he was throwing the football wrong when she'd never played. Not once. "I'll hold the baby."

Angie nodded and strode away.

He looked down at the kid. It happened so fast. Surely there was someone who would take him.

He was at a family function. Everyone held babies at these things. They passed them around like candy.

He glanced around but no one was close. They were all in little clusters, all talking and having a great time.

A short cry grabbed his attention.

He looked down and Nicky was staring up at him with big wide eyes and a trembling mouth that let him know he could do much worse than that little cry if he didn't get what he needed.

"I thought your mom was breastfeeding."

Like the baby would answer him.

Damn it. He winced as the answer hit him. "She probably pumped and now it's in the bottle, and I know I'm supposed to be cool with everything, but it's gross, kid. She's my sister. Nothing is supposed to come out of her boobs. It's like she doesn't have boobs."

That mouth opened again, and he'd been right. Nicky could amp it up when he wanted to.

Still no one came to his rescue.

Deke had that ick-came-out-of-his-sister's-boobs bottle in his nephew's mouth as fast as he could.

Someone would save him. No one was going to leave him sitting here with a baby. He was fucked up. He wasn't supposed to hold sweet little helpless babies.

He'd been helpless. Like this baby.

Nicky's chubby hands came up and over Deke's as though he wanted to make sure the bottle stayed right where it was. As if he wanted his uncle to stay right where he was.

Here. With his family.

He had been helpless. He'd been a baby, and his father had held him and fed him and changed him. His mother hadn't cared that he couldn't fight, couldn't take care of himself.

He was a grown man, but did that matter?

Something loosened inside him in that moment, something that previously made his chest tight. He wasn't sure what it was, but it didn't matter.

He sat there, staring into his nephew's eyes. He hadn't really looked at the kid before. He had Angie's eyes.

The future was right there. Right in his hands.

"Hey, do you want me to take him?" His father was there. "Nicky can be a handful."

Deke stared down at his nephew, who was managing to grin around the nipple. The kid was cute. "Nah. I'm good. I could use some water though."

He might try the pills. What could it hurt? It would make his parents feel better. It wouldn't be for him. It was for them.

His father jogged off, obviously eager to help.

Deke sat back, a weird peace coming over him.

He still wished he could have seen Maddie, but maybe it was all for the best.

When his sister Ashley exchanged Nicky for her daughter, he grumbled.

But he fed that one, too.

Chapter One

Fourteen years later
Dallas, TX

Madeline Hill stood outside the upscale apartment building and stared up.

Deke was in that building. He lived right here according to all her research. Fourteenth floor. All she had to do was walk in, find the elevator, search for 14B, and knock on his door. He would open it and she would see him.

Or she could knock and knock and he wouldn't answer because he was on a date or out with friends or he could see her through the peephole and hide because she hadn't seen him since she'd left for college.

Weariness battled with adrenaline, and it was making her feel like the world was about to explode. Of course, she was the one who'd pushed that button, so she had no one to blame but herself.

Her cell phone buzzed and she pulled it out of her pocket like it was a lifeline, praying it was her mom or dad or even work. Anything that would give her another fifteen or twenty minutes before she had to explain to Deke why she needed his help.

Before he probably laughed at her and told her to take a hike.

She grimaced at the name. Daniel Gray was her latest experiment in modern-day dating. She'd put herself out there on a dating app specifically made for men and women in high tech and science fields. After a couple of truly awful experiences where dumbass men tried to explain her own field of expertise to her, she'd matched with Dan. He was in biotech and a good listener. Five dates in and he hadn't even tried to make a move on her. It was comforting. He was easy to be around.

She was totally uninterested in him. She wished she wasn't, wished he could be the guy who made her heart race, but the chemistry wasn't there.

She let the call go to voice mail. She wasn't going to ghost the guy, but it wasn't a love match.

Would it be if she gave it time? If he'd come into her life before she'd found herself here, standing on the precipice of being near Deke again?

Not that it would matter. They'd made their choices a very long time ago, and she was at peace with the fact that Deke had done her a favor. He'd been right to break it off, and she was grateful to him. Over the last couple of years she'd even gotten to the point that she didn't think about him every day. Once or twice a year she got wistful about him, but she'd moved on.

This was a mistake. Bringing him back into her life was a huge mistake, and maybe one she couldn't afford.

A text came over her screen, this one from her boss. Nolan Byrne. He was one of the world's most successful inventors.

And Maddie was worried he was also a killer. He was the very reason she was standing here.

Thanks for the new reports. Good work on the interface. It looks like we're on track for launch. Changing the world, baby!

He called everyone *baby*. Men. Women. His cat. She didn't read a thing into it. He was a genius, and she'd learned oftentimes genius came with weird habits. Male geniuses were especially likely to indulge their own oddities. The women, well, they were still women, and there were expectations even on the most gifted. She stood on the steps that led to the building and quickly typed her response.

Awesome. I'm super excited about it.

One of the ways to deal with Nolan was to be as over-the-top enthusiastic as he was. She sometimes thought of him as the tech version of Willy Wonka, and the rest of them were Oompa-Loompas just trying to get by while making all the candy and singing all the songs.

I'm excited about meeting your guy and getting into that club. Enjoy your vacay, M. See you back here on Monday. I'll take your guy to lunch. N signing off!

Fuck. Fuck. Fuck. She grimaced and sent off a quick round of smiley face emojis and little suns since she was supposed to be in Sedona on a girls trip this weekend, not visiting her long-lost ex-boyfriend who might be the only person in the world who could get her out of the corner she'd placed herself in.

Why, why, why had she done something this freaking dumb?

She was going to lose her job and if she did, she might never find out what Nolan was up to.

Well, until the world exploded.

Yes, this was something she had to do. It didn't matter how embarrassing it was going to be. Two people had lost their lives to whatever Nolan was plotting, and she wasn't about to let more victims get sucked in.

She strode up the steps, forcing her feet to move. She pressed the button on the elevator, got in, and pushed number fourteen. When the doors opened, she strode out even as her heart started to pound.

When she got to his door she heard the sound of laughter coming from inside and hesitated for a moment.

He had people over. The clock was closing in on midnight and he had guests. Probably a girlfriend. She should...

She knocked on the door. She hadn't come here because she was trying to reignite a flame. She wasn't here to have fun and catch up. She was here because people's lives were on the line and Deke was the only person in the world she trusted who had the right skills and connections to help her.

She put a hand on her backpack strap to stop the fine tremble that had come over her.

She was wearing jeans and a T-shirt and sneakers. In the last eighteen hours she'd been on three different planes in case anyone was following her. She'd had little sleep and was pretty sure her hair was going everywhere.

So different from the polished woman she'd wanted to show him fourteen years before. He was getting the full-on real-world Maddie Hill, and she was a hot mess, but that was okay because she was over him now, truly and fully.

Right? He was probably a hot mess, too.

The door came open and she realized she'd been halfway right in her assessment.

He was hot.

So freaking hot.

Somehow she'd thought he would still be the man Angie had described all those years ago. Broken, tragedy etched on his face. She'd been told he'd gotten better, left the military, found a job in Dallas and was doing well.

He looked like he was fan-freaking-tastic, and she was a mess who had to tell him she was also an idiot who'd done the stupidest thing in her life and she needed him to save her.

That suddenly seemed like a terrible idea, but she didn't have another one.

He stood in the doorway, staring at her like she was an alien being who'd dropped down from space.

There was nothing else to do but brave her way through and pray he could help her out for old time's sake. "Hey, Deke."

He wore a white dress shirt that had probably included a tie at one point. It was unbuttoned at the throat, but the collar was a little wrinkled as if Deke had pulled a tie through it before he'd tossed it aside. Black slacks and dress shoes completed the ensemble. "Hey."

Well, at least he didn't slam the door in her face.

She heard someone laugh in the background and glanced up and down the hall. Despite all her subterfuge, she was still a little worried that her boss would figure out she wasn't where she was supposed to be. She'd made sure her cell would show her in Sedona. She'd left her personal phone in a hotel room she'd rented and then written a code that duped her phone and sent it to the burner she was using. She knew the tech and had carefully researched how to fool anyone who might casually try to figure out where she was.

But if someone was physically following her, she was fucked.

"Can I come in? I'm afraid I've got a problem and you're the only one who can help me." She prayed he would help her and that he didn't laugh in her face and send her on her way.

She also prayed her intel was correct and she wasn't about to embarrass the hell out of both of them.

"I am?" He shook his head as though trying to clear it. "I mean what kind of problem?"

His dark hair had the faintest hint of gray right at his temples, but otherwise she couldn't see the years on him. Oh, he was definitely more masculine than he'd been, but it was hard not to see the youthful Deke she'd loved so much.

But she was over him, and this was nothing more than a job. "The national security kind." He was quiet for a moment, and she felt another surge of panic at the idea of him closing that door. "I'm in over my head. Please, Deke."

She hated begging, but she couldn't let him shut her out. Not when there was so much on the line.

He stepped aside, opening the door wide and letting her in.

Relief flooded her system and she walked inside. The minute he closed the door behind her, she felt some modicum of safety.

"I'm sorry it's so late. I just got into Dallas, and I came straight here." She'd taken a cab and paid cash.

"Are you okay? Is someone following you?" Deke moved to the end of the entryway. "Hey, MaeBe, can you hop online and check the CCTV cams around the building? Go back at least fifteen minutes."

Maddie followed him and found herself staring into his living room/dining area. It was a big space with a couple of armchairs and a comfy-looking couch. Everyone seemed to be congregated in the dining room, however. Deke had a big table that was covered in…holy shit. Deke Murphy played board games?

Deke Murphy was a jock who played football and baseball and effortlessly won at both. He was the popular guy who everyone looked up to. She was the nerd who played board games.

A pink-haired young woman popped out of her seat as though she'd just been waiting for something to go wrong. "Sure thing, Deke. Am I looking for anything specific?"

"I'd like to see if anyone might have followed my friend here," Deke replied.

"Something going on?" A man with piercing green eyes and super-short dark hair asked. He looked military.

There were several women and men around the table. The men were all dressed in a similar fashion to Deke, dress shirts and slacks. The women were in cocktail dresses.

"I don't know yet, but I want to be careful." Deke gestured her way. "This is an old friend of mine from high school. Her name is Madeline Hill."

A stunningly gorgeous blond guy whistled. "The Maddie Hill?"

"Not now, Boom," Deke said with a shake of his head. "Maddie works for Nolan Byrne."

A collective gasp went through the room, and she realized where she was. She was in a hall of geeks. Her people.

She hadn't expected them to be Deke's, yet here she was in a room full of people playing an economic game based around small woodland creatures and their railroads and who likely worshipped Nolan Byrne.

"Who's that?" Except the gorgeous blond guy who seemed to know who she was. He was also huge. Like he was probably taller than she was right now and he was sitting down.

"Dude, even I know that and I'm usually the dummy of this group," the man with the military cut said.

"Not if I'm here," Blond Hunk shot back.

"That's why I said *usually*," Military Cut replied.

"Don't be rude," Pink-Haired Hacker said to Military Cut, and mentally Maddie put them together. There was something about the rebuke that screamed girlfriend.

That wasn't the only conclusion Maddie could draw. There was no question in Maddie's mind what Pink Hair did for a living. She'd basically walked off the pages of a techno thriller. Pink Hair worked in cybersecurity, and likely for the same firm as Deke. They weren't two people who looked like they would fit together except for the forced proximity of work. It could make for unlikely friendships.

"To answer Boomer's question, Nolan Byrne is a god of the tech world." The man who spoke was leaner than the rest and had what looked like a Red Vine in his mouth. He talked around the candy like he'd done it a million times. "He started out in the gaming world, made his first billion by inventing the chip that powers most virtual reality headsets now. He then moved on to smart cars."

"I want a Byrne so bad," Pink Hair said with a sigh. "I can't afford one, but I want it. It fully integrates with everything. Like I could plug it into my smart home and tell it to charge up and I don't have to do anything. It's that cool. It's also got a hands-free drive function. I can't believe you…" Pink Hair stopped and frowned suddenly. "He's evil, isn't he? Damn it. I should have known."

"I didn't say that," Maddie stammered.

"Of course he's evil," a feminine voice said. She was a pretty woman wearing a cardigan over her dress. She had a heavy cane leaning on the table at her side. "He's managed to make billions of dollars in three different tech fields. He's barely forty. I assure you he's stepped on people. He's into satellites now, isn't he?"

"Yes." Maddie was on the team that was set to launch the first new model in six weeks. She had six weeks to figure out what was wrong with that satellite.

"Baby, just because a tech guru tried to kill you doesn't mean Deke's high school girlfriend is here because her tech guru is a bad guy," Red Vine said, winking Cardigan's way.

"Girlfriend?" Military Cut seemed interested again.

"Hey, can we focus?" Deke stepped in behind Pink Hair. "You got anything?"

"No one except her for the last hour. The building's quiet. She waited on the steps for a long time, though. She's nervous about seeing you," Pink Hair said.

"I was…I was trying to remember if this was the right building." Who the hell were these people and why was she slightly afraid of them?

"They all look similar in this part of the city." Deke was obviously trying to smooth things over for her because that was a complete lie. The buildings were all arty and different. "Maddie, let me introduce you to my friends. This is MaeBe Vaughn. She and Hutch are part of McKay-Taggart's cyber team. McKay-Taggart is…"

She knew exactly who they were. "The company you work for."

He nodded. "Yeah. I'm on an investigative team. I often work with Brian Ward, but we all call him Boomer."

The blond hottie waved. "Hi, Deke's old girlfriend."

Deke ignored that entirely. He quickly pointed to the rest of his friends. Hutch was the guy with the Red Vine. His wife was Noelle, and she was in biotech. Kyle Hawthorne was Military Cut, and he was a bodyguard.

MaeBe closed her laptop and slid it inside what looked to be a well-worn bag, slinging it over her shoulder. "If someone's following her, they aren't sticking close. All is quiet outside." She turned Maddie's way. "Do you have a cell?"

Maddie pulled out the piece of crap she was carrying. "My cell is in a secure location. I have it forwarded to this burner. I've got someone I trust moving it around."

Her cousin thought she was running some tests and that was why she needed to take the cell phone to the spa and a couple of other places Maddie was paying for before bringing it back to her hotel room every night. She'd thought it was a weird request but had been thrilled at the thought of a paid vacation with her boyfriend.

"She's good," Deke said. "She knows what she's doing when it comes to tech."

"Well, some of it, anyway." She didn't want him to think she was some super expert who didn't need any help. After all, she desperately needed his. "I've worked in high end and experimental tech for years. I'm excellent with robotics, but I had to figure out how to deal with the cell."

A smirk hit Deke's gorgeous face. "You were always good on your feet."

He'd been good on his feet. She remembered a time when he'd simply picked her up and slid her onto his dick and fucked her without her feet ever hitting the floor.

The boy had been good, and now she was wondering if the man wasn't even better.

Of course he would be. Practice made perfect, and he'd had years to master the art of pleasure.

And this was exactly why she should have hired an actor.

She felt her whole body flush and was almost certain the man knew exactly what she was thinking, but she needed to get to the heart of the matter. "I'm sorry to disrupt your..." It wasn't a game night. They wouldn't be dressed the way they were. This group had been at some sort of event. "Were you at a wedding? Or was it a graduation? It's Thursday. Odd day for either."

"See, I told you she was smart." Deke's lips quirked up. "It was a wedding. It was scheduled for Thursday because the groom is a sentimental man. This is the same day his parents got married. His dad died. He wants to make the day happy and special again."

"And the bride is super cheap, and getting married on a Thursday night is hella cheaper than Friday or Saturday," Kyle explained before holding up his hands as though to ward off attack. "Hey, Tessa's words, not mine."

Deke rolled his eyes and sighed. "And it's not a problem. We were about to break up. Unlike the bride, we still have to be at work tomorrow."

"Which means whoever has the most points right now wins," Kyle said.

Noelle's eyes narrowed. "It means the game didn't conclude."

Hutch stood. "Come along, my overly competitive love."

"Uh, pizza. We called in pizza." Boomer suddenly looked crestfallen.

"Hey, there's a twenty-four-hour diner on the way home." MaeBe stepped up beside Boomer. "We can get some late-night breakfast."

"I could eat," Kyle said, stretching. "What do you say we move this party?"

As the rest of the group started packing up, Hutch moved in close to Deke. "You need backup?"

Deke looked her way. "Do you think you need more of a bodyguard than me?"

She shook her head. She wasn't sure she needed a bodyguard at all. "I just need to talk to you."

"Call us if you need us." Hutch patted his arm in a friendly gesture that made her think they were long-time friends.

She didn't know who his friends were. She didn't know what his life was like, with the exception of stories she heard from her mom when she went home. And that one little thing Angie had let slip when they'd had lunch about six months ago.

It's the craziest thing, but I'm almost one hundred percent certain my brother joined a BDSM club. Like years ago. He wore this T-shirt with a logo for a club in Dallas called Sanctum, and when I looked it up all I could find was some stuff about this underground sex club. I asked him and he told me to mind my own business. It's weird, right?

She'd done her own research. That was probably why she'd been dumb enough to step into the trap she had. She'd been able to find out that Sanctum was in fact a BDSM club. The membership was supersecret, but she'd determined that the building itself was owned by Ian Taggart—Deke's employer.

She'd been curious, and then she'd been arrogant.

Deke said good-bye to his friends. She heard the door close, and her tension ratcheted up by a mile.

She was alone with the man who'd taken her virginity. Well, she'd given it to him. And he'd given her his. They'd been virgins together. It was weird to be standing here, and the stress of the day threatened to overwhelm her.

"All right, to what do I really owe this pleasure, Maddie?" Deke asked in that deep voice of his. He'd had it even in high school. "And it is a pleasure. It's good to see you. It's been a long time."

So long. How had she let all these years go by and not called? She'd even stopped asking about him. Angie had been the one who brought him up when she'd been in LA and they'd had lunch. Maddie had sunk into her career and become everything she'd hoped to be. The girl she'd been, the one who'd loved the boy he'd been, had been forgotten. "Yeah. It's been a long time."

He shook his head. "How have you... I'm sorry. This isn't a friendly visit. How can I help?"

Had she thought even for a second that he would turn her away? He wasn't that man. He was a good man who took care of the people around him, and she felt so alone. She didn't know a single man like Deke Murphy, and she'd stayed away from him. She'd let years go by because it was easier than admitting she'd made a mistake when she'd

43

shut him out.

They'd been friends. Good friends. They wouldn't be again. They couldn't be more than old friends who met up every now and then when they were in their hometown at the same time. Their chance was gone and it wouldn't come again, but he was still a bastion of everything that had once been good and safe in her life.

The world went watery, and she couldn't hold it back another second. "I need you to be my Dom."

His jaw actually dropped.

And that was the moment she burst into tears.

* * * *

Deke stood there for a moment, completely unsure of what the hell to do.

I need you to be my Dom.

What did she mean by that? Because she couldn't possibly mean what he thought she meant. Maddie Hill couldn't know what that word meant. And then there were all the tears.

She'd burst into tears, and not the pretty kind. Maddie almost never cried. At least she hadn't when they were kids. Her tears built and built and built until they came out like a chaotic waterfall of pure emotion.

"I'm sorry," she said, obviously trying to get herself under control. "I'm so sorry. I didn't mean to do this. It's been such a long day."

"It's okay." He said the words even though he knew she wasn't. This was a Maddie he knew well.

Anxiety. She'd had it as a kid, but they hadn't known what to call it. She'd been the smartest kid in town, pushed by everyone to greater and greater heights, and it had taken a toll on her. Even he'd pushed her. She would work and work, and then she would do this. She would hold it all in until it erupted, and she wouldn't acknowledge that she'd felt the attack coming but kept going. Sometimes he would see her rub her chest like it was far too tight for her to breathe.

And even as a dumbass kid, he'd known there was a price to be paid to be as talented and driven as Maddie was.

"Hey, come here." He hadn't known what to do then, had viewed those outbursts as one of Maddie's weaknesses. He would step away when she had these episodes and joke with his friends that she was probably on her period. He'd been an asshole. He'd been wrong, but he'd learned a lot since then. "Let's breathe together. You're having an anxiety attack. I know them well. So let's breathe together and get through it."

She shook her head. "I can stop."

Still so stubborn. She still needed to be Super Girl, or maybe he should call her Wonder Woman because she was definitely not a girl anymore. "I know you can, but I can help. I've had many a panic attack. Come on, Maddie. I've been in therapy for almost twenty years. Let me use some of it. Breathe with me."

Her hands squeezed his. "Okay."

"Close your eyes and concentrate on your breath." He'd been through this with the therapists he'd seen since he'd been rescued. At first it had been a rotating door through the Army care he'd been given, and then the solid presence of Kai Ferguson in his life. Kai was the therapist who worked with McKay-Taggart, and more importantly with Sanctum. He now had a clinic here in Dallas that specialized in trauma and PTSD. "Let it fill your chest and nothing else matters. Everything else can fall away because you can handle this."

Her breath hitched. "You don't even know what it is."

He lowered his forehead to hers. Physical touch had comforted Maddie back in high school. If she stepped away from him, he would back off, but he wanted to help her any way he could. "I don't need to. I know you can handle it. I'll help you."

She sighed and seemed to relax slightly. "Just like that?"

"Just like that." What had it taken for her to come to him? He'd broken her heart. He wasn't going to make it hard for her. "I'm going to help you. That's not even a question, so put it out of your mind.

Now take a breath. Feel it inside your chest. Nothing else matters but that breath."

She took a shaky breath, but he could feel her start to steady. She leaned against him and breathed in and out, each breath slower and more deliberate than the last, each one bringing her closer and closer to the calm she needed.

"You're okay. You're safe here," he promised, trying to keep his voice soft.

Maddie was here. Maddie was here and she needed his help, and damn if his stupid heart didn't thud at the thought.

Maddie's shoulders came down as she continued to breathe, and for a moment he could feel them synching up, their breaths matched and in harmony, as though she could breathe in that placid piece of himself and it soothed her.

She might not be calming down if she knew there was a part of him that hoped her situation was really fucking bad, like end of the world, throw them together for weeks at a time and if the world's going to explode, we might as well sleep together bad.

Because he wanted her. Maybe it was the fact that he'd attended a wedding this evening and that had him thinking about his shitastic love life, but he didn't care. He'd thought about Maddie for the first time in forever and she'd shown up on his doorstep looking like the sexiest, slightly rumpled lady genius he'd ever seen.

Fate. That was what had happened tonight. Pure fate.

I need you to be my Dom.

The words had gone straight to his dick. It was a damn good thing that he hadn't hugged her or she would have felt what that sentence had done to him.

Careful. He needed to be careful with her. From what his sisters had told him, she wasn't married. She'd been engaged a couple of years back, but they hadn't even sent out invitations. She might have a boyfriend.

He didn't care. If she was here, he was going to do his level best to work his way back into her life. He'd been a decent boyfriend to her in high school—dumb assholery not withstanding—but he was so much better now. Smarter. More open. He'd learned lessons from all his dumbass friends.

Slow down, man. You cannot just throw her on the couch and fuck her. Not yet.

"Okay, I think I'm good." She took a step back and brushed the tears off her cheeks.

"I'm glad." He was the one who needed control now.

He had the sudden urge to grab his phone and ask the women in his life how he should handle this. Not the guys. They were mostly dumb, even the ones who were already married. Big Tag would yell at him about condoms. Michael would overthink the whole thing. But the ladies would take it all seriously.

He might have gotten too invested in the McKay-Taggart carpool text group. The fact that he was the only male on the list and he had zero children probably had gone to his head.

First he needed to figure out what the problem was.

"I'm so sorry. I'm exhausted. I've been up since…" She glanced down at the smart watch around her wrist. "It's over twenty-four hours now. I couldn't sleep last night. My flight to Sedona was at six this morning, and then I had to meet my cousin, get her and her boyfriend checked into the resort and get to my flight to Chicago by noon, and then I turned around and came here."

"Why the extra flight?" He moved to the couch, offering her a seat.

She yawned behind her hand. "In case someone was physically following me. I thought I would be able to recognize if someone was on all three planes. I picked seats in the back of the plane and made sure I didn't get on until right before they were closing the doors."

"They don't have to physically follow you. They could track your records." He hoped she'd truly thought this through. Yes, she was a genius, but that was in science and technology. Sometimes an Ivy League education didn't translate into street smarts.

"Which is why I bought fake identification," she replied.

47

What the hell was Maddie Hill doing buying a fake ID? He had about a million questions. "Let me see it. Maddie, that's dangerous. You can get into real trouble. If TSA figures out you're flying with false ID, you can get put on a no-fly list for the rest of your damn life."

She huffed and slung her backpack off her shoulder. She was still sniffling but seemed better than before. "I paid for the best. I did a ton of research and found someone good."

She pulled out her wallet and handed him her ID.

It was a perfectly legitimate-looking California driver's license. He checked the back. She was right. Whoever had done this had been a master at his craft. "Okay. This guy seems to be good."

Her nose wrinkled in that way that let him know she was annoyed with him. "Girl. Woman. She's excellent. She typically works with women running from abusive relationships. She helps them get away when everything else fails. Charged me ten times what she normally does. I paid it happily because I happen to know she also does it for free when a woman has no money."

Ah, there was the girl he remembered. He handed back her fake ID. "Now why don't you tell me why you need a fake ID? Who are you trying to evade?"

She sat back, weariness apparent in her every move. All she seemed to have with her was that backpack. She set it on the floor at her feet. "My boss. Something's happening at Byrne Corp."

"Okay." He pulled his cell phone out of his pocket and quickly dashed off a text to both Ian and his partner Alex McKay requesting a meeting. "I'll get you into the morning conference. At McKay-Taggart we have a morning conference three times a week where we can present cases for consideration. Can you explain it all there? We can go over it in the morning, but they'll need a complete rundown of what you suspect is happening so we can come up with the right team."

Her eyes had widened. "Team?"

"Yeah, you need an investigative team, right?" He was already thinking about how he would handle the meeting. He would need to make certain Big Tag understood this was about more than just his dick because Big Tag was definitely going to accuse him of that. "That's why you came to me. Are you in immediate danger? I can make sure you're safe here tonight, but we'll hire an extra guard if you need protection twenty-four seven."

"I don't think anyone knows what I'm doing. I don't have friends at the office, so I haven't talked to anyone about it. I know I seem paranoid, but I'm only being careful. The project is at a delicate stage, so I think caution is a good thing. I know something's wrong, but I can't get to the system I need in order to figure out what's happening." She yawned again. "But I didn't come here to hire McKay-Taggart. I'll figure this out on my own. I need you to...this sounds so stupid."

Ah, so they were getting back to that one little word that had shaken his world. "Just say it."

She seemed to steel herself. "Okay. But it is stupid. It's...I needed to get closer to Nolan and I found out that he was interested in certain topics and liked to talk about them."

Damn it. "Let me guess. BDSM? Nolan Byrne is in the lifestyle?"

She seemed to consider how to reply. "No. He's interested in the lifestyle. He's a weird guy. He goes through these phases, and then he tends to surround himself with people who are similarly minded. Like a couple of years ago he was completely obsessed with competitive biking. Suddenly no one was driving to work. They were all biking and wore the worst shorts. It was not a good time to be there. Chess was a good year of his life. The breakrooms were covered with dudes playing chess. Often it's because he's seen some movie or read a book that catches his imagination. Everyone knows that one way to move onto whatever team Nolan's interested in is to talk about his favorite subject of the moment."

"He openly talks about his sex life?"

She shook her head. "Oh, no. This one is kind of a secret. I was reading a book about BDSM and his assistant caught me, and she was the one who mentioned he was trying to get into a club. Not just any club. Apparently there are many around the LA area, but he wants access to the one in Malibu."

He knew it well. He had a couple of friends who played there. "The Reef?"

Her eyes widened. "It's true. You are a BDSM guy. BDSM person."

"We tend to prefer to call ourselves Doms or tops." He remembered his recent mistake. "I personally identify as a Dom. Many men are subs or bottoms. Same for women and nonbinary people."

A brow rose over her eyes. "That's awfully forward thinking for a guy from Calhoun, California."

"I've learned a lot over the years. You'll find I'm pretty open to whatever makes a person feel happy and complete. Especially when it doesn't affect me in any way. I can only truly understand my own experience. If a man feels wrong in his body and feels better as a woman, who the hell am I to say he's wrong. How does her happiness make the world a worse place?" BDSM had smoothed so many of his edges, teaching him to not merely tolerate differences, but to find joy in them. He now had friends of all kinds. "So why were you reading about BDSM?"

Her face flushed slightly. "I had a friend who talked about it. I was interested in the theories behind it."

Liar. He still knew her tells, and the flush was proof she wasn't telling him the truth. He had the insane urge to lower his voice and explain to her that lying wasn't acceptable between them. He could explain that if he was going to be her Dom, there would be rules, and he would be happy to discipline her when she broke them.

Or she was simply embarrassed to be sitting here talking to him about something that was often viewed as sexual. "Okay, so you told Nolan Byrne you were reading up on the lifestyle so you could get some time with the boss? Has he hit on you?"

"What? No. Nothing like that." She pushed her glasses up.

"Really? Because I've been in the lifestyle for a very long time, and I would be surprised if a single Dom didn't hit on a cute little sub."

She grimaced. "He might think I'm more in the lifestyle than I really am."

His stomach dropped. "So you told a man you're suspicious of, a man who has a mega shit ton of money and power, a lie about your lifestyle in order to get close to him so you can prove he's doing something wrong?"

She shrugged and yawned again. "Maybe."

He groaned in frustration. "Maddie, what did you tell him?"

"I got antsy when we talked about it. Look, I've been around this guy for five years. I stayed out of his direct orbit because he can be hard on his people. But I needed to get close to him. I need access to his private system. So when I got the chance to move to his inner circle, I took it. I told him I've been in the lifestyle for years and that I have a Dom." She looked him in the eyes, a grimace on her face. "In particular I told him my Dom is you."

Deke had two reactions to her words. His dick practically jumped for joy. His heart did a little flip, too, because damn she was bringing back all his emotions. He'd loved her, like soul-deep teenaged loved her.

His brain was trying hard to tap those brakes. There was something going on with Maddie and he needed to be professional. She seemed to have a real problem if the expensive fake ID was any indication.

"Okay, you need someone—me in particular—to pretend to be your Dom so you can get your boss into The Reef to build enough trust with him that you can get close to his private system?" He wanted to make sure he fully understood the situation she was bringing him into.

She sighed with seeming relief. "Yes. I'm so glad you understand. I've got six weeks before launch, and I probably really only need you to come out maybe once or twice. I'll pay all your expenses, and I've got a guest room you'll be perfectly comfortable in. We can talk about compensation, too. I would prefer to pay for this as a project rather than by the hour, but I can be incredibly generous. I'll need you to broker a deal with whoever owns The Reef. He seems to not like Nolan at all, and we'll probably need to do a small scene or something. I've studied up on everything, so you don't have to educate me."

Oh, he was going to educate her. Did she think she could treat him like some kind of prop? Did she actually believe he would sit back and look pretty and be quiet? "If you want my help, we'll bring it to the group. I'm not for hire by the hour, Maddie."

She seemed to have trouble keeping her eyes open. "Good. Like I said I would rather make it a project. So I need to talk to the group in order to hire you? I don't know how your company works. Do you have a pamphlet or something with costs?"

Should he explain that he would be taking over everything? And she would be hiring way more than him. In his brain he was already putting together his team. He would need backup, and this was a tech job, so MaeBe would be getting out of the office. Of course if he took MaeBe he would have to take Kyle. "Don't worry about the costs. We'll work something out, but I need you to understand that I'm not going to be a prop. I know you're incredibly smart and independent, but you came to me for a reason."

"Because Angie told me you were a Dom, and I thought it would be easier to work with someone who knew about the lifestyle," she admitted.

A few things went through his head. First, he was having a long talk with his youngest sister because she needed to keep her mouth shut, but the second was all about timing. "I take it this came out when she was in LA right before Christmas?"

He'd heard all about Angie's trip to the big city when he'd gone home for the holidays. He'd also heard about how amazing Maddie was and how successful she was.

"We had lunch. Don't be mad at her. She just thought it was weird."

"And when did you start to suspect something was going on with Byrne?" He was about to prove he could put pieces of puzzles together too.

"A few months ago," she replied. "That was when I realized we have two employees who've gone missing, and they all touched the satellite project."

"But you didn't know about Byrne's obsession with BDSM at that point."

"No. I found that out when I got caught reading that book."

"And you were reading that book because someone you're friends with is in the lifestyle. Who might that be?" He waited, and sure enough she flushed.

"Uhm, her name is Joanna."

Now he did lower his tone. "That's a lie, Maddie. We're going to start now. If you want to play the part of my sub, then we're going to set a few boundaries, and lying is one of them. Why were you reading that book? Shortly after you found out I was in the lifestyle."

"I was curious." She bit her bottom lip. "I don't know. After Angie told me you were in the lifestyle, I was curious, and when the chance to get close to Byrne came up, I sort of told him this whole crazy story about my Dom and how we were trying to get into The Reef too. For a while we just talked, but now he wants to meet you, and I can't put him off anymore."

"All right. I believe that." Actually, when he thought about it, there was no one in the world who'd needed a good top more than the Maddie he'd known in high school. She'd needed a partner who could remind her she was more than her big brain, that she was worthy of care and rest, that she didn't owe the world everything she had.

She frowned at him. "And I know what you were doing. That was your Dom voice, and we don't need rules because we're not really going to be a D/s couple."

She would find that working with him on an op would be a whole lot like being a D/s couple. Oh, not with someone like MaeBe or Charlotte or any of the other highly trained women he worked with. But this was dangerous and outside Maddie's area of expertise. "I've done this job for more than a decade, and then there's all my military training. Did my sister happen to mention I was on a CIA special ops team for a couple of years?"

"No."

At least Angie had some discretion. "I was. I assure you I've worked more corporate security cases than I can remember. You were worried enough about your safety that you spent thousands of dollars trying to cover up where you were going. How much more dangerous is it going to be when you get into Byrne's private system? I'm going to be honest with you, Maddie. I'm going to take over now. I know you're smart and I'll follow your every order when it comes to launching a satellite, but you're going to follow mine when it comes to this."

"Or?" She got that stubborn look on her face. "I assume there's an or."

He hated the fact that he wasn't going to be able to ease her into this, but he knew her. At least he'd known her, and Maddie required firm boundaries or she ran over everything and everyone in her way. "Or I'll call in the authorities and probably blow it all to hell."

"But he'll have warning," she argued. "He'll be able to hide what he's doing."

He shrugged. "Then you should let me do my job. You need to understand that this isn't my job right now. I don't have skin in the game beyond making sure an old friend of mine is safe, and that will be my primary goal if I'm not in charge of the mission."

"Your way or the highway, huh, Deke?"

"I'm not trying to be a dick."

"And yet you've managed."

"Is the situation dangerous?"

She sighed. "Yes."

"Do you have security training?"

"No." She slumped against the sofa. "Fine. I think I probably knew you would be a dick about it and take over, and somewhere in the back of my head I know I'm not ready for this. But you have to understand that it is important to me."

"I'll do anything I can to help and that includes protecting you." He watched her for a moment. "It is good to see you."

Her lips curled up slightly. "You, too, Murphy."

A gentle chiming sounded through the apartment.

Damn it. He'd forgotten about the pizza. "Stay here. I ordered some pizza a while back."

She winced. "They weren't really going home, were they?"

"It's okay." He stood up and stared down at her for a moment. Damn but she was still so pretty it hurt. She hadn't been the cheerleader type or the glamourous girl, but she'd been the one who caught every part of his soul and had once held his heart in her little hand. "I'm glad you came to me."

She gave him a half smile. "I didn't know who else to go to. It won't be too much trouble. I promise. You'll see. I've got it all planned out and taken care of."

Sure she did. He had zero doubt that she would know exactly how to deal with the computer system, but she had no idea how complex an op like this could get. He hadn't even delved into the details of why she thought her boss was doing something that could threaten national security, and he was certain it would be a delicate op.

After all, they were dealing with one of the smartest men on the planet, and likely one of the most ruthless.

"Well, we can talk about that over pizza. A whole lot of pizza," he said. He might be eating pizza for the rest of time. Or he could invite Boomer over tomorrow and it would be gone in one night.

"Good. I'm starving," she said with another yawn. "I didn't eat most of the day. I was too nervous."

"There's plenty." He walked toward the hallway, reluctant to take his eyes off her in case she disappeared.

He opened the door, paid the guy, and headed back in with all freaking five pizzas, one of which was covered in something called srirancha, a combo of sriracha and Ranch dressing that MaeBe craved like Hutch did candy. It was also something Deke wasn't going to touch because he didn't like his gut going up in flames.

He wondered if Maddie had expanded her culinary horizons past the casseroles and meat and potatoes they used to eat in their hometown.

He stepped back in, ready to offer her anything she liked.

And that was when he realized she was asleep on his couch.

He sighed and put the pizzas down.

He had a guest room, and it looked like it would get some use tonight.

The girl he'd loved was now a woman in trouble.

He wasn't going to let her down.

But she might not like how he did it.

Chapter Two

Maddie followed Deke out of the elevator. She was surprisingly awake, probably because she'd actually slept the night before. She'd made a nominal protest when Deke had picked her up and started carrying her to his guest room, but it was all for show.

He'd taken over, and while she knew the feminist in her should be railing at the constraints, she also figured the feminist inside her respected a subject expert, and Deke had been right about that. She didn't really know what she was doing, and that could be dangerous.

"So you came here after you left the CIA?" She followed him down the hall, trying to make some small talk to cover the fact that she couldn't take her eyes off him. It was weird. It wasn't normal. She kept trying to act like she had some semblance of sense, but every time she tried to focus on something else, her eyes drifted right back to him. She'd watched him make eggs and toast and bacon like a teen girl at a boy band concert.

"I kind of fell in here and it stuck," Deke allowed. "Two of the guys on my team are the big guy's brothers. When things came apart, we all ended up here. I don't think we were ever officially hired, but after a while Charlotte took pity on us and I'm still riding that wave of sympathy ten years later."

"So it's a security company?" She kind of wanted to keep him talking. It was weird when he fell silent because then she didn't have an excuse to stare at him.

He stopped, turning her way, a brow cocking over his piercing eyes. "Seriously? So you read up on BDSM because you were curious about what I was doing, but you didn't check into the company I work for before you came to find me and ask me to help you out?"

He was killing her. The old jock Deke would have smiled and accepted anything she said as fact. It wasn't like he hadn't been smart back then. He had. He just hadn't used his smarts very often. He certainly wouldn't have challenged her like this.

The new authoritative presence did something for her, and that was dangerous.

Unfortunately, he was right. "Fine. Of course I read up. I was making small talk."

He grinned, an open, happy expression that also made her heart do a flip. "Tell me what you've found out."

"McKay-Taggart is considered a boutique firm."

He snorted. "Please tell my boss that."

"Well, it is. It's a small company, but it's considered one of the premiere security services in the world. The company offers everything from bodyguards to high-end personalized security services. You have a highly regarded investigative team, and the rumor is you often work with intelligence agencies. I can give you a rundown of the finances. They're quite healthy."

"There's the smarty pants I remember." He stopped right outside the big bank of floor-to-ceiling glass doors. The entryway looked sleek and modern. "All right, I'm going to bet we're meeting with Big Tag. If I could, I would pick Alex, but Ian's going to have heard the gossip that we used to date and he'll move heaven and earth to be here this morning."

"Who would tell him?"

"Everyone you met last night," Deke admitted. "This place runs on gossip. Let me show you."

He slapped a key card over the security system and the door came open, allowing them into the lovely lobby where a woman with dark hair and a sunny smile was at the reception desk. Deke walked right up to her. "Hey, Yasmin. What's the word about me and the lady I'm bringing into conference this morning?"

Yasmin's eyes lit with apparent glee. "Oh, so many words. Some people are saying she's your old high school girlfriend and she's recently discovered the company she's working for is evil and she wants to stop them. But I've also heard the rumor that she might actually be the head of the evil company and she wants to start a new group of super-soldiers, and you're her first victim."

"What?" Maddie asked, horrified. "Why would anyone think that?"

Deke simply shook his head. "Happens more often than you think."

"Oh, and there's already a betting pool going, and I'm supposed to offer you these." Yasmin pulled out a box of…

"Are those condoms?" She felt her whole body flush with embarrassment.

Deke held them up. "They are indeed, and you need to get used to weird sex talk because it flies around here constantly. Sarcasm is the language of this particular land." He looked down at the box and nodded. "Hey, the old guy must be in a good mood. He gave me extra larges. If he's pissy, I'd get smalls."

"Those wouldn't…" Yep, she blushed again.

Deke snorted and slid the box into his laptop bag.

"Well, it's not like it probably changed," she said under her breath. "I don't think they get smaller as you age."

"They do not," he agreed.

"So it's the first one?" Yasmin asked. "Because I could use some insider info. Summer camp is not cheap."

Deke leaned over and asked her a question Maddie couldn't hear.

Yasmin whispered something back and Deke nodded. "I would definitely bet on that."

He straightened up and glanced down at his watch. "We should hurry. He'll give us hell if we're late. Are you ready?"

She wasn't. She wasn't ready at all. "Sure."

She could absolutely present her case. That wasn't what worried her. It was what came after. It was turning everything over to Deke and what that would mean. It would mean that Deke could do the security heavy lifting. It would also mean being vulnerable to the man who'd broken her heart before.

"Murphy," a deep voice said as they entered the main offices. There were rows of offices down one side and roomy cubicles in the middle. A big man with blond hair leaned against one of the cubicle walls, a mug of coffee in his hand.

A stunning woman with strawberry blonde hair joined him. "Deke, it's good to see you this morning. And your friend."

Maddie stepped forward, holding out a hand. "Madeline Hill."

"I'm Charlotte Taggart. This is my husband, Ian." The woman shook her hand. "And are you planning on twisting Deke's soul for your own terrible purposes?"

"Not at all." She did not get the humor in that statement, but it was obviously amusing to everyone else. "I have a problem with the company I work for. I suspect my boss might be doing something he shouldn't. I need some help proving it, though."

"Let's move into the conference room." Ian Taggart had a couple of inches on Deke. "I've assembled your chosen Avengers, Deke. Do you really think you're going to need all three of them? Sending Boomer out into the field can get expensive. It's way cheaper to feed him here at home."

She followed when Deke walked into a big conference room. There were already people inside, some of the people from the night before. MaeBe Vaughn was seated with her laptop in front of her and the guy named Kyle at her side. She also recognized the man named Boomer.

60

Ian Taggart moved through the conference room, taking the place at the head of the table. His wife sank down to the seat at his side.

Deke held a chair out for her. It was the chair directly across from Ian Taggart. Luckily the table was long enough that there was plenty of space between them. The head of the company reminded her of a lion. It was probably the color of his hair. Or maybe the hard look in his eyes as he stared at her like he could see deep in her soul.

"So the going rate for four employees twenty-four seven isn't cheap," Taggart began.

"Ian." Deke sat beside her.

"I was hoping we could negotiate a project rate." She wasn't some shrinking violet. She'd worked in big tech for years, and she'd had to stare down bigger assholes than the one in front of her. Getting a good deal was an artform.

"Has anyone mentioned who she's investigating?" Deke's question held an air of expectation.

MaeBe's eyes had gone wide. "I thought for sure you would have told him. I was wondering why he was so calm."

Charlotte Taggart sat up straight, her hand going to the landline phone that sat on the conference table. It likely linked to an inhouse communication system. They used something similar at Byrne Corp to conference in people in different buildings on campus. Charlotte's hand hovered close to the system. "Who does she work for, Deke? I wish I could guess, but the truth is my husband has a whole lot of triggers."

The boss's blue eyes rolled. "I do not have triggers. I have a couple of people I don't like."

"Yeah, it's called the phone book," Kyle said under his breath.

"Uh, I think you really hate this one, boss," Boomer added. "But I also forgot who it was. I was hungry when she first showed up. Did you try the srirancha?"

"I don't know what that is." They were all weird. "I work for Nolan Byrne."

Ian went still. Like preternaturally still. Like he was being so still

61

because he was about to murder someone still.

"Shit," Charlotte said and picked up the phone. "Yasmin, we have a meltdown. Yeah, bring the good stuff. Everything you have."

The conference room walls were made of glass, and no one had closed the shades, so Maddie was able to see the receptionist fly past, sprinting on her way to wherever she was going.

Maddie leaned toward Deke but did not take her eyes off Ian. He hadn't moved, but his face was going red, like he was a tea kettle rapidly heating up. "Is he okay?"

"Nah. He's working his way through something. Don't worry. When he explodes, it's usually pretty funny." Deke sounded amused, but then she was starting to remember that the world had always amused this man. He'd gotten through some tough times by never taking anything too seriously. "What is your tolerance level when it comes to curse words? He's big on the frankenswears."

"Oh, I've heard them all. What did Nolan do to him?" Nolan Byrne was known for his perky nature when it came to reporters and for being utterly ruthless in all other regards.

Charlotte winced. "We try not to say that name."

"He stiffed Big Tag on a bill," Kyle said with a shrug. "My uncle holds grudges over tiny things."

MaeBe gasped. "You are so bad."

"It was a hundred and twenty-five thousand fucking dollars and fifty-nine cents." Ian finally exploded. "This company built the security system for one of that cockwaffle's companies. Built it. Installed it. Trained his security team on how to use it, and do you know what he did when the bill came due?"

Oh, she could bet. "He had his lawyers tear apart the contract and bilked you out of everything he still owed you?"

"He called me incompetent," Ian said, his voice low. "Fucker. I should have shoved my fist up his asshole and then smashed his face with my fist so he could taste his own shit."

Boomer's eyes lit with recognition. "Oh, that guy. Yeah, we hate that guy. I almost sniped him but Charlotte said no."

"And that is why we fail," Ian announced.

The doors came open and Yasmin rushed in with a box. She set it on the table and opened it, passing the contents to Charlotte.

"You took him to court," Kyle said with a seemingly sympathetic shake of his head. "You did all you could do."

Charlotte's eyes narrowed as she opened…was that Scotch? "I will not protect you from him."

Kyle shrugged. "It was a very mature decision. I mean, the old man's been out of the game for a long time."

"Old man?" Ian started to turn on the dude who did not seem to be able to read the room. "I will show you how much of an old man I am. I don't think your momma spanked you enough."

"Ian, drink." Charlotte managed to get the glass in her husband's hand before he could stand up. "See. Good Scotch. Old Scotch. Expensive Scotch."

"Is he okay?" She looked to Deke, who was grinning ear to ear.

"He will be. Charlotte knows how to bring him down," Deke said.

That was the moment she realized she'd reached for his hand. At some point she'd put a hand on his. She'd done it unconsciously, as if her body remembered that he was safe, that he would protect her.

She eased her hand off his.

Charlotte's blouse seemed way less buttoned up all of the sudden, and she had a cookie in her hand as she moved into her husband's space, lowering herself onto his lap. "There you go, baby. Scotch and a lemon cookie. That feels better now, doesn't it?"

The big guy's free arm wound around his wife's waist, and he seemed to relax. "And boobs. The boobs are a big part of this protocol of yours."

"So we don't need the stun gun?" Yasmin actually had one in her hand.

This was the weirdest place.

"I think we're good." Charlotte seemed perfectly happy to conduct the rest of the meeting while her husband treated her like a teddy bear. "So you are Deke's high school girlfriend and you now work for that man. We're going to call him *that man* from now on, and we will not mention legal fees anymore."

"If it helps, I think he's likely doing something illegal. I think he might even be working with a foreign government, but I'm not totally sure," Maddie explained. "I need to get onto his private system to figure out what he's doing."

"Wait." Ian seemed more interested now. He hadn't let go of his wife, but he was sitting up again. "This is about Nolan Byrne going to jail? What do you suspect he's up to?"

"I work on the satellite team," she began.

"That's his new thing, isn't it?" MaeBe asked. "I know that I'm supposed to hate the guy, and I think what he did is terrible and an awful thing, but he's kind of a big deal in the tech world, so I know more about him than just how terrible he is."

"He's a fuckcake," Ian grumbled. "But maybe he's a fuckcake who I might be able to send to prison. Please illuminate me on how a new satellite is going to screw over the world. Is he using it to spy on his enemies?"

"I don't know," she admitted. "It's supposed to be going up basically as a test. It's the first of its kind and if it works, the technology could potentially be used to streamline space travel."

"So this isn't your run of the mill communications satellite?" Kyle asked.

"No." She hesitated, looking to Deke. "I'm breaking my contract even talking about this."

"You can trust them. I promise you that even if your boss turns out to be entirely innocent, Ian will keep his mouth shut. What you say doesn't go past these conference room walls. He won't use you to get revenge."

"No because I'm not a shitgibbon asshole," Ian replied, picking up another cookie. "Yasmin, thank you for the save. I'm good now. Please tell me there's extra in there."

Yasmin put the stun gun away. "Of course. I keep these close by in case of Boomer. Here you go. I made them myself. They're called *sfouf*. It's a kind of cake with turmeric. It tastes better than it sounds."

She handed a container to Boomer, who opened it with relish. "Thanks, Yasmin. Smells great and I'm hungry."

"You're always hungry," Ian said with a shake of his head. He kissed his wife. "Go on, baby. I'm ready to get serious. Yasmin, go ahead and close the blinds and let everyone know we're not to be disturbed. And maybe pull a nondisclosure for all of us to sign. Will that make it more comfortable for you, Ms. Hill?"

It looked like the antics were over. "I suppose. I'm nervous because I take my contract seriously. But then so did Justin Garcia and Pam Dodson."

Yasmin exited and then the blinds started to run down, shutting the conference room off from the rest of the office. Charlotte sat back in her own chair, and all of the focus was back on Maddie.

"He means what he says," Deke offered. "He'll have us all sign nondisclosures, but if you would prefer we can wait until Yasmin has them printed out."

"Also, Deke would punch us if we talked," Boomer added. "And let's face facts, I'm probably going to forget most of what you say because it's going to be a lot of technical stuff, right? Yeah. I won't get it, so I won't be able to tell anyone about it. I'm going to do what I do best. Sit here, eat some cake, and look pretty." He shrugged. "I'm comfortable with my role on the team."

She trusted Deke. "All right. The satellite is run by an AI that is beyond anything we have today. Byrne is basically taking the self-drive function of his cars and using them to power and maintain the sat. So instead of a human operator on the ground deciding on the upkeep, Clarke makes the decisions and uses his resources to do the work."

"Clarke?" Charlotte asked.

MaeBe raised her hand and bounced like a kid in school. "Is it for Arthur C?"

It would be so good to have someone on this team of Deke's who

65

understood her world. "Yes. Arthur C. Clarke. He was a science fiction writer. He's also responsible for conceptualizing the geostationary satellite communication system we use today."

"Smartie pants," Kyle said under his breath. "All right, I'll be the dummy of the group and ask the question. How is this different from what we do now? I mean I can't believe we send a repairman up to space every time something goes wrong with a satellite."

"Up until a few years ago if something went wrong with a satellite or it ran out of fuel, it was simply decommissioned. There were no repairs. If something went wrong the satellite was either flown toward the atmosphere where it would burn up or it was sent to what's known as a graveyard orbit," Maddie explained. "That's an orbital path roughly 23,000 miles up. It's far enough that the debris doesn't impact spacecraft."

"And they eat the cost?" Ian asked, a brow rising over his blue eyes.

"Yes. And the cost is sometimes billions of dollars. So a few years back DARPA began working with a private firm on a project known as RSGS. Robotic Servicing of Geosynchronous Satellites," she explained. "We believe in the next decade there will be a booming business concerning space, including satellite maintenance and repair. It would absolutely include human technicians along with robotics. Byrne wants to streamline the process by building satellites that do their own work."

"You mean he wants to shut out DARPA and own the industry for himself," Ian countered. "Why would anyone build a billion-dollar product they then have to pay to maintain when he can do it for you for free? Well, beyond the billion. And if he has proof of concept, I would bet he suddenly looks real good to any country thinking about, say, building a spaceport in the future."

Maddie nodded. "Yes. What we're working on could transform the space industry."

"I have questions," Deke said. "I get that an AI can make decisions, but how can it repair itself? Are you launching the satellite with extra parts?"

"Yes, in some cases, but obviously that could be cumbersome," she replied. "Especially in the cases of large parts. For some smaller pieces, a 3D printer would be used. For larger parts, we've designed a scavenger drone."

MaeBe whistled, obviously impressed. "It can get to the graveyard orbit?"

"That is the plan. There are more than 3,000 decommissioned satellites in orbit. Most of them are there because they ran out of fuel. The parts are still good. Clarke would search for a usable part and send the scavenger to do its thing."

"Damn." Deke put a hand on hers. "I knew you were smart and that you could change the world, but damn, baby." He shook his head and sat back. "Sorry. Old habit. I'm just...I'm really proud of you."

She had the sudden urge to lean into him, to get his hand back in hers. Maddie tried to shake it off. She was annoyingly emotional around him. "Thanks, but I'm a little worried that all my hard work is being used for something it wasn't intended for. Not that I could tell you what that is."

"When did you start to suspect something was wrong at Byrne?" Charlotte asked.

"A few months ago. I've had this project in my head for years." She'd been a workaholic. "I thought up the concept of how the AI would work when I was in college, but Byrne gave me the chance to really test it out. I've worked sixty hours a week for years on this project, and I was hyperfocused on what I was doing. The satellite project is made up of twenty different teams and over three hundred people. On big projects like this, often one hand doesn't know what the other is doing."

"I'm sure Byrne likes it that way," Ian added. "He gets to put everything together and take all the credit."

"The base of the AI is a combination of his work from the self-driving cars and my own work." She wouldn't ever take credit where it wasn't due. "I brought my ideas to the project and found a way to elevate the base AI. I streamlined Clarke's processes and I believe what we have is the most well-developed AI on the planet. But I understand the industry, Mr. Taggart. At this point in my career I'm compensated with money, not prestige."

"You were telling us how you became suspicious," Deke prompted.

"A few months back a man on my team named Justin Garcia wrote me an email requesting a meeting. He said it was important and that he would rather talk to me off campus. I was busy that day but agreed to meet with him for coffee the following morning. He didn't show. He didn't come to work that day and after a week, we found out from his girlfriend that he was missing," she explained. "A couple of days later, his body was found in an area of LA known for illegal drug buys and gang activity. But I knew Justin. He wasn't the kind of guy to be so reckless. Still, the medical examiner found fentanyl and heroin in his system, so I have to assume that one of the nicest men I ever met ended his life in a flop house doing poorly cut drugs."

"He was on your team? Did he work on anything sensitive?" Kyle asked.

"Everything we work on is sensitive, but he was working on the audio system. It's considered glitter. You know, like sprinkles on a cupcake. Clarke doesn't need a voice to talk to home base, but it's one of those things that makes the project more interesting to the public. It's like those freaky robots that look like hellhounds that are going to kill the world so they make sure they can do goofy dances. Justin was in charge of giving Clarke a human voice."

"Maybe he can sing to us before he takes over the world and nukes us all from space," Ian said with a shake of his head. "Sorry. I watched too much *Terminator*. Please proceed."

Taggart wasn't the only person who had reservations about what she did. Her father questioned her all the time. It made for fun holidays. "Three weeks ago, Pam Dodson went missing. I don't believe for a second that she would up and quit and walk out on her kids. She has two, and I know she and her husband were having trouble, but I can't buy the idea that she left a note saying she needed to find herself. She wasn't that person."

"Sometimes people do things that seem out of character," Charlotte mused. "We can't truly know what's going on in a person's head. Does the husband believe it?"

"I went by their house after she disappeared. He gave me some song and dance about how she'd been talking about taking a sabbatical from her boring life and going hiking." She hadn't bought anything Matt had told her.

"Okay, I understand that two people going missing in the same company in such a short amount of time seems odd, but I don't see how they connect except that you knew both of them." Deke had sat back, studying her.

"Pam was also working on audio." How did she explain that this was an instinct? She was a scientist who believed in logic and hard facts, but she knew something was wrong with the project. Something dark. "Specifically on the way Clarke targets the transfer of audio, how he changes frequency for private messaging. When I tried to access her work, I found out someone had wiped it off her laptop. Everything. All of her notes. Her messages—even the ones to me— were all deliberately erased. She's not working on new tech. What Pam does has been around for a long time. Why erase her background work? She wasn't finished. Someone has to take over and now they have to start from scratch."

"Why do you think it wasn't an accident?" Taggart asked. "I know most research and tech companies have protocols including securing data when an employee leaves or is fired."

"There's no reason to secure this data," she countered. "None. It actively hurts the project, and it wasn't an accident. I was able to find the order to erase her systems. It came straight from Byrne himself."

"How did you find the order?" Deke asked.

"I was left in Byrne's office alone for a few minutes and I rifled through his notes," she admitted. "He doodles a lot. He's the kind of guy who's always got to be in motion. He's never still. Even when he's in a meeting, he's got a notepad and he's drawing or sometimes making notes to himself. I looked through his notebook and he reminded himself to erase Pam. As far as I know he'd never met Pam. Why would he be concerned with a fairly low-level employee working on what was a basic system?"

"I agree that seems odd, but all of this is circumstantial. Pam is not an uncommon name. He could have been talking about a voicemail or some project notes you don't know about. What do you think he's doing?" Taggart asked.

There was a level of disbelief in Taggart's tone that made her gut twist. "I'm not sure, but it has something to do with the audio team, and I think it's curious that he's been to Beijing five times in the last year. I know he works with manufacturers there. Most of the processors used in tech come out of Asia. But he lied about where he was going at least twice. He told me he was going to be in South Korea meeting with investors. I know he was in Beijing. I know it because of some texts he sent me."

"He texts you personally?" Deke asked with a frown.

"Like I told you, we've gotten to be friendly in the last couple of months. In this case, he was sending me pictures of a dinner he was having. Like I said, he was supposed to be in Korea, but I know the restaurant he was in. I recognized it. He was in Beijing at a place where the manufacturers always take clients. I've been several times. He was drinking their signature drink."

"All right, but there are a lot of reasons he might not want an employee to know where he is," Taggart allowed, his disbelief obviously not moving an inch. "Look, Madeline, there's no one on the planet who would like to send Byrne to jail more than me, but I can't justify the potential lawsuit Byrne can bring down on all our heads with this little evidence that he's doing something wrong. Deke, I can give you some time off to help her, but I'm not going to send a four-person team out in the field."

Crazily enough, that was kind of what she'd planned, but now she panicked at the thought of being out there alone. Her initial idea had been to hire Deke as a bodyguard, and she would handle the investigation on her own. But she'd spent the whole morning reconsidering. After all, she hired subject experts all the time. How was this different? She had more money than she could reasonably spend. It seemed like a good call to ensure her safety and to do things right. "I can pay. I'll pay upfront."

Taggart stood, closing the notebook he'd had open in front of him. "It's not about the money. It's about exposure. I have to safeguard my company, and the reward in this case isn't worth the risk. If you have anything else, I'll reconsider, but at this point, we would simply be providing you cover so you can go through your boss's information on a top-secret project based on the thinnest of evidence."

"He meets with this woman." She sought her brain for anything else she could give him that wasn't simply her hunch. "I don't know her name. He doesn't introduce her. I think she might be with the government. He meets with her regularly, and I think she'll show up next week if my schedule is correct. She might have something to do with what's going on. I'm almost certain she was who he met in Beijing."

"I would assume a man like Byrne has many government contacts." Charlotte stood beside her husband, a sympathetic look on her face. "We can always revisit the situation if something new happens. And if you're worried about your personal safety, we can assign a bodyguard rotation so you're never without protection."

Frustration welled inside her. She knew something was wrong but she didn't have solid proof, and she wouldn't get any if she didn't have help. Deke had convinced her this morning. He'd laid out all the ways his company could help her, and now it seemed like a mistake to go any other way.

"Why do you think she's with the government?" Deke asked as everyone started to get ready to leave. Everyone except Boomer, who was still working on Yasmin's treats.

"It doesn't matter." She sighed and sat back. All of her

subterfuge had been for nothing. She would have to go back home and figure out another plan.

"It was nice to meet you." MaeBe clutched her laptop to her chest. "Deke can give you my phone number if you need any help."

"And Ian's serious about the bodyguard." Kyle followed MaeBe. "Give us a call if you need anything."

She needed help but she wasn't going to get it.

"Hey, I'll talk to him." Deke pushed back his chair. His jaw was tight, a sure sign he was upset. This morning obviously hadn't gone the way he'd thought it would, either. "Do you have a picture of this woman? If she's with the CIA, Ian might know her. Even if she isn't, I know some people who can figure out who she is. We've got a couple of days before you're due back. I can still make this happen. There's a company here in the building that specializes in finding missing persons. Their facial identification software works magic. If we prove there's a foreign agent at work, Ian will approve the op."

She shook her head. "You think I haven't tried facial recognition? She wears these glasses. It's some kind of tech I've never seen before. The glasses themselves look normal until any kind of camera hits them. They use some kind of light that distorts her face."

"Whoa." Boomer's eyes had gone wide, and he looked to Deke. "Remember Hutch's case?"

Deke was on his feet, shoving the chair back. "You've got yourself a team. I promise. We'll be going back to California with you. Give me five minutes."

He strode out the door.

"What did I say?" Those words appeared to have worked some magic.

"The big boss doesn't like unsolved mysteries. Relax. You'll get what you need." Boomer held out the box Yasmin had given him. "Want a *sfouf*? They're delicious."

She took one and sat back, hoping Deke was right.

72

* * * *

Deke raced out of the conference room, brushing past Kyle.

"Don't schedule anything for next week. We're still going to California." There was no way Ian turned him down once he'd shared that last bit of news.

"The old man sounded sure," Kyle replied. "And I've got some plans for next week, so I'm not all that upset."

Even better. If he could avoid Kyle and MaeBe drama, he would be so much happier for it. "Cool. I'll take Jamal."

Jamal likely was on assignment since the man never stopped working, but Kyle could take it over. And Jamal wouldn't freak out anytime MaeBe stepped away from her computer. He would call it a win.

"I'd still like to go," MaeBe called out.

He heard Kyle say something, but he didn't have time for it. Ian had walked out with his lemon cookies and his expensive Scotch and his wife's boobs. If the big boss shut the door to his office, it could be hours before it opened again. No one in the world had more office sex than those two, and they were serious about it.

He got to Ian's office just as the door was starting to close. He slammed a hand on it. "The woman Maddie saw is the same one who was working with Jessica Layne."

Hutch's wife, Noelle, had worked for the tech guru Jessica Layne, head of Genedyne. The mystery woman had been paid big bucks to tank Noelle's potentially world-changing technological advances in favor of keeping up profits for her multinational corporate clients who could have been eclipsed by the advance.

It had been very reminiscent of the way an old foe had operated—one Ian had thought he'd taken down years before.

Big Tag's face went blank as if he was trying to come up with any kind of reason to keep closing that door. He finally gritted his teeth and growled.

And opened the door.

73

"Fuck." He allowed Deke in.

Charlotte was already on the couch. Big Tag's office was basically a suite. It contained his big desk, a sitting area with a couch and a love seat, and it had its own full bathroom. Deke happened to know that big couch opened to a foldout bed Ian did not mind using in the middle of the day.

Tag lived the dream, in Deke's opinion.

"Are you talking about the woman we couldn't ID?" Charlotte sat up straighter. "The one who had tech that fooled Adam's facial recognition?"

"We better be because otherwise we're ruining a perfectly good morning." Tag closed the door behind him. "I was serious about the time off, Deke. You can go out and gather more intel. We have no verification we're dealing with the same woman."

"I don't think we need more. You've heard the rumors. There's a new group filling in the void The Collective left behind." He understood why Tag had turned down the assignment. He'd been worried that would be exactly the case from the minute Maddie had told him who he worked for. "I know what Byrne almost did to this firm, but if he's in league with that group, we have to find out. The technology Maddie is working on could be a giant leap forward. That group will kill it if it benefits them."

"You know I don't back down from a fight, but I'm also not putting everyone's jobs at risk over a hunch." Tag joined his wife.

"It was a hard time in our lives, and honestly, I don't want to revisit it." Charlotte put a hand on her husband's leg as though giving him her comfort.

Deke remembered the time well. Four years before, Byrne had not only tried to stiff the company out of the remaining bill, he'd tried to alienate them from potential clients. He'd used his influence to cost McKay-Taggart. The company had taken a hit, and Charlotte had lost her mind when she'd found out Ian had been talking to Boomer about sniping the man from a distance. They'd eventually settled out of court and things had calmed down, but he understood why Tag wanted to stay away from the man.

"I can do it completely off the books." Deke took a seat across from the Taggarts. "If anyone asks, I worked alone."

"But you're not going to work alone or you wouldn't be sitting here," Tag pointed out. "You want a team."

"I'm the only one who'll have any contact with Byrne. Boomer's there as my backup. I need MaeBe, but she's strictly behind a computer," he promised. When he thought about it, he didn't really need a bodyguard. He or Boomer could handle that part. Keeping the team small and agile was to his benefit. "I can get the team down to three."

"You know they're a package deal. You get MaeBe, you have to take Crazy." Tag knew exactly who his nephew was and didn't mind putting that out there.

"I'll make sure Kyle stays out of trouble." He couldn't let Maddie go back alone, and if he was going, he wanted a team in place. Especially if he was right and they were dealing with the same group who'd worked with Jessica Layne's company. Because of the contracts in place, Noelle's breakthrough in helium tech was still out of her hands. She'd found new work, but the trouble had set her back years. He didn't want that for Maddie. If he could prove something illegal was going on, he might be able to get her out of the contracts and free up her research.

"All right. What exactly did she say?" Big Tag sat back.

"I asked her about the woman she's seen with Byrne. She doesn't have a name. I asked if she's got a picture because we could take it down to Adam," Deke explained. "She said she'd tried to grab a shot from security cams, but the woman is wearing glasses that disrupted the images."

Charlotte frowned. "Like the woman who worked with Layne. That tech isn't available to the public, so we have to assume she's at least with the same group even if she's not the same person. I know you don't like coincidence, but..."

"A woman with crazy secret tech shows up at the side of another billionaire tech giant? Yeah." Tag sighed and shook his head. "I don't want to get into this."

But he would because Tag wouldn't trust anyone else to do it. "I will make it my mission in life to get a good shot of this woman if you let me go and bring a small team. Maddie said she should be coming to Byrne sometime in the next week or so."

"She can't know the schedule." Tag seemed to be looking for a way out.

"I think we have to take the chance. If The Collective is up and working again, we have to know," Deke pointed out.

"The rumor is they are calling themselves The Consortium now. Like changing their name means they're invisible again." Tag growled a little and took a sip of Scotch. "I hate the fuckers, and if Byrne is one of them, we do need to know. He's shooting satellites into space, and if he has his way, he'll control access to space itself. He'll fucking privatize the moon and charge us all for the tides."

Charlotte stood, straightening her skirt. "I'll go and talk to Genny about travel and per diems. Are we sending the whole crew Deke asked for?"

Tag nodded, reaching for his wife's hand and giving it a squeeze. "Give him whatever he wants. But if he wants MaeBe, he has to take Kyle. I'm not going to listen to my nephew whine that his emotional support hacker is in another state."

She winked his way. "Will do. And Deke, we'll expect regular updates. I mean the text group, not Ian. We're all boring married women. We need some drama. I want to know the minute Kyle and MaeBe throw down. Like I want to know before they do."

He wasn't sure how he was going to make that happen, but he would do his level best to provide his group with some entertainment. The group had started out as a way to easily connect a bunch of moms to help with carpool and bake sales and other kidcentric activities, and like all things McKay-Taggart, had quickly dissolved into an amusing shitshow of gossip and speculation and well-meaning nosiness. He fucking loved it. "Will do, boss."

Charlotte strode out.

"And there goes the best part of my morning." Tag set the Scotch down with a sigh. "I won't see her again until we go home, and then we'll be all about the kids. Getting old and responsible sucks ass. All right, Deke. You're the most reasonable of all my employees. Tell me what you think."

It was good to know the boss believed in him. "I think Maddie is the smartest person I've ever met, and if she believes something is wrong, then something is wrong. I'm going to explain to her that we will work this op for her, but we have our own mission and that's to ID the woman meeting with Byrne."

Ian stared down at the Scotch but didn't pick it back up. "You're not worried she's involved?"

Deke shook his head. "Not at all. She's solid, boss."

Ian's head cocked as though he was considering the situation. "How do you know? You haven't had a relationship with her since you were both in high school. There are a lot of years between you and the girl you remember."

"She's stayed somewhat close to one of my sisters. She and Angie even kept in touch while Maddie was at Yale." Sometimes he thought his sister had done that so she could tell him about the amazing things Maddie was doing. Not to make him feel bad about himself, rather to let him know he'd made the right decision all those years ago. "Maddie is incapable of doing anything truly morally wrong. It's why she's here."

"She could have gone a lot of places," Ian pointed out. "She could have called the FBI. She didn't. She came here, or more importantly, she came to you."

"I'm likely the only person she knows with the skills required to do the job. Again, I'm sure my sister has told her all about my adventures in the private security world." Sometimes he wondered if Angie would do that to let Maddie know he was still available. Or to remind her she'd made the right choice.

"So this is simply a guy helping out an old friend. You don't still

77

have feelings for her."

He wasn't about to lie to Ian. There was zero point. "Oh, I'm planning on using this time to see if we can finally work. I'm not going to lie to you or myself. It's always been Maddie for me. I've had some girlfriends over the years, and I never could bring myself to commit to them because in the back of my head, I've always wanted Maddie. We were on different paths in high school, and I broke it off with her so she didn't miss out on an enormous opportunity."

"What was that?" Ian asked.

"She had a full-ride scholarship to Yale, and she wanted to defer so we wouldn't have to spend a year apart. She wanted me to follow her."

"And you'd actually slept with her by then?"

Tag was an asshole. Deke flipped him off. "We were in love, but even as a dumbass kid I knew Madeline Hill wasn't meant to marry her high school boyfriend and stay in her small town. That's where we were headed."

"All right." Ian conceded. "What's the cover story? Is there a cover? I don't know what the basis of the op is. Are you staying in the background?"

Even if he wanted to, that wasn't possible now. Maddie had set the parameters before she'd even known what she was doing. "She got into Byrne's inner circle by telling him she's in the lifestyle. I'm going in as her Dom."

A brow rose over Big Tag's eyes. Way over his eyes. "I'm sorry. Byrne is interested in BDSM?"

"Apparently. Maddie used that as her in, but talking to him about it in a hypothetical way isn't working anymore. She's told him a whole lot of stories she made up. I'm sure she did her homework and sounded like an expert, but he's pressing to meet her Dom."

"And that would be you. Who I assume she never actually thought she would have to introduce," Ian continued. "Tell me something. Did she even change your name?"

"I don't think she's shared much about me, but no. She told

Byrne that her Dom's name is Deke." And wasn't that interesting? "We can have one of the techs build a fake history for me in case he wants to dig into my background."

"Let's invite him right here to Sanctum, and I'll introduce him to our ways."

Yeah, he was sure his boss would love to get his torture on, but it wasn't going to happen. "He wants to visit The Reef."

"Seriously?" Tag's head fell back. "Once again BDSM saves the world." He brought his head back up and his eyes pinned Deke. "You know who runs The Reef now? Angelo DeMaris stepped down three years ago and they voted in a new president. It's the first time a submissive has ever held that crown. Don't get me wrong. Subs do a lot of the organizing and the work, but they don't usually technically run the club."

But Kayla Summers-Hunt wasn't any old sub. Once she'd been a CIA operative sent on the most dangerous missions. She'd infiltrated Chinese intelligence and worked undercover for years. She was a badass who'd ended up married to one of Hollywood's most successful leading men and living a beautiful life in Malibu when she wasn't with her husband on a movie set. "I was hoping you could ask her for me."

"She's got a kid now. The last time I talked to her, she was settling in to doing the mommy thing. I don't know how she's going to react to bringing a potentially dangerous op into her club." Tag pulled out his phone and slid his finger across the screen. "It's a little early on the West Coast, but I can leave her a voice mail. You need to think about how you're going to handle it if you can't get Byrne into The Reef. Oh, hey, Kay. I didn't think you would be up."

Deke sat back. He wasn't sure what he would do. He would have to come up with a good reason they couldn't go since Maddie had already told the man she had a way in. They could string him along for a little while, but eventually he would want in.

"I wanted to talk to you about an op," Tag began. "I know you're out of the business and I need you to feel free to say no…"

There was a feminine screech, and Tag pulled the phone away from his ear. Deke could hear Kayla from where he sat.

"Oh my god! Yes! Yes! Do you need an assassin? Because it's been so long. I love being a mom, but I miss my old job." Kayla went on, but Tag simply shrugged his way.

"You've got your op."

Deke breathed a sigh of relief. He had his chance. He wasn't going to waste it.

Chapter Three

"So this is what a BDSM club looks like?" Maddie stared up at Sanctum like she expected it to transform into something else any minute.

Which just proved that she didn't know as much as she thought she did. That was the trouble with geniuses. They often thought book smarts were everything. Deke meant to prove her wrong.

Deke stood back, allowing her to take it all in. He hadn't spent time with her in over a decade, but some things didn't change with Maddie Hill. She still studied the world around her carefully when she deigned to look up from studying books. She often missed what was going on around her because she was so focused on what truly interested her. Half the time in high school he would find her reading a book while she walked down the hallway and he would have to save her from taking a fall.

"This is what Sanctum looks like. I wasn't around when it was founded. From what I understand, Big Tag bought the building for fairly cheap. It was once a soda bottling factory. Big Tag and the other founding members refurbished it and turned it into a club."

Sometimes Sanctum had felt like his second home. "This is the second version of Sanctum though. I never actually saw the first. By the time I was hired on and got my membership, McKay-Taggart was a huge financial success and Ian built his version of a pleasure palace."

Her eyes widened slightly, and then she was back to staring. "They redecorated?"

"Oh, they pretty much rebuilt from the ground up. One of the guys on my CIA black ops team turned out to be a double, and he blew the club up. With people in it." Deke did not remember that asshole with fondness.

Now Maddie turned his way. "What?"

He shrugged. "It happens. Nobody died. Well, the traitor did. Jake got shot. Ian actually made it out with his dessert intact. Sat right down on the rubble and ate it. The silver lining was it proved I wasn't the traitor."

It was weird to think that once he was on the other side of an MT investigation.

"Why would they think you were a traitor?" The question had an air of violence about it. Like Maddie would take on whoever had thought he was capable of turning on his country.

She'd always been a fierce woman. It was one of her many charms.

It seemed like a lifetime ago. "At the time I fit the profile. The CIA team I was on had a leak. Someone was giving out important intelligence and actively working against us. Big Tag had a couple of brothers on the team, so he stuck his nose in. They thought they were looking for someone who'd been turned while in captivity. I spent a couple of months as the guest of our enemy while I was in the Middle East. It isn't completely unheard of for a person to break under torture and do things they normally wouldn't. Three of us had been captured at some point. Me and Boomer and a guy we called Ace."

Her expression softened. "I know. I mean I knew about you. Not about the others. I'm...I don't even know what to say about that.

There's no *I'm sorry* that feels like enough."

"It was a long time ago and like Sanctum, I'm all new and spiffy again." Thanks to many years of therapy and the love of his family. Being around his nieces and nephews had done him a world of good. "Are you ready to see the inside?"

Her face flushed, and she went back to staring at the doors. "I don't know. I'm still trying to get over how normal it looks. I thought it would look more like a nightclub, I guess."

Deke tested the door and found it locked. Whoever Big Tag had sent to let them in wasn't here yet. "I've found the club's exterior charms usually reflect whoever built the place. Like this one. It's utilitarian on the outside, but there's a surprising amount of whimsy on the inside. Clubs are all different, though there are some things that are pretty much the same. You'll find lots of the same equipment like benches and St. Andrew's Crosses."

"I've been reading books and watching documentaries so I could converse with Nolan." She glanced around while Deke started texting.

"Sorry, someone was supposed to meet us here to let us in," Deke explained. "The Domme in residence is not in fact in residence at the moment. She's a lawyer and she's got a big trial coming up, but someone should be here soon."

"It's bigger than I thought it would be."

"That's because most clubs aren't run by ridiculously successful and obsessively competitive people." Deke shot off a couple of texts and hoped for the best. The Ferguson Clinic was next door, and some of the people who worked there had keys and the alarm code to the club.

"I'm surrounded by those kinds of people." She put a hand on the strap of her bag.

She *was* that kind of person. She'd always been competitive. He'd been the star football player but he'd been the laid-back one in their relationship. "Well, then we know what kind of club you're going to enjoy."

She took a long breath, the sun hitting her hair in a way that brought out all the different colors in her brown tresses. It was ridiculous to call her hair brown when it was a wild and lovely mix of chestnut and honey and auburn. "I think we should talk about that word you used. Enjoy. I'm not here to enjoy myself. I'm here to get a job done. I need you to make sure I know the basics, but I don't think we should get too physical."

He'd been almost certain they would have this conversation at some point, but it still felt like a kick to the gut. He hadn't been able to stop thinking about her, and she didn't want him to touch her. "I will absolutely not lay a hand on you if you don't want me to. Anything that happens between us will be consensual, but you have to know how physical D/s can be."

He had a couple of days before they needed to be back in California, and he intended to spend them working with her, building their cover as a couple.

And if that led to something more real, he was pretty sure he would be okay with that, too.

"I know there are many ways to practice," she replied, a prim set to her mouth. "I've read up on this, Deke. I know what I'm doing."

Ah, there was the arrogant academic. He wished that part of her didn't make him hot, too. "I'm sure if I gave you a quiz, you would know every single answer. But D/s isn't something you can think your way through. No one's going to give you a test booklet with multiple choice questions and an essay for extra points. The way you'll be assessed is based on our physicality. Did you tell your boss our relationship wasn't physical? That I simply top you for accountability purposes?"

The arrogant look fled, and she bit that plump bottom lip the way she always did when she was trying to think her way through a problem. "Accountability? Like you punish me if I don't get enough work done? I read about that. There was a section in a book I read about businesspeople who need someone watching them to stop them from procrastinating. It was on the history of the Dominatrix."

He was sure she'd found that book illuminating, but it didn't help her in this situation. "I know some people who hire a top to help them, but how do you think the punishment works? Also, I'm not that kind of top. I don't live the lifestyle twenty-four seven. Most people don't. I play. Do you understand what I mean by that?"

She nodded. "You are a sexual top. You don't have D/s relationships outside the club."

"Or the bedroom or wherever I and my partner choose to play. I can very likely handle the role of hands-on twenty-four seven if I need to, but I have to know what you've told your boss and how you think punishment will work if I don't put hands on you."

"In the book, the Dominatrix sometimes sent her clients into time-outs," she offered. "Humiliation was often a consequence."

He frowned her way. "Do you think I'm going to make you sit in a corner? Maybe eat your dinner from a dog bowl?"

"No. Of course not. But spanking also seems a bit extreme."

"Have you tried it?"

"Have you?" Maddie countered.

"Absolutely."

That seemed to stump her. "Seriously? You let someone spank you. Like you're a naughty kid?"

"No. I let someone spank me like I'm an adult who consented to it." He was surprised at her tone. "I've experimented in a lot of ways when it comes to sex. Being comfortable with my body and my sexuality was an important choice for me to make."

"I guess I didn't know you weren't comfortable with it. You always seemed to be."

"Well, you can't always tell what a person is feeling. That's something I've learned along the way. It's precisely why D/s works for me. There's an added layer of intimacy to the type of D/s I practice," he explained. "Maybe it's years of therapy, but I've learned you can't get anything out of an experience unless you're willing to admit the things you want. It's just as important to be honest about the things you don't like."

"You're talking about sexually?" Maddie asked.

"In this instance, yes. But it works in all aspects of life, I've found." He needed to steer her back to the question at hand. They had very little time when it came to preparation. They needed to decide on a course of action when it came to their fake D/s relationship. "How much does Byrne know about me?"

"He knows you're my Dom. He thinks you work in security. I kind of told him you were a bodyguard. I didn't want him to think you were involved in investigations."

"Good. Bodyguards are supposed to keep their mouths shut and not ask questions." He wished he could have controlled that particular narrative, but the truth was no one would buy he was some IT guy. He didn't have those skills. Bodyguard was a good way to go. "It's close enough to the truth that it shouldn't trip me up. Now how have you explained why I don't come up to the office?"

She shrugged. "You're working. I'm working. We're busy."

"But we have to meet with him. He'll have questions about our relationship that we'll need to be able to answer."

"I think he'll be more interested in what you know about D/s."

"He'll want to watch us as a couple," he corrected. "That's how he'll learn. We need to have a basis for the type of relationship we have. Have you been pretending to take calls and texts from me checking up on you? Because that kind of relationship wouldn't be kept to after hours."

"I didn't tell him that. I…I…" She groaned and leaned against the stone walls. "I pretty much made it sound like a fucking romance novel. I made it all the things you said because I didn't like the thought of anyone having control over me in real life. So yes, I told him you were my boyfriend and that we played."

He'd thought as much. He rather thought she was playing out a fantasy. He was fine with that. She was his fantasy, too. The trouble was she'd always been way more stubborn than he was, and it was obvious she would fight him on this. If he had time, he would take it slow, give her all the space she needed. But they were on a clock and going into a dangerous op. He was going to be blunt with her. About everything. "Did you tell him we don't fuck?"

Her cheeks went the cutest pink. "No. Of course not. But I also didn't go into detail with him. I didn't talk about sex. We mostly discussed the lifestyle in intellectual terms. You know when you think about it that way, he might buy the idea that we aren't physically close."

"Is he a man?"

Her eyes rolled. "Yes."

"Then he thinks we're fucking, and he'll be able to tell we aren't. If he's studied for any amount of time, he'll be able to catch on that we're uncomfortable with each other. Or rather that you're uncomfortable with me."

"Why just me? Why would I be the uncomfortable one?"

"Because I'm not uncomfortable at all. I still remember exactly how good it feels to be inside you, Madeline. I remember everything about fucking you. I'll be perfectly comfortable sliding back into the role of the man who makes you come. I don't think you can say the same."

The pink deepened to red. "I...I...Deke, it's not like I could forget. You were my first boyfriend. But we've both moved on. We've had other partners."

"I've never loved any one like I loved you." He wasn't going to lie to her. Not about this. "Every sexual partner I've had since paled in comparison to what we had."

Her eyes slid away from him. "I didn't come out here to reconnect with you in that way."

Yet she'd used his name when she'd needed to come up with a fantasy Dom. She'd studied up on the lifestyle because Angie mentioned he was in it. Not the other way around. "Would it be bad? We're adults. We're about to be put into a very intimate situation. I'll need to stay at your place, be close to you when we're at The Reef. I'll pretend to be in your bed. Why not simply be in your bed?"

"I have a boyfriend."

He hadn't known that four words could gut him quite the way

those did. He stopped, trying to process them. All of his plans were upended with those four words. They needed a new plan. "Does Byrne know about him? He didn't question why you had a Dom and a boyfriend."

"No. Nolan hasn't met Dan." Something about the tight set of her jaw made him wonder. "He's not in the same field so he hasn't come to any of our functions. Yet."

Was she fucking lying to him? Her eyes had slid away when she said the word *boyfriend*. He could figure it out very quickly. "Well, I think we should call him and bring him in on the plan. He must be worried sick. I can teach him how to top you. Obviously the man you're sleeping with would be a better fit than an unwanted old flame."

"What?"

Yes, there was the expression he'd been looking for, the one of surprise and a bit of panic. The question was did this man exist? "I can bring him up to date. What kind of work does he do?"

Maddie's jaw had dropped. "He can't... Deke, I'm not involving him in this."

"What do you mean? If he's your boyfriend, he's not going to take kindly to another man touching you. I can pose as his mentor. A lot of D/s couples have mentors, especially in the beginning." It would kill him to train another man to top her, but he would do it if he had to. Her safety was more important than what he wanted.

He'd taken one look at her and been fifteen fucking years old and head over heels in love. They weren't kids anymore. Time and distance and life itself had seasoned them in different ways, and if she had a man she cared for, he wouldn't shove himself back into her life.

He'd sacrificed his needs for her once before. If she was in love, he could do it again.

But if she was being a scaredy cat lying coward, then all bets were off.

"Dan doesn't know," Maddie admitted. "I haven't told him about any of this."

"You haven't told the man you're sleeping with that you're going to try to catch your boss doing something that could affect national security?" How the fuck close could they be if she hadn't mentioned she was in trouble? "Where does he think you are right now?"

"I didn't exactly tell him. We're not at a place in our relationship where I feel like I need to tell him everything. It's a new relationship."

Every instinct inside him flared. "But you are sleeping with him."

"I don't see how that's any of your business."

"If I'm running this op, everything about you is my business."

"You're not really running it for my good, are you?" Her shoulders squared, a sure sign she was ready for an argument. There was nothing she liked more than a good argument, and he used to never give her one. Back in the day, he let her walk those pretty feet all over him. "You're here because your boss wants to know who my boss is meeting with."

He'd explained that his goal would be twofold—help her find out what Byrne was doing and identify the woman he was meeting with. She had an appointment with Adam Miles tomorrow morning to tell him everything she could remember about the mysterious lady. "I would have gone back with you either way. I wouldn't have left you alone."

That seemed to deflate some of her bravado. "And I appreciate that, but I meant what I said. I didn't come back for a reunion. That was over a long time ago, and it's best left in the past. I think we need to keep things as professional as possible, and that means I'm not going to talk about my relationship with Dan. I will tell you that we haven't been dating long, but it's something I'm pursuing. I'll let him know I've got to keep my head down for a couple of weeks and it should be fine."

"So you're not sleeping with him."

She groaned, a deeply frustrated sound. "No. No, we haven't gotten to that part yet. I don't just fall into bed with a guy. We've been on a couple of dates and he's nice. He's also patient, so he won't be involved in this op. You are my subject matter expert. I think I've studied enough that I don't need this training, but if you do then I'll give it a go. If you think we need to be a bit on the touchy-feely side, then we'll go that way, too. I want this to work. If my boss believes we're a D/s couple and we can get him into The Reef, he'll lower his guard around me."

She was once again trying to logic her way through. In the distance, he saw a familiar car turning into the parking lot. The sleek Mercedes pulled into the parking space next to Deke's SUV, and Adam Miles hopped out of the backseat and immediately went to open the passenger side door.

He waved Deke's way even as he held a hand out for his wife. "Hey, sorry we're late. I had to finish up a phone call. We heard you needed someone to come open the club and maybe help with some training."

Jacob Dean shut the driver's side door with a smirk. "He thought we could get some fun time in on the company dime."

Serena Dean-Miles was a pretty brunette with a smile a mile wide, but then she had two husbands who adored her and a couple of kids she loved. "And I heard someone say the new girl knows about satellites. I thought I could ask some questions. Hi, I'm Serena, long-time sub. I have two Doms, so I've pretty much been through it all. What do you know about lasers in space?"

Oh, boy. "Serena, this is my friend Madeline Hill. Maddie, how much did you really read up on D/s? Any fiction?"

"Of course," Maddie replied.

"Then you might want to call her Amber Rose."

"Amber Rose? Soldiers and Doms Amber Rose?" Maddie got that spark in her eyes that every romance reader seemed to get when they figured out who Serena was. "Oh, my god." Her voice went low. "I love her books. What do I say?"

"I think you'll find she's easy to get along with. Let's go and tour the club and then we can start training." It would be good to have Serena talk to Maddie. Serena wasn't joking about being a long-time submissive. Perhaps she could convince Maddie there was more to D/s than what she read in some nonfiction book.

"Come with me." Serena held up the keycard that would let them all in. "We can get some work in before the club opens tonight. According to Ian, we don't have long to get you up to speed, but I think we can do it. And if I can sneak a few questions about satellites and artificial intelligence in, I would love you forever."

"I have tons of questions, too." Maddie seemed much more animated. She followed behind Serena.

"Hey, do we really think she's seen our mystery woman?" Adam held back, allowing the women to go ahead of them.

"I think she's seen the same tech Hutch saw." Deke watched as Maddie walked through the doors, her hips swaying.

He hadn't been lying to her. He still remembered every inch of her body, still could hear the way she moaned and how she clutched him right before she came.

If she wasn't sleeping with this guy, she was fair game. She hadn't gone to that Dan person. She'd come to him when she needed help. She hadn't even told Dan Whatshisname. He needed to find out what Dan's last name was so he could run an incredibly invasive check into the man's life.

"When we take a dinner break, I'll have her take a look at the sketch we did from what Noelle could recall," Jake promised.

"You really couldn't find her from that sketch?" The company Adam and Jake ran were the best in the world at finding missing persons.

"No. We haven't managed to match the sketch to any kind of a credible lead," Adam admitted. "It can be hard to work from a sketch. We also have to consider the fact that Noelle didn't spend much time with her and eyewitness observations can be faulty sometimes."

"We have nothing else to go on," Jake agreed. "If we could get a real picture of her, I think we could ID her."

"So what I need is as good a picture or video as you can get for me," Adam explained. "You'll have to catch her when she's not wearing the tech."

"So I need to get her to take those glasses off." He wasn't sure how he would do it, but he was willing to try.

"You're going to have to find a way to follow her. She'll trip up at some point, but finding her and then not losing her is going to be your best bet," Jake continued. "Figure out where she's staying and camp out."

"That's what Boomer and Kyle are for," he admitted. "No one on the planet has more patience being in a perch than Boomer."

Boomer used to be the best sniper in Special Forces. He could take a person out at four thousand yards. Because of the classified nature of his work, he didn't get credit, but luckily, Boomer didn't mind getting paid off in food. Give that guy a couple of pizzas and he was happy. Sometimes Deke wished he had that man's metabolism. As for Kyle, he could be ruthless as hell.

Somehow they would find a way to figure the mystery out.

"As soon as you have something, send it my way." Adam patted his shoulder, a friendly gesture. "How close you want to get to this woman? Because I have a couple of scenarios in mind."

So close there was nothing between them. So close she would remember everything he had to give her.

"Just the basics this afternoon." He wasn't going to overwhelm her. "Then we'll stay and watch the scenes this evening and see where that takes us."

"I heard a rumor that she used to be your girlfriend," Jake said. "I'm surprised you're taking it slow. You always seemed like a guy who went after what he wanted. Unless you don't want her anymore."

"She's dating someone. Someone she called her boyfriend, but then she didn't bother to actually tell him what's going on in her life. She seems to think he'll take her brush off and won't care that she doesn't see him for a couple of weeks." He wasn't sure how much he believed her when she said she wanted to try with this guy. She'd never been a good liar. He believed this man existed, but not that she was invested in him.

"If she's sleeping with him, then it's casual," Adam mused.

"She's not." He did believe her on that count. "I would bet they've been on a couple of dates and she's using him like a shield."

Adam shrugged one shoulder. "She didn't run to him, man. I would not let that get in my way."

"Yeah, we all know about that." Jake's eyes rolled. "But in this case, I agree. She used you as cover, not the guy she's seeing. She's about to get a crash course in corsets, spanking, and walking with butt floss between her cheeks. Ian said she's a total newbie, and he wasn't sure if he would call her submissive."

"Oh, sexually she's entirely submissive. She requires it. We didn't know what to call it when we were kids, but all our sex was D/s. It was awkward D/s, but D/s all the same. Maddie needs to be in control of her career and her life, but she also needs someone to force her to take care of herself, to pay attention to something beyond her big old brain." He sighed. "At least she used to be."

"Ah, that type doesn't change." Adam started for the doors. "Serena requires two. See where you are at the end of the weekend and don't push too hard. Let her come to you. I bet she will."

Deke wished he was half as certain. He followed the guys in, ready to start this particular op.

* * * *

Maddie breathed in as Serena Dean-Miles proved she had some serious upper-body strength as she pulled on the corset. "Does it have to be so tight?"

"Oh, you'll love how pretty it is," Serena assured her. "And most of the time I've found that when I begin the evening in a corset, I rarely end in one."

"You change?" She hoped so because she could barely breathe in this sucker.

"Well, if by change you mean end up naked, then yes." Serena tied off the back of the corset. "There you go. I went easy on you."

93

Maddie rose to her feet, trying to get used to the sensation of being caged in a corset. "This is why they do the corset thing, isn't it? It's so we're so uncomfortable, we would rather be naked than in this thing."

"I wouldn't put it past some sneaky Dom to come up with that plan." Serena had walked her through the club while the guys had been outside talking. She'd given her a brief history of the place and then brought her down to the locker room to try on what she called "proper fet wear."

"Proper fet wear," it seemed, included a lot of uncomfortable-looking costumes. She'd been given the choice of a PVC body suit with all the wrong cutouts or a selection of corsets. Serena had explained that they kept the small wardrobe of new fet wear for visitors who weren't prepared for the club's rules. No street clothes were allowed in the dungeon when the club was open.

The club wouldn't open for a couple of hours, but she was supposed to start getting used to playing the role she needed to play.

The role of Deke's submissive.

Had she thought about this at all? Or was she running on pure instinct? It wasn't the way she usually worked. She was logical. She didn't leap without looking. And then she only leapt after making a very thorough study of what she was leaping into, including a decision matrix that weighed the pros and cons of leaping at all.

Yet she'd dove right into this stupid lake. She'd taken the plunge without a second thought.

What's your Dom's name?

Deke. His name is Deke and we've been friends for a long time, but D/s really took our relationship to another level.

Why? Why had she said that? Why couldn't she have come up with some other name? Some completely falsified construct that allowed her room to maneuver?

"It gets easier," Serena assured her. "You get used to it, and there are some things you'll even come to love about corsets."

"Like what?"

"It changes your posture for one thing. Feel how straight your back is. I like the sensation. I spend all day hunched over a computer and when I put on a corset, I get to become someone else."

"You get to pretend?" Maddie had friends who cosplayed a lot. She could understand the concept, though she'd never particularly wanted to dress up herself.

"Not pretend, exactly," Serena mused. "I put that wrong. You would think a writer would be careful with words. No. It's not pretending, not at the core. Sure, playing out scenes can be fun. You pretend to be the nurse and your husbands are doctors who need some special time. Or it can be fun to be the virginal villager who gets pillaged hard."

Maddie couldn't help but snort at the thought. "I don't see myself doing that."

"You never know what ends up floating your boat. Or long boat, in the Viking scenario," Serena replied. "You get two kids in and suddenly it's freeing to be Helga with the braids and the intact hymen. But I digress. What I was trying to say is that the pretending isn't about leaving yourself behind. It's about finding parts of yourself that don't get attention. I write all day. I write about romance and sex, and there's still a part of me that needs both romance and sex. I write words, and words don't fulfill our physical needs. It can be easy to get stuck inside your head and forget you have other parts that need tending."

"That's what a vibrator is for." A vibrator didn't care that she worked late and knew more science than it did. She'd found men often took offense.

Serena's lips quirked up. "Oh, baby girl. I used to be you. Okay. Let's try something. I want you to close your eyes and take a deep breath. I'm going to take your hand and you follow me. I won't let you trip."

But she tripped so easily, and she often did it with her eyes open. "Why?"

"Because I want to show you something," Serena explained.

"Come on. I promise I won't let anything bad happen, but it will work better if you don't open your eyes until I tell you to."

"I don't see how this is supposed to help me with training…" The other woman's eyes had narrowed, proving she absolutely wasn't one of those submissive outside the bedroom types. And she was a brilliant author who actually lived the lifestyle. "Sorry. I'm not used to being out of control."

She closed her eyes and felt Serena's hand take hers.

"I understand the need for control. It's precisely why a lot of powerful women enjoy submitting when it comes to sex." Serena moved slowly, guiding her only she knew where. "Although you'll find the right Dom tends to quietly top you outside the bedroom as well."

"Why would you want that?"

"Oh, for things we can't do for ourselves," Serena said. "It would be great if we were all completely perfect when it came to balance, but most women find it hard to ever put themselves first. I used to work all day. I mean from the minute I got up to right before bed I would have my computer on. Shortly after we got together Adam started making dinner at night and he asked if I wouldn't mind not bringing the computer to the table. I said yes, of course. And then we would watch a movie and Jake would rub my feet, and that's not conducive to working. Slowly but surely I found myself working normal hours and enjoying my time off. And weirdly I became more productive."

"They trained you not to work after dinner was served," Maddie surmised. "Well, I don't have anything to do, so work is kind of comforting."

"Only until you know what real comfort is." Serena stopped. "Now I want you to think about yourself. Think about how you look, how you present yourself to the world. Think about how you dress and how you want others to see you. Think about the secret you, the Madeline you only share with your lovers, and I don't mean the kind that require batteries. Even if you haven't had one in a while, think about a time when you enjoyed someone in bed. It could be a man or a woman. It could be more than one, just a simple time when the world melted away and nothing mattered but how your body felt."

Electric. Young. So filled with potential. Nothing had mattered when Deke kissed her. Her brain went on the fritz the minute he put his hands on her, and while she was with him, she could let go of all her worries and cares and simply be. She'd been able to breathe in those moments, able to float when she so often felt anchored to the ground.

I've never loved any one like I loved you.

And he'd still left her.

I'll pretend to be in your bed. Why not simply be in your bed?

Why not prove to herself that the memory was false and the sex wasn't that good? Why not take what he was willing to offer and be the one to leave him this time?

Serena continued. "Think about the difference between the professional woman you are every day and the secret, intimate woman you get to be when you walk into this club, when you share yourself with your Dom. Now open your eyes."

Maddie opened her eyes and stared for a moment, completely shocked at what she saw.

She was a woman who wasn't defined by her body. Not in any way. Her body was nothing more than a tool to house her brain. She wasn't soft and sweet. She was logical and sometimes cold. In the last few years, she'd traded any sexuality for a hard exterior because she'd learned that the men in her world would view her sexuality as a weakness to be pounced on.

There was nothing cold about the woman in the mirror. The corset was a deep sapphire that brought out the blue undertone of her skin and pushed up the breasts she would normally call small and made them plump and ripe. Her hair wasn't in its usual bun. It flowed around her shoulders. Her waist was nipped in, giving her an hourglass shape any pinup girl would envy.

The woman in the mirror was ready for a sensual experience, but it went beyond sex. There was a soft, vulnerable look in her eyes brought on by the memories of how long and well that man had loved her.

And an aching sorrow that couldn't be denied because he'd left her.

This was who she was when no one else was around. Softer than normal. More vulnerable. A hundred times more afraid.

"You look gorgeous." Serena was smiling.

She did look pretty. It made her think maybe she didn't need to breathe. "You picked a good color for me."

"Most jewel tones will look good on you. I thought we should try the corset because I find putting one on tends to be a good way to bridge the two worlds," Serena explained. "How do you feel?"

She wasn't sure. She wasn't sure she liked how stripped down and real she felt. But she couldn't deny that this part of her existed. It made her wonder how long she could keep this softer Madeline buried around the man who was the reason she'd buried her in the first place.

"I'm good."

"Liar," Serena said with a good-natured grin "It's hard to take the first step."

"I'm only doing this for research. And for the mission."

Serena leaned in. "That's what I said fifteen years, two husbands, and two kids ago. Be careful, Maddie. You might end up like me." She chuckled. "Now come on. I'll take you upstairs and we can practice your greeting. In most formal scenes, the Dom and sub have protocols for how they begin. I'll show you some simple ones that should pass with anyone who watches you."

The idea that someone would be watching made her gut turn. She wasn't used to being in the spotlight. Quite the opposite. She was the brains behind the spotlight.

But Serena was right. Nolan Byrne would be watching. He would know if she was lying and then everything would fall apart, and she would have brought Deke into all of this for nothing.

"I'm ready." She had to be.

She followed Serena out, trying to listen to every word the woman said, but all the while she couldn't help but wonder.

If she had a secret self, a sexual side that lived under the covers of clothes and layers of polite personality, did Deke have one, too?

Would she even be able to survive Deke's dominant side? Because if she fell for that man again, she might never get back up.

* * * *

Nolan Byrne often thought that he might have been more happy had he led a normal life.

Then he looked around his palatial Malibu estate and remembered how much it sucked to be poor.

"I'm going to need to see those quarterly reports next week. You know that, right?" a soft feminine voice said.

He only knew her as Jane. It was the only name she would give him, but then the group she worked for believed deeply in the shadows of the world. It was in the shadows they worked their magic, making the world move this way or that. Not even he was sure who all was on the board of the "company" Jane represented.

He only knew she was powerful and he wanted her.

He meant to have her.

She was going to make him a legend in the scientific world, and he would make her his queen.

After he convinced her he could give her what she needed, of course. "I'll have them ready for you. I'm surprised you agreed to meet me here."

She was stunning, truly the most beautiful woman he'd ever seen, and he'd been around Hollywood stars. They all flocked to him now that he was worth a couple of billion dollars. Of course they wouldn't have paid any attention to the college kid he'd been, sitting on his computer night after night writing code instead of dating.

He was under no real illusions that any of the women he slept with now were interested in more than his bank account.

But Jane was a different story. Jane wasn't interested in money. She wanted power, craved it, and that was something he could respect. That was the kind of thing a real partnership could be based on.

That and the fact that he wanted to bang her so bad he couldn't see straight some days.

A wisp of a smile crossed her lips and she sat back. They were on the veranda, with its sweeping views of the Pacific Ocean. He'd thought about a house on the beach, but all California beaches were public, so he'd settled for the canyon, though the denial of any of his impulses rankled.

"I thought I should see this view you always talk about," she murmured, her eyes on the ocean. "Also, you should know that my handlers don't know I'm here. They think I'm back at the hotel."

"Handlers?"

"Eyes, really. They don't send one to physically watch me all the time, but they do always have eyes out there waiting for me to trip up." She took a long breath, her chest moving, and he could see the faintest edge of her bra and the creamy mounds it covered. "Did you contact your friend? Do you think she can get us into The Reef?"

At least he had good news on that front. A year and half into his very frustrating relationship with this woman and he finally had a way to get to her. He moved to the seat next to her, easing down. He wished she'd chosen the big sofa where they both could sit, but Jane often frustrated him. He rather thought that was her point. "Madeline is surprisingly good at doing what she says she's going to do."

"Why is that surprising? She's a woman in a man's world. I assure you she wouldn't have lasted long if she didn't deliver," Jane replied. "We don't tend to fail in an upward fashion the way you men do."

He held back the need to correct her. He supposed some people would call one bankruptcy a failure, but he'd still managed to come up with the idea for the processor that revolutionized the video game industry and then turned smart cars into geniuses. "Well, she's a good enough employee. I don't have to worry about her taking credit."

"You pay her well enough to forego it, and women don't tend to have the egos men have," Jane agreed. "I think you were smart to elevate her the way you have. If you're loyal to her, I think she'll be an excellent C-level one day."

He gave her a noncommittal grunt because he would never promote little Maddie past where she was right now. In fact, he intended to fire her as soon as the project was done because she didn't have the ruthlessness he needed for his closest advisors. Maddie was quick witted and pleasant to be around, but there was a core of morality in the woman. She would be perfectly horrified if she knew what he planned to use her AI for.

She would give him all kinds of lectures about democracy and fairness and all the other bullshit intellectuals tended to spit.

He knew what was coming. Democracy would inevitably fail because people were morons and needed to be ruled.

He was going to be the one who ruled them all. Or at least be a member of the cabal who secretly ran everything. He would do this one little thing for them and then he would be in. Once he was in, he would do what he always did. He would backstab his way to the throne, and the woman beside him would take her crown, too.

"Let me know when she's back in town." Jane turned his way. "Did you read some of the materials I left for you? I know it might seem odd but…"

"It doesn't seem odd at all." He leaned in, giving her his most sincere gaze. He didn't want her to think for a moment that he found her proclivities disgusting. He didn't. He had at first, but then the whole concept made sense. BDSM was a way for a woman like the one in front of him to accept her natural place—at a strong man's feet. Jane was smart and gorgeous, and she'd bought into the idea that she was as good as any man. D/s allowed her to be the woman she truly was, the way she was always supposed to be. Submissive.

He didn't buy the stories about her. There were rumors that she was dangerous. Oh, she had ties in the world that could certainly be dangerous to his future plans, but she wasn't capable of real physical violence. He was sure she could shoot a gun and probably had some self-defense skills, but a woman like Jane was built to please a man.

A man like him.

He simply had to prove to her that he could handle what she needed, and that meant getting into that fucking club she wanted to see.

A shy smile came over her face and the sun hit her in just the right way that he would swear he could see the hint of a scar running up her neck. Then she moved and it was gone. "I'm glad to hear it. I like you a lot, Nolan. I fought to keep this assignment because I think we could have something good."

But only if she got what she wanted. "She went on a spa trip with a friend of hers this weekend, but on Monday we're supposed to talk about getting together with her Dom." He had to shake his head at the thought. "I was surprised to find out she had one. She's so buttoned up. I'm a little worried about who this man is going to end up being."

"You might be surprised." She leaned in, giving him the faintest hint of the perfume she wore. The scent made his cock tighten. "Maybe Maddie has some secrets of her own."

"She better not or I'll have to kill her like I did the others," he admitted. "I'll be happy when the damn thing launches and I don't have to worry about getting found out."

She moved in closer, so close he could feel her breath on his lips. "I'll be happy when it's over, too."

He started to lean in and she stood, the prize taken from him once more.

Frustration welled like a snake ready to strike, but he shoved it all down. He could be patient.

She stared down at him, an earnest look on her face. "It means the world to me that you're willing to do this. I need…boundaries and rules. The last man I loved, well, to say he broke my heart would be the least of what he did to me. Having a contract between us, knowing how we're going to proceed, it means everything to me, Nolan."

This was why he didn't walk away from her. When he saw the barest glimpse of her vulnerability, his whole being sparked. He stood but didn't move too close to her. "Of course. I want to show you not all men are like your ex."

"Oh, there's no one like him. No one on earth," she said and then shook her head. "Thank god. I don't think the world could handle another him. I know I couldn't. It's time for me to find some joy, and that starts with beginning our journey."

"She'll be back on Monday. I'll speak with her and perhaps we can have dinner sometime that week." He hated how eager he was, how she could lead him around by his dick. "Do you think we'll talk to the board and tell them of our plans?"

She dangled more than her body in front of him. She dangled all the possibilities of his world, the rare land left to conquer.

Another smile curled up her lips, a secretive one that always made him think about wrapping his hand around her throat and proving he was man enough for her. "I think it's almost time to reveal all the plans. It's almost time to come out of the shadows and see what happens."

She walked away, her heels not making a single sound though he knew they should. It unnerved him how quiet she could be.

Nolan sat back as the sun started to go down, lighting the world in a spectacular show.

He would have her. She was fit to be his queen, and she would take her place.

If she didn't, he would destroy her and find another one. After all, women were mostly interchangeable.

When his butler came to let him know his guests for the evening were here, he put on his shiniest face, the one he showed to the whole world.

Just a few more weeks and everyone would meet the real Nolan Byrne.

He couldn't wait.

Chapter Four

"How much do you know about Byrne?" Adam sat down on the bench beside Deke's locker. Adam's own was at the front of the locker room beside Jake's, where the original Sanctum members kept a whole row.

Deke's was located in the back with the "riffraff," as Big Tag called them. In true Tag fashion, though, the riffraff lockers were just as spiffy.

He wondered if Maddie was impressed with the women's locker room. It was far more plush than the men's, but they didn't have a massive TV so they could watch football or play video games when the night wasn't going the way they'd hoped. More than once a couple of the guys would find themselves without play partners and end up virtually shooting some dude in Minnesota on the big screen.

The women had their choice of partners. Almost always. Sanctum had too many dudes.

"I know he pissed off Big Tag. I know Hutch and MaeBe think he's some tech god." He still wasn't sure how Maddie saw the man. She was obviously willing to entertain the idea that he could be a bad guy, but he wasn't certain she was sure.

"Oh, he is. He's a complete rock star in the tech world. His history is fairly common for that type. Byrne came from a solid middle-class upbringing. His parents were both white collar, but they divorced when he was in his teens. That was around the time he sold his first app, a game that made him some money, and he started a company with a friend of his," Adam explained.

Adam knew a lot. "You sound like a fan."

"Oh, I think the man is brilliant. I also think he's one of the most dangerous men on the planet," Adam corrected.

Deke hung his shirt up and reached for his vest. He'd already changed into his leathers and boots. He'd meant to spend this time planning some lessons for Maddie, but when Adam talked like this, he tended to listen. Adam could be a jokester, but he knew his stuff when it came to technology and men like Byrne. "Because of the tech he's creating?"

"Because I believe that he's a sociopath with absolutely no feelings or empathy for anyone around him," Adam explained. "I wasn't working for McKay-Taggart when they took the job for Byrne's company, but I made sure I met him. I spent some time with him, and he is excellent at looking like the happy-go-lucky, slightly goofy guy you see on TV. But there's a deep well of darkness in the man that scares me."

"Maddie thinks he might have had some employees killed." That wasn't exactly how she'd put it, but when it came to work, he was a worst-case scenario guy. In his daily life, he was a positive thinker, hence him already putting the idea of her boyfriend behind him. But when it came to an investigation, if someone was missing, he was always looking for a killer first.

"I wouldn't put it past him at all, and that's one of the reasons I wanted to come talk to you. Ian loses his fucking mind at the thought of the man. He'll rant and rave about the money Byrne cost him, but that's not the danger you're going into. I've talked to Chelsea about this, and we'd like to be looped into any technical intel you find."

Deke closed the locker door, suspicions starting to play in his head. The last thing he wanted was to get caught between Ian and Adam. "What are you asking me to do?"

Adam stopped, seeming to think about what he said next. "Look, what I'm about to tell you is somewhat classified."

"Then maybe you shouldn't tell me." He worked corporate investigations. Sometimes he did trace jobs for wealthy people who wanted to make sure their kids/spouse/business partner weren't doing something they shouldn't. He'd left the Agency, and he didn't want to go back. McKay-Taggart was out of the spy business—at least they were out of the business when it came to the CIA. He couldn't say the same for Adam's business. While the other partners in Miles-Dean, Weston, and Murdoch ran the business side of the firm, Adam Miles and Chelsea Weston were the brains behind the technology that fueled the company. Chelsea once ran her own department for the CIA, and most of the people he knew still thought she did jobs for them from time to time.

When it came to the Agency, he was happy to be left in the dark.

"You're going to be difficult," Adam murmured. "Would you change your mind if I told you that I believe your girl might be involved?"

"What do you mean by that?" His every instinct flared, and he realized he'd never stopped being protective of Maddie. He was ready to throw down with a man he admired at the very thought that he might accuse Maddie of something.

Adam stood, meeting his gaze. "I mean that roughly two months ago there was a cyber attack on three nuclear power plants. One in each of the three largest nuclear power producing countries in the world—the US, China, and France. The Agency contacted one of their best contractors in a desperate attempt to shut down the attack."

A shiver went up his spine at the thought. There was zero question who the contractor was. It had to have been Chelsea Weston. At one point in time, she'd been the world's premiere information broker, and that included superlative hacker skills.

Ransomware attacks had been on the rise for the last decade, mostly by organized crime who were emboldened by the ease of cryptocurrency. They could get paid, and as long as they were smart about it, the currency was untraceable. But the targets were usually soft—hospitals, businesses, even individuals. Hell, he knew some public figures who'd had their social media hacked and paid thousands of dollars to get it back. A nuclear power plant would have spectacular security. At least he hoped it would. But there was an easy way to deal with a ransomware attack. "They didn't pay straightaway? I thought most companies plan for those kinds of attacks. There's insurance for it now."

It was expensive as hell, but some businesses found it necessary.

"They didn't ask for ransom."

That chill was positively a freeze now. "If they didn't want money, what did they want?"

"On the surface, it looks like they wanted to cause a meltdown at three power plants, possibly killing hundreds of thousands of people," Adam replied quietly. "Chelsea got it under control here in the States, and by then they'd brought me in and I walked our French counterparts through the solution while Chelsea dealt with the Chinese. All of our plant security has been hardened, but there's a part of me that wonders if what happened that day wasn't a test for something more."

"Something more?" This was exactly the kind of shit he didn't want to get involved in.

"I don't know, but my instincts tell me this was a trial, and Chelsea agrees with me. I would bet this isn't the first time they've used this particular system, but they wanted to see how quickly we can shut them down," Adam explained. "We believe the same group that attacked the power plants was behind more than fifty smaller attacks across the world in the last six months. All of the previous attacks were minor headaches, but the thing that connects them is the mode of attack."

"I don't understand what this has to do with Maddie. She doesn't

107

write that kind of code—certainly not ransomware or malware."

"I assure you she could. She might not deal with basic coding anymore, but I looked her up and she could easily learn anything she needed to. A ransomware attack would be basic for her. However, it wasn't that kind of attack," Adam replied. "The plants were attacked by what I can only describe as an artificial intelligence."

Fuck. He felt his jaw clench. "She did not do this. She would never do anything like this, Adam. I know her."

"You know who she used to be." There was a deep sympathy in Adam's tone. "I understand that you were close back in high school, but it's been a long time, and you've both changed. Can you honestly say she knows you? The Deke Murphy who went through the military and the Agency? The one who's been in Dallas for over a decade?"

"The core of who I am hasn't changed." There was zero chance Maddie Hill had anything to do with an attack that could kill people. "And it hasn't changed for her either. She is incapable of this level of evil."

"All right. Then I believe someone might be using her work for criminal purposes I don't even understand at this point," Adam allowed. "I get that you like the lady, that you're probably still half in love with her, but she's in a dangerous position if she's working with Byrne."

He didn't want to even think about Maddie being involved with people who could try overloading a power plant. "Why do you think the AI that tried to take over the plant is Maddie's?"

Adam leaned against the locker. "Chelsea managed to keep records of some of what she did. She's been examining the code, and she says some of it is very similar to Byrne's previous work."

"Okay. Then Byrne is the problem, not Madeline." He was completely sure of that.

Adam's dark head shook. "But Madeline is the head of his artificial intelligence team, and she's the one working on the AI for the satellite system that—if it works—will likely form the basis for all US satellites in the foreseeable future. If this works, Byrne will likely be given anything he wants to build satellites for this country, and if that AI does what I suspect it does, think about what kind of access that will mean."

It meant Byrne would have his hands in all the nation's security systems. "Then maybe what I should do is pull Maddie out of that company altogether and let the Agency handle it."

"We don't know if the Agency is handling anything at all. Why do you think I'm asking you? Do you think we haven't tried to take these questions to them? Our only contact is Drake Radcliffe, and he's not answering Chelsea's calls at the moment," Adam shot back. "He told her she's overreacting and to stand down."

Deke didn't see the problem. He'd met Drake Radcliffe a couple of times, and though the guy was young, he seemed solid. Drake was in his late twenties now, but he'd started working for the Agency years before. He was their wunderkind, and he'd been the one handling Chelsea for a while now. Chelsea and Adam weren't direct employees. There would be a limit to what the Agency would tell them. "Then he's handling it. You know they can be secretive bastards."

"They can also go bad." Adam's eyes had taken a steely look. "You should know that better than most. You watched what the Agency did to Ten Smith. They chose to disavow him when he wouldn't allow Hope McDonald to continue her work. They chose Levi Green over Beck and Solo. Do you honestly believe Drake is incapable of turning? Hell, he might even be under orders to let this thing play out. If the government believes the tech is worth it, they'll sacrifice lives and cover it all up. He's been acting weird the last year or so. He's distracted by something, and I worry when a man who has always been so focused is acting even slightly out of sorts."

His head was spinning with the implications. "Again, then maybe I should pull her out."

"Then they would know something is wrong and they'll go underground," Adam argued. "We'll lose our chance to figure out what they're trying to do."

Deke shook his head. "This is far above my paygrade. Talk to Tag, man. I'm not a spy. I never really was. I was muscle for way smarter guys than me. I'm going to do the job Tag asked me to do. I'm going to protect Maddie, and I'll try my damnedest to ID our mystery lady, but I'm not going to work behind Maddie's back. Let's sit her down and tell her what we know."

"Absolutely not." Adam's whole body had gone tense. "I know you believe in her, but she can't know what I just told you. It could get me and Chelsea in serious trouble. If you won't do what I need you to do, I'll find another way, but you can't tell her." Adam put his hands up in obvious defeat. "I'll talk to Ian."

"I'm not coming off this op." He wasn't going to let anyone use Maddie. He would bring her in if he needed to, but he wasn't going to go around her and potentially ruin her career. "If Tag pulls me, I'll make sure she stays out of this. I'm not trying to be difficult."

Adam's eyes rolled. "Well, you're doing a spectacular job of it."

How to make the guy understand that this was more than a job to him? "I care about her."

"I get that."

"You also aren't even sure it's the same," Deke pointed out. "Look, she's trying to get onto Byrne's system. That's what you really want, right? You want a peek?"

"Yeah. I'd like to see what the man's doing."

"I'm going to have MaeBe help her. Maddie has skills, but I bet MaeBe's the better hacker," he pointed out. He could still salvage this. He just needed to get Adam to compromise with him. "Do you trust MaeBe?"

Adam nodded. "Yes."

"Then I'll talk to MaeBe and direct her to grab copies of anything she thinks is suspicious. But Maddie's going to know I'm doing it. She needs the information, too. MaeBe will keep a copy on her system, and we'll go from there. I know you have to look at this situation with a cynical eye, but I would bet my soul that Maddie has nothing to do with this. She's working on our side."

"I hope you're right." Adam backed away as he spoke.

He felt bad. He knew Adam was trying to do what he thought was right, but he couldn't get into the mud again. "I'll talk to Ian with you. We can restructure things and come to some kind of compromise."

"I'll deal with it. Honestly, it was a long shot, and you're right. We don't have the kind of proof we need to put the company at risk," Adam conceded. "But my warning is still real. Watch your back with Byrne. He's capable of anything." Adam's expression cleared. "Now let's go teach your girl a little bit about D/s."

"Adam, you don't have to help me. I get why you came down here now, and I will also understand if you want to walk away."

Adam's head shook. "There's no price for my help. I know we're not exactly the best of friends, but you've been around for a long time. You have to know we don't work that way. I might not be a member of your team, but we are all still family. Chelsea and I will figure this out. And spending time with Madeline might ease my worry."

Deke heard the door to the locker room open. "She's a good woman."

"I hope so." Adam nodded his way. "I'll go get dressed. I thought we would start by talking about protocol."

"Oh, I assure you she knows all the technicalities of D/s. She's a quick study when it comes to the intellectual parts. She probably knows more than you or I about the philosophies behind the lifestyle. It's the physical and emotional aspects she'll struggle with."

"Then let's combine the two," Adam offered. "We can make her comfortable by lobbing her questions she can easily answer and then hit her with the reality of how physical D/s can be. You really want this woman?"

"I do." He wasn't going to lie. "She got away once. I don't want to let it happen again."

"All right, then. Let's see what we can do." Adam rounded the corner and then stopped. "Hey, Kyle. I can't imagine what you've come here to talk to Deke about."

"Uh, obviously I'm going to talk to him about the op and how he plans to use MaeBe," Kyle replied.

Deke groaned and let his head fall back.

It was going to be a long day.

* * * *

Maddie felt the hard wood beneath her knees and tried to get her back to straighten up the way Serena had directed her to. After they'd handled her wardrobe, Serena had taken her up the stairs and through the big dungeon to what she called the training room. Unlike the rest of the dungeon this space had a door and a solid wall of mirrors so she could watch herself fuck up.

"Think of it like there's a string that runs through you and it lifts you up all the way from the base of your spine to the top of your head," Serena advised.

This was a lot like the yoga classes she signed up for, went to two, and then found a reason to skip. Although at least at the yoga class she got to wear comfy clothes. No one told her she had to stretch a corset around her body while wearing nothing else but underwear.

If she had known she would get down to her undies, she probably wouldn't have worn pink cotton granny panties.

"Relax, Maddie," Serena said, her voice matching the meaning of her name. Calm. Peaceful. Serene.

Maddie felt a little like her own nickname. Angry. Not angry, exactly, but frustrated and self-conscious. "Do you want me to relax or to sit up straight?"

A low chuckle came from Serena. "You're going to have to learn how to do both and how to moderate your tone unless you like being spanked."

Maddie stopped and looked up at her new mentor. "He's not going to spank me."

She had a hard time believing that Deke spanked women. He

wasn't like that. He was normal. Except she could see it in her head. When she'd first started researching D/s, she'd been able to close her eyes and see Deke staring down at a woman's bare ass draped over his lap. He would touch her, stroking the cheeks before he brought his hand down.

The woman was always her.

A brow cocked over Serena's eyes. There was nothing about the beautiful woman's stance that told Maddie she held an ounce of self-consciousness. She wore an emerald green corset and what was probably considered proper underwear for the fet set—a teeny, tiny thong that proved Serena Dean-Miles believed in a certain grooming routine that Maddie needed to get on board with if she was going to wear anything close to that thong. "So you're going to hang out with a guy who is into the lifestyle and will probably want to watch the two of you practice, and you're not going to be spanked? Because that part isn't always about punishment. It's actually rarely about punishment at Sanctum. It's play. You're not planning on playing?"

Maddie didn't like the fact that she was challenged at every turn here. Every time she opened her mouth someone pointed out that she was a dumbass and all her plans were stupid. Not in an impolite way, but that was how it felt. "I guess I didn't really think about the physical part. Nolan is more of an intellectual person. We talk about D/s."

"Yes, that's usually the first step. There's a lot of talking in D/s, but at the heart it's a physical thing," Serena said. "Why do you think he's interested in the lifestyle?"

"There's a woman he likes, and she's involved in D/s." He'd talked about his relationship with someone named Jane. "She apparently wants a Dom, and she won't have a relationship with him until he's been cleared by a trusted top. It seems weird to me, but he's weird, so it tracks."

It was obvious Nolan was deeply involved with this woman, so involved he would do almost anything to be with her. That was when she'd realized she could use her fake D/s status to get into Nolan's inner circle and have a shot at figuring out what happened to her coworkers.

"So this guy wants to learn how to have a D/s relationship from you and your Dom, and you don't think he'll want to study you? You don't think you'll have to scene for him?"

She wanted to growl. She hadn't thought at all. She'd fallen down a rabbit hole with no plans about how she would get out, and now she was here and Deke was still so delicious it hurt to look at him and she was in panties never meant for the masculine gaze. And she'd told her boss that she liked a good spanking. For that alone she could be fired, much less actually getting spanked in front of the man. No. There had been no thinking on her part, and it wouldn't do any good to take it out on the woman who was trying to help her. She settled back on her heels and drew her shoulders straight, lengthening her spine. "I will most likely have to do that, so I'm going to stop fighting."

"Oh, I doubt that very much," a deep voice said.

A deep, rich as sin, masculine voice that practically stroked against her skin. She closed her eyes because Deke was behind her, and she wasn't sure she wanted to see him in a set of leathers. Somehow she got the feeling he wouldn't be wearing the male equivalent of her granny panties.

"You will probably fight me the whole damn time," Deke said with a chuckle. "It's all right. I like a good fight. Serena, you look lovely and do your Masters proud. I appreciate you working with my submissive."

That sounded formal. She forced herself to open her eyes. She noticed Serena's head had dropped as though she was following some sort of protocol. Yeah. She knew about protocol, and her brain was on the fritz. She'd studied for months but was finding the practical application of all that reading and watching a bit hard. She lowered her head, trying to keep her spine straight and her hands on her thighs.

"I'm enjoying spending time with her, Master Deke," Serena replied. "We were going over proper form when greeting one's

Master in a formal setting."

"You should have gone over proper presentation in a formal setting. The corset is lovely, but what the hell, Maddie?" He'd dropped the deep tone and sounded more like the Deke she knew.

She brought her head up now because no amount of protocol would stop her from defending her sad-sack undies. "I wasn't planning on getting half naked and…"

Yup. She shouldn't have looked. She should have kept her head down, eyes closed, and then she wouldn't have the sight of Deke Murphy—former high school goofy jock—looking like a decadent sex god in leather pants and a vest with no shirt on. It showed off his chest. The man had not let himself go. Not in any way. She'd been in love with the boy.

The man was even more devastating.

"And?" He stared down at her.

She'd been saying something. "And I hadn't done laundry in a long time."

His lips quirked up in a smirk that shouldn't be so freaking appealing. "So you have a bunch of sexy underwear at home?"

He would probably look through her drawers. He seemed way more nosy than he'd been before. "Not really."

"You will when I'm done. I understand you want to be comfortable in the normal course of your day, but when we're playing, I dress you. You'll be dressed to please me, to show off every inch of your beauty."

She rolled her eyes. "Yeah, I'm not…"

Serena hissed in a way that told her not to finish that sentence.

She didn't. Just sat there and tried to figure out what the hell to do next. The lifestyle was pretty clear on one thing. Every body was welcome. Slim, fat, disabled, scars, or perfect skin. They were all to be considered beautiful and worthy of worship and pleasure. It was one thing she wanted to actually take away from this. "I'm sorry, Sir. I was about to say something I shouldn't. I'm trying to wrap my brain around the fact that my body is beautiful, but I've got a couple of decades of societal norms pressing down on me."

"Your boyfriend doesn't tell you how gorgeous you are?" The deep voice returned.

He kept going back to her not-exactly boyfriend, who she hadn't even kissed yet and never would now. "We haven't slept together. He doesn't know."

Deke knelt down, his hand going to her chin, lifting it so she had to look him right in his gorgeous eyes. "You look amazing, Madeline. You're sexier than you were in high school, and I thought you were the sexiest, most beautiful thing I'd ever seen back then." He let the moment hold, their eyes locked on each other before that smirk was back. "But the panties are going to go as soon as possible."

"I apologize, Master Deke," Serena said with a chuckle. "We have corsets and fet wear for guests, but undies are a bit more personal. I'll have someone go by a store and buy something more suitable for tonight."

"You don't have to do that. I can run by a Target." She didn't want to put anyone out.

Deke stood again. "Nope. First of all, the garments she's talking about can't be bought at a big box store, and second, you're in hiding. I don't like the fact that you came from the airport to my place alone. Any number of cameras could have caught you. You stay with me while we're in Dallas. I don't want to chance someone seeing you and reporting back to Nolan Byrne that you weren't where you said you were."

"How would he see me here?"

"Oh, any number of ways," a new voice said.

Maddie looked in the mirror and saw the door had come open again.

Serena gracefully dropped to her knees, her form exquisite. A dark-haired man in similar leathers to Deke stepped up next to her, placing his hand on her head with a gentle touch.

"You are perfect in every way, my love," he said before turning his gaze on Maddie. She recognized the man as one of Serena's husbands. Adam Miles. "Depending on how paranoid Byrne is, he could have systems that sweep across the country scraping CCTV cams for data. It's certainly what I would do if I suspected you of anything."

"I don't think he suspects me. If I had to guess, he thinks I'm quite naïve." She didn't like it, but it worked in her favor this time. "I know he can make ruthless business decisions, but he's good to his employees. At least he seems to be. That's what I need to find out—if this is Nolan or if there's someone else pulling the strings at Byrne."

"Well, now Mr. Byrne isn't the only one who thinks you're a bit naïve." Adam was staring at her in the glass of the mirror.

"Adam." The name was a warning on Deke's tongue.

Adam held a hand out, helping Serena to her feet. "We'll meet you on the main stage. Jake is getting everything ready. We'll go over the equipment and see what she knows. We'll talk about a contract between the two of you. I want you to have a physical one in case Byrne would like to see it. Tonight she can watch the scenes and you can talk about your cover."

He led Serena out of the small room and toward the stairs.

"That seemed tense. Did something happen?" Was she already causing trouble for Deke?

"You need to spread your knees wider," he murmured, watching as Adam and Serena disappeared. The door closed, and Deke's shoulders seemed to relax. "He's upset that I'm unwilling to do some dirty work for him. He thinks your boss is behind some attacks on critical targets and that Byrne's using your AI."

She gasped and started to get up.

"No," he commanded, his hand coming to her shoulder. "If you want me to explain, you'll do as I asked."

She wasn't sure she liked the sound of that. "I have to do things your way."

"When we're in a dungeon or on the mission, yes, Madeline." He had a confidence about him that had been absent when they were kids. It wasn't that he'd been insecure. He'd been a boy, and now he was a man who'd gone through the crucible and come out on the other side.

Sometimes her heart ached that she hadn't gone through it with him, but he'd been the one to make that choice. He'd chosen to leave her, chosen to not seek her out later on. She had to remember that. He was the subject matter expert, and he was nothing more than a tool to help her accomplish her goal. Therefore she should choose to do as he'd asked.

Ordered. In a super-sexy voice.

She moved her knees further apart, trying to find that peace Serena seemed to have around her. She straightened her spine and took a long breath, trying to let go of the tension that seemed to plague her every day.

"Adequate, but we have to get you comfortable with yourself. I wouldn't buy that you've spent any time at all in the lifestyle right now," he admonished. "And you should know that I was just told you could cost me my job. The man you met sometimes works for the government. His partner is Charlotte Taggart's sister, and she used to be one of the CIA's top analysts."

"What does that have to do with Clarke?" Her heart raced at the thought of someone misusing her work. She wanted to get up but if he was right, then it was more important than ever that she learn how to fool Byrne into believing the stories she'd been feeding him.

"The AI used in the attacks is very similar to your work, though I'm going to admit that I don't understand how Adam can tell," he replied quietly. "What I did get him to admit is that they don't have enough data to truly know."

She took a deep breath and let the panic seep away. Often if one didn't work in the industry, they didn't understand the way things were. This Adam person could be the rock star of the facial recognition world and not have the knowledge he needed to understand what she did. What she did wasn't magic. She stood on the shoulders of others. "The base work has been available for a long time. Byrne has no reason to risk putting Clarke out there and potentially allowing someone else to steal it. We don't have a patent yet. He would do anything to protect what will likely make his company not billions of dollars, but trillions of dollars over the next thirty years. I don't trust him, but I know the one thing he'll protect is his profits. And I protect my research. It doesn't leave the lab."

"Like I said, I think Adam's fishing, and I told him I'm unwilling to put you at risk," Deke explained. "I'm trusting you not to let anyone know what I've told you."

He was risking his job for her. She was back in his life for a couple of hours and he was already putting her first. If only he could have put her first when they'd graduated. "I won't. I promise. I understand why your friend wants to look into it, and I'll share anything we find with him, but I can't open the project to anyone. I'm under a strict contract, and I could lose everything. I'm willing to risk it but not purely out of curiosity."

"I understand. I'm letting you know I won't steal it from you. Not for anyone. When you and MaeBe get into Byrne's system, if you find something relevant, you'll turn it over."

"Is that an order?"

He shook his head. "No. It's a fact. If you find out Byrne is endangering people or betraying his country, you'll turn him in."

Her heart twisted at the absolute trust he was showing her. He was saying and doing all the right things, being the exact person she'd dreamed of. "I work in a world where most people will do anything to get ahead. I mean anything. So how can you be so sure I'll do the right thing simply because it's the right thing?"

His lips curled in that half smile he got when he was sentimental. How could she still remember every one of his smiles? "Because you're Madeline Hill and you always will be."

The words brought tears to her eyes because sometimes she wondered. "I don't know about that. I feel so far away from that girl I was. There are days she feels like a dream I had."

There were days she could still feel the cool grass under her feet as she ran across the yard of the house she'd grown up in, her father chasing her while she giggled madly and the world seemed warm and cozy. Some nights she woke up and she could still feel how Deke would hold her, how much space he took up and how she adored the way she tucked under his arm.

And there were days and weeks and months that went by and she didn't think about them at all, times when her research was all that mattered and someone had to remind her to eat. They were exciting times.

They were lonely times. They felt infinitely lonelier now that he was standing in front of her.

He held a hand out and helped her up. When she was on her feet, he didn't release her hand. He brought it up to his chest, palm pressed to his warm, muscled flesh. "It was a long time ago, but it feels like yesterday to me. I trust you to always do the right thing. I hope you can trust me."

She could trust him with anything but her heart. That had to remain true. "For the mission, yes. I'll follow your lead, but you have to know that I'm not going to fall for you again. I'm a different person when it comes to that part of my life."

"Then you don't have anything to worry about," he promised even as he stepped back and her hand fell away. "I've heard your warning and know what I'm getting myself into. If I do fall for you, it's on me."

She frowned at him. No matter what he said or how accepting the D/s world was, he was totally out of her league. Even more so as an adult. "Deke, I'm being serious."

"I am, too. I've told you there isn't anyone who compares to the way I felt about you. Maybe it was first love. Maybe it was teenage hormones. I don't know, but I'd like to find out. We're about to play a role that puts us in very intimate contact. Even the training is going to be intimate. I think it's inevitable that we wind up in bed together, and I'm not going to fight it."

"Well, I am." She didn't pretend that there would be nothing to fight.

He stood over her, his eyes warm and inviting. "Tell me you

don't want to know. Tell me you didn't read those books and think about what D/s sex would be like."

She couldn't. She'd read the books and thought about what it would mean to be tied up and helpless with a man she could trust, to be able to let go of every single worry she had and concentrate on pure pleasure for an hour or so.

What Serena had said finally sank in. Yes, she was playing a role, but what she was truly doing was unleashing a part of herself that never got fed. What she would be doing was fulfilling needs she hadn't dreamed of, but that had always been there, simmering under her shiny, intellectual surface.

"I think it would be a bad idea for us to go to bed together. I know we need a certain level of intimacy in order to fool Nolan, but it has to stop there."

Deke took a step back. "I won't do anything without your permission. Consent must always be given, and even if we're in a heavy scene you can stop me with a single word. We should agree on a safe word."

She hated that he sounded hard again. Not cold, but he'd put his Dom hat back on. He was in teaching mode, and for a moment they'd felt like something more.

Which was precisely why she needed to keep her guard up. At least she knew about safe words, and she knew they would have a contract. Those were things she could deal with. Those were logical things, steps they needed to take.

"I won't say anything about Adam." She needed to let him know that just because she couldn't take that risk with him again didn't mean she didn't care. "I need you to know that I have your back out there."

"And I have yours." He held out a hand. "So we're friends?"

She shook it, trying not to think about how big and callused it was, how she'd loved the feel of those hands on her body. "Friends."

She couldn't help but feel like she'd slipped right into his trap, and if she wasn't careful, she wouldn't even want out of it.

"Come on. We're going to let Jake and Adam and Serena show you the ropes a bit. I want you to sit on my lap while we watch them. It's good practice to get comfortable with one another again."

His hand held hers, surrounding her with his warmth. Didn't she want to know? It wasn't like anything could come of their going to bed together. He'd made it plain that he wasn't about to follow a woman around, and he had a job here in Dallas. She lived in California. What was the real danger in sinking into this role he wanted her to play?

"Okay, I suppose I should do that. I think once Nolan knows you're in town, he'll want us to spend an evening with him. We really should look like we're physically comfortable with each other."

He stopped and loomed over her. "I agree with that assessment. We need to be comfortable showing a lot of affection to each other. Unless you told your boss I'm a cold, formal top."

Well, if she'd known she would have to produce him, she would have. She sighed. "I didn't. I pretty much said you were perfect and that you keep me close and like to touch me a lot." She didn't want to examine why she'd built a dream Dom in her head. She definitely didn't want to think about why he'd taken far more than Deke's name. "I described you as possessive but not overly so, just enough to let me know you care. I said you were quite affectionate and that while you absolutely had hard and fast rules, you were indulgent with me. I think I was trying to keep him from going overboard when it comes to the woman he wants to top."

Yeah, that sounded good.

"Or you're falling back on what you know." The expression on Deke's face let her know she wasn't fooling him for a second. "You pretty much described our prior relationship to a *T*. I was affectionate and indulgent, and I was absolutely possessive, though I think I hid my caveman side from you back then. I won't now. Now I understand there's a place for my inner caveman. I can control him so he gets let off the leash every now and then. I've found it helps to keep that particular beast fed."

"Well, you were possessive to a point, weren't you?" It was so good to remind herself of what had happened, of how he'd wrecked her heart when he was just a boy. How much more damage could the man do? "You let me go when you thought it was time. I learned that lesson from you. Let's get to work."

If anything happened between them it would be temporary, and as long as she remembered that fact, she would be fine. She would complete her mission and perhaps if she did indulge in sex with Deke, she could get on with her life.

He'd always been there. He'd always been the shining star she compared every man to. Maybe if she let herself spend this time with him, she would see that memory wasn't reality.

She could move on. If she realized Deke wasn't the perfect man she'd built him up to be, she might be able to consider a good man like Dan Gray. She would see that the spark between them wasn't as important as relatability and reliability.

"Maddie, we should talk about that." For the first time Deke didn't look like he was completely in control.

She shook her head. "Nope. That's going to be my one rule. No talking about the past. I mean, it's inevitable that we will refer to things that happened when we were kids, but we're not rehashing the end of our relationship. It's done, and there's nothing we can do about it."

"Yes, there is. We can talk," Deke insisted.

She pulled away from him. Luckily she'd learned his language. "I'm afraid I need to make that a hard limit. I think you'll find you can talk me into trying a lot of things I shy away from initially. I'm incredibly curious, but not about this. It's ancient history."

"It doesn't feel like ancient history. It still feels like it's between us."

"Hard limit, Deke." She wasn't going to listen to him rationalize leaving her behind. Or rather forcing her to leave him. He'd had the comfort of home and family, and she'd been shipped out into the big bad world without even being able to call him. He'd made that happen, and all anyone would talk about is how lucky she was to have a boy willing to sacrifice for her.

He'd sacrifice *her*, and he wasn't capable of being honest about why he'd really done it.

He held his hands up. "All right. We won't talk about it. But I'm serious about the rest. I'm going to get you comfortable with me. You're going to tell me everything you've ever said to Byrne about me. We have two days before we fly back to California. I'll take you to work on Monday and you'll introduce me. So we should get started."

She followed him out but wished she hadn't put that grim look in his eyes. She let the regret go. He was right. They had work to do.

Chapter Five

The lights from the hamster wheel cast neon shadows all through the lounge. Sometimes Deke was absolutely certain Big Tag had placed the human-sized wheel perfectly so part of the big lounge acted as an audience space to watch whatever dumbass was running that night. Sometimes it was subs who pissed off their Doms. Sometimes it was Doms who made a bad bet. Of course, sometimes it was members who preferred Sanctum to a gym and they legit were just working out.

He wasn't sure why Jesse Murdoch was running like there was no tomorrow, but his best friend, Simon Weston, was laughing his ass off as the lights changed from yellow to green to blue. Probably some kind of bet. He couldn't be sure because he was trying to avoid Chelsea Weston. He did not need her backing up Adam's previous arguments. Chelsea could be…intimidating, to say the least.

He glanced over to where Maddie sat at a table, laughing with MaeBe and Kori Ferguson. They'd spent all afternoon training with the Dean-Miles trio, so when the lights had gone down and Sanctum turned into a serious club, he'd given her a little time off. She was sitting at a table twenty feet away having a glass of wine and sharing a charcuterie board. They'd had dinner brought in earlier, but she hadn't eaten much.

She was nervous. He could feel her anxiety all through the training sessions. She'd been stiff and precise when she should be loose and flowing. He needed to find a way to break through her walls and get her to relax around him or they would look exactly like what they were—an awkward couple of used-to-be lovers.

He fucking wished Michael Malone was here. Mike had been one of his closest friends for over a decade, but no he had to go and find a girlfriend and be all happy and shit. It was the theme of his life lately. He'd watched Hutch settle down, and then Tessa Santiago had found her professor, and the man he'd thought would die a bachelor had hooked up with a Hollywood star and they'd taken off for Miami after David and Tessa's wedding for a long romantic weekend.

Big Tag wasn't even available for advice this evening. He'd started only coming to Sanctum once a week, and tonight wasn't his play night.

He'd seen Boomer around, but he wasn't sure Boomer was the right guy to give him advice when it came to this. Boomer's longest relationship was with the staff at Top who fed him a couple of times a week.

If only Maddie was a taco, then Boomer would be his man. Other than that, he had a whole crew of happy couples and that one threesome. Not a one would want to sit around and bemoan fate with him.

"All right, we have the plane for Sunday night." Kyle sank down onto the chair beside him, a bottle of beer in his hand. "Once we get to the client's place, I'll check her security system and do a walk-through to make sure she's not bugged."

At least he could depend on one person to not be happy. Unfortunately, Kyle wasn't exactly his close friend. He wasn't sure Kyle was close to anyone with the exception of MaeBe. "I thought you didn't come to Sanctum. Shouldn't you be at The Club?"

Kyle and his brother, David, played at Sanctum's rival club, The

126

Club. Yes, someone should have thought out that name, but most people didn't question the Dom who ran that particular dungeon.

"My mom's in New York with Sean. They're meeting with investors or something. I'm not sure. The upshot is I can be here and not have to worry about running into my mom's boobs." He took a quick drink as though he'd seen a few things he couldn't unsee. "Your girl has done well for herself. I got the blueprints for the house she owns and damn, she's got some room, if you know what I mean."

He turned Kyle's way. "You did what?"

"Who do you want on logistics? Me or Boomer?" Kyle asked.

If he let Boomer handle logistics, they would all have food and weapons and maybe nothing else. "I kind of thought I would handle it."

"When were you going to make a bunch of reservations? I kind of think you need to spend every second you have trying to make sure you look like a functional D/s couple," Kyle replied. "You know I have done this before."

Kyle was an enigma. Technically he was a bodyguard. Technically he'd been Special Forces in the Army. He called himself nothing but a grunt, but the word around the office was Kyle had worked for the Agency, and not the way Deke had. Kyle had been on the path to become a full-on operative, but he wouldn't admit it. Not even to his family. If he could take someone else, he would, but Kyle was Ian's brother's stepson, and he tended to get his way when it came to assignments. "All right. Does Maddie know you have her floor plan?"

"Where did she expect us to stay?" Kyle asked. "Because I don't think we're going to be much help if we're holed up at the Holiday Inn Express on the freeway. We should warn her about Boomer's appetite."

"I'll take care of it." Boomer wasn't so bad. He wasn't picky. He just needed vast quantities of food.

"Relax, man. I was joking. MaeBe and I have a plan. We're going to hole up on Madeline's second floor. She's got two bedrooms and a big loft up there. Boomer and I will share, and Mae will have her own room. We'll use the loft as our office space, and Mae and I have a list of hearty casseroles we can easily make to feed the Boom man. You are in the downstairs guest room, and we're going to stay as quiet as possible. Unless she's bugged, and then we'll have to figure out where to go from there. How do we explain me, MaeBe, and Boomer if the big boss man shows up at her place?"

He'd already thought through that particular scenario. It was important they all had the basics of their stories straight. "You and Mae are a D/s couple we're friendly with. Kayla is putting your name on the books at The Reef. When we get to LA, I want you to familiarize yourself with the place. You'll take MaeBe out there and let Kay show you around. Boomer's my brother. From what I understand, Maddie doesn't have a lot of friends who come over. She works a lot."

"Then why the four-bedroom house?" Kyle asked. "You know it's in a nice neighborhood, right? That house is worth three million dollars. It's not a particularly big house, but it's in LA."

"I'm sure she sees it as an investment." He was probably right about that, but the number shocked him a bit. She was in her thirties, and she could afford three million for a house. He thought he'd saved well and he couldn't even think about buying anything more than his condo.

It was intimidating, but then he'd always known what she could do if given the chance.

You let me go when you thought it was time. I learned that lesson from you.

The words had haunted him all day. She still thought he'd planned to break up with her, still thought he'd gotten something out of it. The accusation had hurt then and it hurt now.

"Well, it's probably a really good one." Kyle sat back, obviously getting comfortable. "I think we'll be okay using it as our base. Any idea how long this job is going to take?"

He kind of hoped it would take a couple of months. It could take that long to crack her shell. It could take forever to really convince her to explore a relationship with him.

Of course, why would she explore a relationship with a blue-collar guy? She moves the world forward and you make sure employees don't embezzle. She doesn't need you for anything.

He forced himself to focus. "Well, that depends on how fast we get into Byrne's personal system and get the information we need. I'm not going to rush it. If we push him, we put Maddie in danger, and as I've already had to listen to you lecture me on how to not place a woman who actually works in security in danger, I'm sure you'll understand that I don't want to put a woman with zero skills in a bad position."

"Yeah, you're not the first person to point out how irrational I am. Mae might have all the training in the world, but she's never been tested, and I'm okay with that. I'm okay if she spends all of her life not going through that particular fire." Kyle's gaze drifted over to where MaeBe sat. The IT specialist wore all black, from her PVC leggings to the corset with gold piping. Her hair was in vibrant contrast to the dark fet wear, and her smile was even more incongruous. She was laughing at something Kori said.

That was when he realized Maddie's smile was slightly uncomfortable. She tugged at the bottom of her corset. She'd changed after the initial session and they'd had dinner with Kori and her husband, Kai, before getting ready for the club to open. When she'd changed this time, she'd put on a new corset—one MaeBe had gone to buy for her along with the ridiculously flimsy scrap of underwear he'd had her pick up, too.

She had not been impressed, but damn he had. Her ass was gorgeous, and he couldn't wait to spank it.

"I don't care, you know." Kyle's eyes stayed on Mae. "What you think. What anyone thinks when it comes to her. She deserves to have someone watch out for her. You know about her family, right?"

He knew a little. "I know her mom died shortly after she graduated from college and her dad remarried a woman she's not

129

close to."

That was how MaeBe had described the situation. She didn't talk a lot about her dad. She often mentioned her mom and how close they'd been once.

"The new wife had a couple of young daughters, and she decided MaeBe was a bad influence on them. She convinced her husband to distance until MaeBe outgrows her rebellious phase. So she lost her mom and her dad over the course of roughly a year."

He hadn't heard that. "The asshole remarried that soon?"

"She's pretty sure they were seeing each other before her mom died. But MaeBe's hair is the real problem," Kyle said, sarcasm dripping. "Anyway, like I was saying, she has no real family, so someone has to watch out for her." He went quiet for a moment and then turned Deke's way. "Besides, I think I'm going to use this op to ease us into a more personal relationship."

Deke groaned. He did not need Kyle and MaeBe drama. "Man, come on. It's an op not a…" There was some hypocrisy right there. Shit. He couldn't exactly come out and say there was only room for one desperate dude going after the woman of his dreams per op. "Just make sure you do your job."

Kyle's lips quirked up. "I will. It's part of the job if we're supposed to be a D/s couple. From the way you look at the client, I assume you'll be doing the same. She was important to you, right?"

"She was the love of my life when I was a kid." He needed to find out if she still was. "I'm attracted to her, but the truth is we live in two different worlds."

"What does that mean? Like she's in LA? I know it seems like a different world, but I've found you can get used to almost anywhere. Except a couple of places in Southeast Asia where the bugs are bigger than my head. Great food, man. I mean spectacular, and the women are gorgeous, but I couldn't get over the bugs."

Kyle's easy words surprised the hell out of Deke. "Since when do you talk about your time in the Navy? I thought that was one of those taboo subjects."

"Since I started to realize that life has to go on and my past is just that. It's in the past." He had a half smile on his face. "I think I'm coming out of my dark and broody period, as my brother calls it. The last year has been one weird calamity after another. I mean it. It's been this crazy string of bad luck for my whole family, and we got through it. We're okay. That got me thinking that maybe I can be okay, too. It also made me think that I take shit too seriously. Including myself and my own damage. Everyone knows I probably wasn't working for the Navy when I was in Southeast Asia."

That was a shock, too. "Yeah, no one buys that bullshit."

Kyle tipped back his beer and looked more relaxed than Deke could ever remember him being. "Well, it's all classified so I still can't talk about it, but I can say that it didn't break me the way I thought it had. There was a woman, and I made a huge mistake with her. She wasn't the person I thought she was and she died. I'm coming to terms with the fact that her death is probably the best thing that ever happened to me because I wouldn't be here if she was alive."

Deke stared at him. Even the lights from the hamster wheel were casting a happy, almost sunny light on the usually dark man. "Who are you and what did you do with Kyle?"

Kyle laughed. "I'm sick of watching all you bastards get your girls and be all happy and shit. How about that? Being around my brother and Tessa, and even my mom and Sean, has made me…soft. I've gotten fucking soft." He sobered a bit. "It's probably all the therapy, too. I wasn't always a secretive asshole. I want to find the guy I used to be and…I don't know…blend him in and figure out who I am now. But mostly I just want her, and I'm tired of waiting. I've always said she deserves better, but I think that woman is going to have to settle."

He was a weird guy, but he absolutely found the Kyle who was enjoying his beer while he stared at the woman he wanted with open longing on his face far more relatable than the dude who played everything close to his vest. "You know you don't need the op. You can just walk up to her and tell her how you feel and she'll jump all over you."

Kyle winced. "Yeah, I haven't had that much therapy. I think I need to ease into it. Playing a couple might help me feel like I can be in a couple. You know, without the whole wake up screaming and trying to kill her thing."

He knew that well. It was probably the kind of statement that would make most people take a step back, but it was pretty standard around here. They'd all seen some shit. "That took me a couple of years. Have you tried holding babies? It worked for me."

"No. I try to avoid all the babies. Luckily my younger siblings are both teenagers and my brother and Tess are far from procreating. I managed to miss out on the poop years, and for that I am grateful."

He could still remember how his sisters wouldn't let him brood in peace. Somehow they'd known how to force him back to reality, to see that there was still good in the world and he could be a part of it.

He'd always wondered if he would have needed those babies if he'd had Madeline. He'd spent every night in that prison he'd been in dreaming she was with him, seeing her open the cell door and leading him back out into the light.

"How long has it been since you've seen her?" Kyle asked.

He let out a long sigh. It was time to be realistic. He didn't want to be the one who was so focused on the woman that he fucked up the op and potentially got her and his team killed. "Almost twenty years. I haven't actually laid eyes on her since the last day of high school. I broke up with her because she was going to pass on a full ride to Yale to stay close to me."

"Seriously?" Kyle's eyes had gone wide. "You must have a very large dick, my brother."

Deke snorted. "We were in love. We were that ridiculous couple who almost never fought. Everything was easy for us until the day I realized I might cost her the future she could have. She wasn't meant to live the life her parents did. She was meant to go to Yale and get a high-tech job and afford a three-million-dollar house."

"Uh, why didn't you just go with her?"

He'd certainly thought about it. "My dad was sick at the time. He had cancer and I needed to help keep the business going. He recovered, but it was too late by then, and she wouldn't talk to me."

"Well, that's ancient history. There's not a damn thing you can do about that now. I think you should do exactly what I'm going to do. You should play your part and figure out if it feels natural to you," Kyle replied, tipping his beer toward the ladies' table. "Right now, she doesn't look natural. She's twelve kinds of uncomfortable, and I wouldn't buy her as a long-time submissive. Not even one who'd played for a couple of months. You have to get her to loosen up."

"I can't order her to relax." It would be so much easier if he could.

Kyle turned his way. "She's not the only one who needs to relax."

"I've been doing this for a long time."

"Yeah, with subs who were only looking for a good time," Kyle pointed out. "That's easy. I can do that, man. She's special. She's important. I watched you with her during the training sessions with Adam, Jake, and Serena. You were tense. What's the problem? Beyond she's the woman who got away and you're worried she's going to figure out you're not the stud you were in high school."

Asshole. "I assure you I'm way better in bed than I was in high school. Hell, I don't think we actually did it in a bed more than a couple of times, and those were quick because one of our parents could come home at any minute."

"Then what is the concern? I'm not seeing it."

Why the hell was he having this conversation with Kyle Hawthorne? He thought seriously about not replying at all, but then he had to admit that he might be the one asking these questions if he was going into an op with Kyle as the lead. They had to work together for the next couple of weeks, and right now he wasn't exactly giving off confident leader vibes. "I'll make it work. I promise. Once I get her in bed, everything will work out."

He looked over at Maddie and she was saying something to MaeBe, a light in her eyes. Then she seemed to remember she was wearing a thong and she went tight again.

He had to get her to relax, to be as comfortable with herself as she'd been when they were in high school. Sex would solve all his problems.

She could talk about dating a guy all she liked, but she admitted she hadn't slept with him. He would bet any relationships she'd had mostly revolved around work and hadn't been hot and heavy.

Not the way it had been with them. They'd made love the first time when they were sixteen and both virgins. It hadn't been great, but they'd practiced and before long they'd gone at it anywhere they could, anytime they could.

They'd once had sex in the storage closet at the First Presbyterian Church during one of his sister's wedding receptions.

When was the last time Maddie had a man so fucking hungry for her?

"Do you think she'll enjoy D/s sex?" Kyle asked.

"I can make her love it. I can make her crave it." He knew that woman, and like he'd told Adam, the core of her hadn't changed. She might have grown and matured, but her deep-seated needs hadn't changed. She was a creature of intellect, and he could make her remember that she could be sensual, too.

Kyle was right. He'd been coming at this from his younger self, the one who worried he wouldn't be enough for her.

If Maddie had come into her own, then he had, too. His needs hadn't changed, but he'd learned how to satisfy them in a way that could serve them both. He'd been tentative with her because her words had hurt his feelings.

Fuck his feelings. He was acting like a lovesick boy, and it was time to be a Dom.

"I think we'll watch some scenes, too." He stood up just as one of the newer members approached the table the ladies were occupying. He was one of the lawyers who worked with the Domme in residence.

He was big and broad, and some women might find him attractive in a douchebag, coming-onto-other-Doms'-subs way.

Of course two of the women at the table weren't wearing collars, but he wasn't in the mood to be understanding.

"Who the fuck is that?" Kyle proved he could be a possessive ass, too.

"Does it matter?" He couldn't remember the dude's name, but he was encroaching heavily. The Dom placed himself squarely between Maddie and MaeBe, giving them both a jerkface smirk he probably thought was sexy or some shit. He leaned over and seemed to be whispering something Maddie's way.

Yeah, that wasn't happening. He crossed the distance between them in a quick order.

"Oh, I'm not sure I'm supposed to do that." Maddie's eyes had gone wide, and she was looking the other man over like he was a popsicle on a hot day. "I mean it's really nice of you to ask, but I'm kind of working."

"Yes, she's working with me. I'm training her," Deke announced.

Kori snorted and her eyes rolled, proving years of marriage hadn't made her any less of a brat. "I can bet what comes next."

"She's not wearing a collar," the douchebag asswipe said.

"How many times have I heard this conversation?" Kori asked to no one in particular.

"Oh, I haven't had time to get a collar," Maddie said. "I just got in last night. We had to send someone out to get these... Do we call them underwear? I'm not actually wearing them under anything. Also, they're not very comfortable."

"You're going to be wearing them under my hand, baby," he promised. "When I spank you. Come on. We're going to watch some scenes, and I promise she'll have a collar on tomorrow."

The guy wasn't at all upset at the cockblock. He simply moved on to the next target. He looked MaeBe's way. "How about you, sweetheart? You need a play partner?"

"Do you need to sleep at night? Because I promise you touch her

135

arm again and you won't because you'll sit up all night worried that I'm going to sneak in and cut off your fingers and stuff them in all your holes," Kyle promised.

MaeBe simply smiled the guy's way as she eased off her barstool. "He's joking, but we are actually supposed to work a bit tonight. We're all MT employees and we have to save the world and stuff. But thanks for asking. I'm here most Fridays."

"Not for a while." Kyle moved in close. He might be a kinder, gentler Kyle when it came to talking about his past, but he was still a raging ball of murder when it came to MaeBe Vaughn. "We won't be back for at least a couple of weeks, so you should find someone else to play with."

The guy put his hands up in obvious defeat. "I will do just that. Have a good night, folks."

"You know you're all the same, right?" Kori simply shook her head. "I will give you the same advice I've been handing out for years. Put a collar on your sub. Something pretty they won't want to take off. And I hope you do it before you get to The Reef because those boys do not play, and you don't happen to be related to or working for the owner. Good luck with that."

Maddie frowned up at him. "What was that about? He was only asking if I wanted to watch some scene with him. Aren't I supposed to do that? When you think about it, I don't really have to watch them with you, right? And I have thoughts about a collar. There's no hard and fast rule about collars. Isn't the lifestyle kind of about making your own rules?"

Kyle snorted and Kori flat out laughed.

"I'm calling my friend, Sarah. She's going to love you so much." Kori had pulled her cell out of her corset and had it against her ear in a heartbeat. "Hey, girl. Wait until you see who's coming your way."

"Kai should spank her more often," Kyle said with a huff.

"She would like that very much." Kori was a bit of a pain slut. But then Kori had been in the lifestyle for a very long time. She knew what she liked. She'd explored pretty much every aspect of her sexuality.

Madeline hadn't. He would bet a turn on the hamster wheel that her sex life had been fairly tame. When they'd been together, he'd been the one to gently push her boundaries. She was submissive when it came to that aspect of her life, and nothing he'd heard made him believe she'd sought out a natural dominant partner. He'd spent the whole day worried about how to reach her without truly grasping the one tool he had.

He could show her how good the lifestyle could be for her.

"I think it's time to start discussing some of those rules," Deke said. "We're going to watch some scenes and then we'll talk. But you should understand the number one rule is that you are with me and there won't be any other Dom who touches you. Is that understood?"

"He was only being nice."

"He was trying to get into your thong, baby," he pointed out.

"Well, it wouldn't be hard," she shot back. "There's not much of it in the first place. It's not exactly a chastity belt."

He moved in, sinking a hand into her hair. He remembered how little of a punishment this would be. He twisted lightly, bringing her up on her toes and lowering his head down so she would have to look right into his eyes. "I don't expect you to be chaste. I expect you to behave like a woman who knows exactly how good it is to be available for her Dom at all times, and I don't mean available to make him a sandwich. By the time I'm finished, you'll appreciate the thong because it means you don't have to do much in order to be ready to take my cock. Am I clear?"

She stared up at him, and he could see the way her gaze softened as he twisted her hair. "Yes."

It was said in a breathless hush that let him know he'd caught her off guard. "Excellent. Then we should begin. The academic part of your day is over. It's time to go into the lab and get some hands-on learning done."

He could speak her language, and he could teach her his.

She grimaced and backed down, a frown on her face. "This is the weirdest lab I've ever been in."

It might be a really long lesson.

* * * *

Three hours later, Madeline had a pit in her stomach as she stood in the living room of Deke's condo. She could feel the frustration coming off of him in waves, but all he would tell her was that he was fine.

Wasn't that the word *she* was supposed to use in a passive-aggressive fashion? Fine seemed to be an all-gender word now.

She sat the bag down on the bar and wondered if she should try to talk to him again.

She'd spent hours watching scenes with him, talking to him about how the scenes made her feel. Well, explaining to him why most of them wouldn't work. They'd watched the main stage where a Dom had walked his pretty submissive through a series of tests that she inevitably failed and was punished for. Normally it would be offensive to watch some poor woman get set up to fail, but the punishment didn't seem to bother the blonde. When she'd dropped the drink she was supposed to gracefully carry on her head, she'd practically hopped onto the spanking bench.

She wasn't sure she understood, and that seemed to bother Deke.

"Do you want anything to drink?" Deke hadn't had a thing to drink while they were at Sanctum. He'd made sure she had a glass of wine, but he'd had water. Now he pulled a beer from his fridge. "I'm going to sit on the balcony for a while. You should feel free to go to bed or watch TV or whatever you do to relax. There's some Pinot on the counter."

The words were all polite, but there was a sheen of ice to them.

She'd done everything he'd asked her to do. She'd sat on his lap despite the fact that it had been awkward and weird. She'd worn the stupid thong even though she'd been heinously self-conscious. When he'd asked her questions, she'd answered them. She'd asked a few of her own.

Maddie had no idea why Deke was so pissed off at her.

"The wine glasses are in the cabinet over the microwave. Good night." He strode away, and she heard the door to his balcony open and close.

She stood there feeling way more vulnerable than she had before.

The night had been so tense. Hell, the whole day had. From the minute they stepped into the club, she'd felt awkward, and she wasn't sure why. She'd studied all the things she'd seen today. None of it was a shock. What had been a shock was how ungainly she'd felt. She was confident. She had a freaking undergraduate degree from Yale and had gotten her master's in aerospace engineering from Cal Tech while she'd been working for a startup she'd made a ton of money from when it had sold.

She'd felt small in the dungeon. Like she was the nerd back in gym class. Of course back then she'd had Deke, who would deal with anyone who tried to make her feel bad.

She stood in his kitchen, the moonlight filtering through the filmy curtains that covered his living room windows, and she wondered who'd decorated his place. It was well done. It wasn't overly masculine. It was comfortable.

Why hadn't she been comfortable in the dungeon? What the hell was she going to do if she couldn't figure out a way to not be so fucking awkward?

Why was he mad at her?

It shouldn't matter. This wasn't her world. It was his. He'd made a conscious decision to belong to the D/s community and she'd stumbled into it for reasons that had nothing to do with her own needs, and now he was pushing her.

When she thought about it, he'd been the jerk. He'd been fine during the day, but after the club had opened, he'd changed. Like the lights going down and music starting up brought about a transformation in him. Like a werewolf on a full moon, he'd gone from mild-mannered, nice guy to a hungry predator who was sure he would get fed.

He'd been bossy and obviously annoyed with her and her questions. He wanted her to simply go along with everything he said, and that wasn't who she was.

She didn't belong here but she wasn't sure what to do, and that was an awful position to be in. This wasn't who she wanted to be, and perversely, she blamed Deke for putting her in the position. He was the one who pushed her to wear things she wasn't comfortable in and then got angry with her that she was awkward.

It would be far smarter to go to bed and start over in the morning, but she couldn't do it. She marched to the balcony doors and walked through.

Deke sat in the shadows, one leg over his knee and a grim look on his face. "Maddie, go to bed."

He said it in that low growl that made her want to obey him and also to defy him just to show him she could. "I don't appreciate the way you treated me tonight."

A brow rose over his eyes, which seemed so much darker in the moonlight. "Then we're going to have a problem because I was nothing but polite to you this evening."

When she thought about it, he *had* been polite, but she'd been able to feel his disappointment. "You were passive aggressive."

"Well, I would think you would appreciate that I managed to not be aggressive, aggressive."

He was frustrating her. "You can't be either. You're working for me, and I expect some professionalism."

He stood suddenly, the move so easy and graceful it seemed almost preternatural. It made her take a step back.

"All right. If that's how you truly feel, then we need another plan. If it helps, I was probably going to suggest another plan anyway. I'll let you sit down with Ian tomorrow and explain that you need a different approach and definitely a different lead investigator."

His words felt like a kick to her gut. "What? You're leaving me because I asked you to be professional?"

"I'm leaving you because you can't work with me." Every word sounded ground out of his mouth. "You don't trust me, and that's why this cannot work. I tried several tactics today. I tried to follow your lead. It got us nowhere. I tried to take the lead. You fought me at every turn."

That's not how she remembered things. "I didn't fight you. I did everything you asked."

"You argued with me constantly."

Once again she felt like a kid in class. She'd been the one the teacher got frustrated with because she wanted to delve deeper into the subject. "I had questions."

"Questions that could get us both killed out in the field."

"You can't expect me to simply follow orders." It wasn't who she was.

"Oh, but I do, and that's why I think the absolute best course of action is for you to stop investigating entirely. I'll let Adam know he can send his own team in if he and Chelsea want to, but you're out of it."

How was she supposed to drop the investigation? "You can't do that."

His face looked like it was made of granite. "Watch me."

He wanted to be stubborn? She could show him stubborn. "What are you going to do, Deke? Kidnap me? Force me to quit a job I worked hard for?"

Was this some kind of revenge for him? She wasn't sure why he would need revenge. He was the one who'd left her, but she knew some men could be irrational about the women in their lives. Even the ones they'd kicked out. It was a surprise to find out Deke was one of those men.

He sank down on the couch, and his eyes went back to the shadows and the energy seemed to flee his body. "For one thing, I thought I'd call your parents in the morning and let them know that you've gotten involved in a dangerous situation. Then I'll call Nolan Byrne and tell him you've lied to him all along and that we have no connection, and he will never be allowed into The Reef."

She stood there for a moment trying to process the threat. He was willing to ruin her career? "How could you?"

He simply shrugged. "It's that or we find someone you can trust enough. Someone you feel comfortable with. Right now, I don't think your plan is going to work. We can try some training with Kyle in the morning. There are a couple of other Doms who might work, but Kyle is already on the team. He would be the easiest replacement. MaeBe can be a friend of yours, and Boomer can be his brother. You never showed Byrne a picture of your Dom, so it could work."

She didn't want to go in with Kyle. She didn't even know Kyle. If Deke called her parents, she would never hear the end of it. They would show up on her doorstep and hound her until she convinced them she was safe—something that might be hard to do considering her situation. If he called Nolan, well, then everything was probably over, including her career.

She'd made a terrible mistake. Coming here to talk to Deke had seemed like a good idea, but it was obviously never going to work. "I'll go. There's no need to have another meeting tomorrow. We can pretend like this never happened. I'm sorry I didn't do what you wanted."

Maddie started to back away.

"I'll call them tonight if you try to leave," Deke vowed. "I'll find Byrne's personal number and I'll have you fired by morning."

She turned on him, an ache inside her opening up. "Why? Why the hell would you do that? Because I didn't obey well enough?"

"Maddie, I already offered to sacrifice a job I adore so I didn't have to lie to you." There was fire back in his tone. "I wasn't joking when I told you what Adam asked of me. Hell, I gave you classified information. It could be more than merely my job on the line. I could find myself in jail or worse. And I knew it when I told you. I made that choice. What do you think I'm willing to do to keep you alive?"

She didn't understand him. The anger and outrage she felt fled, and she had to face the fact that she didn't know what she was doing and she couldn't get anything at all done without him. "What did I do wrong?"

He sighed, a weary sound. "I thought you were submissive and you're not. I was making assumptions based on who you were in high school and how our sex lives went back then, and I was wrong. Someone could teach you to play the role, but it would take far more time than we have. I say we give Kyle a shot to see if it's just me you're opposed to and if it doesn't work, we figure something else out."

She felt frozen in place. "I sat on your lap like you asked me to."

"You complained the whole time. You were uncomfortable, and it was obvious to everyone around us," he explained. "You flinched when I touched you. I assure you Byrne will notice that you find touching me distasteful."

That hadn't been the problem. Not at all. Everywhere he'd touched her, her skin had lit up and something warm had built inside her. She'd worried that damn thong she'd been wearing would show the world exactly how much she'd liked him touching her. Her arousal had spiked when his hands moved over her, and she'd been forced to refocus her attention to the task at hand or she would have forgotten the assignment entirely. "I was trying to concentrate. You wanted me to watch the scenes."

"Yes, and I felt your distaste for the scenes, too."

"I didn't…" How did she explain this to him? "I wouldn't say I found them distasteful. It was surprisingly different to see it happening in person. I've studied. I've read up, and it's not like I didn't go out and watch some porn."

He pointed her way as though she'd just made his point. "Ah, there it is. There's the derision."

"What's wrong with porn?" She had no idea why she couldn't reach him.

"It's a loaded word and you know it. It's also not what we watched tonight."

He was making her so frustrated. She hated this feeling. It made her feel small and powerless. "Then what did we watch, Deke?"

"We watched people connecting. We watched people enjoying their sexuality. There's nothing wrong with porn. It has its place, but that's not what D/s is about."

"It can be. There don't have to be all these feelings involved. Sex can just be sex."

"But we weren't having sex," Deke pointed out. "We weren't even having a pleasant conversation. You want to walk in and fool a man who's considered to be a genius and you can't even act like you enjoy being around me. You flinched every time a sub got spanked and you closed your eyes when Alex put Eve on the St. Andrew's Cross. Every single question you asked I found somewhat insulting. Do you honestly think the subs are allowing their dominant partners to hurt them in a way that doesn't give them something they need?"

Tears pricked her eyes. "I wasn't trying to insult you. I was asking questions. I don't know how to not ask questions."

He leaned forward, his head coming up to lock eyes with her. "It's not going to work with me. There are only a few Doms who can do this job. I'll let you meet them tomorrow, but there's very little time to find someone acceptable and train you properly. Unless you can get another two weeks out of this impromptu vacation of yours."

She wasn't sure how everything had gotten so out of control. She'd known he was upset with her, but not that he was dumping her. All she'd done was ask a couple of questions. And refused to even consider relaxing her guard around him, which kind of defeated the point.

Had she spent the whole night fighting him because she wasn't sure how to deal with the things that truly bothered her?

"You know I can't do that."

He sighed again and sat back. "Then go to bed because we'll have an early morning. I'm sorry I made you uncomfortable. I mean that, Madeline. I hated that…it hurt that we didn't connect the way I thought we would, and I'm sorry if I was having trouble communicating that to you. Despite all the therapy, I'm still a man and my feelings got hurt. I should have been kinder about it."

Maddie sat down across from him. It would be easy to agree with everything he said, but she wasn't exactly without blame here. Communication was everything when it came to D/s, and she hadn't done a good job either. She didn't want to admit why. Honesty would make her more vulnerable, and that was what she'd been trying to avoid. She was doing what she always did, plowing her way through and trying not to feel too much.

There were three choices in front of her. She could allow Deke to pick another investigator for her to work with and see if not having emotional baggage with a guy made it easier to be in a thong in front of a ton of people. Choice two was to give up her whole career because walking away from or being fired from a major project six weeks before launch would make her unemployable for a long time.

Or she could face the truth. She was sitting in front of the man who'd helped form the base of her sexuality, who'd been her lover, who'd left an indelible imprint on her, and she was scared of being hurt again.

Despite the fact that she'd spent all day trying to intellect her way out of the situation she'd gotten herself into, she couldn't even think about the first two options. Seeing Deke's anger deflate had blown away her own, and she was left with an ache that had never really gone away. She'd merely managed to ignore it for a long time. Years, when she thought about it.

"I was scared today. I was out of my element, and it's been a long time since I felt that way. I didn't handle it well."

"Which is why we need to find a different solution to your problem," Deke replied. "There's not time to teach you how to act like you enjoy D/s...relationships. It would be one thing if you'd introduced me as a vanilla boyfriend. We could get through that. I know a lot of couples who aren't particularly affectionate. Hell, even if you hadn't brought the club aspect in we might have been able to make a go of it."

"Deke," she began.

"Hey. It's not your fault. This isn't your thing."

"But how can I know if I don't try?"

"I'll help you no matter what."

"By calling my parents?"

"I know that feels harsh, but I'm serious." He obviously wasn't backing down on this. "I know he's your boss, but if you're right he's responsible for the death of one, possibly two people, and if he thinks you're on to him, he'll likely do the same to you."

She needed to make sure her own work wasn't being compromised. Deke was right that he'd put his own career on the line. He'd told her something he hadn't been forced to. He'd been honorable, and she'd fought him every step of the way today because she'd been embarrassed.

"I was freaked out by being nearly naked in front of strangers." She waited for him to nod and tell her that was another reason her dumb plan couldn't work.

Instead he put the beer down and his hand was suddenly covering hers. "Of course you were. I pushed you on that, and I wish I had more time to get you used to it. I'm sorry if that made you uncomfortable. I know I pushed the hell out of you tonight, and I feel like shit about it. You had a safe word, but you're not used to using it. Maddie, I would never want to force myself on anyone."

Damn it. He'd totally misunderstood her. "I was uncomfortable on your lap because I wanted to be more comfortable."

His hand didn't move, and she gripped it. The last thing she wanted was for this amazing man to think he'd violated her in some way. "What does that mean?"

Was he going to make her say it?

She didn't want to, but he thought he'd been a creep and he so wasn't. He was a man who read body language, and he'd totally gotten hers right but for all the wrong reasons. "I didn't...I wasn't wearing pants so you would have...known. Everyone would have known."

That hand on hers tightened. "Known? Known what, Madeline?"

Okay, now he was a jerk, but hiding from this hadn't worked for either of them. "Known that I was thinking about sex. It embarrassed me, and I tried to cover it by asking you a ton of questions. I also at one point recited the periodic table in my head so I wouldn't think about sex."

He released her hand and studied her for a moment. "Do you want to move on with me?"

"Yes. I know I screwed up tonight, but I can do this. I can absolutely pretend to want you."

He huffed, but there was a hint of a smile on his face. "Maybe I started in the wrong place. I panicked in a way. I wondered if maybe today wasn't the only time I pushed myself on you."

"What do you mean?"

"Given how you reacted today, I have to wonder if I made you do things you weren't ready to do," he said quietly. "When we were younger. The sex we had back then, it was actually quite close to D/s sex. Not with bondage or protocol, but I was definitely in charge."

"Deke, that was the best sex of my life." She wasn't going to lie to him on that point. He'd never been anything but amazing to her when it came to sex. Making love. That's what they'd done. She had friends who talked about the shits their high school and college boyfriends were, but she couldn't say the same of Deke. "I mean the first time kind of sucked, but then you made up for it."

"I figured out how to get you off first." There was a light in his eyes again that did something to her heart. "I was worried you would never want to do it again."

He'd convinced her to let him try. He'd laid her out on a blanket and eaten her pussy until she'd screamed out his name, and then she'd been addicted to him. "You didn't force me into anything. You didn't manipulate me. You gave me pleasure. I promise at no point in time today was I worried you would hurt me. I was self-conscious. I'm not sure how to overcome it."

"I should have waited until we were alone to try a little intimacy. Can we talk now? Not in an academic way. I want to sit here in the dark and talk to you about what you saw and what you felt today. You weren't scared of me?"

She managed to not roll her eyes. She'd done a number on him. She needed to show him. She stood and moved to him, shifting so she could lower herself down onto his lap. "This is how you wanted to talk, right?"

His arm curled around her waist. "I did. We need to look like a couple."

Somehow it was easier talking to him in the intimacy of the warm, dark night. Here in his space, she felt more settled, more like herself than she'd been before. "Well, we never had problems with that, did we? I remember my dad asking if you needed to hold my hand all the time."

He chuckled. "I think he asked if I would die if I didn't hold your hand because I did it so damn often. I got a lot of lectures on keeping my hands to myself."

She breathed in the night air and his scent filled her, too, taking her right back to a good time in her life. She couldn't fool herself that her relationship with Deke had been anything but lovely until the end. "I'm fighting getting close to you because I'm afraid."

"Of what?"

"I'm afraid I'll get hurt again. I'm afraid I won't fit in and I'll look ridiculous. I'm afraid I will fit in and I'll like it and there won't be a place for me when this is all over. I'm a big bundle of nerves, and I'm reacting poorly."

"We should have done this first. I should have turned off the lights and put my arms around you and talked about this like a friend and not a mentor. I know you're scared, but I have no intention of hurting you. It's the last thing I want to do. It was the last thing I wanted to do then."

She felt herself stiffen. "I don't..."

"Want to talk about it," he finished for her. "Let's view this as a moment out of time. There are zero expectations on you. I'll take what you willingly give me. I won't push you further than you're willing to go on the personal front. When it comes to the mission, I have to push you, baby. You have to understand that he's going to know if you're not comfortable in normal club settings. We don't want him asking questions. We want him to trust us enough that we can get him to organize a play party at his house. That's where you'll get to his personal system."

It was kind of brilliant. And it could absolutely work, but only if she convinced Nolan she was who she'd said she was. "I'll be better tomorrow. I promise. We have a day and a half, right? We don't have to leave until Sunday afternoon. I promise I'll be what I need to be."

"Not when you're so tense I can feel it coming off you." His mouth was close to her ear, warmth sparking through her. "I can think of a way to help you relax and make you comfortable around me. I'm your partner in this. I understand that you have no interest in an emotional relationship with me."

"I didn't say that. I said I was scared of it. I'm also not in a place where a relationship would work for me. It's why I'm not going to see Dan again." That was a little fib. She wasn't going to see Dan again because she knew she would need time and space before she could consider dating anyone after seeing Deke again. "I need to concentrate on work. Besides, you live here and I live in LA."

"Exactly. It can't work, so why should you be afraid? You know it's not going to be long term. It's a job." A big hand was on her thigh.

Being with him alone in the moonlight was doing something that the club hadn't been able to do. It was making her soften up, making her brain a little fuzzy at the sound of his voice, the touch of his hand.

"Part of this job is honoring the contract we signed this afternoon." His words were rumbled along the side of her neck, every single one seeming to find a straight line to her traitorous pussy. Maybe not traitorous, exactly. Sentimental. Her pussy was sentimental, and he was a really good memory.

The contract they'd signed had been a basic D/s contract. The Dom would take care of the sub and yadda yadda, sex could happen or not happen, yadda yadda, rules, yadda yadda, punishment. It had an end date. Their D/s relationship would terminate when the job was done.

He was so big and warm and he smelled good. She'd spent the last few weeks on edge, and that all seemed to melt away now that she was here with him. She turned her head his way, appreciating the hard line of his jaw.

"So you're saying we should work within the parameters of our contract and not worry about what happens after."

His hand moved along her thigh, making her breath catch, making her remember all the parts of the contract that had been about sexual contact.

She could stop it at any time, but she couldn't seem to remember why she would want that. Oh, in the back of her head a whole lot of warning bells were going off, but it was easy to ignore them now that they were alone.

"I'm saying this is a couple of weeks where we get to enjoy each other again," Deke murmured. "In a new way. I'll be your top and you'll get to know one person in the world has your back completely. If you can trust me."

"I trust you. I wouldn't have flown halfway across the country if I didn't. I trust you even though we haven't seen each other in years." She let her head drift back to rest on his broad shoulder. "I'm sorry for how I reacted today. I didn't mean to make you feel bad. I don't deal with stress well."

"One of the clauses in our contract talks about comfort," Deke pointed out. "I remember well how stressed you can get. Your brain rarely shuts down. Will you give me permission to try an experiment? You can stop me at any time."

"Are you going to touch me?"

"Yes. I'm going to slip my hand under your panties and then I'm going to find your little clit and I'm going to rub it and tease it until you forget to think about everything that went wrong today."

She couldn't even hear the alarm bells anymore. If they were going off, it was such a distant thing that it no longer mattered. She wasn't sure how she'd gone from arguing with the man two minutes before, to feeling guilty about the way she'd treated him, to her whole body going soft and willing from his words. "That would probably make me stop thinking about how scared I am."

"I need you to spread your legs for me."

He'd asked to do this very thing at the club and she'd struggled with it, but now she simply did as he commanded.

"Very good." His hand ran up her inner thigh, brushing against her pussy. "We talked about some of the philosophy behind Dominance and submission when it comes to sex, but I don't think I plainly put why I enjoy it."

"I would think it's the orgasms."

He nipped her ear, a sharp shock that made her squirm. "No sarcasm right now, brat, or we'll move to punishment instead of reward. Do you want to try a spanking this evening or would you like me to fulfill part of my contract with you?"

His hand was so close. She wasn't about to tell him that even the tiny bite he'd given her had done something for her. She would bet a lot that he already knew exactly how she would react. Like he'd known just how to tug on her hair to light up her senses. "The contract thing. Definitely."

His fingers slipped under the waistband of the silky lingerie she wore. She was fairly certain her granny panties had been tossed in the trash, but she'd been left with a box of gorgeous undies she likely would never have bought for herself.

"One of the reasons the subs I know enjoy a night in the club with a Dom is that they get permission to let go," Deke explained. "Of course you don't need permission, but some of the submissives find it hard to enjoy themselves on a physical level because they can't shut their brains down. They worry. They overthink. Does that sound like someone we know?"

"Yes."

Another nip. "What do you call me?"

They'd talked about this during the sessions this afternoon and she'd called him Deke all night. Now that she was sitting here with him, she could see that she hadn't truly opened herself to the experience. He was giving her a way to connect to him safely. In these moments, he wasn't Deke and she wasn't Madeline. Not wholly. Like Serena had said. They could be different versions of themselves. "Sir. I call you Sir."

"And I call you... What do you want me to call you?"

She was supposed to pick a pet name, a way to put some distance between her different selves. When he called her by this name, she could let go of her daily cares and concentrate on serving Sir.

When she'd read about subs doing this, she'd scoffed a bit, but now she understood. This wasn't about the Dom having a servant. It was about two people choosing to fulfill each other's needs.

"I like it when you call me baby." What she didn't tell him was that she never let another man call her that. She'd told herself it was because that had been his nickname for her and he'd left her. But what if it was because she didn't want to be anyone else's baby?

"Baby. You know it's easy for me to call you that. You're Sir's submissive right now, his baby. Sir wants you relaxed. Sir wants you to be able to sleep tonight so we can work tomorrow. All you have to do is follow Sir's orders. You don't have to think about anything else. I want you to let go. There shouldn't be a thought in your head. Just feel."

She wasn't sure she could manage the whole not thinking thing, but she could concentrate on him. This was what she'd needed for a long time—a safe place to simply be for a moment. Her days had become long and arduous, with nothing to truly break them up. She loved her work, but she needed this, too.

The arm around her waist shifted up and he cupped her breast. She bit her bottom lip to keep from begging him for more. For all she'd been worried about being naked before, she hated the blouse and bra between them now. Her nipple was hard, and she wanted to feel his palm against it.

"Sink into that place where nothing matters but the sound of my voice, the feel of my hands on you. I'll do it, too. I'll find this space in my head where I don't worry or feel self-conscious because I know the only thing that matters is giving you what you need. We can spend hours here." His finger slipped over her clitoris, a feathery brush that made her legs shift again, offering him more and more. "Do you understand, baby?"

"Yes." She'd understood it in an academic fashion, but this was something more visceral. This was real, and she could feel herself relaxing in a way she hadn't for years.

Not since Deke used to take her someplace private when she got all wound up. She would fill with anxiety and worry, and he would lay her out and eat her pussy until she couldn't see straight and then the world didn't seem too much to handle. Then she felt more confident, better able to think her way through the swamp her brain could be at times.

He was right. They'd been practicing a form of this long before they knew what to call it.

He nipped her ear again. "Yes?"

"Yes, Sir." He seemed to be a very bossy Sir when it came to this. He would want her to practice and to be perfect when it came to how they played.

"Better." He licked the shell of her ear, a shiver of pleasure running through her. "You'll find I can be a very generous Sir when you're a good girl. Of course when you're a bad girl, I'll have to lay you over my lap."

She'd watched several subs being spanked this evening. She'd wondered what it would feel like to be over Deke's lap. "What will you do to me?"

A big finger settled over her clit and started to rub, gently at first, and stronger with each rhythmic pass. "See, that's a question I like. What will I do to my wayward sub? First I'll stare at your naked ass because you won't be wearing a stitch of clothes when I punish you. You'll be naked, and I'll have access to every inch of your gorgeous skin. I'll make you hold on to my ankles while I prepare your ass for the discipline to come."

"How will you prepare me, Sir?" He seemed to like her asking the question with a breathless curiosity. He was rubbing her just the right way, the tension building like she was a bottle of champagne waiting to pop.

"I'll caress you. I'll inspect you. I'll make sure your legs are far enough apart that I can see your pussy peeking out at me. I'll want to make sure you're nice and wet when I start spanking you, so I'll likely have to play around, sliding my fingers all across your labia and clitoris. My fingers will be wet with your arousal. You'll be able to smell yourself right before I send that first smack across your cheeks."

She'd questioned whether she would even want to try spanking, and now she could see it in her head, feel it in her pussy. His words opened an ache inside her, a place she hadn't known existed that suddenly needed to be filled.

"I'll slap your ass and make you count each smack, knowing that if you're good and you take what I give you, there will be pleasure at the end, a reminder of how good it can be to obey me in this place we made for ourselves. You'll want to do my bidding because it will always lead to good things for you. I'll worship you with everything I have in this secret place between the two of us. I'll always give you this when you need it."

A single finger slipped inside her pussy, and he bit her ear gently as he pressed on her clit. It sent her over the edge, waves of pleasure coursing through her system, making her blood pound, making her feel alive for the first time in forever.

She stiffened and then it was like every muscle in her body relaxed and she was languid, his arms the only thing holding her up.

He chuckled and eased his hand out of her undies. "Do you feel better?"

She felt like that was a very good appetizer and she was ready for the main course. He was right. They could view this as a moment in time that didn't have to lead to anything in the future. They could enjoy each other. "So much better, Sir."

"I do, too," he said and straightened up. "That was a good first step. We'll try it again at Sanctum tomorrow. You good to go to bed?"

"Yes." She was definitely good to go to bed with him. She'd been dumb to think it was avoidable. She scrambled off his lap and stood on wobbly legs. He could carry her there and rip her clothes off for all she cared. She wasn't even certain why she'd wanted to avoid this outcome.

He stood up and she could see his erection against his jeans. That was one thing that definitely hadn't been a false memory. His cock was big, just like it had been all those years ago. She could feel it in her hand. She'd loved stroking him and getting her mouth on him.

Oh, she wanted to feel his mouth on her.

"We're wheels up at eight in the morning." He put a hand on her shoulder, an earnest expression on his face. "I think if we get in a good ten or twelve more hours, we'll be ready for at least a first meeting. Thank you for trusting me, Maddie. I can't tell you how much it means."

She stared at him for a moment because he did not seem like a guy who was about to sweep her off her feet. "I'm glad. This was…training?"

"This was exactly what we're supposed to do. I think it was a great first step. I can't tell you how relieved I am. I thought I would have to turn you over to Kyle, and I did not want to do that."

Then shouldn't he take her to bed? "I didn't either. I wanted you. I want you."

His lips curled into a bright smile. Not a sexy, I'm-about-to-get-inside-you smile, more like a teacher whose student finally passed a test. "I'm glad because no one is going to watch your back the way I will. I promise, follow my lead and I'll do everything I can to protect you and get the information you need. I'll see you in the morning."

He squeezed her shoulder briefly and then turned and walked

back inside.

What the hell had just happened? She'd had her mind blown and he'd been totally in control.

He was supposed to be. He was the Dom. He was supposed to stay in control so she didn't have to be. It was part of the exchange.

So why did it feel like she'd missed something?

Maddie sank down on the couch and reached for Deke's beer. He'd abandoned it so now it was hers. She took a long swig. Her body still felt spectacular, but her brain had turned on again.

It was going to be a long night.

Chapter Six

Sunday afternoon, Madeline was still frustrated. Not at the training she'd gone through in the last thirty-six hours. She'd been surprised to find she'd enjoyed herself for much of it. Once she'd relaxed and decided to honestly try to let go of her preconceived notions, she'd been able to sink into the role. There had been no more orgasms, but she'd gone with Deke to a play party and had seemed to pass all his tests. She'd enjoyed talking to the men and women of Sanctum, listening to their stories, and really opening herself to the experience.

Nope. She was frustrated for the basest of all reasons. She was sexually frustrated.

"Hey, you don't do that again."

She glanced up from her seat on the private plane they were taking back to LA and saw MaeBe turning to Kyle.

"Do what?" The young woman with the vibrant pink hair seemed genuinely confused.

Kyle frowned down at her. If she hadn't really watched the man over the last couple of days she might be concerned for Mae. He was intimidating when he wanted to be. He could also be quite handsome and charming and so obviously into the hacker. "We talked about this. We're not breaking cover unless we're absolutely certain no one is around. I know this is a private airport, but there are still cameras. You don't carry your own bags. That's my job and you should have stopped and let me help you on the stairs."

Maddie expected this would be the time that MaeBe pointed out she was perfectly capable of getting herself up the stairs. Instead the other woman merely turned her Dom's way.

"Of course, Sir." MaeBe handed over her backpack. "I won't forget again." She smiled sweetly up at him. "I was overly eager to get the op started, and I forgot our protocols. I want you to know that I appreciate everything you do for me."

When she went up on her toes and kissed his cheek the scary dude practically melted. His jaw went tight, and a flush stained his cheeks. But he simply nodded, holding the backpack. "See that you don't." He carefully placed the backpack in the overhead bin and closed it. "I'll be right back. I'm going to warn the flight attendant that Boomer missed lunch. Deke is making sure all our equipment is on board. You two stay out of trouble."

MaeBe snorted as Kyle exited the small but luxurious plane. "Like I'm ever allowed to get into trouble. You get one little stab wound and everyone freaks out."

"Stab wound?" She'd come to enjoy MaeBe's company. The woman was a bit younger than her but so sunny she was a genuine pleasure to be around. Normally Maddie would worry that happy smile was a mask, but she was trying a new life skill—optimism.

Mae grinned as she sank down onto the seat across from Maddie's. "Yeah. A couple of months back, I got between a friend of mine and a creepy stalker guy. Lucky for me he was bad at stabbing. Missed all my vital organs, and now I have a cool scar and Mr. Grumpy became even grumpier. Though he seems to be in a good mood lately."

She wasn't sure she would recognize the differences in Kyle's moods. He seemed to frown. A lot. "You're handling the whole thrown-together-fake-relationship thing well."

MaeBe shrugged. "Oh, it's so not fake. It's more of a fake fake-dating situation, but then I think we've been doing that for a while."

"So he's dating you but pretending to not date you." She couldn't quite get a handle on their relationship dynamic. They were obviously into each other, but they didn't seem to be dating in a traditional sense.

"That sums up my life since meeting Kyle. He says we're just friends and then pays for everything and makes sure he always walks me to my door and is way too into my business. He acts like he's my boss when I don't even work in the same department he does. But I put up with it because I know it bothers him when he's out of control. Like I would let some random friend have any kind of control over how I do my job," MaeBe said with a shake of her head. "That man adores me and I adore him, but he's got some serious baggage. This whole op is his way of sneaking into a real relationship with me. I've been waiting a long time for this. My patience is going to end in wedding bells, you wait and see."

It was odd. She'd only known the woman for a couple of days, but it felt like longer. They'd been in the training trenches together. MaeBe had been the one to walk her through things the day before. She'd been the one to sink to her knees beside Maddie when they greeted their Masters. "That's great for you."

MaeBe's expression softened. "He's a great guy. Weird, but he's also my best friend. Sometimes I'm oddly grateful we got this time together. If he'd been less traumatized, we probably would have ended up in bed the first night we met and I would have freaked out and run from him like I do sometimes. Instead, we built something."

The last few days had been one long reminder of how she and Deke had influenced each other's lives. "Deke and I have known each other since we were kids. He used to stop anyone who tried to bully me."

"He's a great guy, too. It's impossible to not like Deke." She glanced toward the door. "Is there a reason you're not climbing that man like a tree?"

Maddie winced. It wasn't like she hadn't thought about it every single minute of the day. "I don't think that's what he wants."

"Oh, hell no. I've watched him watching you."

Well, Mae wasn't there at night when he sent her to bed alone even though she'd pretty much done everything she could to let him know she was willing. Well, everything but telling him she was willing. "He's playing a part. He seems very dedicated to his job."

"He's not usually," MaeBe mused. "Deke is a good guy and he works hard, but he's not obsessed with his job like some of the guys. He doesn't work constantly. He takes all his vacation days. He likes to have fun and spend time goofing off with his friends. And he's also not obsessed with being a Dom. I've been going to Sanctum for a couple of years, and I would call him a casual top. I've never seen the man be so serious about protocol."

"That's because of our cover."

MaeBe groaned. "Why am I the only smart person?"

"Hello, master's degree from Cal Tech. Yale alumna."

MaeBe's nose wrinkled. "Well, I have a degree from UNT and I know when a guy likes me."

"Who likes you? Don't let my nephew know. I've buried all the bodies on my property that I can, and he doesn't own property. We're all full on the murders," a deep voice said. "I suppose we could go the acid route, but I'm getting too old to put on a hazmat suit, and Charlie doesn't like it when I use her soaking tub to disintegrate the bodies of my enemies."

Ian Taggart stood at the front of the plane, a big cooler in his hands.

MaeBe turned her boss's way. If she was concerned he'd overheard her, she didn't show it. "I was talking about Kyle. He's using the op to turn our fake relationship into a real one. I firmly expect at some point he'll say he needs to sleep in my bed because of danger or something and then oops, how did that get in my vagina? Don't worry. We have condoms."

The biggest smile came over Taggart's face, transforming his normally taciturn expression into something swoon worthy. "You are the smartest of my employees, Mae. I assure you that everyone will be thrilled when he finally just moves in. I'll send a fake assassin your way, and you'll be engaged by the end of the year."

"I welcome the assist, boss." MaeBe gestured Maddie's way. "She doesn't think Deke wants her."

Taggart snorted and set down the cooler. "Dumbass."

The guy did not have a way with words. "I'm not pulling this theory out of thin air. I practically begged him to take me to bed Friday night."

"After your bratty performance?" Taggart asked. "Yeah, honey, that was punishment."

She felt heat scorch her cheeks. "I wasn't trying to be bratty. I was feeling self-conscious and it came off as arrogant. I've been perfectly nice since and he still high-fives me and tells me good work. It does not feel like a sexy relationship."

Taggart chuckled and leaned against the side of the plane like he owned it—which he did since she'd been told it was his company jet. "Have you said 'Hey, Deke, let's hug this out and by hug I mean I want to hug your dick with my vagina'?"

He was a terrible man. He also made her laugh because she kind of liked his put-it-all-out-there attitude. "No. No, I have not said that to him."

"There you go. Problem solved." Taggart looked pleased with himself.

"She's not going to come out and say it," MaeBe argued. "And she shouldn't because that would totally put Deke in the better position. I do have a suggestion, though. Deke and Kyle have a lot in common these days. I think Deke is also using the whole fake D/s relationship, we-have-to-train-to-fool-the-world thing to get his hands on you. He wants you hot for him."

"Well, it worked." It was strange, but she felt comfortable talking about this very intimate subject with two people she'd only known for a couple of days. Spending so much time in Sanctum had loosened her up. It was sex and love and relationships. It was something that should be talked about. It was okay for her to want things.

It was okay for her to want Deke.

"Deke's being a sneaky bastard. I approve," Taggart announced. "I think Mae's about to advise you that you can be sneaky, too. Despite Friday night's bratastic display, you've done well. You've been a good student and done everything Deke's asked of you. But I think you're the kind of student who goes for extra credit."

Mae pointed her boss's way. "That's exactly what I was going to say."

"We're practically family," Taggart said with an affectionate grin. It was obvious he liked MaeBe and approved of her relationship with his nephew.

"Well, I am not practically family and don't possess the Taggart family hive mind," Maddie pointed out. "You're going to have to use human words to explain this plan to me."

Taggart chuckled as though the whole conversation amused him. "When Deke walks on this plane, greet him with the type of affection he wants Byrne to see. Play your part. Sit on his lap. See how he likes having you as his sweet sub. Like this one is doing. Play his game."

"I'm dedicated to our cover," Mae said with a nod. "That means being the best sub I can be and making sure my Dom has everything he needs."

Actually, that wasn't a terrible idea. How long could he hold out on her if they were constantly affectionate? "So I should do all the things he trained me to do even though we're not in public. Because I need practice."

"Exactly. Turn this shit around on him." Taggart straightened up, his gaze going to the door as the plane shifted. "Hey, guys. Charlie made sandwiches for the trip."

A long sigh could be heard, and the plane moved again as Boomer stepped inside. "Tell her thanks for me. I'm starving. I was going to stop and grab something but I got caught in traffic."

162

Taggart patted the even bigger guy on the shoulder. "There's chips and cookies in there, too."

Boomer picked up the cooler and moved to the back of the plane as Kyle and Deke stepped into the cabin.

"Thanks for letting us use the jet." Deke looked delicious in a plain T-shirt and jeans. "It's going to be easier to keep Maddie off the radar this way. I'm worried Byrne knows where she's been."

"I'm not," MaeBe countered. "She showed me what she did to cover her tracks, and it's a solid plan. Her cousin is even taking the phone with her back to LA this afternoon. According to her phone locator records, she's had a nice spa vacay and is getting back right on time."

Her cousin was dropping the phone into her mailbox, and she would be there an hour later to pick it up and resume normalcy.

"That's good to know. I'm still happy we're on a private plane." Deke shook Taggart's hand. "I'll update you as soon as I have anything. Thank you, Ian."

"No problem, man. Tell Kayla hello for me." Ian stepped back. "And figure out one other thing for me."

"Why Byrne wants into The Reef." It wasn't a question out of Deke's mouth. It was a statement, proof that he'd been thinking about it for a long time.

"It's where Jane wants to go," Maddie explained. For some reason Byrne's mystery lady wanted to see The Reef.

"But you haven't actually met Jane," Taggart pointed out.

"You don't think she's real?" It was a scenario she hadn't thought about at all. "Byrne didn't know I was reading up on D/s. I don't see how he could have planned this."

"Just keep an open mind and let my team do its job." Taggart backed away. "And Boomer, you ready?"

Boomer already had a sandwich in his hand. He gave his boss a thumbs-up. "I have a rifle and a camera. I'm good with both, boss. I'll get any shot we need."

She wasn't sure she wanted to know what other shot they might need. She knew they wanted a picture of the woman who visited Byrne at the office every couple of months. It was probably best she put it out of her mind. According to MaeBe, Boomer was excellent at a couple of things. All children adored him. He would eat almost anything. And he could take people out from long-range distances.

"We're good to go," Kyle promised. He sank down in the chair next to MaeBe's.

"Don't worry about anything, boss." MaeBe threaded her arm through Kyle's and put her head on his shoulder. "My Master will make sure I don't do anything fun."

Kyle's eyes rolled but he did nothing to detach the woman holding on to him. "Brat."

"You guys stay safe." Taggart slapped the top of the plane with an open palm. "And don't wreck my plane."

The plane had eight seats, and she'd put her backpack on the seat next to hers. Deke stored his own carry-on and looked down at her. "You okay? The pilot's finishing up and the flight attendant is getting more food. She should be here in a minute."

She wished the very sight of that man didn't make her heart race. Over the course of the weekend, she'd gotten two more texts from Dan. Why couldn't he do it for her? "I'm good."

Deke seemed almost disappointed by her answer. He nodded and started to turn. "Let me know if I can do anything."

She watched as he sank down on the chair in front of her.

Mae and Kyle were quietly chatting. Boomer had what seemed like a never-ending pile of sandwiches to keep him company. Was she going to sit here and...what? Work? She wouldn't be able to concentrate. She'd been given instructions on what would happen when they got back to her place. MaeBe would take over the security system and the cameras on her doors before they even approached the place. Then Deke and Kyle would enter the house and check for whatever they were going to check for and then perhaps she would be allowed in.

Her stomach was in knots. She had to go in to work tomorrow

and act like she hadn't spent the whole long weekend in a thong pretending to be something she wasn't.

That might be the wrong way to look at it.

What if she wasn't pretending to be something she wasn't but rather finding a part of herself she hadn't realized existed? What if she'd spent the weekend experiencing something new and exciting? Something she might enjoy if she let herself?

She already felt closer to these people in a few days than she did to her coworkers, and she'd known them for years. The act of being stripped down in the physical sense had done something to her emotionally. She didn't open herself to people because she was afraid of being hurt. She kept telling herself that friends didn't matter because she had her work.

But damn it, her work wouldn't make her laugh. Her work wouldn't tease her and remind her that she could watch a movie every now and then. Her work had no balance to it. Her work wanted everything she had and only fed part of her soul.

She glanced over and MaeBe was looking her way, giving her an encouraging smile. She winked and then shifted her focus back to Kyle, turning her face up to his. "Master, do you think there's champagne on the plane?"

Kyle's lips turned up in a superior smile. "Do you think I would let this plane take off without your favorite drink? When we get going, I think you'll find the exact champagne you like."

"You are very good at pretending to be my Master." MaeBe cuddled close.

That got Kyle to stiffen as though he hadn't expected those words.

She was right. He wasn't pretending. Or rather he was pretending to pretend.

She could do that. Did she want to do that?

Did she want to take this time with Deke and enjoy him for as long as she could?

The night before she'd dreamed about slowly turning into her own AI, all intellect and no feeling. It was a dream she'd had many times over the years. In the dream she would be happy at first because if she didn't feel, then there would be no pain or anxiety, no awkwardness or loneliness.

No joy. No love.

She could exist forever and be utterly meaningless because in the end, life wasn't measured in achievements. The work she would do might live on, be built on, but who she was would be forgotten. In the dream she realized that memories, knowledge, success meant nothing without feeling behind them.

Sometimes it was her father's face she saw, he who pushed the button that freed her from the cold place she'd confined herself to. Sometimes it was her mom.

Mostly it was Deke.

She stood and moved to his aisle. "Sir, I think I need more practice. Also, sometimes I get nervous on flights. I know a lot about what can go wrong from the engineering side. Way too much."

"Do you want to sit with me? We can talk about the op more."

She didn't want to talk about the op, and it was obvious she needed to take a tiny bit of control. She sat on his lap, her arms going around him. She let her head find his broad shoulder and her breathing evened out, the dream she'd had the night before leaching away, warmth taking its place. "Tell me about your nieces and nephews. Are they being terrible? Angie tells me about her kids, but I haven't heard a good Sylvester story in a long time."

His arm wound around her waist, the other hand finding the outside of her thigh, holding her close. "Oh, that boy is so much trouble. Sweet kid, but I don't think he has a brain. Last time I was home, he got stuck in the dog door and his sisters tried to grease him up with a stick of butter, but he wouldn't budge. And then the dog, who couldn't get out to pee, forgot all about the bathroom and just started licking the butter off."

She laughed and relaxed and realized this plan might work. Unless that was a gun against her butt.

She wiggled a little, and Deke's hand tightened.

"You're playing with fire, baby," he whispered against her ear.

"I'll be still, Sir," she replied. "Tell me more."

She settled in. This might be one time she wouldn't mind getting a little burned.

* * * *

Something had changed, and he wasn't sure if he should thank the universe or curse it because his cock ached from hours of touching Maddie, holding her hand, taking care of her. He stood on her back patio and wondered if he even had the right to change the rules of the game on her.

He'd told her it was all practice for their ruse, and she'd done what she always did when she went all in on a subject. She'd been an excellent student and wanted to go in as prepared as possible, and he was trying to figure out a way to get into her bed tonight. It had been all he could think about during the flight.

Then he'd gotten to this ridiculous house and wondered what the hell he had to offer a woman who could afford this place. It wasn't just nice. It was lush, luxurious. He was in what she'd called the outdoor living space, which included a sparkling grill and kitchen, a pool, and hot tub.

"Damn, man. This place is nice, but we need to talk about your girl." Kyle strode out, obviously appreciating the amenities.

"Are we secure? Did you let Boomer and the women in?" He turned and sure enough, he could see Maddie talking to MaeBe in the kitchen, gesturing around as if to familiarize the other woman.

Boomer slid out the big floor-to-ceiling glass doors. He'd slept most of the flight but then he'd probably needed his rest to digest his lunch.

"We're all secure. I checked the whole house. No one was listening in, but Mae did find something suspicious on Madeline's alarm system," Kyle explained. "The only camera is on the front door, and someone had piggybacked off it."

"Do they know we cut them off?" He didn't like the fact that someone had been watching her, seeing who was coming in and out of her home.

"Nah, Mae took care of it," Boomer said. "She told me she's duped some footage she found on the backlog and that should work until she can make a twenty-four-hour fake. She's not concerned. I'm going to take the room over the front door. I can get on the roof from there if I need to. I'll go over the whole house in the morning and build a couple of stashes in case we need them."

Boomer would make an assessment of points of ingress and hide some weapons where he thought they would be easy to get to.

"How big is that room? Please tell me there are two beds," Kyle pleaded.

"There's a frilly daybed that won't fit either one of you and a couch," Deke announced. "Just sleep in Mae's room. You won't sleep if you don't."

"I'm not ready to sleep with her. I wouldn't be able to keep my hands off her if we're in the same bed," Kyle shot back, and his eyes went steely. "Especially since MaeBe's gotten spectacularly handsy this afternoon, and I know who to blame. You need to get control of your sub. She's got to be the one who convinced MaeBe she needs to be physically stuck to me at all times. It's very disconcerting."

Yes, it was hard to be so freaking horny. "Why would Maddie convince MaeBe to do that?"

"I don't know, man. You should figure it out because she's obviously being a bad influence," Kyle replied. "Mae's a sweet girl who would never put me in a tough position."

"I think she's trying to get you into any position at all," Boomer offered. "I don't think she would be picky. Missionary. Doggy style. Cowgirl. Reverse cowgirl. I don't think she cares."

Kyle's eyes rolled. "She's not even thinking that way. She doesn't know how I feel about her."

"Well, she knows how she feels about you." Boomer ran a hand over his head with a groan. He usually kept his sandy-colored hair in a military-style cut, but in the last year he'd let it grow out, and he seemed to be growing in a beard. "And I don't think you're as good at hiding stuff as you think you are."

That was when Kyle ignored Boomer, who really did have a point.

"Talk to your sub," Kyle ordered. "There's zero reason for us to be uncomfortable when we don't have to be."

Kyle strode away, going back into the house.

"I'm pretty sure it was MaeBe who told Madeline how to get under your skin," Boomer said, looking out over the pool. "This place is real pretty but something's missing."

"What do you mean by *get under my skin*?" He wasn't going to question Boomer on the whole MaeBe thing. MaeBe was way sneakier than Kyle gave her credit for. She was on a pedestal with that man. MaeBe played board games at least twice a week, and she was excellent at strategy games. She could work an end around any strategy Deke could come up with. She might not always win, but she came close.

"It wasn't just MaeBe."

Deke groaned. Only one other person had been on the plane besides the five of them. "Big Tag is a meddling old man, and I'm going to tell him that."

Boomer shrugged a big shoulder. "It's your funeral. I might have overheard them. I started up the stairs to the plane and stopped because they were having a very interesting conversation. MaeBe's fucking around with Kyle. Or rather MaeBe's done fucking around with Kyle. She's planning a wedding."

"It couldn't happen to a more deserving guy. I want to be there when he wakes up and has a wife and kid and wonders where he lost control." He hoped Kyle ended up with as many kiddos as his meddling uncle and they caused just as much trouble. "Why would they tell Maddie to sit on my lap and take every chance she has to brush her body against mine?"

It had been an uncomfortable flight.

Boomer stared at him. "Dude, I'm supposed to be the dumb one."

"You're not," Deke started.

Boomer waved him off. "I make up for it by being an amazing guy. I'm not the brightest bulb, but I know my worth. I'm not sure you do when it comes to this, brother. You are crazy about this woman, and you're acting like you don't have anything to offer her."

"Sex. I can offer her sex." Did she want sex? He'd given her the one orgasm to prove to both of them they could still connect, but then he'd backed off. She'd been plain that she didn't want to trust him. He'd told her they could enjoy each other knowing it wouldn't go anywhere.

Then he'd held her and he'd wanted more. So much more.

Boomer huffed. "I'm calling Kai."

He did not need a therapy session. "Just say what you need to say."

Boomer was one of his oldest friends. They'd been like brothers for over a decade. He'd nursed Boomer through many a head injury because he seemed to be the guy who always took one to the noggin. And Boomer always supported him. When Deke's family home had flooded, Boomer had gone with him and worked for days cleaning the place out and helping his family. He would listen to Boomer.

"She was disappointed you didn't take her to bed Friday night. Apparently you had some kind of encounter."

He shrugged. "Yeah. I figured out she was acting like a brat because she was self-conscious. When she gets anxious it can be hard for her to settle down. So I thought I would handle both problems with some play. She sat on my lap, and I got her to relax in a very physical way."

"Well, you didn't whisk her away."

He'd wanted nothing more than to take her to his bed, strip her down, and get inside her. But he'd known he would be wanting far more than sex. "I didn't think that would be a good idea."

"Well, she thought you didn't want her. Big Tag and MaeBe

convinced her you do, and now she's... I don't know, the word *pretending* was said a whole lot. Like pretending to pretend. It got confusing there, and I was pretty hungry."

That little brat. "MaeBe is the bad influence. She's topping from the bottom and showing my sub how to do it, too."

"So top her from the top," Boomer suggested.

"What?"

"You know, turn it around on her. The way I see it the two of you are in a standoff. Neither one of you wants to be the first one to say 'Hey, I like you. Let's go to bed.' So she's trying to tempt you. Tempt her. You have charms, Deke. I've found it helps if I show a little maleavage."

"Dare I ask what that is?" Deke was fairly certain he didn't want to know.

Boomer undid three of the buttons on his shirt and spread the sides out a bit to show off part of his pecs and the curve of his muscular chest. "It's better with a V-neck, but when I wear one to work Big Tag slaps me upside the head and calls me a himbo. Masculine cleavage is a thing. And your forearms. See, you roll up your sleeves real slow, give 'em a show, and then you do something manly with your arms. I like to pick up something heavy."

Deke couldn't help but laugh. This was another thing Boomer did well. He took a rough moment and turned it into something fun. "Okay, I can probably show her my charms, but it doesn't fix the problem. She doesn't want a long-term relationship with me, and I can't blame her. Look at this place. I can't even come close to offering her something like this."

"Dude, you're going to make her give up this place and live off only your income?" Boomer asked. "That seems dumb. I don't think she's going to go for that. This place is nicer than yours. You should pick this place."

Well, that was moving fast. "Very sarcastic of you, but I have a point. She's in a different league than me financially."

"Do you ask the women you date how much money they make

and then compare salaries? Like how close does she have to be?" Boomer kept up the sarcasm. "Because I've been forgetting to do that."

"Of course I don't ask them about their finances," Deke said with a sigh. "I'm just saying I don't bring Madeline anything financial."

"And I'm saying the fact that you think that way is your problem, not hers. Personally I'm going to go with the flow. If I meet a lady who wants to stay home and take care of our house, then I'll work real hard to make that happen. If I meet one who wants to work, then we'll divide the household chores and go from there. She wants me to stay home and take care of the kids, she's going to find out my biggest secret."

Deke felt a smile cross his face. Only a couple of people knew Boomer's deepest held secret. "You'll cook for her?"

He happened to know that Boomer was an excellent cook, but the women of MT liked to feed him and Boomer liked to make people feel good.

"I will," Boomer agreed. "I can't bake to save my life, but I can make a meal. My point is who does what jobs doesn't matter. I don't want a wife who stays at home or a wife who needs to work. I want a wife who loves me, and I want a family. The rest is window dressing."

Put so simply, Deke knew that was what he wanted, too. What he'd always wanted. "I don't think Maddie shares your vision."

Boomer gestured toward the back of the house. "Then it's only because she doesn't know how nice it can be. Look around that house. You know what's missing?"

"Nothing, from what I can tell." She had everything including a tricked-out media room with a massive TV and movie theater style chairs.

"There's no pictures," Boomer replied. "She's got one picture of her mom and dad and nothing else. She's got paintings, but I would bet those are more investments than anything else. She doesn't have pictures of her friends. I'm starting to think she doesn't have any."

But Maddie had friends in high school. She'd loved hanging with her girlfriends and going on double dates. She'd loved parties.

Over the last couple of days, they'd talked about the op mostly, but at night she'd asked him about his life. When she talked about hers, it was all work. She hadn't mentioned friends she went out with. She hadn't mentioned friends at all.

The idea that Maddie was lonely made his heart ache.

The idea that she was manipulating him oddly didn't irritate him. She wanted to get into bed with him, and she could tell herself it was all about sex. Hell, he'd propped that door open with the whole live-in-the-moment bullshit he'd spouted.

Now he had two things to give her. Pleasure and companionship.

The money disparity still worried him, but he would think about that later. Right now, he was going to concentrate on rebuilding their connection. They had some time. He wouldn't rush her, but he also wasn't going to let her slip into his bed and slip out without giving something back.

"Hey, I was going to order some dinner since it's getting late." Maddie had opened the glass door and stood there watching them, the light from the pool casting shadows across the beautifully landscaped yard. "I've got a bunch of delivery menus if you want to look."

Boomer turned. "I could eat."

Boomer walked back into the house. Through the windows he could see MaeBe already had her laptop out. Kyle stood behind her, his hands on her shoulders. Boomer immediately started picking up the menus Maddie had left out.

It was a cozy scene.

"I like your friends a lot." Maddie joined him at the edge of the pool, her arms wrapped around her torso as if she didn't trust herself not to put a hand on him.

Had he been reading her body language all wrong?

"They like you, too." He turned her way. "I think they're going to enjoy staying in this amazing house you have. Boomer will spend all his time sitting in the hot tub eating sandwiches if we let him."

Her lips turned up in a grin and she relaxed. "I'm glad to hear it. I think he might spice the place up a little. Give the neighbors something to look at. This is a quiet neighborhood. It could use some scandal."

Like the neighbors could see anything. The backyard had been meticulously designed for privacy, complete with lush, tall bushes and a ten-foot fence, but he could play her game. "I might try the hot tub myself."

He watched as she seemed to make a decision.

Her chin came up, a challenge in her eyes. "Yeah, I think that might be a good idea. We could sit in the hot tub tonight, if you like. I'm now used to being mostly naked a lot of the time, so a swimsuit should be easy."

"You won't be wearing a suit, baby."

She bit her bottom lip, her tongue darting over it. "Okay. I should get used to being around you like that. I thought today went pretty well. The practicing part, that is. I talked to MaeBe, and she and Kyle are trying to keep up the illusion even when they're alone. She thinks it will help them look like a couple."

Little liar. He knew damn well Kyle wasn't on board with that plan, and MaeBe was going to get spanked at some point. Which would likely lead to exactly what that brat wanted—Kyle Hawthorne in her bed.

Maddie was going to get spanked, too, but he wasn't in a hurry to call her on the manipulation quite yet. She was trying to tempt him. He could have told her all she had to do to tempt him was exist, but he might have more fun playing her game.

"I agree." He turned to her, getting into her space. "You know what we haven't done yet? I haven't kissed you. Not properly."

Her eyes went wide, and he could see he'd surprised her. Had she not thought he could play this game, too? "You think we'll need to kiss in front of my boss?"

"I think we need to be prepared to." He'd had his hand on her pussy, but he hadn't put his lips on hers yet, and that seemed like such a mistake. He used to kiss her for hours. They would park by the lake and make out until they couldn't stand it a second longer, until the windows of his old truck were glossy with steam.

She seemed to think about it for a moment and then she nodded. "Yeah, we should be ready for that. Wouldn't want it to be awkward."

That was exactly what he wanted to hear. He reached out and let his hand find her neck, running back and cupping her nape. He gently drew her up on her toes. "We need to look like we've done this a thousand times."

"We have," she whispered.

It was good that she remembered, too. He lowered his head, brushing his mouth over hers, and all the years between them melted away. Her hands came up to clutch his waist, and she pressed her body to his. Fire lit through him, and he knew he wasn't going to be able to wait. They had to find a way to get into bed and soon.

She groaned when he dragged his tongue over her bottom lip.

"Let me in, baby. Let me taste you," he whispered against her mouth as he tangled his fingers in her hair and tugged a little.

A gasp went through her, and her hands tightened, her mouth opening.

He let his tongue surge in, finding the velvet warmth of her mouth and stroking his tongue against hers. He moved his free hand over her back and down to the curve of her ass, cupping her there and locking her against his rapidly heating body.

She broke away suddenly, stepping back and reaching into the pocket of her jeans. "Sorry. I...my phone is vibrating. I'm pretty sure we've got the kissing thing down."

His whole body revolted at the distance between them, and he was pretty sure his cock was going to wither and die if he didn't have her soon.

She frowned down at her screen. "Damn it. I have to deal with this, Deke. Uhm. Can you call in dinner for us all?"

He could make a meal out of her. He nodded, well aware every muscle in his body was tense. "Yeah. I'll try to find a delivery service that can handle Boomer."

In a minute. He definitely needed a minute.

He watched her stride back into the house. She said something to MaeBe, who glanced down at her screen and nodded Maddie's way.

Deke turned back to the pool and wondered how cold it was. He could just fall forward and cool his dumb ass off.

When was the last time he'd kissed a woman the way he had Maddie? It wasn't like he hadn't had sex while they'd been apart. He'd had his share. He'd had some long-term relationships, and not one of them had him panting the way he did after that woman.

He took a deep breath because it probably wasn't a good idea to jump in her pool fully clothed the first night he was in her house. He'd meant to fluster her, and he was the one who was trying to make his brain work again. He sat down on one of the plush chairs that surrounded what he suspected would be a fabulous fire pit when it was lit up.

He could see himself here, cuddling up with her after a long day at work. She would come home and insist she should probably work a little more and he would tell her she'd done enough for the day, and they could sit out here and talk. He would hold her and she would relax, and at some point they would have kids who would run and jump into the pool and force their parents to have some fun.

He could see their lives.

What if he couldn't get her to see it? What if all she would ever want from him was sex?

"Hey, Deke, I think you should get in here," Kyle called from the doorway. "You won't fucking believe what's happening on the front porch."

"Where's Maddie?" He was on his feet in a heartbeat. What had happened? He'd thought she was going to make a phone call. Had someone shown up? Was Byrne already here?

"She's on the porch, and her boyfriend is here," Kyle said with a frown.

"What?" He could feel his blood pressure tick up.

MaeBe was watching the screen of her laptop. "She told me it's the guy she's been seeing. It's why I didn't send Boomer with her. He showed up and... I've only met the man once. It's not my fault I didn't recognize him."

She turned the screen his way, and Deke saw Maddie talking to a man.

A familiar man.

He was so fucking dumb. "She told me she'd started dating someone very recently. Someone named Dan Gray."

"You know he likes his color names," Kyle said.

On screen, the man who'd called himself Dan Gray...and Mr. White and Mr. Black and any number of colorful surnames, reached for Maddie's hand.

"Oh, that is not fucking happening." Deke started for the door.

Well, at least he could let Adam know he didn't have to worry about the Agency.

They were already fucking here.

Chapter Seven

Maddie walked away from Deke, deeply thankful that her phone had vibrated and saved her from what might have been an awkward sexual encounter since she'd stopped caring about anything the minute he'd kissed her. That text coming through had been a reminder that they weren't alone, and she was actually in her backyard.

The man kissed like a god, like every romance hero she'd ever dreamed of all rolled into one.

"You okay?" MaeBe was staring her way as she walked back into the kitchen.

She wasn't the only one. Kyle had a smirk on his face, and Boomer wasn't looking at the three menus in his hands.

Yep. Everyone had seen her, and they would have seen her climbing up his body and trying to get inside his pants if she hadn't been rescued.

Although it appeared she was about to have another awkward situation that would likely be watched by her new friends. They might pop some corn and enjoy the trash fire that was her life.

"I'm good." She held up her phone and prayed she didn't look like a woman who'd recently had a tongue halfway down her throat. A sexy, talented tongue. A tongue that had licked pretty much every inch of her body at one point in time, and didn't she fucking remember. "I kind of ghosted this guy I've been seeing for a couple of months. I didn't mean to, but things got real at work, if you know what I mean."

"There's another man?" Kyle lost his smirk. "Does Deke know?"

She was so glad she'd told Deke about Dan Gray. Oh, he'd figured out she wasn't all that into him very quickly, but she didn't have to explain the guy away to the man in the backyard. "Yes, he knows about Dan. We casually dated for a couple of weeks. Nothing serious, but I think he's worried about me. He's apparently outside and wants to talk."

MaeBe glanced down at her screen. "Yeah, someone's pulling up in your driveway. Does this guy drive a Prius?"

That was Dan. She strode toward the front door. "Yeah. He's nothing to worry about, but I don't want to have to explain Deke to him. Or any of you. He knows I live alone and don't have many people over, so if he sees you he might have questions I don't want to answer. I'll get rid of him. I'm going to tell him I can't see him again. He's a nice guy. He'll leave as soon as he realizes it's not working for me."

"I'll be on the roo…in my room," Boomer offered like that was a normal thing to announce. "Just going to go hang out up there until dinner."

"I think that's a great idea," Kyle agreed.

She wasn't sure why Boomer needed to be in his room, but she had a guy to break up with. It was a surprise that he was here. She thought he could take a hint, but she wasn't worried. Dan was a logical guy, and they'd been nothing more than friendly dinner companions.

She smoothed her hair, put her phone back in her pocket, and opened the door, stepping onto her porch. Dan was just getting out of his car. Maddie walked across the yard to join him. The further she kept him from the house and all its new and never talked about before occupants, the less chance she would have some explaining to do.

After all, she was about to have to tell a guy who liked her that it wasn't going to work out.

She wouldn't tell him the reason why she couldn't even contemplate a relationship with him was standing in her backyard, and she would probably get naked in a hot tub with him later on tonight.

Daniel Gray stopped when he caught sight of her. He wore khakis and a button-down shirt, his uniform. He was as tall as Deke but leaner. His dark hair and gray eyes should have her sighing.

But he seemed dull next to Deke.

He was exactly the right man for her. It was like someone had checked off a list. Intelligent but not arrogant. Good job but willing to listen to her work stories, too. Handsome but not overwhelmingly so. Not intimidated by her.

"Madeline." He put a hand to his chest. "I swear you've given me a heart attack the last few days. Where have you been? You don't answer my calls or texts. I was worried something happened to you."

She should have talked to him. This would have been easier over the phone, but she hadn't thought about anyone but Deke. "I'm sorry. I was out of town. I went to a spa with my cousin. It was one of those wellness places where you have to lock up your phone so you can be present in the moment or something like that. I was going to call you tonight but time kind of got away from me."

"I've been so worried about you." He took a long breath. "You just disappeared. Are you sure everything is all right, sweetheart?"

"Yeah. It came up suddenly and we hadn't talked in a couple of days, so I didn't think to tell you I was leaving town. We didn't have a date set up." She was kind of surprised he was reacting this way. She'd gone days without talking to him before and he hadn't been worried. Half the time, she thought he was the one avoiding her.

"I'm sorry about that. I had to do some traveling myself," Dan admitted. "I know I've been kind of drifting in and out but I'm clearing my schedule for the next several weeks, and I am going to concentrate on you. I know you're under a lot of pressure at work, and I'm going to make sure you relax. I was hoping we could spend some time together this weekend, but I'm glad you got away. Did you already eat? I would love to take you out, or we could order something in and you can tell me all about your weekend."

It was oddly aggressive for Dan. She'd always kind of gotten the idea that he could take her or leave her. Not that he didn't like her, but he was always so casual. "I'm afraid I've got some work to do. We're scheduled to launch in a couple of weeks, so any time off is going to be hard. It's why I jumped on this weekend when I had the chance."

His jaw tightened, and even in the moonlight she could see the resolute look in his eyes. He straightened the glasses he wore and moved in close. "Maddie, I think I've played this the wrong way. I've played it cool when that's not at all how I feel about you. I'm sorry. I should have shown you."

He reached out for her hand, taking it in his.

Alarm bells started to go off in her head, and unlike with Deke, she could hear these perfectly. "I think you played it right because we've got a nice, friendly thing going."

He stepped in, coming into her space. "No, I've definitely given you the wrong impression. Let me correct that mistake."

Suddenly he was leaning over, his nicely shaped lips swooping in to cover hers.

Wrong. Wrong. Wrong. It felt wrong to have him kiss her. Not an ounce of arousal went through her, just a terrible sense of alarm that she was definitely breaking the rules and her Dom was going to spank her, and maybe not sensually.

She pushed at his chest, and somewhere in the background she heard the door slam open. "No. I don't want you to kiss me."

Dan stepped back and started to open his mouth when he looked over and his jaw dropped. "Fuck. Deke, I did not know you were going to be here. I am working and you need to…"

Deke walked right up to Dan and punched him straight in the face.

Maddie gasped. "What are you doing?"

Dan was on the ground, holding his nose. His glasses had come off and they were somewhere on her yard. He couldn't see, and he would likely call the cops and then it would be all over the neighborhood that Maddie Hill had two men fighting over her on her front yard. One of her coworkers was two doors down. She didn't know Sharon all that well, but the one thing she did know was that the woman liked to talk. A lot.

Deke stood over Dan, his hands both fists. "How long have you been here? How long have you been trying to fuck her for intel?"

Maddie stopped looking for Dan's glasses. What the hell did that mean?

Had Dan called Deke by his name?

Dan—who often joked that he wouldn't recognize a gym if he got lost and walked into one—kicked up and caught Deke in the gut. He did one of those kung fu, Bruce Lee things where he leapt to his feet from his back and turned the tables on his opponent.

Deke was the one on the ground now, and Dan stood over him.

"You know why I'm here. I'm absolutely certain you're here for the same damn reasons," Dan said, his tone deeper than she'd ever heard from him. He talked about how bad his eyes were, but he didn't seem to mind the loss of his glasses.

Deke nodded, his head hanging. "Yeah, I know. I'm sorry, man. She means something to me, and I think you know that, too."

Dan seemed to relax and held out his hand. "Of course I know. I know everything about her."

Deke took his hand, allowed Dan to help him up, and then punched him again. "Then you know you should have fucking called me. I'm not going to let you use her."

"What is going on?" She wasn't sure how they knew each other, but it was obvious they did, and they didn't seem to be friends.

"You are going to pack your shit and go home. Get off my op."

Dan growled the words. "Or I'll have you taken out of here, and you won't like where I put you."

Deke reared back again, and that was when Maddie's heart nearly stopped because when Dan's hand came up there was a gun in it. She caught the glint from the porch lights and in her mind's eye, saw Dan shooting Deke and his life ending right here and now. She wasn't thinking. Instinct had her running across the grass and throwing herself in front of Deke.

Deke's arms went around her and then the whole world was moving, turning and twisting as they both hit the ground and he rolled over her. Her breath fled as Deke's whole weight crushed her into the ground.

"It's a taser, Deke. I wasn't going to shoot you," Dan was saying.

"This isn't a taser." Boomer's voice could be heard from somewhere above her. "I will shoot you if you make another move, and I won't miss, man. I've got him, Deke. You can get up and get Maddie inside. The neighbors are starting to get interested."

"What the hell were you doing?" Deke rolled off her and was on his feet faster than he should have been. He held his hand out.

"I didn't want him to shoot you." Her heart was pounding, and she still didn't understand what was going on. "Dan has a gun."

"We all have guns. But he's holding a taser, and he's not going to fuck with Boomer, who absolutely will shoot him if he makes a wrong move," he said as he hauled her up. "Don't you ever do that again. He could have hurt you."

"I wasn't planning on hurting her, asshole. I was going to tase your balls so you didn't hit me again," Dan hissed Deke's way.

"You leave and don't you ever come back, Drake. I see you around her again and I won't care who'll come after me," Deke promised, getting in front of her. His big body was a wall between her and a man she'd never known.

Since he had another name and knew things he shouldn't know.

"I'm not leaving. You have no idea what she's involved in," the man whose name wasn't Dan said.

"And he's not going to discuss it on the lawn." Kyle was on the top step, his arms crossed over his chest. "Get inside, now. All of you."

"He can leave," Deke offered.

"He can't, and you know why. Drake, get in here. Deke, get your caveman under control because if we don't take this scene inside, we'll be dealing with the cops soon." Kyle's words were quiet, but there was no doubt he understood the danger they were all in.

They weren't going to figure out anything if the police showed up. Especially not if they started wondering why she had a two-hundred-pound muscular hottie hanging off her roof with some kind of rifle.

How had he gotten a rifle into her house without her knowing it? How the hell had he gotten on the roof? She'd been pretty sure those windows didn't open.

"Fine, but he makes a wrong move and I won't be responsible for my actions." Deke grabbed her hand and gently dragged her close. "She's not some pawn for the Agency to use."

Agency? What Agency? Did Dan/Drake work for a competing tech firm? Her stomach turned because she would absolutely get fired if she'd been the idiot who dated a corporate spy.

Boomer's face suddenly came into view. "Hey, I ordered Chinese and burgers. I did not order for him."

What was he hanging from?

"Is he okay?" They would need an ambulance if Boomer fell.

"He's fine." Dan/Drake strode up the steps to her door. "Even if he falls on his head, that one just gets back up and starts eating again."

Boomer disappeared and Kyle ushered her mysterious former date into the house, and she was left with Deke, who started to lead her inside.

"You were dating a CIA agent, baby." Deke led her up the stairs. "We're going to talk about your taste in men."

Not a corporate spy. A real spy.

She forced herself to move as she realized her whole world had upended.

Again.

* * * *

His heart was still pounding as he walked back into Maddie's house.

She'd thrown herself in front of him. Anything could have happened. He'd realized the weapon in Drake Radcliffe's hand had been a taser. It was practically a toy in their world. It was what they used when they wanted to make a point but not actually hurt the target.

And yes, on some out-of-control Saturday nights there were dumbasses who played with them. He wasn't one of those men.

But Maddie had thought it was a gun. She'd thought he was about to be shot, and she'd thrown her body over his.

She'd nearly given him a heart attack, but he knew exactly who to take all his stress out on.

She pulled at his hand as they entered the hallway leading to her great room. "What is going on?"

Deke took a deep breath. None of this was her fault, and he wasn't about to take his anger at the Agency out on her. He pulled her close, wrapping his arms around her. "I'm sorry. My adrenaline's up. Help me calm down."

She softened immediately, hugging him and rubbing her head against his chest. "Of course. It's okay. I was scared, too. I didn't know he carried around a taser. I thought he worked in biotech. He's supposed to be a research scientist not a spy. I guess that's why he was so willing to listen to my work stories."

She'd been running on instinct, and her instinct had been to protect him. He needed to train her to protect herself instead since he was the one with all those skills, but damn it had felt good.

He'd been pissed as hell at Drake, but Maddie had risked her life for him.

If that wasn't a shot, he didn't know what was.

"His name is Drake Radcliffe. He works for the CIA, and he's been with them since he was barely out of diapers."

"I heard that, Murphy," a loud voice called from the kitchen. "How about we keep classified information classified."

"If you wanted to keep your identity on the down low, you shouldn't have tried to take advantage of her." He kissed the top of her head and lowered his voice since it seemed Drake had superhearing. "Do not trust him. We might have to work together, but you need to understand he's got an agenda."

"I'm not going to trust that man. He lied to me and went totally against the terms of service for the dating app. It clearly states that you have to use your own name," she replied.

He smoothed a hand over her back and felt her starting to relax. "I assure you that when they go to block his profile, it will already be gone. He'll have protocols in place to clean up any hint that Dan Gray had ever been on the app. Maybe you shouldn't try to find love online."

She huffed and took a step back. "Well, I wasn't finding it anywhere else." She frowned and glanced down the hall. "Is he the one who was watching my door?"

It was a pretty good bet, but at least now they could know for sure. He reached for her hand again, happy when she let him entwine their fingers. He tugged her close. "We'll ask him, but it would be a good idea to let him believe we're together. I don't want him thinking he can drive a wedge between us and use you the way he planned to."

Drake would still try to find a way, but he needed to keep Maddie as close as he possibly could. He'd wanted to give her more time, but Drake showing up meant time was something they didn't have. It also meant that there was no question something bad was happening on her project. Drake's involvement proved she'd been right.

"Okay," she replied.

She was right back to nervous again. He squeezed her hand. "Let me handle this. It's going to be all right. This is exactly what I'm here to do. I'm here to protect you and handle all the crappy security stuff. I'll deal with him."

She sniffled and seemed to find her footing again. "Good. I think I'm going to open a bottle of wine while you deal with the spy guy."

He led her into the hallway and down to her kitchen where Drake was sitting at the bar. Kyle stood at the refrigerator, the freezer door open.

"Well, I guess you don't work in biotech." Maddie frowned Drake's way.

Drake's expression softened. "No. I don't. I'm sorry, Madeline. I needed to figure out what's going on at Byrne with the satellite project."

"How about asking her?" Deke did not understand the spy's need for subterfuge.

"Because she could have been in on it." Kyle pulled an ice pack from the freezer and handed it to Drake. "He doesn't have years of history with her, man. You know how the Agency works."

They worked in the shadows and didn't care who they hurt. "So you tried to get in her bed? You know what that makes you?"

He was feeling mean.

"It makes me effective at my job." Drake put the pack over his nose. "Or it would have if I'd really tried. I thought I could get close to Madeline without hurting her, but I had to figure out what she knows."

"Nothing. I know nothing." Maddie found a corkscrew and started working on a bottle of Pinot. "I didn't even know who I was dating, so I'm pretty sure I can't help anyone at all."

"You know more than you think," Drake said. "I need you to understand that I decided you're not involved in what's going on. I will admit that I went in with some suspicions, but getting to know you has led me to believe you're not capable of what I think Byrne is planning."

"And what is that?" MaeBe came down the stairs, Boomer following her. She frowned Kyle's way. "I assume it's safe enough

187

for me to come back down now?"

So Kyle had sent MaeBe up to her room when things had taken a nasty turn. Deke would bet that had gone over sensationally.

Kyle didn't look at all worried about that expression on her face. "Yes. Now it's safe."

"Hey, MaeBe Vaughn. You are looking good, girl," Drake said with a nod.

"If you don't want that ice pack shoved up your asshole, you won't look at her at all." Kyle stared at Drake.

MaeBe's eyes rolled, and she joined Maddie. Yeah, she would probably need a lot of wine to survive Kyle.

Drake ran a hand over his hair, smoothing it back. "You have spent far too much time with your uncle. As to MaeBe's question, I'm not about to show my cards until I know we're working together and not against each other."

Deke had a few questions of his own. "If you did any research at all on Maddie, you knew her connection to me. So why the hell didn't you call me when you found out she was involved in something dangerous?"

"Well, first of all, I absolutely knew the connection. I also knew you haven't spoken to her in over fifteen years. You know most of us move on from our high school girlfriends." Drake sat back. "Secondly, Big Tag has made it plain that he doesn't want to work with me."

"I think that is more about the Agency and his history with them than you." Deke was fairly certain Drake was the only CIA employee Big Tag could stomach for short periods of time. "It's not like you haven't worked with us lately."

After all, Drake had worked with Chelsea a few months back. While Chelsea wasn't an MT employee, she was definitely in Tag's family. Drake had also been pivotal in taking down Levi Green—a man Tag had considered extremely dangerous.

"Given what I knew about Madeline's connection to Deke, I rather thought if I brought Big Tag in, I would lose control of the op.

This particular mission requires finesse, and your team isn't known for its subtlety," Drake explained. "There is a delicacy to the matter."

Deke could figure out what was so delicate. "Who's invested in Byrne? I'm going to assume the people you're working for have some sort of financial stake or they would just walk in and get what they want."

"Of course they do. Byrne's companies make billions," Drake admitted. "And that's precisely why there are people in the upper echelons of my agency who don't want me investigating at all."

"Are you sanctioned to be here?" Boomer asked. "Or have you gone rogue?"

"Hey, why is the CIA involved?" Maddie poured a glass for herself and one for MaeBe. "Shouldn't some FBI agent have been creeping on me instead of you? Aren't you supposed to only sleep with foreigners for information?"

"Oh, she's going to fit in nicely," Drake cracked. "No one's going to call the FBI in for the reasons I just gave you. Too many politicians are in bed with Byrne. Hell, I'm sure Byrne going down would affect the bottom lines of a lot of FBI agents, too. I'm authorized to investigate anything I find interesting, so don't bother trying to get me off the case. All I have right now are suspicions. I'm pretty much doing three jobs at once, and I'm tired and getting old since I had no idea Madeline was in Dallas. I take it there was no spa."

"I went to Dallas to get Deke. I think something's wrong at the office, and he's the person most likely to know how to handle the situation," Maddie admitted.

"And all those times I asked you about work, you didn't think to mention your suspicions?" Drake asked. "We were getting close."

She shook her head. "No, we weren't. You were nice and all, but I was planning on ending it even before I found out you're a spy."

"Why?" Drake sat up straighter, a look of genuine confusion on his face. "On paper I'm perfect for you. I made sure of it."

She shrugged. "I bet you did. Did you manipulate the app so we would match?"

"Believe it or not, I didn't have to do much to get us to match." Drake slid off the chair, letting the ice pack drop to the counter. "We share a lot of the same interests. I am mostly the man I presented to you."

"The one who bored her?" Deke couldn't help the dig.

"I didn't say that." Maddie frowned his way.

Deke stared at her for a moment, and she finally winced, a sure sign that he'd been right. Maddie didn't need someone exactly like her. She needed her natural opposite, and that was him, not some overly educated asshole with a ton of old money behind him. Drake was connected in the DC world. His family was powerful in both the business and political worlds. He'd heard rumors that Drake's mother was a senator. Samantha Radcliffe of Virginia. He wondered what she thought of her son running around the States playing James Bond.

"Like I said, I slow-played it, and that was why it failed," Drake summed up. "I thought slow was the way to go with you. You didn't seem like someone who fell in bed with the first set of abs you met. I didn't get a chance to show you mine. They're spectacular, by the way."

"She's with me, and not in a just-for-the-op way." He would lie to Drake all day if it meant keeping Maddie safe from him.

It also wasn't a terrible way to stay extra close to her. He got the feeling Drake was about to dig in like a tick.

Drake's gaze shifted between the two of them as though he was sizing up the situation and looking for a way around the problem he faced.

"Baby, I think you should come here." He hoped she caught on to his use of *baby* because this was their first real test.

"I don't think he's going..." Maddie's eyes widened, and she hurried to his side. "Oh, this is one of those times, right? I'm supposed to obey you now."

Drake groaned. "Well, of course. I should have known the ridiculously smart scientist would go all Fifty Shades on me. Honey, if that was all it took, I can tie you up right."

Strangely, with her arm wrapped around his waist, his inner caveman was easier to control. "I think she'll pass on that. So you understand that if you want access to what Maddie knows, you go through me."

"Fine." Drake seemed to get serious. "Madeline, what do you know about Justin Garcia?"

Maddie tensed beside him. "I know he worked on the communications team with the audio portion of my AI. He was fine tuning what Clarke will sound like when he talks to home base. I know he wasn't a regular drug user and yet they treated it like it was no big deal that he died in a flop house."

"And Pam Dodson?" Drake prompted.

"She also worked on the comms team, and I don't think she's hiking to try to find herself," Maddie replied.

"No, she's not. She was going to meet me the day she disappeared," Drake revealed. "I'd been working her as an asset since she joined the team. I led her to believe I was an investigative reporter doing research on Byrne. For the first year or so what I got out of her was gossip. I wanted to keep the lines of communication open in case something did go wrong. Three weeks ago, she contacted me and asked me to meet with her because she'd learned some information that could put Byrne behind bars."

"And what was that information?" It was time to see if Drake was truly willing to play ball.

Drake's shoulders shrugged. "I don't know because when I got to the motel we were meeting at she was dead."

Maddie gasped. "Someone killed her?"

"Either that or she stabbed herself with that knife." Drake's casual tone let Deke know he'd seen his fair share of bodies. "I didn't stick around. I left the motel, but I waited and watched because I wanted to see how they dealt with her body. A few hours later a cleanup crew showed. They were professionals. They took the body, cleaned up the room, talked a bit with the staff to make sure no one remembered something they shouldn't. And that was when my journalist identity started getting hits."

"Hits?" Maddie asked.

"He peppered records and documents on that ID around the web," MaeBe explained. "He would want to look real. Like I'm sure there's an Internet footprint for Dan Gray."

"Not anymore, there isn't," Drake replied. "I had my techie erase it all about two minutes after I realized my cover was blown. I sent her a signal, and I assure you she's done her job. But the point is they knew Pamela was about to give me real evidence about what Byrne is planning."

"What do you think he's planning?" Kyle asked. "I know you wouldn't be out here if you didn't have some kind of idea."

Drake went quiet, and for a moment Deke worried he wasn't going to talk. "Have you heard of Havana Syndrome?"

"Of course." Years before there had been complaints from members of the US Embassy of a mysterious attack. They'd been woken by terrible sounds that brought on bouts of nausea and vertigo. Over the years more and more of these attacks had been reported, and the long-term neurological problems had been documented and called Havana Syndrome. "I thought they'd determined it was likely microwaves."

"Attacks like these have been happening for far longer than the incident at the embassy in Havana," Drake explained. "The Agency has records of similar incidents going back decades. Those were single spies, usually working in remote places. We believe that the attack on the embassy is proof that the technology has evolved. Since then there have been several more mysterious attacks. None of which we can prove."

"I don't understand what this has to do with our satellite," Maddie said. "We obviously don't have microwaves on board."

"Would you know?" Drake asked. "I'm not talking about something that blatantly looks like a laser beam. We know so little about this technology that it's impossible to say what it is we're looking for. Most of the people I've talked to think I'm crazy."

"I don't." Deke was with him on this point. "We've been tracking a woman we believe is working with a group called The Consortium. She has tech we've never seen before and can't explain. It's far beyond anything that's on the market today or even close to being released."

"She was involved in a case we worked with Hutch's wife," MaeBe offered. "That case was about high tech, too. We believe the group she works for was paying to slow down technological advances so they could profit for longer off contemporary tech."

Drake's jaw had gone tight. "I would like anything you have on this woman. Do you believe she's been meeting with Byrne?"

"I know someone is." Maddie put her glass on the bar. "A woman comes to meet him. She's never on his calendar, and she doesn't talk to anyone else. According to his secretary, Nolan books the appointment himself and simply tells her to block off the time."

"One of our goals is to get a decent picture of this woman so we can ID her," Deke admitted. "So what do microwaves have to do with the attacks on the power plants?" He wasn't sure he understood the connection.

"Adam's been talking. I should have known he would. I would have only dealt with Chelsea if that had been possible, but we were out of time. The attack was controlled by an artificial intelligence that resembles Madeline's prior work. I think this was a test of the system." Drake walked up and grabbed a glass, pouring his own wine. "As to your question, Madeline, I believe the two are going to be used in conjunction, with the AI controlling the microwave weapon, taking over the systems of whoever they want to target before they attack. Taking control of smart systems in homes or businesses could let the AI know if the targets are actually in the building. This is all conjecture, of course, combined with some of the intel I've put together. Since you were working on the AI, I had to make sure you weren't the one in control of the weapon."

"I haven't seen anything like that, not in the plans, not on what we've put together so far." Madeline had paled, probably at the thought of her work being used in such a potentially violent way.

"They likely won't change anything until right before launch," Deke explained. "I suspect you'll turn in your finished work, and then I assume there's a launch team."

"Yeah, but the heads of the departments should all be on that team," Maddie argued.

"Has he named the team? Announced who's on it?" He didn't like to shake her illusions, but she had to be less naïve.

"No." Her face fell. "He's really doing this, isn't he?"

"I think he's doing something, and it's not going to be for the good of our country. Whether Drake is right or not is the question. And the only way we're going to find out is to get into Byrne's personal system." It was exactly what he was here to do, but now he wasn't sure he wanted Maddie to be the one to do it. Luckily there was a real live spy here, and he could do the dangerous stuff.

"I need to get into his personal office. The one at his home." Drake seemed to be on the same page. "And that's why it's best if I'm the one dating Maddie. She can introduce me as her boyfriend, and I'll work on the man. I've studied him. I can talk to him, get him to trust me, and then get on that system. MaeBe can work tech for me, and I'll get what we need to put this guy away and make sure a dangerous weapon doesn't go into orbit around the planet."

"He's got a point," Kyle said. "Not about being Maddie's boyfriend. That won't work, but I would way rather we risk his life than hers."

"Thanks, buddy. I appreciate your support." Drake sighed. "Why can't it work?"

"Because we've already set up our cover, and you're not taking my place. Byrne is hot for a woman who's interested in having him top her," Deke explained. "Maddie and I are going to mentor him. Kyle and MaeBe are friends of ours who've been in the lifestyle for a while and who are regulars at the club Byrne wants to get in to. You'll have to settle for sneaking in when we go to his place."

"Are you fucking kidding me?" Drake's head fell back on a groan. His head came back up, a gleam in his eyes. "But he hasn't met you yet. I can answer to your name, and I've got Master's rights at a lot of clubs."

He wasn't going to punch the man again. He turned to Maddie. "You want to go in with this guy, baby?"

Her eyes rolled. "No. Obviously not."

He shrugged Drake's way. "She's not comfortable with you, and she's a terrible actress. It wouldn't work."

"I'm not that bad," Maddie complained.

She was. She was pretty awful, but he could make it work. "Byrne wants to bring his lady friend to The Reef."

Drake whistled. "So he wants to bring some random woman to a club that just happens to be run by an ex-operative."

"It's also a bunch of Hollywood stars' home club." MaeBe had moved closer to Kyle while Boomer stood near the stairs, watching the whole scene playing out. "She might want to meet one. She might be using Byrne to get in so she can find a movie star hottie."

"Somehow, I don't think it's that easy." Drake nodded as though coming to a decision. "All right then. I'll go in with MaeBe. We can have a few practice sessions, but we don't need much. We both have plenty of...hey!"

Drake's chest took the full power of the orange Kyle had just fastballed his way.

"He's got more fruit," MaeBe said, taking a sip of her wine. "Maddie's fruit bowl is full of citrus. He's not going to let me go in with you. I think you get to be the bartender or something."

"I'm always the damn bartender." Drake smoothed out his shirt. "Fine. I'll hang back with Boomer. It'll be a good way to make sure he doesn't snipe me."

"I'm good at hand to hand, too," Boomer offered. There was a chiming through the room and Boomer perked up. "That should be the burgers. I hope I ordered enough."

"All right, let's sit down and talk this out." Having Drake around

195

would give him more options and potentially keep Maddie from having to do the really dangerous stuff. It also meant he would have to watch him like a hawk.

"Which room is mine?" Drake asked.

"Uh, the one at your house," Maddie replied.

"He's going to want to stay close." Deke didn't want the fucker around twenty-four seven, but it would make it easier to watch him.

"MaeBe, you got any room?" Drake ducked when a lemon went flying his way. "I'm just kidding. Jeez, Kyle, take a joke."

Kyle would never joke about MaeBe.

"I'll go and get the downstairs guest room ready for you," Maddie offered. She went on her toes and whispered in Deke's ear. "He won't buy the whole we're together thing if we're in separate rooms. I'll move your stuff into mine. Keep him occupied for a couple of minutes."

She strode away.

Deke looked to the man who'd just handed him the keys to the kingdom. "You'll be in the room down from ours. Now I want a rundown on everything you know."

Drake sighed and started to talk.

All in all, not a bad night. And it wasn't over yet.

* * * *

Nolan Byrne stared down at the laptop screen.

He'd sent off a text to Madeline Hill earlier in the afternoon to see if she'd made it back to LA on time. She'd read it and ignored him until now.

If he didn't need the little bitch so much, he would fire her. Unfortunately, she was too important for all his future plans to deal with her properly.

His phone vibrated right before the message popped up on his screen.

I'm back and I had a lovely time. Deke is in town this week. He would like to meet you before he talks to the woman who runs The Reef. They have some requirements that have to be met before they allow guests in, but Deke is sure we can work something out. I was hoping we could have lunch soon. Thank you so much for the time off. I needed to relax.

If he hadn't been able to track her phone, he would be suspicious. She'd suddenly needed a spa trip right before the biggest launch in company history? He supposed if she'd been doing something she shouldn't have it would have been better to claim a family emergency. Instead she'd explained she was exhausted and the opportunity to go to a spa with her cousin had come up.

He had friends everywhere. Well, connections. He wouldn't call anyone his friend. The idea of friends was nonsense, a social construct meant to force people to behave in a certain way. Connection was a better word for it. He knew people who owed him favors, and one of them was a higher-up at the cellular company who serviced Madeline Hill's phone. It was easy to track it, and she'd spent the whole weekend at the hotel, only leaving it once to have brunch at a place in the city.

If only he could track Jane the way he could pretty much everyone else in his life.

Was that why he was so fascinated with her? She was the one woman who could actually play his game.

The phone rang before he could message Madeline back. He glanced down and the number was unavailable. His heart rate actually ticked up. She was the only thing in the world that could throw him off, make him feel anything at all. There were times when he was sure once he'd had her, he would be able to move on with his life, get back to normal. He would see she was just a woman like the rest, and life would settle back down.

Sometimes he resented her every bit as much as he wanted her.

Still, he found himself taking the call when he should show her it

197

wasn't like he sat around waiting for her. He had a business to run, after all. "This is Byrne."

"Is your friend back?"

No sweet hellos. She'd explained that once they had a proper D/s relationship in place, he could guide how she greeted him, how she related to him in every way. She'd offered him the world, but only after she'd danced to his tune.

He hoped she enjoyed pain as much as she claimed to.

"Yes, and she's with her Dom. I'm going to meet him for lunch sometime this week." It annoyed him to no end that he couldn't simply buy his way into this club she wanted to go to. Hell, he'd thought about buying the building and forcing the fuckers to let him in. He would be making a note of everyone who tried to keep him out. They'd learn what happened when a person didn't show proper respect to the king. "I could set up the meeting in a private dining room if you would like to join us."

Because she almost never would meet him in a public place. Another intriguing thing about her. She was a puzzle he wanted to solve. Then he could likely play with her for a while and toss her out when he got bored.

"I can't right now. I'm not in town," she revealed. "I'm on another job, but I need to send you the final code for the project."

"I thought you would bring that yourself."

"I'm sending a courier. You're going to have to work on it a bit to ensure it's properly integrated with the AI. The group doesn't want there to be any problems. Unless you'll let me send one of our people out there."

He wasn't going to let anyone touch his tech. "I don't think that's a good idea. Not until I've been invited into the group."

Not even after he was invited in, but he wasn't about to tell her that.

"I can understand why you're wary," she conceded. "So you're going to have to be the one to ensure everything is properly integrated before launch. We won't exactly get a chance to tweak it once it's up in orbit."

"I'll deal with it, Jane. When are you back in town?" He didn't want to wait until he was invited into The Consortium to finalize his relationship with her. He wanted her to wear his collar when he walked in to that first meeting, wanted to show them all that he could master their queen.

"I'll be in this weekend. That would be a good time to meet with Madeline Hill and her...friends," she said, suggestion plain in her tone.

He needed to get that invitation to The Reef as quickly as possible. "All right. I'll arrange it. It looks like I've got a few more hoops to jump through before they let us in. I thought perhaps we should practice. We wouldn't want to look completely green now, would we?"

"Oh, I think we'll figure it out," she replied. "It's not hard. But you should start looking for a collar for me. I want something lovely, something that shows the world how good it is to be your submissive, Nolan."

When her voice went soft and sexy, he felt it in his dick. It wasn't the first time he'd bought her jewelry. She'd been very specific about what she'd wanted then, so he liked having some freedom when it came to her collar. "I'll have it by the time we go to the club."

"Excellent. And, Nolan, watch who you hire for the next few weeks," she said, her tone going back to professional. "The launch is soon, and you have to know that there are people watching. I would be especially careful about bringing in new security."

That was an odd request, but one he could grant. "I'll freeze hiring for a few weeks. We have to concentrate on our plans. By the way, should I expect any scrutiny over the disappearance of that woman?"

He couldn't quite remember her name. Something with a *P.* She'd had a husband and a couple of kids. That could make things messy. She'd had to be dealt with since he'd discovered she was meeting with a reporter. She'd stumbled across some of the changes he'd made, and the girl had been too clever for her own good.

He'd turned the whole thing over to Jane.

"The husband has been properly handled. He understands if he says anything at all, we'll kill his children." Her tone didn't change, stayed the exact even keel. "He took the money and he's said all the right things to the police. I don't think they were madly in love. He had a woman on the side. Lucky for us, his wife was estranged from her family, so no one's looking for her. I have to go. I'll contact you later this week. And I'm serious about the hiring. There are people out there who are looking for me, and if they place me close to you the first thing they'll do is try to hire on at the company. I'd rather they didn't find me until I'm ready."

He had questions, but he knew she wouldn't answer them. "I'll be careful. I want this to work as much as you do."

Because if this worked, he would truly be the king of the fucking world. He would be the man who controlled who lived and who died, and he would do it with the stroke of his keyboard.

"See that you do."

There was a click that let him know he'd been dismissed.

Bitch. He would show her. He would become her Dom and then her god.

He set the phone down and messaged Madeline back.

He would jump through her hoops, and then she would find out how fast that hoop could tighten around her throat.

Chapter Eight

Maddie sat on her bed and rethought every decision she'd made tonight.

Mostly she rethought the decision to bring Deke into her bedroom. How the hell was she supposed to climb into bed with him? Maybe she could sleep in her reading chair. Or out on the couch in the living room. In the moment it had seemed like such a good idea, but now the reality of the day set in. It pressed on her chest and made her feel like she couldn't breathe.

The door to her bathroom came open and Deke was standing there wearing nothing but a towel around his waist. He had another towel in his hand, and he ran it over his dark hair. He looked far too good to be true, every inch of his body muscular and fit. "You doing okay? Everyone in their rightful places?"

Her evening had turned into one long mission briefing where she hadn't understood half of what they were saying. She'd spent most of her time trying not to show how worried she was. And watching Boomer inhale an unholy amount of food. She'd eaten next to nothing. How could she think about food when the world was falling apart and it might be her fault?

"Yes. Although I think Kyle's worried Dan is going to try to sneak into MaeBe's room and...Drake." She felt herself flush remembering how the man had tricked her. "His name is Drake."

Deke stepped in front of her. "Hey, are you okay? I'm sorry it got out of hand. I didn't mean to talk for so long. I just wanted to make sure our Agency friend understands the plan."

She nodded. "It's okay. I'm glad we're getting to bed early. I've got a lot to do in the morning. I've already heard back from Nolan. He wants to meet you tomorrow."

His hand came out, brushing over her hair. His tone went deep and smooth. "Then we should get some practice in. I was hoping we could get into the hot tub, but I don't trust Drake not to try to join us, and then I'll have to kill him."

It was hard to believe that it had only been a few hours before that she'd thought seriously about getting into the hot tub naked with him. That moment seemed like it was a world away now. "I'll be all right. I don't think we'll be doing a scene tomorrow. I think the most we have to worry about is coffee."

"No, but how we present ourselves as a couple is important. And I also think you've had a rough day, and this doesn't have to be about training. I'm using the word to make it easier for you to give yourself permission to relax."

He didn't understand her at all. "I don't think I need to relax. I think I've been far too relaxed. I've always thought I was a smart woman, the kind that would notice if someone was going to use her work to kill people."

"You did." Deke's steady tone grated on her, showing her how calm he was when she felt like falling apart. "You noticed something was wrong. You can't be this hard on yourself."

But she could. It was the one thing she absolutely knew how to do. "I thought someone was trying to steal the tech or sell it to some other country. I never dreamed they would use my work to... I'm not even sure I understand what they're trying to do."

She stood, her gut churning. Anger and confusion warred with the guilt she felt.

They'd used her work to try to blow up a nuclear power plant and kill thousands of people and she'd just sat there at the dinner table.

She should have known. It wasn't like this hadn't happened before. Time and time again scientists had made breakthroughs only to have their peaceful work perverted for the industrial-military machine.

"Hey, it's going to be all right, Maddie."

She turned on him. "No, it's not. Do you know how long and hard I've worked for this?"

"I do."

He couldn't possibly know. He couldn't understand what she'd given up. A life. Friends. Lovers.

Him. Except she hadn't given him up. He'd given up on her.

"You can't understand."

"I don't have to understand to sympathize. Of course you're upset. So let me help you," he said in a tone she was sure was meant to soothe.

"By doing what?" She practically spat the question at him. "What is the great Deke Murphy going to do to make me feel better?"

"I'm going to spank you and then I'm going to fuck you, Madeline."

She stopped in her tracks.

"You feel out of control, and there's nothing you can do about it tonight." He stood there with his perfect body and gorgeous face. "So let someone else be in control for a while. Don't think about anything else but me and you and how good we can make each other feel."

It was a trap, but she wasn't sure it was one she could avoid.

"I can't just lie over your lap like some wayward child." She couldn't wrap her brain around it.

He moved in again, and there was a darkness in his eyes that made her step back, one and then two steps until she hit the wall, and still he moved in. His shoulders had come down, but not in a relaxed fashion. Oh no. This was the stance of a predator who knew he was about to take down his prey.

"Tell me what you need," he ordered in a deep tone.

"I need for none of this to have happened."

He slapped at the wall behind her. "I can't fix that for you. Tell me what you need here and now. This doesn't work if you aren't honest. Honest with me. Honest with yourself. What do you need to get through the night? Don't think about tomorrow. We'll deal with tomorrow when it comes. I'm talking about tonight. What do you need to let me in?"

Her back was against the wall, and he loomed over her. Honesty. What was her first instinct? Was it to push him back and get him out of her space? No. She didn't want him to leave. She wanted what he'd promised her, but she didn't want to ask for it. "I'm angry and I can't seem to scream or cry. I'm stuck in a corner, and I don't know how to get out."

His hand came up, circling her throat. If anyone besides Deke had wrapped a big hand around her neck she would have fought. Instead, she felt her nipples go hard, the tension inside her beginning to transform. "You need someone to fight. You need someone to make you cry. I can do that for you, and then I promise I'll make you come and then I'll hold you all fucking night long and I won't take a single thing for myself unless you say it's okay. This can be nasty and rough. It can be anything you need. You need me to be the bastard who forces you to submit, I can do that. It's all an illusion because you can stop me at any time. It's play, but it can get you where you need to go."

She wouldn't have to ask him? Wouldn't have to beg? She couldn't beg right now. "This doesn't change anything."

That hand moved to her hair, tangling his fingers in. "Of course not. It's only play. It's nothing but me being your Dom. What's your safe word?"

Was she really doing this? Was she going to let him spank her? Was she going to let him prove to her that she wasn't alone? That he could handle her damage?

Something fierce had awakened inside her, some piece of herself she hadn't known existed. "Red."

She'd gone for something simple, not really thinking she would ever find the need to use it. Now she wanted to push herself to the brink.

His hand tightened, lighting up her scalp. Arousal started to pulse through her, warring with the anger she felt, mixing inside. Was it all right to let off steam this way? She was feeling raw, and she could yell at him and probably say things she didn't mean. Or she could play this his way.

She pushed against him. "Fuck off, Deke."

He didn't move at all. Not an inch. He was a hunk of stone, offering her some really weird shelter from the storm inside her head. "That's not your safe word."

It felt good to push at him because every time she did, his hand tightened on her hair, and she loved the bite of pain she got from it. "Fuck off. I don't want you here."

He pressed his body against hers, giving her no more space to fight him. "But I want to be here, baby, and there's not a damn thing you can do about it. Stop cursing at me or you're going to find out what happens when you disobey. I've been indulgent to this point, but you're going to meet the real Dom tonight if you keep pushing me."

He was so close, and all the man was wearing was one of her towels. He smelled like her soap, and he was staring down at her like he could eat her alive.

She went up on her toes, getting as close to eye level as she could. "I said fuck off."

She gasped as he tugged on her hair, harder than before, and his gaze went positively glacial.

"I'm not joking with you. I'm feeling savage tonight," Deke admitted. "If I scare you in any way, you use your safe word."

She struggled against him, needing to keep the tension between them. What she couldn't accept from him tenderly, she found she could handle with a little hate between them. "Let me go."

His hand tightened again, a jagged thrill of pain racing along her skin. "Tell me you'll use it."

He was frustrating her. How could she lose herself in the play if he constantly reminded her it wasn't real? "This is all consensual, asshole. I'll use my safe word if I need to, but right now I'm thinking I won't because you're soft, Murphy. Maybe you're the one who needs a safe word."

His lips curled up in the most wicked smirk. "Oh, there's nothing at all soft about me right now, baby. And you push me harder and we'll talk about more than a spanking. We'll talk about how well your asshole is going to take a plug."

That was something that normally she would roll her eyes at, but in the heat of the moment, she kind of wanted to try it. The anxiety that had threatened to tear her up moments before seemed to recede, and she could focus on her anger. And her desire.

She wanted a fight, especially one where she knew the person she was fighting would never hurt her. She pushed at him again and managed to bring her leg up, kneeing his thigh.

His hand left her hair and captured her wrists, hauling them up above her head while he pressed his body against hers, getting both his legs between hers and holding them apart so she couldn't get another kick in. "Do not try that again, baby."

She could feel the press of his cock against her belly. He was so big, and she was utterly helpless against him. He could do whatever he wanted to her. Just like her boss. Just like the whole fucking world seemed to be.

She'd been so alone without him. She hadn't realized it. She'd managed to put those feelings in a closet and lock them up tight, convincing herself that she didn't need him, that he was some childish fascination.

He was everything, and in that moment, she hated him for being so important, resented him for coming back into her life to show her everything she'd missed.

It didn't matter that once she'd tried to do the same thing to him. It didn't matter that she'd gone to him. It made it worse because he hadn't come looking for her. He'd been content to never see her again.

"I hate you."

His eyes closed but not before she saw the pain there. When he opened them again, they were full of stubborn, steely will. "It doesn't matter. I'm in charge, and you're going to obey me. I think it's time I showed you what happens to little brats who don't mind their Masters."

He stepped back, dropping her hands and leaving her off balance.

"You are not my Master." She struggled to straighten up and growled the words his way before glancing toward the door. She wanted to run, to have him chase her through her house. He could pull her down on the soft rug in the living room and spread her legs wide and impale her on his cock. Her heart raced, pure arousal flooding her in a way it never had before. It was mixed with all the noxious emotions she'd felt for weeks, but somehow it wasn't toxic.

Deke pulled the towel off and then her eyes weren't anywhere but on that stunning body of his. His cock was long and thick, erect against his taut belly. He reached into his bag and pulled out a length of rope. "You should understand that if you run, I'll chase you, and I won't care that there are other people in the house. They don't matter right now. I won't care if they're watching. I'll still spank you until your ass is red, and then I'll force you on my cock. You can scream and moan and call out and I won't care unless they try to stop me. You're the only one who gets to stop me."

He would do it. He would spank her and fuck her in front of whoever was there, not because he was an exhibitionist but because he didn't care about anyone but her. No one mattered to him in this moment except her.

That made her mad, too. If he'd cared about her half as much in high school, they would have had years together. They would have had a family. She wouldn't be so fucking alone.

She rushed at him because if he thought she was going to sit there and be a good girl and let him tie her up, he didn't know her. She pushed at him, this minor violence all part of the "play." It didn't feel like play. It felt like fucking therapy, and he was the only one she could ever share this with, ever allow to see her stripped down to her core.

When he was gone, she would be alone again, and that made her angry, too.

She pushed at him, tears starting to blur her eyes, but he was too fast. He had her hands in his and dragged her to the bed, straddling her and holding her down as he wound that rope around her wrists.

"That's right, baby. You fight all you like. It's going to end the way I want it to," he said, his face a hard mask.

He was so gorgeous, and she was probably a mess. She pulled at the rope, but it held her fast. He sat on top of her, his cock thrusting up from a nest of well-groomed dark hair. He reached down and pulled at the sides of her shirt, ripping it open, buttons pinging as they hit the floor. He cupped her breast through her bra.

"Are you going to behave?" He asked the question as he pushed the cup down, freeing her breast. "We can get to the part where I eat your pussy faster if you like."

She couldn't. She wasn't sure she should go there with him. It was one more temptation she could have avoided. "Get off me, asshole."

He tugged her nipple between his thumb and forefinger and twisted. "If you keep it up, I'll have you in clamps. They'll bite into your nipples and get them ruby red for me."

"Promises, promises." She couldn't let him get tender on her. She needed this fight between them, needed him to break her walls down. She couldn't bring them down on her own, and those walls were holding something she needed to purge.

He eased off her and caught her when she tried to roll off the bed. He hauled her up and had her over his knees in a heartbeat. She'd put on pajama pants earlier, trying to cover for how long it had taken to shift Deke's luggage to her room by changing clothes. The stretchy material made it easy for Deke to pull her pants down and off her legs.

Vulnerable. She felt so damn vulnerable.

Then she felt pain because Deke's hand came down on her ass.

No one had ever spanked her. Not her parents. Certainly not a boyfriend. The sound cracked through the air as he slapped her cheeks again. Then she gritted her teeth and blinked back tears.

"Is this what you want, baby? You want me to be the bad guy?" Deke's hand came down again. "I'll be the bad guy. I'll be the one who makes you cry. I've done it before. I'm always the bad guy."

He wasn't. He was the best man she'd ever met, and that was what made it so hard that he hadn't loved her the way she'd loved him.

Now she was alone, and he'd only come out here to save her damn life, and it was so screwed up.

He spanked her over and over, and the wall finally broke. Tears dripped from her eyes, and she let them go. He was here with her in this one moment in time, and it was safe to let it all go. She sobbed, and it took her a moment to realize that Deke had stopped spanking her. Somehow he'd managed to turn her over and settle her on his lap, his arms coming around her.

"That's good, baby. Cry all you like." He held on to her, his voice cracking like he was about to cry with her.

It was the closest she'd felt to another human being since…since him.

Him. Always him.

He had her out of the ropes with a few pulls, and she followed her instincts. She wrapped her arms around him and held him close, letting out all the fear and anxiety of the last few weeks, purging it from her soul so she could function.

She cried for the longest time. All the while Deke sat there, holding her and rocking with her.

She finally laid her head on his shoulder, a beautiful sense of peace coming over her.

"Are you all right?" Deke asked the question as he brushed back her hair.

She was still wearing her bra, which had one cup out of place, and that was the only clothing she wore. Her face was probably a mess, and she was sitting on top of the hottest man she'd ever met. He was naked, too. It was weird and should be awkward, and it was so comforting she never wanted to leave this place.

She was tired and spent and still needy.

"Do you want to take a shower, baby?" Deke asked, the low rumble of his voice seeming to roll across her skin.

She'd purged one need but another remained, and she was done fighting it. "I don't want a shower."

"All right. I'm going to get you in bed and then I think I'm going to go for a jog," Deke replied.

"You promised me, Deke. You've made good on half of it," she pointed out. This was Deke being Deke. She didn't take it that he didn't want her. She could feel his cock, and he wasn't trying to get out of sex with her.

"Nothing else has to happen. I need you to understand that."

She was going to have to show him she was okay and perfectly capable of making terrible decisions all on her own. She slid off his lap and unhooked her bra before walking to the side of her normally lonely bed. All the bad shit was gone now, and arousal was the only thing she felt.

Arousal and the need to be close to him. A relationship wouldn't work this time, either, but she wasn't going to sleep alone while he was here. He was it for her, and she would take any time she had with him. She was done denying herself. She would deal with the heartache later.

She wanted him now.

Maddie laid down on the bed, all her inhibitions gone. They'd shared something far more intimate than sex. Now she wanted the fun part. He stood at the end of the bed, his cock still hard, and watched as she spread her legs wide for him.

"I think you said something about making a meal out of me." She laid back, ready to take everything that man had to give.

* * * *

Deke felt every fiber of his being go insane with wanting.

Madeline Hill was laid out and waiting for him, her lovely body still flush from the emotional time they'd spent.

She'd sobbed in his arms, and his heart had broken. He'd held her and wondered who'd been here for her in the years he'd been gone. He'd found a whole other family. Who'd held her and promised her everything would be all right?

Her tears had gutted him for another reason, too. He'd been the bad guy, the one who pushed her until she cried. He seemed to always be the bad guy with her, but here she was, opening herself up to him, giving him what he wanted.

His body was beyond eager. His soul was wary. "You're not mad at me?"

She'd read a lot about the lifestyle, but she wasn't experienced. The scene they'd just played out had been a heavy one. It wouldn't have surprised him if she'd asked him to leave and let her recover on her own. He would do it. He would put on his clothes and go sit outside until she let him back in. Or sleep on the couch and deal with the ramifications.

She sighed and rolled over, propping her head on her hand. "You want to talk now. So much talking in D/s. No. Why would I be mad at you? You did what I asked you to do. I needed to cry. It's hard for me. Especially when I'm anxious. I internalize a lot."

"It was a heavy scene. It didn't scare you?"

"I found it surprisingly hot. I think I might be a little freaky. I kind of liked you manhandling me," she admitted.

"Kind of?" He climbed on the bed with her. "I think it was a little more than kind of. I think you liked it a lot." They did need to talk

211

about the scene, but that didn't mean he couldn't give her what she wanted. He could multitask. He put a hand on her ankle, running his palm up her leg. "I think you've always liked some role play with your sex. Even when you're not emotional."

She allowed him to roll her on her back, her eyes drifting closed as he stroked his hand over her silken skin. She was calm now, her whole body relaxed, when she'd been a bundle of stress before. "I suppose you could say all my sex has been vanilla up until now. Although we haven't actually had sex. It might be fun, though."

He would love to play with her, to sit down and plan out scenes or let things happen organically. He would love to explore how creatively he could fuck her. She had a big imagination and was a total geek, so he could see some cosplay in his future.

If they had a future…

There was one thing he needed her to understand. He cupped her breast, loving the softness of her skin and the way her nipple had peaked against his palm. "You are not responsible for anything that is happening now or what the people who are using your technology do with it."

Her eyes opened. "I know that logically. It's different emotionally, but, Deke, I don't want to talk about that. Not tonight. I feel good right now. I want to stay in this place with you."

He wanted to lock down the relationship, but it was too soon for her. She'd come so far in the course of a few days. She'd vowed she wouldn't sleep with him much less share a room with him, and here she was. He could win her over. All he needed was a little time.

And a whole lot of pleasure.

He needed to show her how good it could be between them.

"You want to stay in the place where you're my sweet little fuck toy and you do anything I ask of you?"

Her gaze went hot, staring at the part of his body that ached right now. "Yes. I'm talking about that place. You're right. It's different in practice. In my head I don't imagine that I'm the woman who needs permission, but I think I do. I think my head goes so many different directions, I need help to focus on this part of me."

The sexual part. The sensual part.

"Good. It's good for you to tell me what you need." He was naked in bed with the most gorgeous woman he'd ever seen, and it was time to take control again. Sex was so much more than pumping his way to orgasm. Sex was long periods of time where he explored his lover's body, learned what made her come quickly, and how to draw the orgasm out when he wanted to.

He'd had Maddie hundreds of times, but she was a different person now and so was he. He got to learn her all over again.

"You're going to do everything I ask you to do, baby. Do you understand? In this bed you're mine. You're mine to fuck and please and spank. Anything I want."

"Yes." The word came out on a breathless sigh.

"This gorgeous body belongs to me." He would bet she didn't think of herself as beautiful and hot and so fuckable she made his dick hard when she walked into a room.

"I think it always has."

Sweet honesty. The crying session had softened her up, and he was going to be the ruthless bastard who didn't let her take it back. He was going to bring down all her walls and not let her build them up ever again. Not for him. "I'll make up for lost time. Starting now."

He brought their mouths together in a long, luxurious kiss. His cock was dying, but he meant to take his time with her. She'd opened to him tonight, and he wasn't going to reward that trust with a quick roll, like he might have when they'd been in high school.

He was going to show her that her Dom was a patient top, that he could lavish her with affection and show her how much she moved him.

He let their tongues tangle, warmth flowing through him as he covered her body with his. He didn't hold his weight off her as her legs opened, sliding over his. "I've missed you, Madeline."

She shook her head. "Not now. I can't do that tonight. I need to be your submissive right now."

213

He wanted to growl with frustration, to force her to admit they belonged together, but if this was all she could handle, then he would top her. "Baby, you're going to let me explore your body. You're going to be still or I'll tie your hands again. When we get into the club, I'll find a bench where I can tie your hands and feet, and you won't be able to move. I'll be able to touch you anywhere I want, play with any soft, sweet part of you I desire."

"I can be still."

His cock was against her pussy, and all it would take was a simple thrust, but he wasn't getting off so easily and neither was she. He kissed her again before lowering his head to her neck, inhaling her sweet scent. Everything about this woman felt like home to him, and he ached that he wasn't the same for her. He kissed his way down her neck toward her breast. "When I'm done there won't be an inch of you I haven't kissed."

He kissed a line to her breast, tonguing her nipple before giving it a nip. Maddie hissed, and he noted her hands fisting the comforter as she tried so hard to stay still.

"One day we'll play a game," he promised as he moved to her other breast. "We'll see how still you can be, and every time you move, you'll get spanked. A little slap to your ass or a snap of my hand against your pussy. By the end you'll be so sensitive and wet that you'll come the minute I slide my cock inside you."

"You want to make me crazy, don't you?"

"I want to make you wild for me," he corrected. "Like I'm wild for you."

She whimpered when he nipped her. "You're not the one getting spanked."

"Hey, if you want to try it, I'll let you." He was willing to go there with her. Only her.

"But you're the Dom," she pointed out.

"We make our own rules." He traced her areola with his tongue. "Nothing is off limits if it brings us both pleasure. I know some Doms who couldn't let their subs take control like that, and I probably wouldn't have been able to years ago. But I could with you. If that's what you wanted, I'd try it."

"You need the control because of what happened," she said, her voice just above a whisper.

He did not want to talk about his time as a prisoner of war. "I'm better now."

"I wish I could have helped you."

"You did. I thought about you every day." It was all she needed to know about that terrible time.

"I wish I could have been there for you." She went silent for a moment. "I'm just glad you're better."

He got the feeling he was missing something, but he didn't want to bring her into the worst moments of his life. It was so much better to concentrate on the now. On how good it was to be here with her. He wanted to move forward, not look back. "You're the one who's better, baby. I bet you are going to taste even better than I remember. And I remember everything."

He moved down her body, spreading her legs wide. He put his mouth on her, kissing her labia and giving her clit a little lick that had her gasping. She was wet, her body ready for him. He could smell her arousal, the scent damn near sending him into a frenzy. He feasted on her pussy, spearing her with his tongue over and over, taking in the honey of her body. It coated his tongue, reminding him of how good it was to be with her.

Being Maddie's man had been the best part of his life. Even though he'd been a boy.

He'd been hers no matter what stage of his life.

She cried out as she came, her body shaking and going stiff before she sighed and relaxed.

It was his time. He pushed himself off the bed and grabbed the condom he'd lain out next to his kit because he was a motherfucking optimist. He dragged it over his dick, watching her. She lay on the bed, soft light from the lamp caressing her skin. She was the definition of temptation with her legs still spread, evidence of her orgasm glistening on her pussy.

"You are so fucking gorgeous." He moved back to the bed, covering her and making a place for himself at her core. "Wrap your legs around me."

She gave him a smile, her eyes soft as she did his bidding, and wound herself around him. "That's an easy order to follow. Oh, god, you're going to kill me, Deke."

He was sliding his hard length over her clit, getting his dick wet. "Never. Look at me."

Her eyes caught on his.

"Hello again, baby." He thrust up, joining them together.

He hissed, trying not to give into the desperate need to fuck her as hard as he could. Instead he kissed her as he eased back out of her body. Kissed her as he thrust in. Kissed her as they found a familiar rhythm, one he'd worried he would never find again. Every sigh from her lips, touch of her hand, connected him to the boy he'd been, formed a bridge between that boy and the man he'd become.

When Maddie tightened around him and called out his name, he couldn't hold back another second. He wanted it to last, wanted to stay in this moment of rediscovery with her forever. But the orgasm bloomed over him, sending him into a spiral of pure pleasure.

He collapsed on top of her, surrounded by her warmth.

"Well I feel better," Maddie said with a sigh.

He chuckled and rolled to the side, keeping his arms around her. "I'm glad I could help, baby."

She cuddled close, and Deke wished the night didn't have to end.

Chapter Nine

"Do you really have to do that so loudly?" Drake walked into the kitchen as Deke was pouring coffee into the tumbler Maddie used for her morning commute. He'd moved his bag from the car the night before. The man packed light, but he was dressed in fresh clothes this morning—jeans and a V-neck tee that would make him look like every other So Cal dude who worked in tech. Drake was good at fitting in. "We all get it. Deke's got a girl now. You don't have to shout it to the world."

"Yeah, man, I could hear you two upstairs." Kyle had already been in the kitchen when Deke had walked out to start breakfast only to find the upstairs group was already at work.

"If you don't like it, you're welcome to find a hotel. It's LA. There are tons of them." He wasn't about to apologize for the night before. He'd woken up to a very cuddly Madeline, and he was happy.

"I couldn't hear you at all." Boomer was at the stove, using pretty much all of Maddie's eggs to make breakfast. "I slept like a baby."

"He is weirdly still when he sleeps." Kyle frowned before taking a sip of his coffee. "I kind of wondered if he was dead, but when I tried to poke him to make sure he was breathing he nearly killed me. He got his whole hand around my neck. Like he could probably touch his fingers to his thumb. Around my neck. It's not like I'm skinny or anything."

MaeBe grinned. "Kyle's been whining about it all morning. I told him there's a saying around the building. Never wake a sleeping Boomer."

"I didn't even squeeze hard." Boomer moved the spatula around the pan and added a bit of milk to the eggs he was scrambling. "I was having a bad dream. I got one real whiff of Axe body spray and realized I wasn't in an Afghani prison and I woke up."

"I do not wear body spray." Kyle's brows damn near met in the middle of his forehead.

"It's a cologne," MaeBe explained. "I got Kyle for Secret Santa last year and I didn't know him real well so I bought him this cologne I like. It smells good."

"Well, it smells way better than the dude who waterboarded me in prison so I woke up, and Kyle and I have an understanding now," Boomer replied.

"Yeah, I know to let him stop breathing in the middle of the night. You know it's not like I don't have bad dreams and shit. I haven't tried to kill anyone over them yet." Kyle sat back down beside MaeBe, who was already on her computer.

"You're not as committed as I am. Hey, do you think Maddie has any bread?" Boomer asked.

"It's in the freezer. I didn't want to waste it while I was out of town." Maddie walked in looking all buttoned up and sexy as hell. She strode to the fridge and opened the freezer, pulling out what looked like a loaf of dark wheat bread. "You should be able to toast it. I'll put in a grocery order this afternoon. I don't have a lot of food. I'm afraid I usually pick up something on my way home."

"Don't worry about it. Obtaining food is one of the many not dangerous tasks I have on my list for today," MaeBe announced. "By the way, I've managed to get into the CCTV system in your building.

Just so you know I'm watching."

Maddie's brows rose. "I would think our security would be better than that."

MaeBe shrugged. "CCTV isn't hard. I would have a much harder time getting into the network. Not that I couldn't, but it could take a while. Speaking of, what do you know about Byrne's personal system? Do you have an idea of what kind of security he uses?"

"I've only been to his house a couple of times. He hosts this party every year for upper-level employees," Maddie explained. "I know where his office is, and I've seen him use the system. I think it's password protected."

"Not a problem," MaeBe replied. "I can crack a code. I'm more worried about biometrics."

He wasn't. If they needed Byrne's eye or fingers to unlock the system, they could take the fuckers. The more he thought about the position Byrne had put Maddie in, the more he wanted to kill the man.

"He didn't have anything like that on the computer when I saw it last, but that was six months ago. He had it at the office the last time the mystery lady came into town," she explained.

"And she's due back soon?" Drake asked.

When they'd explained the mysterious visitor and how they believed she might be connected to another case they'd worked, Drake had listened intently. He had not, however, offered up his own information. Maybe he didn't have any, but something about the way he'd gone still had made Deke wonder.

"She's shown up on a regular basis for the last eighteen months." Madeline opened the bread and slid two slices in the toaster. "If she's on the same schedule, she should be back either this week or next."

"You've been working on the satellite project for longer than that," Drake prompted.

"Yes. I've been working on it for almost four years," she replied, getting the butter from the fridge. "But she didn't show up until eighteen months ago. At least that was the first I heard of her, and I think I would have known. Nolan's secretary can be gossipy.

Everyone in the company thinks she's either from the government or another corporation who wants to buy out Byrne—which is ridiculous. There's not enough money in the world to make Nolan give up his company. It's his everything. And some people think she's a sex worker."

"I doubt that very much." Somehow he didn't think sex workers came equipped with off-market tech that allowed them the freedom to move around without the cameras being able to capture their faces.

"And I doubt she's with the government," Drake added.

"How can you possibly know that?" Boomer asked. "I get that you're connected, but you can't know everything that's going on. She could be Department of Defense or NASA."

"I'm certain because if the Agency doesn't have that tech, no one in the government does." Drake sat down at the bar and studied the group for a moment. "I'm going to share classified information with you because I think you're my best shot at identifying this woman. A few years ago I was made aware of a clandestine group of some of the world's wealthiest business leaders who work together to maintain power. They're a new version of a group McKay-Taggart took down ten years ago. We always knew they would come back in some form. I sent out two of my best operatives at the time. They worked their way into one of the lower levels of the group."

Kyle frowned. "Me. He's talking about me."

MaeBe's eyes widened. "Seriously? You're doing this now?"

One big shoulder shrugged. "You know I worked for the Agency. Everyone suspects it. I'm trying to be a better Kyle, and that means admitting I was one of Drake's operatives. It seems to be connected somehow to this case."

"He's right." Boomer turned off the burner. "If I'm pretty sure of something, then everyone else knows. He's got that Agency look about him."

"There is no Agency look," Kyle insisted. "Anyway, when I was in college I would come home for the summers, and one of the perks of working for very little money at my uncle's business was reading the case files."

Drake's head shook. "Classified information was in those files."

"Yeah, my uncle's not big on that. Anyway, I had read a bit about the group called The Collective. When I started working for the CIA, I recognized some of the same methods and manipulations coming from a new group."

"Kyle is the one who identified The Consortium, and he and his partner at the time began working to collect data on the group," Drake continued.

"You never mentioned a partner." MaeBe looked up at Kyle.

"I don't talk about her. She's not a good memory." Kyle's jaw went tight, and he didn't meet MaeBe's gaze. "She ended up turning and joining the very group we were trying to bring down."

Drake took over. "The operative is now deceased, but the group is still working. I've sent a report with all the relevant information to Alex and Big Tag that they will be forwarding to all of you. This group likes to use female liaisons to negotiate with the corporations they work with. Many of these women were recruited from intelligence agencies across the globe."

"What do these liaisons do?" Maddie had a concerned look on her face.

"Any number of different jobs," Drake explained. "We're certain they negotiate to buy emerging technology in order to keep it off the market in certain cases. They also engage in corporate espionage if they're dealing with a company outside the network. We're fairly certain they've assassinated three heads of corporations around the globe so they could install their own more friendly CEOs."

Maddie paled. "That woman who visits Nolan has killed people?"

"It's very likely." Kyle had both hands palms down on the bar as though he needed the support to remain standing. "This woman is dangerous. It's why we need to get that picture. We need to identify and track her."

"Kyle, are you still working for the Agency?" Deke needed to know where Kyle's loyalties lay.

His hands came up. "Absolutely not. I left all of that behind when I came to McKay-Taggart. The only reason I'm talking about this now is it came up on this case. I talked to my uncle and Alex a bit about what I know after Noelle's case, but most of this stuff is highly classified and had to come from Drake. But there's no question that I would go back in if I thought I could take that group down."

"Because they killed your partner?" MaeBe was looking at him, concern clear on her face.

"No." Kyle's tone had gone flat, his expression hollow. "They didn't kill Julia. I did. And I would do it again in a heartbeat. I would kill them all. I'm going to get ready to head out to The Reef when Deke gets back from dropping off Madeline."

MaeBe stood and started to go after him.

"Not now," Kyle said. "Give me a minute. You should get ready, too."

Kyle strode up the stairs.

"Well, there's the broody bastard I know." Boomer shook his head. "Who wants toast?"

Nothing shook Boomer, but Deke required some clarifications. He turned to Drake. "Kyle was your operative?"

"They both worked under me. At the time they were my most trusted agents," Drake replied evenly. "I knew Julia quite well. At least I thought I did. I didn't realize what was happening with Julia until it was far too late to save her. Kyle was forced to kill her during a mission when she turned on him. That's all I'm willing to say. We will focus on this mission and once we ID the woman, McKay-Taggart along with Kyle will be out of it."

"But Kyle said he would come back." MaeBe sniffled and wiped away a tear. "He said he would leave and go back to the CIA if it meant taking these people down."

"I assure you, he won't be allowed to," Drake replied. "His stepfather would filet me. No. This is as close to The Consortium as I want Kyle Hawthorne to be. And I'll take some toast, Boomer. MaeBe, why don't you show me what you've got. I'd like to familiarize myself with the building Maddie works in."

He moved closer to the hacker, and Deke was grateful she had something to do.

Deke took Maddie's hand and led her out of the kitchen. "Are you okay?"

"Well, it feels more serious than it did before," she admitted. "Is there any way Nolan isn't in on this? Could this woman be using him? Misrepresenting herself?"

"He's hiding her identity. I don't think he would if he didn't know she's doing something potentially criminal." He wanted Maddie prepared, and that meant keeping it real with her. If he could keep her from this, he would, but naivety could put her in danger.

She nodded. "All right. We should probably go. I don't want to be late."

He hated how closed off she was again. Like the night before hadn't happened. He should have hopped in the shower with her. He should have fucked her until she couldn't do anything but smile at him and feel relaxed.

He tugged on her hand, bringing her into the circle of his arms. "It's going to be okay. I promise you."

"You can't promise me that, Deke." But she didn't pull away. "You can't promise me the company will still be standing at the end of this. You can't promise me I'll have a job. My career has been everything for the last decade of my life."

"No, I can't promise you Byrne's empire won't crumble if he's involved with something criminal, but I'll protect you and your work." He would do anything for her. "I've got friends who can help you. All I want you to do is focus on staying safe. We take Byrne and his friend to The Reef on Friday night if everything goes well today. Hopefully we get an invite to his place soon after. We're going to let Drake work his magic. You won't even have to get close to the system. We'll let the others handle it while we provide Byrne with a distraction."

"I don't have to get into his office?"

223

"No. You'll stay with me," he vowed.

He felt a shudder go through her. "Good. I have to admit, everything I've found out about what Nolan might be into scares the crap out of me. I'm not a spy. I'm in over my head."

He hugged her close. "I'm not going to let anything happen to you."

She held him for a moment more and then stepped back. "All right. I'm glad you're coming in with me. Are you ready?"

"Of course." He was supposed to meet Byrne this morning and perhaps have coffee with the man. It would be hard to leave her in the building when it came time to go. "If you need anything, text me or flash a sign to the security cameras. Someone will be watching. I promise."

It was a promise he meant to keep.

* * * *

Maddie was still thinking about the night before as they walked out of the elevator onto her floor, her hand in Deke's. It did not get past her notice that every head turned as she started down the hall.

She supposed her coworkers were surprised to see her with a guy since she'd never brought one to the office. Or a party. Or any kind of event. As far as any of them knew she was in a relationship with her computer.

Then there was the fact that Deke was gorgeous and she was kind of a geek.

It was high school all over again.

"Morning, Madeline." Kelly Vinson looked Deke up and down as she walked by, her arms full of files.

"Morning." She felt awkward in a place where she normally held a lot of power. She nodded to a couple of the guys on her team, who stared openly.

"My office is in the back corner." She led Deke along.

"This whole place is nice," Deke said. "You've come a long way from Calhoun High."

She opened the door to her office and felt like she could breathe once she was inside. "It doesn't feel like it today. Everyone was looking at me."

"Yeah, I noticed. You don't normally bring men up here, do you?"

"Never. I've dated, but I kept those two parts of my life separate."

Deke got into her space. He seemed to do that a lot, as if he needed to be close to her. He put a hand on her hip and drew her in. "Kiss me."

She didn't even try to fight the instinct to obey that command. When Deke kissed her she forgot about everything else. The world seemed to melt away. She went on her toes and pressed her lips to his. She'd decided to live in the moment. Even if they got the information they needed soon, Deke wouldn't be leaving for a while. He'd explained that he would need to stay close until there was some sort of conclusion, and that could take months.

She'd woken early and laid there, acknowledging that there was no way she wouldn't end up in bed with him again. As long as they were in close proximity, she would give in to his temptation. After the night before she wasn't sure why she'd tried to stay away.

He'd given her everything she'd needed the night before. Well, everything physical. He'd shut her down when she'd wanted to talk about what had happened to him in Iraq. It had been good to be reminded that those years apart were a closed door between them.

His hands found her hair and he took over the kiss, his tongue surging in. She let her whole body go soft.

This was what she needed. She needed to let go of the emotional stuff and concentrate on how good he could make her feel.

"Knock, knock."

She gasped, pulled back, and would have fallen on her ass if Deke hadn't caught her.

Nolan stood in her doorway, a big smile on his face. It was an odd expression, though one she'd seen a thousand times. She'd never been able to properly explain what bothered her about her boss's smile before. It was out of synch with the look in his eyes, as though he'd trained himself to smile even when he wasn't feeling it. He was in his normal uniform—pressed jeans, button-down, untucked shirt, his brown hair in an almost military cut.

"Nolan." She straightened her skirt, hoping her hair had survived. Deke liked to sink his fingers in. "I'm sorry I didn't hear you come in."

"I can understand why." He moved into the office, holding out a hand. "I'm Nolan Byrne. You must be Deke."

Deke smiled and gripped Nolan's hand, shaking it. "Yes, Deke Murphy. It's good to meet you."

"Oh, no. It's good to meet you." Nolan stepped back, nodding his head. "I can't tell you how happy I am that you're an actual real person."

"Of course he's real." Maddie frowned her boss's way. Had he thought she'd made him up? She kind of had, but he couldn't know that.

"Well, we've never seen our Madeline with a guy before." Nolan smiled her way. "She's married to her job. I'm glad to know she's got some balance in her life. Work-life balance is so important. I was glad she got to spend some time with her cousin this weekend."

Her heart rate ticked up. Did he know something? Or was he just being a decent boss? Were they all wrong about him? "I appreciated the time off."

"You earned it. You've barely taken a vacation day since you started," Nolan said. "I suspect that will change, though it's going to have to wait until the launch."

"We're working on her taking more time for herself." Deke put an arm around her shoulder.

Nolan winced slightly. "Well, I'm afraid we need her around here for the next few weeks. We've got a big launch coming up."

"Yes," Deke agreed. "I've heard a bit about the project, though I

226

have to admit, I don't understand about half of what Maddie says when she starts talking tech."

"Yes, she's very enthusiastic." Nolan turned to her, hopefully with a problem she could solve so she didn't have to stand here and feel awkward while her boss talked to her... She wasn't sure what she should call Deke. But it was weird listening to them talk. "I was hoping to catch you before you got your day started. Naman is having some problems with the audio integration. I thought you might help him out. After Justin passed, he was shifted in to the position, and it's been a struggle to figure out exactly what Justin was doing. He was brilliant, but the project notes he left behind aren't great."

Oh, she would love to get a look at his project notes. And the code. If she had Justin's original code, she and MaeBe could compare it to whatever became the final code. It could tell them a lot. "Of course. I'll go down and talk to him."

"And I'll take your guy for coffee," Nolan offered, sending her stomach plummeting.

"What?" Logically she realized this was exactly what she was supposed to be doing, but the thought of Deke alone with Nolan sent a shock of panic through her. It wasn't because Deke couldn't handle himself. Physically he could take Nolan down in a heartbeat, but they would be talking about...her. "I thought I was going to join you guys."

Deke leaned over, brushing a kiss over her forehead. "Nolan and I have a few things we need to talk about before we go into the club. I'll pick you up this afternoon."

"Don't worry." Nolan started to back away. "I promise I'll take care of him."

There was a knock on the door, and Naman was standing there with two coffee cups in his hands. "Hey, Madeline. I brought you a latte in hopes that I can bribe you into looking over a few things for me."

"She's all yours," Nolan promised as he walked out.

She wanted to run after him, but Deke was already gone.

227

And she had work to do. She gave her coworker a smile and accepted the offering. She would need the caffeine. "Of course."

Fifteen minutes later she was in Naman's office. The audio team had a whole floor to themselves, with small lab spaces and a few individual offices, but for the most part it was a shared space. Naman, as the new lead, had taken over Justin's office, and there were still touches of the man lingering.

She stared at the picture of Justin in his cap and gown at his graduation, his mother and father standing proudly beside him.

"They died a couple of years back," Naman said quietly. "He didn't have any other family. His girlfriend took a few things, but she let us keep some of the pictures. We were his family, this team. It's been hard on us. I understand that things change, people quit, and employees retire or move on. But losing two members in a single year has been difficult."

Pam Dodson was gone, too. "I was surprised to hear she would just walk away."

Naman leaned against his desk. "She'd been acting weird. Pam was always a little on the eccentric side, but I thought she adored her kids. I didn't know her husband very well. Pam was secretive the last few weeks she worked here. I think she might have been having an affair."

Or meeting with a CIA operative, not that she could tell anyone about Pam's connection to Drake Radcliffe. "That might explain her leaving. I didn't know her as well as I knew Justin."

Naman's lips pursed. "I knew Justin quite well. He's been my boss and friend for many years. I still believe there's something more to his death. He wasn't a man who used drugs. I know what they say, but it seems... I'm talking out of hand. I'm sorry. I shouldn't take up your time."

She didn't want to end this conversation. "It's okay. I thought his death was suspicious, too."

Naman's gaze went to the open door. "I didn't use that word."

"No, I did." She lowered her voice. "Justin asked to meet me off campus the day before he died."

Naman shook his head. "I don't know anything about that. He hadn't mentioned it to me. I know he was having some problems with the calibrations on the system. He was worried about some of the code."

"What part?" She should have done this in the first place, but she felt better knowing Deke was around.

"I'm not sure. I can't find all of his notes. After he died, security came in and took his computer away. When the files he was working on were transferred to me, some of them were missing. I know because I worked with him on protocols that no longer show up in the project. I had to rebuild them all from scratch, which is why I'm having the trouble Nolan talked to you about."

"Why wouldn't they send you all of Justin's work?" It didn't make sense. They couldn't afford to restart a single part of this project if they wanted to launch on time. This wasn't some softball, let's-see-how-this-goes kind of launch. There would be a media circus surrounding Byrne's revolutionary satellite going into space. It wasn't something they could delay at this point. They needed every system working.

"No idea. I asked about it and was told this was all they found," Naman replied. "Someone is lying, and I can't figure out why. I also can't waste time investigating. Not if I want my project bonus. I have three girls to put through college. I need this job."

What he wasn't saying was that anyone with the power to delete those files also had the power to fire him. Or worse. Before she'd known the real stakes, she'd had to consider what she was risking with her investigation—the livelihoods of everyone in this building. "Of course you do. We need to buckle down and get through the next couple of weeks and then we'll deal with whatever we need to deal with."

"Yes." Naman let out a sigh of relief and moved to his laptop.

"It's been hard since we started testing the systems. I swear there must be something going around, and I would like to complain about the timing. The last thing I need is every member of my team going down to some weird virus."

"Virus?"

Naman started pulling up his files. "Yes. It seems to be going around this part of the building, but it doesn't seem to be terrible. I had two engineers go down with nausea and dizziness. The same thing happened with one of our admins this morning, and two more last week."

"When did you begin testing on the audio?" She hated to think that people were getting sick because of the project, but she had to consider it after what she'd learned from Drake about Havana Syndrome.

Naman stopped, his gaze coming up. "We've tested all along, but we've been testing the vocal components the last couple of weeks."

"Where do you do that?" They wouldn't test it in the open.

"In one of the labs," he replied. "We have soundproofing in a couple of them. It cuts down on outside noise so we can isolate Clarke's voice." He frowned. "You think there is a connection?"

She thought there were all kinds of connections she'd missed. "Have you done any of the testing yourself?"

"No, I've been working on another part of the project. Madeline, they're not working on what I would consider an important part of this project. It's literally choosing which voice to give Clarke. They're modifying certain tones to be more soothing. It's the cupholders on the car."

Which meant they would be pretty and overlooked by anyone who was smart enough to figure out what was being done. The "cupholders" would be the perfect place to hide a bomb because they were innocuous. "Could you send me whatever you have on that particular project? I'd like to take a peek."

"Of course. It's your AI we're giving a voice to."

"I'd also like to talk to anyone who's been in those labs."

"Well, it can't be the labs. I can give you a list of who's been sick, but I know at least two of them shouldn't have been in the labs. It's got to be a bug." Naman started typing again. "Now this is one of the protocols I'm trying to rebuild."

He turned the screen her way and she got to work.

It was going to be an interesting day.

Chapter Ten

"Thank you." Deke took the coffee from what appeared to be Nolan Byrne's personal barista. As they'd walked through the building Byrne referred to as his "campus," Byrne had pointed out all the amenities available. They had their own cafeteria, gym, childcare. There was a whole floor of the twenty-five-story building called the "chill zone" where his employees could hang out and destress.

McKay-Taggart had something similar except it was pretty much where employees could punch each other in the face.

"Will there be anything else, Nolan?" The barista was young and like many of the employees here had a smile on her face and seemed to worship her boss.

It was Stepford Wives weird, and he was happy Maddie hadn't bought into the sunshine Byrne seemed to blow up his employees' asses.

"I think we're good now, Cindy. Thank you," Byrne said as he sat back.

They were in Byrne's office, a massive space complete with a pinball machine and a full-sized video game console, and this living room area where the man apparently entertained clients. Cindy strode back out of the office where she would pass through the elegant reception area with the three assistants her boss employed. He'd explained they all handled different parts of his life.

Deke got the feeling he was about to get to know a side of Byrne's life not a lot of people knew existed.

"So Maddie told me you've been topping her for the last year or so." Byrne grimaced slightly. "Am I allowed to talk about this? I waited until we were alone. I don't mean to come on too strong. I can do that when I'm enthusiastic about a thing. I'm incredibly interested in the lifestyle."

"I'm absolutely fine talking about it," Deke assured him. If there was one thing he was confident about it was his ability to sit in a chair and talk about shit most men wouldn't. Years of therapy had taught him how to do it. In some ways, D/s was therapy for him, too. Having control over his sexuality, being able to explore it, had helped understand the sides of himself he would rather hide away. A memory of Maddie asking him to talk about the worst time of his life flashed through his head. She never had to know about it. He'd dealt with what had happened to him, and she never had to hear a word about that time.

"Good because there are definitely parts of this I don't want to talk about with a woman who is a friend but also an employee," Byrne said with a wince. "I have to be careful. I don't want to offend anyone."

"I'll give you my cell number. Think of me as your mentor while you're being considered for membership at the club," Deke offered.

A chuckle huffed from Byrne's chest. "It's so weird now to be 'considered' for membership. I'm usually the one who decides who gets in and who's kept out."

The smile was still in place, but there was a tight set to the man's jaw, as though he was working to keep that happy-go-lucky expression in place. It was his mask, that smile of his. "Clubs like The Reef are usually very exclusive. Most of the clubs I've been in are started by a group of people who pool their cash to buy a place to play. They aren't typically concerned with making money."

"Everyone is concerned with money. Why else would a club charge fees?" Byrne asked, one brow arched over his eyes.

"The same reason you have building fees with your condo. The equipment has to be kept up. There are property taxes and upgrades to be made, but most clubs aren't as expensive and influential as a place like The Reef," Deke explained. "All clubs are going to be careful about who they invite in for memberships."

"I was surprised at their refusal to even meet with me," Byrne admitted. "I'm not used to being turned away these days. It reminded me a bit of junior high all over again. I wasn't the most popular kid. I have some triggers when it comes to being denied."

He would bet it had been a very long time since Nolan Byrne was denied anything he wanted. The world he'd built catered to his every need. "The Reef has some very high-profile members. They have to be careful about their privacy. It's precisely why it would be a good place for someone like you to play. They know how to protect their members."

"Yes, they appear to have many lawyers, too. I received the packet the manager sent me. Is Kayla Summers-Hunt the wife of Josh Hunt?" He held up a hand, waving it. "Don't worry. I signed everything and sent it back to her. I've actually met her before, so I'll recognize her and Hunt as well. I didn't see a problem asking, since I'm being allowed in."

"It's fine. If you've signed everything and she's cool with you coming to her club, then she'll be fine with you knowing who she is." He'd gone over all of this with Kayla. In the beginning her husband's involvement with BDSM had been a tightly kept secret. It still wasn't something he talked about a lot, but he wasn't afraid of people knowing he and his wife played. "Yes. She and her husband play at The Reef, along with some other actors you'll likely recognize. Discretion is important."

"So no one is allowed to take pictures," Byrne asked. "I would definitely not like my private life plastered around the world. There are no cameras in the dungeon?"

"There are security cameras directed outside the building. None inside. The security team isn't paid. They're volunteers from the membership. For the most part anyone working in the club also plays there. It's another way to keep our members safe."

"What happens in the club stays in the club. That's good to know," Byrne mused. "I suspect it would be easy to blackmail members if video or photos got out."

He wanted to be careful. Deke could understand that. "I assure you no one will be taking pictures or videos."

"Good." Byrne sat back. "I read that cell phones weren't allowed on the dungeon floor, but I wanted to make sure. I can't imagine what would happen to my stock if pictures of me spanking my girlfriend got out."

"Have you? Spanked her?" He needed to play this like he was truly mentoring the man. "Maddie explained that your girlfriend is a long-term sub. Has she taught you anything? From what I understand you haven't had any formal training."

Byrne set his mug down. "Jane's been in the lifestyle for a couple of years. I'm afraid her last boyfriend wasn't the best Dom. He was controlling and abusive. They had a toxic relationship. She trusted him wholly and he betrayed her in the vilest manner, from what she's told me. Jane was broken for a long time. She's trying to take back this part of her life. Before I met her, it wasn't something I would have considered, but I care about her. If this is what she needs, then I want to be able to give it to her."

There was an earnestness about his words that might have worked on Deke had he not known much of Byrne's openness was a façade to draw in the wary. "Do you feel like dominance in the bedroom is something that works for you?"

Nolan's lips quirked up. "I'm finding that letting my slightly darker side come out is refreshing. I'm afraid I'm known as a pretty happy-go-lucky guy."

"Oh, I don't think a man gets to your position without some dominant tendencies," Deke murmured.

"Well, I certainly have a side that wants to dominate the tech world," Byrne allowed. "And I've been known to be a bit ruthless when it comes to a business deal, but this is my first time taking my dominant tendencies into a more intimate setting. As for your prior question, we're still at the talking stage. I'm looking forward to having a formal mentor. You've been in the lifestyle for a while according to Madeline."

"More than a decade. I came to it through a group of friends who were involved," Deke explained. "Though now I look back on my younger days and realize there was always some component of Dominance and submission to all of my sexual encounters. I simply didn't know what to call those instincts."

"So you and Madeline…" Byrne let the question dangle.

But Deke knew what he was asking. "Even when we were young we had roles we naturally fell into. When we reconnected, it was easy to see it had always been that way between us. Knowing who we are and what we want has been good for us this time around. I think you'll find D/s facilitates communication between you and your partner."

"Oh, yes. Jane likes to talk." Byrne sat back. "We communicate quite well. Jane is fragile in some ways and mighty in others. Getting to know her, to talk about her needs, has made me think a lot about my own. It's made me consider needs I didn't realize I have."

"Yes, when we really talk with our partners, I think the relationship is strengthened. I know it has for Maddie and myself. We've found a good place for both of us through careful negotiation," Deke explained. "I'll be happy to talk to you about contracts or anything else you're interested in. Do you have one with Jane?"

"No, and that's a problem for us." A sigh went through Byrne. "She doesn't want to sign a contract without a mentor in place. So you can understand how important this is to me. We are reaching a point in our relationship where I would very much like to move forward, and the lack of a contract is an issue."

"Well, let's start talking then." It was good to know Byrne was horny. He could use that. "We'll go to The Reef on Friday. You mentioned you'd sent over the nondisclosures. Has Jane signed?"

"Yes. She sent them as well as filling out all the necessary paperwork for the background check," Byrne replied. "She's also talked to them about a particular request. She'd like to wear a mask as part of her fet wear. It's important to her. She's working with a therapist, and they believe this is a part of taking back her power."

"Wearing a mask?" He'd heard it all, but he wasn't sure how the two connected.

"Yes, she felt like she had to wear one for her past Dom," Byrne explained. "When she feels comfortable, taking the mask off will be a signal that she's truly my submissive. She will take off her mask and I attach my collar. It's going to be a ceremony not unlike a wedding. Like I said, I care about this woman. I want to give her what she needs."

He didn't see a problem with it as long as Kayla didn't. There was one dude at Sanctum who liked to wear a full-on rubber suit that covered every inch of his skin. Well, his dick hung out, but the rest was totally covered. "Will she be wearing it in the locker room?"

"Of course not. I understand she needs to prove she's the person whose background has been checked. Otherwise, she could be a reporter," Byrne allowed. "No, I understand the idea of walking into the club as who you are and changing into who you want to be."

There was some truth to his words. "You'll be going in as visitors, but hopefully they'll talk to you about a full membership after you've attended a few times."

"I hope Madeline and Jane can be friends." The smile was back on Nolan's face. "And that you and I can be, too. You know what they say. It's lonely at the top. I'm very excited about our trip on Friday. I'm having a little dinner party on Saturday and I was thinking you and Madeline could come. It's just a celebration of getting that much closer to the finish line. It's all coming together. In the next couple of months, this company is going to be bigger than Apple, bigger than anything they've ever seen."

The man had ambitions. Deke had to temper his own enthusiasm because getting invited to Byrne's for a dinner party might be their ticket to his private laptop. "Yes, Maddie tells me this satellite project is going to be important. We would love to help celebrate."

"It's going to change the world." There was a fervent look in Byrne's eyes. "It's going to change how we use satellites and make further space travel more than possible. It's going to help make it cheaper and more accessible."

"It's going to make you even wealthier," he pointed out.

Byrne huffed. "Not just me. I'm the idiot who tempted my higher-level employees with stock options."

He wasn't sure what that meant. He didn't want to ask but found himself compelled to. "Stock options?"

"Yes. Hiring a truly exceptional subject matter expert can be a lot like an auction. Everyone wants this one person, and we all have to outbid each other. Like with Madeline." Byrne whistled. "I'm not joking. She's a thoroughbred in our world. I knew I needed her AI knowledge, but so does everyone else. It came down to me and a dude named Drew Lawless. I offered her less upfront salary but more stock options."

She'd been offered a job in Texas? Andrew Lawless was a client of McKay-Taggart. More than a client, really. His sister was married to one of Tag's brothers. "Wow. I didn't know that had been a choice for her. I'm surprised she didn't take the bigger salary."

"Madeline's savvy when it comes to money. She knew those options would make her rich, and it's about to pay off. Not like it hasn't before. I mean, you know all of this. She's worked for me for five years, and those options have made her a millionaire a couple of times over. I pay the woman three hundred grand a year straight salary, but the stock is the gem in that contract. She's held on to them. When this project launches, Byrne stock will go through the roof. She'll go to bed with her paltry ten million and wake up to a hundred, and then I'll have to find another way to keep her. You are a very intelligent man to pick her up again. She'll keep you in style for the rest of your life."

A pit opened in his stomach. He made what he'd thought was a good living, but he was pretty sure Maddie made his whole yearly salary in a week or two.

He was right back in high school. He'd heard it all the time. He was the beauty and she was the brains. Wasn't he lucky to have someone to help with his homework since he was a dumb jock who was dating the girl who would one day rule the world? Was this how it would always be with them? He was the dude who carried her purse.

"I think I can take care of myself," Deke said evenly. "But I'm very proud of Maddie's achievements. She's done well for herself."

"She's done well for the world," Byrne corrected. "So let's talk about what I should expect from this contract. I'm eager to get everything in place. I want my sub to feel safe with me."

Deke forced his insecurities down and started to talk.

* * * *

Nolan watched the man Madeline had selected to top her as he went on about hard and soft limits. Something about the man was sending him warning bells.

He was too attractive for Madeline. It wasn't like his AI expert was garbage in the looks department, but Deke could have been a male model. He was tall and incredibly fit, with all-American good looks and an easy smile.

He was exactly the kind of man Nolan hated. He was the kind of man the world handed things to. He would bet not once had Deke had his head held in a toilet. No. He would have been the asshole on the other side, the cool kid, the kind who casually stepped on his smarter, better peers for the simple fact that he was considered more handsome. Even if he hadn't been, he'd almost surely turned a blind eye.

"You'll need to go over all of this with Jane," Deke was saying.

"Of course." He wasn't exactly listening to the man, rather studying him. He'd made a direct hit with the news of Madeline's wealth. Deke hadn't known how well she'd done, and it had bothered him.

Nolan understood the impulse. He wouldn't be in a relationship with a partner who was more successful than him. It created an imbalance, or rather the wrong balance. The power should be in his hands. Always.

As Jane would soon learn.

The question now was what would his little AI tech learn?

He'd been thinking a lot about just how Madeline had manipulated him into giving her those stock options. If she left the company or was fired before the launch, she would have to sell them back. Oh, she would still make a lot of money, but nothing like what she would after the launch.

He had to play his cards right, make the timing line up, because he still needed the bitch. But it might be good to have some leverage on her.

Or he could make it all up, and who would question him? Anyone who did could be handled. Permanently.

Including the man in front of him.

He let Deke talk, all the while planning on how to get rid of them both. After he had what he wanted, of course.

* * * *

Maddie opened the door to her office several hours later. Lunchtime had come and gone, and a quick glance at the clock let her know that the building would be emptying soon. The day had gone by in a rush. Between working on the problem Naman had presented and trying to track down the information she needed, she'd gotten very little of her own project work in. She'd found a thread and started to follow it through.

She was more sure than ever that something bad was happening.

"Lock the door, Maddie."

She gasped and then breathed out a sigh of relief because it was Deke. He sat on the small couch that ran along the left side of her rather large office. She mainly worked in the tech lab on this floor, but she kept the office for when she needed quite time or to speak privately. "I didn't think you would be here until five thirty."

He stood, his big body uncurling with predatory grace. There was something dark in his eyes. "I finished up with your boss and then headed out to The Reef to update Kay and make sure she's gotten all the paperwork we need to do a background check on Jane. Traffic was hell."

"Welcome to LA." She knew Dallas had its own issues, but LA was all over them in the traffic department. There were times she'd been stuck for so long that she'd thought about homesteading the 405.

His lips didn't tick up even a centimeter. "When I realized I didn't have time to make it back to your place and come to pick you up, I decided I would wait here for you."

He seemed pissed about that. "Sorry to inconvenience you. I could have caught a ride with someone."

"That's not the problem. It's not inconvenient for me to drive you. That's a pleasure for me. That's absolutely part of my job while I'm with you, and I don't mean that in a professional way. Taking care of you is more than a business to me." He frowned. "But we do have to talk about the job. What did you do today, Madeline?"

She froze at the deep sound of his voice. That was his Dom voice, the one she'd gotten so acquainted with over the course of the last week. It was the voice he used on her when he wanted to get serious about play. "I worked."

"Not in this office you didn't." He stepped closer to her, and it took a lot to not cede her space. "Nor were you in your tech lab."

Her first instinct was to ask how he knew she hadn't been where she was supposed to be. Then she remembered what MaeBe had told her. "Someone was watching me."

"All day. We told you that would happen when I ordered MaeBe to take over the CCTV cameras in the building," he replied simply, looming over her. "I've been in touch with her this afternoon, and she had an interesting report for me. I understand why you went to the audio team. Byrne asked you to work with them. What I want to understand is why you spent time in human resources. You also went to two other floors and spoke with people who are not your employees. What happened?"

She wasn't sure why he'd brought out the big bad Dom. It wasn't like she'd left the building or done something dangerous. "I was talking to Naman, who leads the audio team now. He said he's had a couple of his people get sick recently, and after what Drake told us about Havana Syndrome, I got curious."

"Damn it. I told them only one thing would take you away from your lab. Of course you did. And that's why you should have waited until you were out of this building and in a safe place to hand over the information to me or Drake or any member of the team. I'm only talking to you about this right now because I checked for bugs fifteen minutes ago. I'm still going to keep my voice down."

"I can't imagine he bugs his employees' offices." Deke was being paranoid. She'd asked a couple of questions. That was all. She'd found the connections between the people who didn't work in audio and the others who'd gotten sick. Every single one of those people had been in the lab.

"I don't care what you can or can't imagine. That man is hiding a whole lot of his personality. Do not believe the happy-go-lucky persona. He's a shark, and if he's working with The Consortium, he's a killer, too. He might not have pulled the trigger himself, but he ordered the killings. I got hold of the medical examiner's report on Justin Garcia. He noted that Garcia showed no signs of long-term drug use. A casual drug user wouldn't know where to find that flop house Garcia was found in, much less a first timer."

A chill went through her. "It might not have been Nolan. He

might not know."

"Don't be naïve. Naïve will get us both killed." His hand went to her hair. "Tell me what you found out."

There was a distinctly sexual air around the man. She could feel it, and the heat in his gaze went straight to her pussy. It was stupid, and she couldn't do anything to stop it. Her whole body was going soft. She'd only had a few days' worth of training with Deke, and she already responded to him like she had in high school. All he had to do was walk into a room and her brain went on the fritz until she'd had him.

He had so much power over her. It scared her. It thrilled her.

"When I was talking to Naman, he told me there's been some kind of virus going around," she explained, her voice sounding shaky. "He said it was a lot of dizziness and nausea. Headaches. There were bad headaches and some disorientation."

"Like the Havana Syndrome victims reported," Deke prompted.

She nodded. "Yes. Just like that. But some of them didn't work with the audio team. I wanted to find the connections. It could just be a virus, but I don't think so after what I learned today."

"Talk to me, baby." His hand twisted in her hair in a way that sent lightning through her system and made her go up on her toes. "I want to know how much you exposed yourself today."

"I didn't at all." Despite being annoyed with the question and his lack of faith in her intelligence, her nipples went hard. "I just talked to some people. I asked a couple of questions. Some of the people who don't work in audio were either involved with someone who was and they were in the lab at some point or security who works on the floor, and there were two people from janitorial who remember cleaning in the lab before they got sick."

"You went to human resources. Did you carefully hack into their systems so no one could possibly know you were there? I'm going to assume you were looking for records of employees using sick days."

"No, I'm the head of the department. I can just ask to see the records," she explained.

"Do you routinely ask to see records like that?" Deke asked the question like he already knew the answer.

"No. I don't have a reason to." It was the kind of thing she would delegate. Now that she thought about it, they had seemed surprised she'd come down herself and not had her assistant send an email requesting the records.

"So it's an odd thing for you to request?"

Put like that it did seem like she could have used more discretion. "Maybe, but human resources isn't supposed to talk about things like that. They won't mention my request. Don't they have an oath or something?"

"Naïve." He stepped back, his hands going to lean hips. "Shall we use your desk or the sofa?"

"For what?" She wasn't sure if she felt relieved or disappointed that he wasn't close anymore.

"I explained when we started this project that there were two places you had to obey me," Deke began. "In the bedroom and in the field. You were in the field today and you disobeyed me."

"How did I disobey you?" He was making her feel like a naughty teenager. Of course all the trouble she'd gotten into as a teenager had been about him. Her dad certainly hadn't punished her the way Deke might.

"By placing yourself in danger," he explained. "You weren't supposed to investigate on your own. You opened yourself up today. What you did could place the entire investigation at risk. What if Byrne hears you're asking about the audio team in a way that raises his suspicions? You're already on his radar."

"You can't know that."

His eyes narrowed. "Baby, explain your stock options to me."

Where was he going with this? "How the hell do you know about my options?"

"Because Byrne made a point to tell me. Outside of Byrne and his board of directors, who has the most to gain by this launch going well?"

"Everyone." The whole company would benefit from it. Not everyone had options, but the company making more money would be good for the employees. Wouldn't it?

"Who has the most stock options?" Deke asked.

She thought about it. Her hire was a little legendary around the building because she'd negotiated hard for what she'd gotten. "It's me. It's me after the C-levels."

Deke nodded in agreement. "He thinks I'm far less savvy than I am. He tried to manipulate me earlier today. I'm not sure if he did it because he needs to be the big man in even casual relationships, but he absolutely zeroed in on the fact that our financial disparity worries the fuck out of me."

"Why would it worry you?" She knew the answer. Deke was proud, but it wasn't like they were trying to get married or anything.

They couldn't if he needed her to make herself small for him to feel good.

"It takes me back to a time when I was nothing more than your dumbass boyfriend," he admitted with a frown. "You have no idea how often people told me the one smart thing I ever did was get you to go out with me. They were joking, and honestly, it's probably true, but it bugged me then and it bugs me now. Your boss easily saw my weak spot, and that's my fault."

"I never thought that." Her heart softened because he was being open and honest with her. This was what hadn't worked for them before. She could remember sitting at dinner with his family and his cousins joking about how he was dating her for her earning potential and how much better she could do. He'd told her it didn't bother him at all if it didn't bother her. She'd known he was lying. His honesty felt like intimacy. Real and true intimacy. "I was always told you were far too hot for me."

He shook his head. "Never. You're so fucking gorgeous it hurts sometimes to look at you, and you are absolutely the hottest woman I've ever seen. No, baby, it's my insecurity, and I'm working on it. I promise. I'm so proud of you and everything you've accomplished.

But I need to admit the feeling so I can process it. Now answer my question. Do you want it at your desk or your couch, because this is happening here and now. You can cry and beg and I'm still going to spank that ass of yours, so you remember what the rules are."

She was about to argue with him when she realized what she'd really done. He was right. She'd exposed herself and the whole team by following her own lead. Susan in HR was a gossipy busybody, but she'd been the only one around for her to work with. She'd been impatient and hadn't communicated with the team put into place to handle the situation. If Deke had done this as a worker on her team, she would be pissed. It hadn't occurred to her that MaeBe could get the same data without anyone knowing.

Beyond that, Deke had been forced to watch her do it with no recourse because she'd stashed her phone in her office. There were some labs where phones weren't allowed, and it could be easier to store it. Her assistant would be able to find her in the office through the comms systems they used, but Deke wouldn't have been able to get in touch with her.

He'd been out of control and worried, and this was how he would want to handle those emotions.

If he'd been a different man she would have walked away, but she trusted him. He wouldn't do anything to hurt her. At its heart this was all play, and he needed to play the same way she'd needed it the night before. His anxiety was high, and he needed to blow off some steam. Controlling her could calm his beast.

It would also probably lead to a mind-blowing orgasm for her.

"The desk." She almost never used the couch, and she wanted this memory. She wanted to sit at her desk and remember how Deke had topped her right here, wanted to be able to close her eyes and feel his hands on her.

"Place your hands on the top of the desk, palms down."

She looked up at him. "Should I take my panties off?"

His hand came up and she could already see a measure of his tension fleeing. "Baby, if I want them off you, I'll tear them off myself. Mind me."

She turned and walked to her desk. Her blinds were open but the floor-to-ceiling windows were tinted, so no one could see in. She faced the window, the afternoon light still glowing and the freeway in the distance. Placing her palms flat on the top of the desk, Maddie breathed in and tried to find that place she'd started to enjoy. Her subspace.

Cool air slid over her skin as he flipped her skirt up. "You need to understand that the most important thing to me about this op is you coming out of it healthy and whole."

"I didn't think I was in any danger."

A hard slap smacked against her ass. She gasped at the pain, but the heat that lingered was pure pleasure. The man knew what he was doing. This wasn't an act of violence or punishment. The way he did it, it was a way to connect, to communicate in their own unique way.

"But you *were* in danger, and we've talked about this. You brought me in to handle this situation for you, and you agreed to my rules. What's my number one rule, baby?"

He'd been clear. He wanted her safe, wanted the investigation in his more experienced hands. "I obey you in the field. In my defense, I didn't consider this to be the field. It's my workplace."

Smack. Smack. Smack.

Oh, he meant those. She shouldn't have tried to be cute.

Still, she could feel her pussy slickening up, her body tightening in anticipation of what was to come.

"Every-fucking-where is the field right now." His hand came down again, this time right in the middle of her ass, and he held it there as though he could keep the heat flowing. "He's watching you. You threaten him."

"I don't threaten anyone."

"Oh, yes, you do. You see what he wants you to see. If he saw through me, then I saw through him, too. There is a core of darkness to that man. He hates anything and everyone who could possibly take him off the mountain he's built. He doesn't want to be the boss. He wants to be the king, and that means controlling everyone and everything around him. It's precisely why he fucks over all of his contractors. He enjoys fucking people over. I bet if I looked at his other companies, he screwed over some people who had stock options. He hates that he had to outbid Drew Lawless for you."

She felt a flush go through her system. "I was doing what every man with my credentials would do."

"I know, baby, and you deserve every single dollar you got, but it bugs him that he had to do it. I'm not sure if it's because you're a woman or if he would hate it coming from anyone, but he hates it. You have to be careful around him."

She'd known the man for years, but she had to consider Deke's words. And her own instincts. Hadn't she always been the tiniest bit wary of Nolan, even in the beginning? She'd wanted to go with Lawless. She'd felt more comfortable with the man, but his company was located in Texas, and she hadn't been ready to be so close to where Deke was. Then the stock options had made the offer more than she could turn down.

Had she let her guard down over the years?

"I'll be more careful. I promise." She could see the logic in Deke's words. This was a one plus one equals two straightforward equation. If something was happening at Byrne, then Nolan was involved. No ifs, ands, or buts. She'd been reckless, and it had scared her lover.

Smack. Smack. Smack. "You have to or I swear I'll tie you up and hide you away somewhere until I can fix this."

"I promise." She braced herself for another barrage.

He sighed and smoothed a hand over the very flesh he'd slapped. "See that you do." His hand slipped lower, delving into her panties and making her squirm. "I don't like how he talked about you this morning. Like I said, you're on his radar. He definitely doesn't like being dependent on someone to get into a place he feels he should be welcome."

How could he sound so calm? Her heart was pounding as he slid a finger up and over her clitoris. He had so much power over her, and she suddenly needed to know she could do the same to him. Deke was a gorgeous man who'd spent years exploring his sexuality while she'd been locked up in a lab pushing her career forward. But she remembered what he used to like.

"Let me make it up to you." She didn't move from her position, not wanting to tempt the Dom in him to start the punishment all over again.

His hand stilled, and she would bet his whole body had, too. "How would you do that, baby?"

"I worried you today. Like I was anxious yesterday. You helped ease my tension. I can do the same for you."

"Again, how would you do that? I'd like to hear you say it."

He wanted her to talk dirty? She could do that. "I'll get on my knees in front of you and I'll lick and suck your cock. It's your choice whether you come straight down my throat or order me to ride you. You can choose if your poor sub deserves any pleasure."

A soft smack against her pussy brought her up on her toes. "Little brat. I'm going to the couch for this. I won't be able to stand up straight for long when you put your mouth on me."

The hand was gone and she felt her skirt drift to the backs of her thighs, and she pushed up from the desk. Her pussy might not be happy at the sudden change of attention, but everything else inside Maddie was looking forward to this encounter. How long had it been since she'd wanted to suck a man's cock? Craved it? It was something she would do with a partner because it was an exchange of pleasures, but she genuinely wouldn't care if Deke came down her throat. There would be a glory in that, too.

Deke sank back against the couch, his legs spreading wide to give her room.

He was so decadently gorgeous. He was the very picture of a Dom waiting for his sub to service him.

"Can I take my panties off now, please?"

He stared at her for a moment and then nodded.

She slowly dragged her skirt back up, hooking her thumbs under the waistband of her panties and easing them down her legs, kicking her shoes off. She might be willing to forgo her own orgasm, but she wasn't going to put obstacles up against one either.

"Fuck, you are so sexy. Always have been," Deke said softly, his hands working on the fly of his jeans.

She wasn't about to argue that she'd been more awkward than sexy in high school because it didn't matter. He saw her that way, would always remember her that way. The same way she remembered him being perfect right up to the moment he took the choice away from her.

She shoved that thought out of her mind. The moment—this one they were living right now—was all that mattered. The future would sort itself out, and they couldn't go back to the past.

She shoved the panties into her bag because she got the feeling she wouldn't be putting them back on for a long time. Her whole body going languid, Maddie moved into Deke's space, dropping to her knees. He shifted, shoving the sides of his jeans down and exposing the boxers he wore. His cock was already long and thick, trying to get past the cotton underwear.

His cock had always fascinated her. Many a long evening had passed while she'd stroked him, adoring how he shuddered when she squeezed him just right. She eased his boxers down and brushed her fingers against the underside, tracing the big vein that ran up to his cockhead.

"Damn it, baby. That feels so good." His eyes were on her, his hands at his sides like he didn't trust himself not to take immediate control and force her to suck him.

He would eventually. He wouldn't be able to help himself, but there was something thrilling about that, too. For now she would enjoy her control. Maddie cupped his balls, gently weighing them in her hand. They were big and heavy, and she loved the way they would draw up, ready to shoot off. She dragged her hand back up to the base of his cock and circled him with her fingers, getting a firm grip. Deke hissed, and she knew that sound. He was ready. She stroked him, watching as his head fell back.

"Does this make you forget all the ways I disobeyed you today?" She knew the answer, but this was part of the play. "Does it make you want to forgive your poor sub?"

His hand finally moved, fingers sinking into her hair just like she'd known they would. There was a fire in his eyes as he gazed down at her. "I'm going to need more than your hand. You put those lips on me."

Two could play his word games. She delicately kissed his cock, brushing butterfly busses up his dick. "Like this?"

He actually growled, the sound making her pussy pulse. "No, not like that, you little brat, and you know it."

She liked this game, liked that they were talking and playing. "How would you like it? Would you like a little lick?"

She lightly traced that vein with her tongue all the way up to the place where his cockhead met, worrying the deep *V* she found there.

"More, Maddie. I want more."

She swirled her tongue around the head, tasting the cream already coating the tip of his dick. "How much more?"

The hand tightened, and a delicious shiver went through her. "I want it all. Give it to me. Suck me deep."

Well, the man knew what he wanted. She kissed his cock and then swallowed him up.

A low groan came from Deke's throat as she worked her mouth around him. She sucked his cock in deep passes, allowing her hand to stroke in time. She licked and sucked until his hold tightened on her hair, and she heard his deep groan as he gently tugged her off.

"I want to be inside you," Deke said.

She wasn't about to deny him that request. Maddie kissed him one last time and got to her feet as he fished a condom out of his pocket. He was always prepared. He had that sucker out of the package and on his cock before she could lift her skirt. She eased down on him like he was a stallion she was mounting, and he was. He was a fucking sexual thoroughbred, and she meant to ride him like one.

His hands gripped her slightly sore ass, the pain reminding her of the connection they'd shared in those moments. His cockhead teased her pussy, and she fitted herself to him. Pleasure swamped her as that big dick started to invade.

"You feel so fucking good." Deke pushed her skirt to the side and gazed down, watching his cock slide inside.

She went as slow as she could, but she couldn't hold out for long. Deke was right about it feeling really fucking good. She moved up and down on his cock, shifting her hips while he pressed up inside her.

He slammed up and stroked deep and a burst of pure pleasure bloomed over her, then Deke had her on her back on the couch, taking the lead. He fucked inside over and over, spreading her legs wide and making her come before he pumped out his own orgasm. He stiffened and fell on her, pressing her against the couch and ensuring that this would be all she would ever be able to think about when she was here.

"Don't scare me again," he whispered as he kissed her neck.

"I'll try."

Warmth and peace spread through her. It felt right to be here with him. As though something she'd been missing had finally settled back into place.

"Did you turn Drew Lawless down because I know him?"

That peace fled, and she felt awkward again. "I took the best offer on the table"

He settled his head against her. "Good. I can't stand the thought you would turn something down because you didn't want to be anywhere near me. I would hate to have been the one to put you here."

But he had in so many ways.

She took a deep breath and tried so fucking hard to let go of the past.

Chapter Eleven

Four days later, Deke walked around the room as Kayla Summers-Hunt stared down at the file in front of her. Her office at The Reef was a bit like the rest of the club—old-school industrial with stained concrete floors and utilitarian fixtures. She'd likely inherited the office from the last president of the club, who'd probably been some serious top. There were a couple of touches that would remind a person the new head of the club was a bit different. On the bookshelves, nestled in with all the serious tomes about the lifestyle, were the brightly colored spines of romance novels. The little Bluetooth speaker sent the latest Korean boy band's hit through the room, and there were photos of Kay and her family scattered around. Kay and her handsome husband holding a tiny baby boy. Kay and her dads. An old shot of Kayla and a group of familiar men caught his eye. He stared down at the picture that had been taken at the London office also known as The Garden. Six men, only four of whom were still alive today, smiled gamely at the camera. Well, most of them did. The Lost Boys, as they'd called them, had mostly gone on to find happy homes, but Sasha and Dante were gone.

"I miss them, you know," Kay said quietly. "Well, not Dante. He was a dickweasel, but I miss the rest of them. Even Sasha. I think I miss a version of Sasha who didn't exist when I knew him. I look at that picture and I sometimes miss the me I was then."

"You want to go back."

She closed the folder. "Absolutely not, but it's okay to get wistful from time to time. I was death in high heels. There was something magnificent about it. I don't think most people ever get to let that side of themselves out the way I did."

"I don't think most people have that particular side."

"I don't know about that. I think we've all got a bit of a predator inside us." She stood, pushing her chair back. Kay was dressed in a chic jumpsuit that likely had a crazy designer label, and she was still in killer heels, her sleek black hair cascading in waves down her back. "My point being that sometimes we romanticize things in our past. Like I know Sasha was a prick who caused almost as much trouble as Dante, but knowing how he sacrificed to save Owen, I see him differently. I see the person he was before all the experiments."

Owen and the rest of the Lost Boys had been tortured by a doctor, their memories erased in an effort to turn them into super-soldiers. "His daughter is doing well. Tasha is a great kid."

Kayla shook her head. "I can't believe she's fifteen. Big Tag has a bunch of teens and preteens. Ten's son is almost a teen. My old mentor John Bishop has two girls. It's weird getting old."

"I think it's weirder getting old when nothing else about your life changes."

"Oh, Charlotte was right." A slow smile spread across Kay's face as she leaned against her desk. "You are in crisis."

He should have known Charlotte would alert Kay. The woman liked to be in the know. He was giving Charlotte regular updates about Kyle and MaeBe. He suspected MaeBe was giving updates on him and Maddie, and the boss lady would want Kayla's opinion of the situation. "I'm not in crisis. I'm good. Maddie and I are good."

There was a brisk knock on the door and then they weren't alone anymore. Drake strode in.

"I've walked the dungeon and I still want to put some cameras in," he announced.

Kay frowned his way. "Absolutely not. I told you that was a hard no. The people in this club voted. No cameras. They will allow you to work your op here, but you're going to have to keep eyes on the subject."

"Subjects," Deke corrected. "I don't know that I trust this Jane person either. Where's MaeBe?"

"I'm here." MaeBe pushed through the doorway, a flush to her face. "Sorry. We were looking around."

"Getting a lay of the land." Kyle strode in behind her.

"They were playing around." Boomer seemed to have found the snacks. He had a bag of chips in his hand. "Did you need to test the spanking bench to make sure it worked?"

MaeBe's flushed deepened. "We were just joking."

"Trust me when I spank her, she'll know it." Kyle had a smirk on his face like that day was coming and fast. "Did he ask about the cameras? Because I already told him you would say no."

"I can't go against the club's rules." Kayla was obviously standing firm. "Not even for an op. Now if you want to put this off and bring in your own crew, then we'll allow you to use the facilities."

"Byrne would know if we brought in a bunch of strangers," Drake argued. "He already knows some of the members here. If he doesn't see them, he'll figure out something is wrong."

"He's aware that Josh and I are members. If we agree to take the chance that those tapes could get out in the public, would you bring in your own people?" Kayla asked.

Her offer was generous and would work, if not for one problem. "He's expecting to come in tonight. I don't think we have time to bring anyone in. Besides, I suspect he knows who plays here and who doesn't. He's got resources most people can't imagine."

"Yeah, like a couple billion of them." Money could buy Byrne a lot of information, even the kind no one should be able to find. No matter how hard The Reef tried, there would be some people willing to talk about the membership for the right price. There were other ways as well. A very good PI would potentially be able to piece together a list.

Drake sighed. "Can't we put him off?"

"He's too smart. He'll figure out something's wrong." He hated every day he sent Maddie into that building because he was more and more certain she was going to get hurt there one way or another. "We need to keep things running so there's no question Byrne has that party come Saturday night."

"What exactly are you worried is going to happen, Drake?" Kayla studied the CIA operative.

Drake shrugged. "I don't know. I've got a bad feeling."

Kay nodded. "Okay, I understand that you need to trust your gut, but it's hard because you won't tell me what you think is going to happen, and I suspect you're not willing to tell anyone else or you would have backup."

Drake's jaw tightened. "There's nothing to tell. Look, I'm worried because I had an operative go bad a couple of years ago, and I think this is the group that turned her. We haven't been able to get any ID on Byrne's contact with the organization, and that could be bad. What do we know about Byrne's girlfriend?"

MaeBe stopped trying to slap Kyle's hands away and got serious. "It's all in what I sent to Kay. Jane Adams. She's thirty-three. She's a consultant. She basically helps companies streamline their processes in order to cut back on payroll."

"I bet she has a ton of friends," Boomer said with a shake of his head.

"Not according to her social media," MaeBe continued. "I've sent you all the relevant data—her birth certificate, social security number, where she went to school and so on. All of it checks out. I even called a guy I know at one of the main social media sites to make sure the timeline was clean."

"What do you mean?" Deke didn't always understand MaeBe's methods.

"She wanted to make sure no one faked the timeline," Kyle explained. "That the posts were made on the days reflected."

MaeBe got the silliest grin on her face. "Oh, you do listen."

Kyle shrugged. "Not according to my uncle, but I listen to you."

Big Tag was right about the puppy love thing being a little nauseating. "So she's on the up-and-up? What else do we know? Anything about an ex-boyfriend?"

MaeBe patted her laptop bag. "It's all in the info I sent you. Her profiles are public, so you can go look at them. She's had one account for twelve years, another for ten. She's got a handful of friends and followers. She lost her mom when she was twelve and spent the rest of her time in the foster system. She managed to get a scholarship and some loans to go to college. She got an MBA in finance while she was working. From what I can tell she does almost everything remotely."

That wasn't surprising. The pandemic a few years back had changed the way people worked. It was much more acceptable to work from home now. It also might be far more comfortable for a woman who basically fired people for a living. "But nothing about the abusive ex."

"Oh, she talks about him, but only in the past tense," MaeBe said. "I can't find any pics of the two of them. She either deleted them or she was extremely private. Most of her Instagram is about her cats. She had two and seemed very attached to them. She doesn't talk about it but there's a post a year ago that says her cats died and she's heartbroken. She went dark for a couple of months and when she came back her tone's been different. I kind of think the ex might have killed her cats."

"The ex sounds like an asshole. Who would kill a cat?" Kyle asked.

Deke happened to know that Kyle was fond of cats, especially his brother's. "Does she talk about her relationship with Byrne?"

"She does not mention him by name," MaeBe replied. "But she has been talking about how positive she's feeling lately and things might be turning a corner. She talked about living well being the best revenge."

"What you're saying is she's got a deep enough footprint that we're not worried she's not who she says she is," Kay said. "But she's the one who wanted in The Reef."

"We can ask her when she gets here," Drake replied. "Or rather you can, Kay. I'd like you to stick close to her, and I'll stick close to Byrne."

It irritated him that Drake was trying to take over. He was responsible for these people. "You can play the dungeon monitor. Byrne doesn't know you. He's not going to relax around you. I'll show him around with Josh, if that's okay with Kay."

"My man is ready for action," Kay promised. "His last three films have been slow-moving Oscar bait. He wants to do some spy work."

He hoped Josh was as good as Kay claimed he was. "All he has to do is follow my lead. My plan is to separate them right at the beginning. Let the subs walk Jane around and Josh and I will walk Byrne through. Then we'll meet back up and watch some scenes. We just have to get through the night so we can get to Saturday. That's the real op."

"I've been studying up," MaeBe promised. "I hunted through a bunch of recent articles on Byrne, and one of them features a shot of him in his private office. It's got this gorgeous view of the ocean in the distance, but it's also got a decent view of his whole system. I managed to isolate and refine that part of the picture. I figured out who makes his components, and I know exactly what I'm up against."

"It was seriously the sexiest thing I've ever seen," Kyle said, his brows waggling suggestively. "She figured out who built his system, got the dude on the phone, and had every single component out of him without even threatening to wrap his colon around his neck or anything."

MaeBe's eyes rolled. "Yeah, it's called charm and finesse, buddy."

It was good to know MaeBe was ready. "I'm glad to hear that. You have everything you need?"

"Yes. It's a complex system but I'm ready. Getting into the room is going to be more complicated," she replied.

"I'll handle that," Kyle promised. "I've got a plan. I wrote it up and sent it to you."

"Uhm, I'll need a copy of that." Drake looked at Kyle like he'd gone insane.

"If Deke sends it, you'll get it," Kyle said with a shrug. "He's my lead on this. He controls the flow of intel."

Kyle had been surprisingly easy to work with. "I'll get it to you this afternoon."

"What should I expect tomorrow night, boss?" Boomer had finished up the chips and was looking around Kay's office like a lion searching for another meal.

"You're going to watch the door." Poor Boomer would be sitting in a perch all night. At least it was California and it wouldn't be cold.

Kay moved to Boomer, threading her arm through his and leaning against him. "I asked our cook to make you a big old basket of all kinds of treats. I'm talking her best tacos and sandwiches and cookies."

Boomer smiled down at her. "Thanks, Kay."

"So we're all good when it comes to this part of the op?" Kay asked, and Deke nodded. "By the way, you did say this Jane woman is an experienced sub, right? Because tonight is Bernie's petting night, and that can freak some people out."

"According to Byrne, she's been in the lifestyle for years." It didn't bother him that she didn't talk about it on her socials. He didn't talk about it either. "If she has, then she shouldn't be shocked. Dare I ask what petting night is?"

"We've got a sub who is totally into petting. If he's been super good or needs some comfort, his top lets him have a petting night. So he gets all tied up, blindfolded, and left in the middle of the dungeon and anyone who likes gets to pet and/or smack his ass. He does it for hours. We'll have a table of paddles and floggers and feathers and soft gloves. And a bunch of treats for people to feed him. He's our pet. I would put it off, but it's his birthday and apparently he had a shitty nose job."

"He got a nose job?" The whole petting thing didn't shock him. He'd seen worse. There was a guy at Sanctum into ball busting. Like his own balls. That dude was never procreating.

"No, Bernie's a world-famous plastic surgeon," Kay explained. "He had a nose job go wrong, and he's going to get hella sued. He needs some petting, if you know what I mean."

"I think it will be fine," Deke replied.

"Good, then we can get to the fun stuff." Kay looked up at Boomer. "Hey, is Deke really doing okay?"

"I'm right here." He knew how these conversations went. Hell, he'd been Boomer in these situations. Many times.

"Nah, he's fucking up." Boomer completely ignored him. Rather like Deke himself had. Again, many times.

Karma sucked.

"Okay, this is where I'm usually the adult in the room and steer the conversation back to the actual case, but fuck it. When in Rome and all. Boomer's right. Deke's fucking up." Drake sighed and sat back on the sofa under the room's only window. "We never do this at the Agency, by the way."

Score one point for the Agency. He sighed. "Fine. How am I screwing up? Because by my count I have everything I want. She sleeps in my bed. She's agreed to let me top her. She's been obeying me in the field. We're good, Maddie and I."

Except he knew they weren't. He could feel something was off. She came to bed with him every night but she'd stopped talking about anything important. She told him about her day, asked about his, but when he tried to broach any talk of a future together, she diverted the conversation. She smiled and happily spent time with MaeBe and the rest, but there was a distance between them that made his heart ache.

He couldn't figure it out, and there was a part of him that was so fucking scared to talk about it with her. Like opening the subject would lead to a conversation he couldn't handle.

"I don't think so," Kyle said with a frown. "Look, I don't want to get involved in some other dude's stuff."

"You get involved all the time," MaeBe corrected. "Like every single time. You're as bad as Big Tag."

Kyle didn't miss a beat. "Like I said, I hate even commenting on someone else's relationship, but I have to say Maddie's not happy."

"How is she not happy?" He gave her like three orgasms a day. He made sure that woman was loose and ready to do anything she needed.

MaeBe frowned thoughtfully. "I don't know that I would say she isn't happy. I would say something is making her restless."

"She's floating, man." Boomer moved to sit on the couch with Drake. "She's not thinking about anything but right now, and you're planning a wedding."

Kyle snorted and then winced when every head turned his way. "Sorry. I just had a vision of Deke in white being left at the altar. It was kind of funny."

"Asshole," MaeBe said under her breath. "Boomer's right. She's not thinking beyond today, and I don't think she's that kind of person. She's a planner. She's got calendars all over her place. This is not a woman who floats through life."

"It's a new relationship." It wasn't, and neither were the feelings they both had. Their history was a strength. It gave them something to build on.

"New relationships don't typically get this serious," Drake pointed out. "I know none of mine have. You two are relying on an old relationship, and one I would bet you never really settled. She talked to her mother yesterday. She didn't even mention you. Hey, skulking around and listening in are literally my jobs."

She hadn't told him she'd talked to her mom. He guessed he could understand it. She wouldn't want to explain the circumstances around how they'd been thrown back together. It would worry her whole family.

Or she didn't talk to her mom about relationships she knew weren't going to last.

There was a distance between them, and he wasn't sure how to broach it. "She won't talk about how we left things. I think she's still angry with me for not allowing her to ruin her future."

Kayla's eyes had gone wide. "I'm sorry. What did you say?"

Boomer groaned and his head fell back. "I'm supposed to be the dumb one."

"Seriously, Deke. You put it that way?" MaeBe was looking at him like he'd grown an extra head.

"I know this situation. He's right." At least Kyle was backing him up. "Maddie was young and in love and not thinking about her future. What was he supposed to do? The woman had a full-ride scholarship to Yale and she wanted to hang out with him instead? It's called sacrifice."

"She was going to turn down Yale?" Kayla asked. "What is in your pants, Murphy?"

He ignored that part. "She wasn't turning them down, exactly. She wanted to defer until I had time to apply to a college close to Yale. Except I wasn't going to go to college. That wasn't for me."

"So you sat down and talked to her about it?" Kay asked. "Did you tell her you wanted to go into the military?"

"I didn't want to go into the military. Hell, I had no idea what I wanted to do I just knew I couldn't..." Deke stopped as the truth washed over him.

Fuck.

"You couldn't follow her around. You needed to stand on your own," Boomer prompted.

"Dude, you thought you would always be in her shadow," Drake corrected with a smirk. "You were an asshole who pretended to sacrifice for her when it was always about your ego."

Boomer sent Drake a death stare. "I was being nice."

"And I was being honest." The expression on Drake's face made

Deke want to punch him. "It's good to see Murphy's a real, flawed human being. He can't stand that the woman he wants is smarter than him."

"It's not that and it never was." He loved Maddie. All of her.

"What are you going to do after the op's over?" Kay asked. "She works out here."

"I don't think Byrne is going to be left standing." He hoped Maddie didn't blame him for that.

"I assure you someone will buy up all that tech. Even if the stock bottoms out. Especially if the stock bottoms out," Kay corrected herself. "They'll want her."

"Texas has a high-tech sector." He stopped himself. "Fuck. You're right. I'm already planning to ease her into my life instead of honoring hers." He sighed. "But there are reasons for that. I've got a good network of friends who are like family. From what I can tell she has no one out here."

"She has the ambition and the job you asked her to put in front of everything else," MaeBe replied. "You told her a long time ago that what she could do for the world was far more important than her own emotional needs. I'm sure you weren't the only one. I'm sure her parents meant well, but she was likely told all of her life that her smarts were her reason for being."

"And the one time she tried to let her heart have its way, her boyfriend gaslighted her," Drake said with a flourish. "Don't look at me like that. Dude, I admit I'm terrible. I'm a liar and I manipulate everyone. I'm honest in my awfulness. You're the wolf in good-guy clothes."

"He's not a bad guy," Boomer argued. "He's just dumb. He didn't even understand what he was doing. He didn't value himself so he decided the best thing he could give her was to sacrifice for her. He didn't realize that he was taking away her choices by making one for her and that it would cost them years. He won't make the same mistake again. He's had a shit ton of therapy, and he knows how to communicate his feelings. He's going to be open with the woman he loves, and they will make the best choice for the two of them."

Yeah, he needed to listen to Boomer more. "I thought I was being open with her."

Boomer seemed to consider the situation. "Have you asked her what's wrong?"

He winced. "No, but I think part of it is she wants me to talk about my time in the military. I don't know that I want to."

"Then give her time and space to figure out if that's something she can live with," Kay said.

"He shouldn't have to talk if he doesn't want to," Kyle insisted. "And it's not right of her to make him. There are things that are personal and private."

"Not in a relationship there aren't," MaeBe said quietly. "Or at least there shouldn't be. I'm sorry. I'm with Maddie. There shouldn't be secrets between people in love. There should be trust and intimacy. Your partner should be the only person in the world you tell everything to. The good. The bad. The ugly." She stepped away from Kyle. "I'm going to go and check on her. She's been in her lab all morning, but it's almost break time. I want to watch over her."

MaeBe strode out of the room.

It was a dramatic kind of day.

Drake shoved himself off the couch. "Kayla, will you show me the outside cameras at least? I want to make sure we've got the most coverage. And get out of this very uncomfortable conversation."

"But I like uncomfortable conversations." Still, Kayla opened the door and followed Drake out.

Kyle was shaking his head. "I get the feeling I did something wrong."

"I think that was MaeBe's way of saying she's not getting everything she needs out of you." Boomer stretched as he stood. "I'm going to check the fridge. I'm getting hungry."

Cowards. They were all leaving him with a confused Kyle. Damn it. He had his own problems. "I think MaeBe is just trying to say you don't have to hide. I'm not ashamed of what I went through. I dealt with it a long time ago, but I'm just realizing that maybe we need to stop pretending the years in between didn't happen. I'm doing that because I know deep down I was wrong not to talk to her more."

"What if I *am* ashamed of what happened?" Kyle's eyes came up, a stubborn look settling in. "What if I'm pretty fucking sure if she knew half the things I did, she would walk away from me in a heartbeat."

"You take the chance." He was going to have to do it. He was going to have to talk to Maddie because he couldn't let her…couldn't stupidly push her away again.

Kyle shook his head. "Or I find another way." He walked over to the desk and pointed at the files MaeBe had given Kayla. "There's something wrong with that chick. With that Jane person."

"What?"

Kyle shook his head. "I can't put my finger on it, but it's there. Something about that picture. I don't know. I've gone over it a hundred times and I can't find a flaw in Mae's research. I think I should go by Jane's apartment. I can get in and see if there's anything unusual."

"Absolutely not. Breaking into a private home is not in the parameters of this mission." The last thing he was going to do was get Big Tag's nephew arrested. "We've got two more nights to get through. We have to get into Byrne's office, and somehow I think he won't invite us to his party if we break into his girlfriend's house. Byrne is the subject. Have you had any luck getting on at the company?"

Kyle shook his head. "Nah. They said there was a hiring freeze."

That didn't feel right. Maddie had been talking about the interns she'd brought in last week. Maybe it was only in security. "Feel free to look into Jane Adams, but you can't break into her place. And I need you with us on Saturday. You're MaeBe's bodyguard. I need her able to work."

Kyle stopped like he was coming up with an argument, and then he backed off. "All right. I'm going to check on her."

Kyle strode out, and he was alone. If he didn't figure out a way to break through Maddie's walls, he might always be.

* * * *

Maddie closed up the lab and glanced down at her watch. Deke would be here in less than half an hour and then they would likely follow the same schedule they had for the last week.

Drive back to her place. Order food. Laugh and talk with the others. He would take her to bed, blow her mind, and then go to sleep. She would lie there wondering what the hell she was doing and then the day would start over again.

Except tonight they would go to The Reef so she would get her mind blown at the club before they went back home and she lay in bed wondering. At least that would be different.

So why was she so worried that after Saturday she would have to make a decision? She wasn't ready to make a decision.

Maybe she wouldn't. Deke could go back to Dallas. She could stay here and deal with the fallout of whatever they found out on Saturday. They could talk on the phone and text. They could spend some weekends together.

They could let it die quietly this time.

She was going to get her heart broken again, and this time it wouldn't heal. Maybe it hadn't ever fully healed from the first time.

He wasn't willing to share those years apart with her. He didn't mind talking about the good stuff. She knew way too many Boomer and Big Tag stories. She knew about Deke's friends and the places he'd seen, but it was all superficial, and now she had to wonder if it hadn't always been that way. Had she been the one offering up her whole soul while Deke gave her sex and friendship and called it love?

What if that was all he had to offer?

She rejected that notion entirely. He wasn't shallow. Not even close.

She just wasn't the person he wanted to share his pain and

266

heartache with. Maybe he didn't want to share it with anyone at all. She wasn't sure she could handle that situation.

Wasn't it better than being alone?

"Maddie, I was looking for you."

Nolan stood outside her office, leaning on her assistant's desk. Jenna had left at lunch for a doctor's appointment, so they were alone in the little space that served as her assistant's office.

She forced a smile on her face. There was a fine tension she felt every time she thought about Nolan now. Deke had convinced her to worry, and now she wasn't sure she had the acting chops to pull off being comfortable around the man. "Hey. I was in the lab. I'm working on the audio problem from my end. I think that's the real trouble they're having. I've got some code I need to fix on my end and then I think the integration should be much more clean."

He seemed to study her for a moment, and then his lips quirked up, though now she found his smile creepy rather than comforting. "Excellent. I've been worried. I know it's small in the big scheme of things, but the voice component will be a big deal to the public." He went quiet again, his gaze seeming to pin her. "You know you're about to be very famous."

"Not really. No one knows the scientists behind a project. I'll just be a member of the team."

"I seriously doubt that. I've been talking to our publicity department, and they think you would be an excellent face for the development team. They love the idea of having a woman in front of the cameras. They even think it might be smart if you handled some of the interviews I would normally do."

He didn't like that idea. It was there in the narrowing of his eyes, the slight distaste in his tone as he said the words. She shook her head. "I'm not good on camera. I'm sure you can handle everything we need. I'm content to stay in the background."

"I'm not sure you'll be able to." He seemed to shake something off and refocused. "Hey, I was talking to someone in HR and she said you were having trouble with employee absences? Is something going on that I should know about?"

She'd thought she'd gotten away with this. Her gut twisted and she was probably getting another spanking because she would bet that someone on the team was currently watching her and would tell Deke, who would want to know what this conversation had been about.

"Naman mentioned he'd had some problems in the last couple of weeks." She hoped she sounded breezy and unworried. "I wanted to check it out. It looks like some kind of bug was going around, but it seems to be better now."

Now that they'd paused working on audio tests while she figured out the integration. Was she about to unleash something terrible on the people she worked with?

She'd talked to a couple of the people who'd been out, and they'd described their symptoms. Some were still dealing with vertigo and random bouts of migraine headaches. They'd been exposed to what she suspected was some form of high-frequency sound wave for mere moments and in a random fashion. What if the sound waves had been directed into their bodies? Clarke could do that. Clarke's systems were built so the AI could pinpoint locations down to a centimeter. It was precisely how Clarke would be able to send the drones to retrieve materials they needed to fix the satellite. It wouldn't take much to use the same system to direct sound waves, pinpointing them to a place on the planet's surface.

Or more likely, to something in the atmosphere. Like a plane. All they would need would be the flight plan and then Clarke could direct the sound waves directly at the aircraft, which could be carrying a bunch of families to Disney World. Or the president. Or any number of world leaders.

"Are you all right?" Nolan's question brought her out of her doomsday scenarios.

"Of course." She wanted out of this office. She wanted Deke to be here, and they would get in the car and drive until she didn't remember LA anymore. They could go home and pretend the last twenty years hadn't happened. She could teach math to a bunch of kids who didn't want to learn math. He could get a job running security for the local grocery store where the worst he would have to worry about was someone trying to steal a couple of beers. They could raise kids and go to family barbecues and allow all of his nieces and nephews to entertain them. They could have a life.

"You seem stressed, dear." Nolan's expression wrinkled into something akin to concern.

Now that it had been pointed out to her, she could see the trappings he hid behind, like a mask that was beginning to fray at the edges, revealing the truth beneath. "Well, it's a big deal. It's all coming so fast, you know."

It felt like it. It felt like life was coming at her in a blinding wave, and she wasn't sure where she'd be on the other side. Conversely, it was going too slow, and she felt like she was caught in a weird limbo. Even if they got what they needed on Saturday night, it wasn't like the world would stop. They would take the data, analyze it, decide what to do about it. No one would be arresting Nolan Byrne on Saturday night.

Deke said he would stay as long as she needed him, but how long could she keep him? How long before she had to make the decision to let him go?

Nolan reached out and put a hand on her arm, an affectionate gesture she wouldn't have given two thoughts about before. Now it felt like a cage. "Don't worry about anything but getting Clarke ready for his big debut. You let me handle everything else. And maybe you're right about staying behind the scenes. It's better that way. I can handle that part, too."

She was going to agree with him on everything. "I would appreciate it. The idea of being in front of a bunch of cameras makes me nervous. I'm a behind-the-scenes kind of woman."

"I'll make sure of it." Nolan stepped back.

"Hey." Deke was suddenly striding down the hall, slowing from what seemed like a jog. "Sorry. I know I'm a little early, but I was hoping I could convince you to come to dinner with me. Nolan, it's good to see you again."

Nolan turned, holding out a hand. "Deke, it's good to see you as well. I was just telling Madeline here that she should relax more. Everything is going to work out exactly the way it should."

Why did that feel like a threat? She moved to Deke's side, slipping her hand into his and feeling better than she had in hours. "Of course it will. We've been working for this for years."

"We're ahead of schedule," Nolan boasted. "I know other companies would burn the candle at both ends and panic, but with the exception of a few bells-and-whistles kind of problems, we're in excellent shape. So we can relax and enjoy this time because we're making history, baby."

He was right back to the man who showed up in interviews, a bright smile on his face—the happy captain of American industry.

"Good, then I'll take her out of here. We're going to do some prep work for tonight," Deke explained.

Nolan nodded. "Excellent. I'm going to do the same. Jane is excited about tonight. We'll see you in a couple of hours then. And Deke?"

"Yes?" Deke asked.

"Thanks for making all of this possible. I can't tell you how much tonight is going to change my life," Nolan said, his tone hushed and fervent.

"I'm glad to help. Everything is ready. We'll be waiting for you." Deke squeezed her hand as though he knew she needed some comfort. "Let's go. I want to spend some time with you before we start our evening with the group."

Nolan nodded her way and stepped back. "Have a good time. I'll see you tonight at ten."

She watched as he walked away.

Deke pulled her into his arms, whispering in her ear. "Are you okay?"

She nodded. "I'm good. But you were right. He knows I was looking into the absences. He asked about them."

Deke's arms tightened around her. "Okay. We'll deal with it. Let's get through tomorrow and we'll discuss how to handle it. You're not working this weekend, so we have some time. Come on. I want to get you to The Reef. I have some other things I want to talk about."

She stepped back and moved into her office, grabbing her purse and then following him out.

No matter what he said, it felt like time was running out.

* * * *

Nolan nodded at the driver. Normally he preferred to drive himself, to be the man of the people he wanted the world to see. But today he needed to ensure privacy for Jane, and that meant her not walking into the office.

Or at least that was what she'd demanded. Normally she met him in his office, walking through the building with the confidence of a woman who didn't care who saw her. This afternoon she'd called and set up this meeting for after work. He rather thought she understood something was off.

He slid into the back of the big black SUV and the door closed behind him.

"Is everything on for tonight?" Jane sat beside him, her hair up in a prim twist. She wore her usual chic skirt and blouse, expensive heels on her feet and a Prada bag nestled at her hip. He'd bought her the Van Cleef and Arpels Alhambra pendant she wore around her neck. She'd been very specific about the one she'd wanted. It had to be the onyx and yellow gold.

I lost my old one, and it meant the world to me. I had to leave everything behind, but this would feel like a new beginning.

She was like everyone else when it came to his money. She wanted her piece, but he could handle that. Money was the building block of what he truly desired. Power.

"Yes, we're meeting them at The Reef at ten p.m. We'll change

271

and then be given a tour." He'd received the schedule from Ms. Summers-Hunt earlier this afternoon. When he took over that club, he intended to ensure that bitch knew she didn't have anything over him. She'd gone on his list. It was a long list of every single person who'd ever fucked him over. He'd crossed a whole lot of them off. Some had gotten off easy. He'd merely screwed them over in a businesslike fashion. Like that sarcastic asshole who'd done his security in the early days. All he'd cost that man was money and a bit of pride.

But some, he intended to cost far more. Kayla Summers-Hunt had made that list along with all the members of The Reef who'd tried to keep him out.

He would have put Madeline Hill in the helpful category, but lately it rankled that she was going to make so much money off his company. And there were other problems to consider.

"Good." Jane sat back as the SUV began moving. "You've done well, Nolan. You've been a perfect partner."

Only the sight of her shapely legs softened the blow of being treated like a fucking lackey. He wasn't her partner. He would show her that soon enough. She'd crossed her legs and the motion slid her skirt up over her knees.

He wished she wasn't so gorgeous. Her body was sheer perfection and her face was exquisite, but then he was almost certain that was artificial. She had some small scars that led him to believe she'd had plastic surgery in the last few years. He should know. He had some done himself, though he rather thought she'd had some radical surgery, not the simple nose job and neck tightening he'd had. He appreciated her perfection no matter how she'd come by it.

Her attitude was the thing that rankled, but he would take care of that soon enough.

"And you were right about Madeline. You told me she might be trouble," he murmured.

"What's happened?"

Oh, he had her full attention now. "Madeline's been asking around about employees taking sick leave. Specifically the ones we tested the initial waves on."

They'd needed to know if the damn thing worked. Of course they'd dialed back on the intensity. He hadn't wanted to have to explain a bunch of employees with fried brains. A watered-down version had done the trick, and it appeared Madeline had solved the issue of how to integrate the weapon into Clarke's systems. He simply had to figure out how she'd done it.

Or force her to do it herself right before he dealt with her.

"So she's asking questions," Jane mused. "I don't like that at all. By the way, I was right to shut down your hiring until the launch. You had an inquiry from a man who used to work for the Central Intelligence Agency."

And now she had *his* attention. "The CIA?"

"I told you they would very likely be looking your way at some point. Don't worry about it. I've got it handled."

"How exactly are you going to handle it?"

"Well, first of all I made sure you didn't hire one of them. Secondly, you'll have to trust that my associates take this project very seriously. We won't allow anything to interfere with our plans, and that means not allowing the Agency to screw everything up. But you have to decide how you want to deal with Madeline Hill. She's becoming a problem. If she's asking those questions, she's starting to put things together, and I don't think she can be bought out. Can we ensure her silence in some way?"

Did he want to? "She cares about her parents, but they're from a small town. I doubt I can simply swoop in and kidnap one without a large media presence coming into play. No. I think we should handle her in a different fashion. The truth of the matter is if she is allowed to keep her stock, she controls a minority share in the company. She could cause me trouble down the line if she chose to."

"I'm surprised you allowed that to happen."

"It hasn't happened yet. Some of those shares only vest if she successfully delivers her AI. She can't deliver it if she's dead, right?"

A brow rose over her eyes, an arrogant look. "You can't afford to kill her. Or did you figure out how to fix your problems?"

Everything seemed to have fallen into place this afternoon. "She's got a solution. All I need is for her to show me how to do it. I'll be the last person to touch the system before it goes into orbit."

"You can't leave this for the launch. I need to take this to my associates very soon. They need to know this is going to work so they can put word out about the service we'll be able to provide."

A service *he* would be able to provide. "I don't know. It seems risky for me to give you something so dangerous when I have no real promise of payment."

She stopped, her body going still. "You don't trust me?"

"I think you've gotten everything you want and given me nothing so far."

One side of her mouth curled up as though he'd said something that finally impressed her. "I can understand that." She turned his way, giving him a better view of the way her breasts rounded. "You've done everything we've asked so far. You've played ball in a most excellent way. How about I set up a meeting with the board?"

A thrill went through his system. The board meant the big guys, the most powerful men in the world. It was what he'd been waiting for. It was the real first step. He would meet with the board, be placed on the board, and then take over the board.

"When?"

If she was surprised by the harshness of his tone, she didn't show it. She merely sat back, her eyes going to the road as her hand drifted up to the pendant at her neck. "Monday. I think Monday will be a good day for a meeting."

"Monday? That's not a lot of time. Should I have the jet ready?" He forced himself to sit back, too. It wouldn't do to look overeager. He had to play this cool.

"They'll come to you," she promised and then shifted again, her expression going soft as she reached for his hand. "Nolan, it's all coming together. Don't worry. I'm here to take care of everything for you. All you have to worry about is the integration."

He felt his jaw tighten. "I'm struggling with it. I need Madeline."

One elegant shoulder shrugged. "So kill two birds with one stone. Force Madeline to do the integration for you and then kill her."

"She'll be missed. She's close to her parents, and I don't think her boyfriend is just going to shrug and let her go." Something about Deke Murphy bugged him, and it went beyond him reminding Nolan of all the assholes who'd been handed the world because they won the genetic lottery.

"Then kill him, too. He's former military," she mused. "Those kind always have problems. Say you were having an affair with her and her boyfriend found out and tried to kill you both." A smile crossed her face. "I like this plan. If we set it up properly, we wouldn't even have to create evidence. Why don't we have dinner and discuss it?"

The offer was accompanied by her hand finding his thigh and stroking upward. His cock immediately tightened, and he didn't even care that his arousal was only partially about the touch of her hand. The vision of killing Madeline Hill was sexy, too. However, there were a few problems with her scenario. "Do you think we have time to set that up? We only have a few hours. The party is tomorrow night. Should we do it then?"

There was nothing he would love more than to deal with his problems quickly, but he had a schedule to keep. He should have put off the business function, but he hadn't wanted to show there was a single moment's strain with the launch. He wanted everyone to know he was the kind of man who could change the world and throw a dinner party while he was doing it.

"Oh, I think that dinner is probably going to be canceled," she said briskly. "I told you I thought it was foolish to have people at your house so close to the launch. You're opening yourself up to spies."

"I only have some board members at this party." They'd had this argument before. "I've had it every year."

It was a way to show his board how much more he had. It was aspirational.

"Well, this year you'll be dealing with a real tragedy. Tell me something, Nolan. Will it bother you if the world thinks you were fucking her?" Jane asked.

"She's passably attractive." There were other reasons to consider the plan. "Also, there will be a lot of people who suddenly understand why I was paying a woman so much. They already think half her work is mine anyway. There aren't many women who can keep up in our world."

"Well, when so many men try to keep them out, it isn't all that surprising, is it?" She crossed one leg over the other, exposing more of her perfect skin. Her legs were long and graceful. "But, yes, you're right. People will say you only hired her because of your dick. You'll get the credit for her work, and she'll be just another woman who tried to sleep her way to the top. That's how the world works, right?"

It was, and he was going to keep it that way. "All right. I'll skip the party. I'll replace it with a wake. And I'll find a way through my mourning. So tell me this plan of yours. And tell me about this."

When she'd crossed her legs, her skirt had come up, exposing the beginnings of a tattoo on her left thigh. He reached out and traced the edges. Was that a *K*?

She shifted again. "That is the only thing I have left over from my former life. It's a reminder of sorts to never trust my heart again. But my brain tells me we could have a perfect partnership, Nolan. So let me tell you how we're going to solve all of your problems in one single night."

He sat back and listened.

Chapter Twelve

Maddie had already had a tour of The Reef, but she hadn't been in one of the privacy rooms. "Okay. I'll bite. Is there a reason we're not going home? I'm nervous, but I thought I would probably eat dinner before we meet Nolan."

Deke had said very little beyond he wanted to stop by the club. She'd gotten the idea he'd planned something when he wouldn't allow her to stay in the car, and then he'd walked past the offices and led her straight to a privacy room.

She wasn't sure she wanted to play right now. Her gut was still in knots, and it all felt like it was about to crash down around her.

Of course, maybe that was Deke's point. She was completely wound up, and in a few hours she was supposed to show Nolan's girlfriend around the place. Deke had always been good at reading her moods. He was trying to get her loose and ready.

"I ordered a large sausage and mushroom pizza just for you. It's in the kitchen, and when you're ready, we'll eat it and share a bottle of your favorite Pinot. But first we're going to do what we should have done in the beginning." His hands went to the back of his T-shirt and he pulled it over his head, revealing that muscular chest she loved so much.

He didn't look like he wanted to talk, and she wasn't sure what he wanted to talk about. "We could have done that at home."

"Where everyone is hanging out?" Deke stared at her, his shoulders squaring in that "I'm about to top you, baby" way of his. "You want me to tie you up with Drake in the next room? He's an asshole and your walls are thin. I would be able to hear him complain about how loud you get."

She rolled her eyes. "My walls are not that thin."

He didn't crack a smile. "I'm asking you for this, Madeline. I need this time with you. We're going into something dangerous tomorrow, and I need to be with you like this."

She sighed and started on the buttons of her shirt. "The pizza better be thin crust."

He'd given her what she'd needed physically over the last week. He'd given her more than that, but she wasn't willing to analyze what it would mean to not have him in her bed every night. It was easy to say she would miss the orgasms, harder to think about how well she slept when she was in his arms.

He could be gone by the end of next week if they found what they needed and figured out how to use it to stop her boss. He needed to know what she'd figured out today. "I think what he's doing is very specific."

"You've got until your clothes are off to talk business. Then it's my time," he vowed.

It wouldn't take her long. She just wanted to put the idea out there and then Deke could decide what to share with the CIA guy and what to hold back. "I think I figured out why he used an early version of Clarke to try to take over the nuclear plants. I think CIA dude is right and it was a test to see how easily the AI can handle heavily guarded systems."

"All right. Take off your pants."

She kicked out of her flats and went to work on the fly of her slacks. "If what he's putting in is a weapon using sound waves, he needs a receiver. He can't simply broadcast into space and make everyone on earth sick. Sound doesn't work like that. He needs to transmit and send it to someone for it to work. It's best if it's someone with specific receivers for satellites. Like airplanes."

A brow rose over his eyes. "I'm listening, but talk quick. I want your bra off next."

He was a hungry man. Seeing her with Nolan must have really unsettled him. Luckily her explanations were fairly straightforward. "Every commercial airliner has satellite linkups. And the planes that carry diplomats and heads of state absolutely do. With the right amount of that sound, they could incapacitate the pilots and bring down whatever airliner they want."

"Fuck." He grimaced but didn't leave his position. "Then it's more important than ever to get into Byrne's system tomorrow night. Underwear, now."

And that was all the business talk she was likely to get. She shimmied out of her undies and was surprised to find she no longer had any self-consciousness when it came to being naked around him. It felt right. She also didn't mind being naked in a room with obvious torture tools. The privacy room had a bed, but it also had several benches that weren't strictly for sitting and a giant *X* on the wall opposite her.

Kink, it turned out, was good for a girl's confidence. Already the awful tension she'd felt was coming loose. She would have to face it, but not for the next hour. The next hour was all about pleasing Deke and letting him please her, too. "So I tell you my boss is probably going to try to kill the president and start a new world order and you just want me naked."

He moved into her space, capturing her wrists. "I want you naked and vulnerable and with no way to run from me. I want you all to myself so I can say a few things I should have been smart enough to say all along. I'll deal with presidential assassination plots later on."

It might be good to give them some closure on that part of their lives. Then they could figure out what they would be after all this was over. Long-distance lovers or maybe friends who hooked up when they could. Or maybe they would move on again and wish each other all the best with no regrets this time.

Except she thought she would always regret not having him in her life.

"I don't think saying it will change anything." She knew what he wanted. He wanted to make his point about why he'd broken up with her all those years ago. He wanted her to agree with him that it had been for the best. He wanted absolution for leaving her. She wasn't sure she could give it. It wasn't kind of her, but it still hurt that he insisted it had been for the best.

"I think it will. I hope the truth will help," he said as he pulled a length of rope from his pockets and started to wind it around her wrists. He bound her tight, though it wasn't uncomfortable, just enough to know he was in control.

He picked her up and carried her across the room, setting her on her feet before reaching up and pulling something down. She heard something snap into place, and Deke gently guided her wrists over her head to the hook above.

There was a table to her left, and she noticed Deke seemed to have set out a whole bunch of items—some she recognized and some she didn't.

The hook was slightly too high for her, and she had to go up on her toes. The stance elongated her body, stretching her. This was what Deke needed? "We couldn't have had this talk at home? It's my home. I could have kicked everyone out."

"At your ridiculously expensive home? The one I could never afford?" Deke ran a big palm down her back to cup her ass.

The words caught her completely off guard, and she felt a flush race across her skin. "No one asked you to afford it."

"No," he agreed as she felt him move behind her. She shivered as he kissed the nape of her neck. "They didn't. Or rather you didn't. You don't need me to be anyone but who I am. You don't care that I never could have bought you these things."

Tears pierced her eyes. Were they actually going to talk about this? She'd been sure this was some bullshit gambit to make Deke feel better about leaving her. "No. I never needed more from you than you were willing to give."

"That's not true. I remember a time when you absolutely needed more than I could give. I think you need more than I was willing to give now, too. But maybe what I'm willing to give needs to equal what you need, and damn my pride. Maybe I've decided that my pride isn't worth losing your love. Not even close." His hands stroked her, brushing across her like a wave of warmth. "I thought we could pick up where we left off, but we never dealt with it. I never dealt with why I really pushed you away."

Oh, this was so much more dangerous than what she'd expected. She tested the bonds, a little impulse to run coming over her. She wasn't sure she was ready for this. "It doesn't matter now."

Yep, he'd tied her up so she couldn't run like the coward she was. Now that she was confronted with it, she wasn't sure she wanted to have this conversation. It would mean she would truly have a decision to make. "Deke, we're not going to solve our problems tonight. I don't know that our problems are solvable. I've thought about this a lot and I'm not sure I can give you what you need, either."

He needed her to fit into his life, and while she liked his friends, she couldn't up and move to Dallas and…she wasn't sure what she would do there.

"You don't know what I need, yet, but I'm going to tell you. I'm going to be honest with you this time. Do you know why Byrne couldn't drive a wedge between us?" He cupped her breasts, rolling her nipples and tweaking them in a way that made her writhe against him.

"Because you saw through him?"

He nipped at the back of her neck. "Because I'm willing to accept my own flaws now. Because somewhere along the way I decided to deal with myself honestly. When he needled me about how wealthy and successful you are, I recognized what I felt as insecurity, and I trust you enough to admit I felt it."

A hard squeeze to her nipples and her whole body tightened. Was this his version of couples therapy? "You have nothing to be insecure about."

"Society tells me differently. Society looks at you and wonders what you see in me beyond some trophy."

Frustration filled her. "Fuck society. I'm not willing to let society vote on my relationship. They can go to hell. I am who I am and you are who you are, and they don't get to change us."

She wasn't going to mold herself into what other people thought she should be. She hadn't been willing to when she was a kid. She wasn't about to start now. People would say what they would say, and she couldn't change that, but she would be damned if she let it force her into a box.

His arms wound around her, pulling her back against him. "You have always been the fiercest woman I know, and I did not deserve you then. I was scared. You would have done exactly what you said you would have. You would have deferred for a year and given me time to get my shit together, and then you would have gone to Yale."

"I would have gone even if you'd told me you couldn't go with me. I would have called and written and loved you from afar, but Deke, I wasn't going to give up my education for you. I couldn't." She had to be honest with him. She'd never understood his argument. It hadn't made sense. Never once in her head had she thought she would stay in Calhoun and raise babies if he wouldn't go with her.

"So I took the choice away," he whispered. "Instead of trusting our relationship one way or another, I broke it. I pulled the bandage off when there wasn't even a wound there. Baby, I was a kid and I was insecure, and I heard everyone around me talking about how the Hill girl was going to end up saddled with me if she wasn't careful. I shouldn't have listened."

"I loved you, Deke. I wanted it to work, but I love me, too. I could have handled long distance."

"We wouldn't have survived. I should have gone with you. I should have been brave. Or maybe it needed to be this way because you were strong and I had to grow up."

"Deke, you don't have to say these things."

She could feel the hard line of his erection pressed to her backside. Despite all the emotions flowing through her, her body went soft and willing.

"I do. I have to let you know that it's not going to be the same this time," he whispered against her ear. "This time I'm not letting my pride get in the way. I'm not letting anything keep me from you. You're the only one who can tell me you're better off without me."

She wouldn't be. She was fairly certain she would be bereft without him, but there was still an ocean between them. He still had his career and she had hers. He was entrenched in Dallas and the closest she might be able to get was Austin. "Our problems are the same."

"But I'm not. I'm better, Maddie. I'm the man for you now. I'm flawed, but I can work on it." He released her and she felt him moving. "I'm going to work on it right now." He stood in front of her, his gorgeous face staring down at hers. "I've figured out that I can give you what you need. You need someone who puts you first. Before everyone and everything else. Before your work. Before all your ambitions. You are my universe, Maddie, and I'm the man who's going to take care of you. Behind every woman who's changing the world there should be a man who makes sure she's got coffee in the morning and who's waiting with a glass of wine and a killer fucking orgasm when she comes home. I'm that man for you, baby. Hold on tight."

He leaned over and she gasped when he gripped her thighs and shifted his body so her legs were hooked over his shoulders and his mouth was right there. Right where she needed it most. He seemed to be done talking, and he was going to prove his words true.

His hands supported her lower back and she clung to the ropes, most of her weight lifted by his muscular body. She was dependent on him, vulnerable and open. He pressed his mouth against her, tongue finding her pussy and licking and tasting.

Her eyes threatened to roll into the back of her head as he worked her pussy. She felt like she was floating and he was the only real thing in the world. Only the stroke of his tongue, the feel of his strong hands, kept her tethered to the earth.

Over and over he fucked her with his tongue, and she lost all thoughts of inhibitions. She wrapped her legs around his head, allowing him all access to her pussy. His hands squeezed her ass, shifting her this way and that, finding the best angle.

The orgasm seemed to come out of nowhere, blasting through her and making her shake. She cried out, holding fast to the bindings as the pleasure rolled over her.

Then he was easing her legs down and lifting her off the hook and into his arms. "I meant to make this last. I meant to torture you for a long time and make you promise you'll let me stay with you, but I can't wait."

You'll let me stay with you.

Not *you'll stay with me.* Not *you'll come with me when I leave.*

"Torture me after," she whispered.

As he moved toward the bed, she realized, this time, they might have a real chance.

* * * *

Deke wasn't sure if he'd reached her, but in that moment it didn't matter. He *would* reach her. Even if she said she wasn't ready for a real relationship, he would move out here and be close when she was.

She was the be-all, end-all of his existence, and he wasn't making the same mistake again.

He strode across the room to the bed and placed her carefully on it.

She was so fucking sexy staring up at him, all languid and

relaxed because he'd eaten her pussy until she'd come all over his face. "Are you going to take these off me now?"

She held her hands up, and that made things very handy for him.

With one hand he gripped her wrists and used the other to attach the bindings to a useful set of cuffs he'd secured to the hook on the bed's headboard. "I'm not done with them yet."

She gasped when he flipped her over and pressed her up to her knees. The cuffs rotated a full 360 degrees for maximum fun.

He kicked off his boots and made quick work of his jeans.

"What are you doing?" She was on her knees, her arms bound in front of her, and she was the most delicious package he'd ever seen. She was sex and love and friendship, and she couldn't get away because he'd tied her up.

He knew he should be feeling anxious about what he was doing, but there was something light bubbling up inside of him. He'd broken free of emotions that he'd dragged around with him for years. Guilt. Regret. Shame. "I'm fucking the woman I love. I'm going to be a trophy husband. I need to keep you properly relaxed."

She craned her head around. "Deke, don't you even say that."

He gave that gorgeous ass of hers a nice smack. "You don't get to tell me what to do when we're in the club. I can have fun with my role as your himbo."

"You are not…" she started and stopped when he slapped her ass again. "Damn it, Deke. We should talk about this."

"You say that because you already came," he pointed out, reaching for a condom. They were going to address that and soon. She was on birth control and he hadn't had a sexual partner since his last checkup, but he'd already discussed a lot with her this evening so he rolled that sucker on and climbed up behind her.

"You're not some piece of ass," she insisted.

That was his baby. He was the one who confessed he'd fucked up their young lives, and she was defending him against himself. She needed to understand that no matter what happened, he was okay with it as long as they were together. "We can play any way we like.

Maybe I like the thought of being your on-call guy. You just call me up and I'll be there, baby. I'll be thinking about fucking you all day."

She whimpered as he forced her legs further apart and gripped the sides of her hips. "It's going to be hard to do your job if you think about fucking me all day."

Oh, she wanted to test him, did she? He rubbed his cock against her pussy. It was so fucking wet, and he could still taste her on his tongue. "Well, it might take me a while to find a job out here unless Big Tag wants to start a West Coast branch. Don't move, baby. Fuck, you feel good."

"Deke, I love that you've been honest, but I'm not sure it can work," she said even as his cock started to penetrate. She took a short breath, her hands gripping the bindings.

He'd done a number on her. He'd lied to her all those years ago, and that could make a person shy about jumping in again. "We'll make it work, and we can go as fast or slow as you like." He gave her a good example of how nice slow could feel. He slid his cock deep inside, letting her feel every inch. "If you want we can get married tomorrow." He pulled out and then back in, three quick strokes. "Or I can find a place out here and we'll date." He slowed the pace again. One easy stroke, and then again. "Any way you like."

The way she was bound made it easy for him to move her body in the rhythm he chose. She sighed as he eased in and out. "You know I like it both ways. All the ways, Deke. All the ways with you."

That was what he wanted to hear. "You don't have to decide. You only have to let me stay close. Husband. Boyfriend. Casual date." He picked up the pace. "I can do them all. I won't stay casual for long. I'll make you want me in your bed every single night. I'll make you think of how good it would be to have me fuck you every night before you go to sleep and to wake up with me inside you all over again."

She pressed back against him. "I think I need fast right now. God, Deke, I need you."

He needed her, too. He fucked into her, giving her what they both required. They needed to be connected. He let himself feel for a moment, feel the way she cradled him, the heat she sent all along his skin, the safety there was in this one woman. She felt so good, but something was wrong with the position.

He pulled out, drawing back so he could manhandle her a little. He'd prepared for this moment.

"Hey," she began.

He gripped her legs and flipped her over on her back, never having to reposition her bindings.

Maddie's eyes were wide as she looked up at him, her legs spread and nipples hard. She loved it when he was the tiniest bit rough with her. With her arms over her head, her body was perfectly laid out for him. She was the most tempting woman in creation, and he was not about to resist.

He covered her body with his, bringing their mouths together. Kissing Maddie made the world drift away. When they were together, the world narrowed down to the two of them, and nothing else mattered. He kissed her even as his cock found her pussy and he thrust home.

Her legs wound around his waist, and she met his rhythm.

Then all he could think about was the woman he'd loved most of his life and how perfect she felt wrapped around him.

Deke moved inside her, letting her silky heat draw him in again and again. He fucked her in the sweetest way, merging their mouths, their bodies, their souls.

She gasped and her legs tightened around him as she came, her whole body going taut. He kissed her, taking in her cries and calls. Then it was his turn. He felt his balls draw up, felt every bone seem to melt as the wave hit him.

He collapsed on top of her, still connected. A sense of peace flowed over him, and he was ready.

Ready to commit to her and everything that meant. Ready to start the rest of his life.

And he was ready to share everything with her.

She was quiet as he unbound her hands and refixed the hook, quiet as he moved to the bathroom and dealt with the condom. His baby was thinking, and he was going to give her even more to think about. When he pulled back the covers, she let him pick her up and tuck her inside. She curled against him when he joined her.

He breathed in her scent, so familiar and comforting to him. He wasn't sure how he'd lived without her.

"I thought we were going to eat dinner," she murmured.

"Not yet." He had a story to tell her. "I was scared when I realized I'd gotten cut off from my squad."

She went still. "Deke, you don't have to tell me."

"I think I didn't want to tell you because I could pretend it wasn't real if you didn't know. Not what happened to me but the fact that you still don't know how close I came to breaking. More than close, really. I was willing to tell them anything. I'd decided to. I wanted them to kill me because I couldn't take another second of the pain," he admitted. She was the first person besides Kai Ferguson he'd ever said the words to. Not even his parents knew what he'd gone through. And yet, it was okay now. He wasn't back there. The memories weren't as sharp with her in his arms. He'd survived and now it was a story, a piece of him that should be made known to the woman who should know all of him.

"Deke," she began, and there were already tears in her eyes.

He brushed them away and kissed her forehead. "The only thing that got me through was the thought that I could see you again. You were in my dreams. I might have been a prideful, foolish boy, but I have always loved you, Madeline. So let me tell you what happened. Share it with me so it doesn't feel like something I should hide from you."

She nodded and settled back down, her arms around him.

And Deke told her everything.

Chapter Thirteen

Four hours later, Maddie still couldn't quite stop thinking about what Deke had been through.

Or what he was offering her. He wanted to stay no matter what happened. Even if they figured the whole case out tomorrow night, he wanted to remain in California with her so they could try to make this relationship work.

I cost us too much time, baby.

He'd whispered the words as they'd lain there in bed. Was it her time to let fear cost them?

"Does it meet your expectations?"

The question brought her out of her thoughts and back into the moment. She stood in The Reef with two women she'd only recently met.

Madeline glanced at Jane Adams and wondered what it was about the woman that felt wrong to her. It wasn't fair or nice because she'd just met her, but Maddie couldn't help but feel like she was missing something. Nothing scary. Jane had been lovely since the moment they'd been introduced, but there was something oddly familiar about her.

"It's everything I thought it would be," Jane was saying, looking around the main dungeon. She gave Kayla Summers-Hunt a wide smile. "Thank you so much for making this dream come true for me."

"I've got to ask why coming to The Reef was a dream for you." Kayla looked spectacular in a peacock blue corset and thong. Her legs appeared long and sleek in a pair of Louboutin stilettos. "I mean, we love it here, but not many people know about it. I've been trying to make the connection."

"Oh, more people know about it than you think. The Reef is considered the best club in California by many in the lifestyle." Jane wore a corset of her own. It was black, and so were the boy shorts and the heels on her feet. Her hair was deep purple and in a bob that brushed her jawline and was almost certainly a wig. By the time Maddie had made it into the locker room, Jane had changed and had an elaborate mask that covered much of her face. "I've visited a couple of the clubs in the valley and one downtown, but I've never been a regular. The Reef is all anyone talks about. It's the pinnacle of where the lifestylers I used to hang around with wanted to be."

"And you?" Kayla asked.

"I wanted to see it. I suppose it's a little bit of revenge because I'm here and he doesn't even know it," Jane replied, touching one of the pillars and running her fingers down it. She seemed completely fascinated with everything around her. Her enthusiasm might have been catching if Maddie wasn't still thinking about how hard life had been on Deke.

The club was starting to hum, the lights low and music beginning to pulse through the building.

"I would ask who your ex is, but I have to be honest, I haven't played outside this club in...well, since I came to LA," Kayla said.

"Malibu, you mean," Jane corrected, her lips curling up in an impish grin. "You, milady, live in Malibu. It's very different from the LA I live in."

"Probably," Kayla admitted. "But it's not like I haven't seen a rougher part of the world. You travel a lot, don't you?"

Jane nodded. "Quite a bit, but it's mostly places like Cleveland or the Atlanta suburbs. Most of the companies I work for are located in boring places. I work from home a lot, too. It can be lonely. I had a bad breakup and I needed to do some healing, so I suppose I hid away for a while and licked my wounds. Tonight is special for me because it feels like I'm taking the first steps to get my life back. I thank you for helping with that, Kayla. And you, Madeline. You have no idea how much you've helped me."

She wasn't sure why Deke was so suspicious of this woman. There was something oddly familiar about her, but she was quite charming. "I'm happy to do it. I know how much D/s has helped me."

It had. She was surprised that something she'd gone into simply thinking it was nothing but a tool had actually transformed the way she thought about sex and her own body. It gave her confidence and made her take her own needs seriously.

Was that why it might be able to work with Deke this time?

Jane smiled. The mask was in the shape of a butterfly on her face, the wings spreading over her cheeks but not covering her mouth. Her lips were generous and perfectly sculpted. "I'm glad to hear that. I'm trying to take back that part of my life." She glanced around. "Where did the other girl go? The one with the cutest name?"

"MaeBe?" Maddie asked.

Jane nodded. "Yes, that was it. She was adorable." She touched the deep purple hair that caressed her cheeks. "Obviously I love her hair, but she just seems like a really fun chick. I don't have many girlfriends. I'm afraid all the women I work with are highly competitive."

"Yes, I saw you specialize in corporate restructuring," Maddie said. "That's got to be stressful. Are there a lot of women in that business?"

"Oh, I've found women are absolutely the best at walking into a situation and realizing who needs to go," Jane murmured. "There she is. I was asking about you. I was just telling them how much I love your hair."

MaeBe lit up as she approached the group. "Oh, thanks. I just had it done. My roots grow so fast I sometimes think I should give it up. It's been so long since I saw my natural color, I wouldn't recognize it. I like yours, too."

Jane reached out, brushing her fingers over MaeBe's pink locks. "I think this looks oddly natural on you. And mine's a wig. I like to be versatile when it comes to how I look."

"Well, this is the place to do it." MaeBe wore a tiny miniskirt and a PVC longline bra along with fishnet socks that came up to her knees and a pair of Mary Janes. Her hair was in pigtails like a naughty schoolgirl. "This is a place to be whoever you want to be."

"I like that," Jane replied. "Though I can't imagine the wife of Joshua Hunt wanting to be anyone else."

Kayla snorted, a sound she managed to make elegant. "Oh, I love that man, but he's human like the rest of us. I wouldn't be anyone but me, however, I do like to play out some fantasies. Let me show you around. We've got some rooms that are specifically for fantasy play. You indicated you enjoy role-playing."

Kayla started to move down the stairs that led into the largest of the dungeons at The Reef. Maddie glanced around, looking for any glimpse of Deke. She hadn't seen him since they'd gone into separate locker rooms and wouldn't until this "girl" time was over.

Kayla started to give Jane some information about the club and Maddie wondered if Nolan was needling Deke again.

The fact that her boss had tried to make her boyfriend feel small pissed her off.

Deke said he was working through his insecurities, but what if he couldn't?

"Hey, are you okay?" MaeBe moved in beside her, her voice going low. "I can handle this if you need to head back to the locker room. Is it something Deke did?"

Kayla had stopped, showing Jane the hallway that led to the offices.

Maddie hung back. "He finally talked about what happened to him during his military days. It was awful, but he seems okay with it. He was calm the whole time he told me the story."

"Well, he's had a lot of therapy," MaeBe replied. "And he took it seriously. He's worked on himself for years. I'm glad he talked to you. He was a little confused about why it was important to share that part of his life with you."

"He told you he was confused?"

"He brought it up to the group," MaeBe acknowledged. "I think the fact that the only person who agreed with him was Kyle made him rethink. My guy isn't the right person to give anyone advice about being open and honest in a relationship, though he's working on it."

She should have known that Deke would ask for advice. He seemed to talk a lot more these days.

He had changed. He was more open, more willing to consider things he would have blown off before. He was ready for a real relationship.

Was she?

"Your guy?" Jane had drifted back to them. "Is he a Dom? I noticed you didn't have a collar. I thought you might be a single sub, which I was totally going to ask you about. I've never played without a Dom. I was going to ask you if it's awesome."

Oh, that didn't sound good for Nolan.

Up ahead, Kayla seemed to have been cornered by another member of the club. She was talking to a man, which had freed Jane up to join them.

MaeBe didn't miss a beat. "Yeah, my Dom and I are having a wee battle about the collar, and I'll probably get a spanking tonight. It's nothing we can't deal with. Master Kyle is thoughtful in many ways, but every now and then we disagree on how to handle things. I want a piece of jewelry as a collar. Something like yours. I love that necklace. It's beautiful."

Maddie had recognized it from Van Cleef and Arpels. It was a classic piece.

Jane's hand went to her throat, fingers brushing the pendant there. "I had Nol…Master Nolan buy it for me. You should tell your Master you want one. Or Cartier makes lovely chokers."

"Oh, my Master is not…well, he's not a billionaire," MaeBe replied. "He's kind of a blue-collar guy. But that doesn't mean I'm wearing a dog collar. I don't care where he found it. It's a dog collar. I know fet wear better than he does. Guys. Especially Doms. They all wear leather pants and a vest and that's all they need, while we have to have a whole wardrobe."

"He didn't buy you a collar?" Jane asked, and for a second her lips curled up. She seemed to realize she was being rude, and a concerned look came over her face. "The way a man treats you is very telling, MaeBe. You should find out if he treats all his girlfriends this way or if it's just you."

Okay. She needed to get this train moving. "They're a new couple. Why don't we go into the touch room? It's interesting. It's being used tonight for a sub who enjoys being the center of attention—good and bad."

MaeBe's smile had been faltering, but she seemed to take the lifeline Maddie had thrown. "Yeah. I saw them setting it all up earlier and it looks like fun. I'll let Kayla know we're heading that way."

As MaeBe went to talk to Kayla, Jane leaned in. "I'm so sorry. I didn't realize that was a problem between them. I'm putting my foot in my mouth."

Maddie waved her off. "Not at all. Everyone talks here. It's okay. MaeBe and Master Kyle are just starting to explore their relationship. It's awkward in the beginning. Tell me. How did you meet your Dom?"

"At work, of course."

"Really? Is there something I should know?" After all, Jane reorganized corporations and trimmed off the fat—which was usually workers who made decent money. She was pretty sure Deke thought Nolan was going to try to cheat her out of her stock. Would firing her work?

Jane laughed. "I'm not working at Byrne Corp. Nolan owns a lot of companies, and I advised him on the organization of a couple of them. We talked and went out and then decided we were compatible. He's a very smart man. Let's go and see this touch space of yours. So this woman likes to be touched?"

She got the feeling that she was missing something, but MaeBe was back.

"He's actually a male identifying submissive," MaeBe explained. "Kayla's handling a problem in one of the locker rooms. She'll be right with us. We can watch the scene until she joins us again. It looks like the club's starting to fill up."

MaeBe was right. There were definitely more people in the club, and some of the scenes were starting up around her. This was why Deke had insisted she spend time at Sanctum. She wasn't freaked out by the fact that two subs were getting their asses whipped by a woman in a leather catsuit ten feet away from her.

She would like going to a club and relaxing and enjoying the freedom she could find here. No one cared that those two people liked the crack of a whip across their bare butts. People watched and cheered them on. It was nice, when she thought about it.

She followed MaeBe and Jane toward the touch room and tried not to gawk at the guy who'd played Dart on TV. He didn't play a superhero anymore, but damn that man still looked good. He had a gorgeous sub sitting on his lap as they relaxed in one of the lounge areas.

Her future was totally uncertain, and all that mattered was how she was going to deal with Deke.

And didn't that tell her something? She wasn't worried about her career. She was worried about whether or not she could trust Deke to stay with her this time.

Could she trust this Deke? It felt like pushing him away would be nothing more than punishment. Punishment to him for leaving her all those years ago. Punishment for her because she'd been stupid enough to think he could love her.

Or she could recognize that she loved him and that was all that mattered. She could take the risk every person in love ever had to take.

She realized MaeBe and Jane had stopped outside a room soft blue light spilled from.

Jane was running a hand over her left thigh, rubbing the elaborate tattoo there. Maddie had noticed it earlier. It was impossible not to see, but she hadn't asked about it. It appeared that MaeBe had.

"I got it last year, right after my very bad breakup." She traced the top of the tattoo.

It was a knife, the hilt pointed toward her hip, as though she could reach down and grab it if she needed. The dagger was beautifully done, ending in a sharp point that seemed to drip blood. The drops formed a pretty rose that wrapped around an ornate *K*. It was a lovely piece of art that also seemed a bit ominous to Maddie. She didn't think the rose was protecting the *K*.

"It's a great piece of work," MaeBe said, studying the tat.

"Thanks. I'm going to add to it as I start the healing process," Jane explained. "I thought I would add the initials of the people who help me get closure. I'm going to put them right on the dagger. So I don't forget."

MaeBe gave her a bright smile. "That's an amazing way to remember the people who help you."

"Yes, I think I'll keep those people with me for the rest of my life," Jane vowed before turning to the entryway. "What are the rules for this scene?"

Maddie was ready for the night to be over. She wanted to see Deke and talk about how they could mesh their lives together. She wasn't sure what would happen after Saturday, but she knew she would have to leave Byrne Corp. She couldn't stay. It would be far too uncomfortable.

Austin wasn't that far from Dallas. Lawless had told her to call him if she ever needed a job.

"No talking inside the room," MaeBe explained. "The sub is tied up and blindfolded. He enjoys the sense of anticipation that comes with not knowing who's touching him or whether that touch will be gentle or sharp. There's a table of impact toys. Any of them can be used. He has a safe word and he'll use it. The woman in the back is his Domme. She's simply there to watch over him."

"He does this often?" Jane asked.

"At least once a month. He's been doing it for years," MaeBe replied. "He's in a high-stress job, and this is how he relaxes. He plays every week, but the third Friday of the month is his touch night. Do you want to go in?"

"Sure. I'll give him a little surprise," Jane said before she walked in.

MaeBe glanced over. "She seems nice."

They watched as Jane moved into the room, the blue light coating her skin as she approached the sub. The sub's mistress stood back, watching but not talking at all.

"I don't know." She was trying not to be naïve. "She's involved with Nolan, so I have to wonder how much she knows about his business. And that tattoo thing sounds more like a threat. Like she's collecting the names of the people who wronged her."

MaeBe frowned. "It is kind of weird to put their names on a dagger. I would not want to be *K*. I think she's got what my boss would call crazy eyes. Sometimes, though, he says I have crazy eyes, so maybe I shouldn't judge. What do you think she's going to do? Soft or hard?"

Jane was looking over the impact toys, her hands brushing over the falls of a flogger.

"I'm not sure."

Jane straightened up, her hands going to the bottom of her corset as though pulling it down, and then she turned, leaving the toys behind and approaching the sub.

Jane touched the sub gently, her palms smoothing out over his back, and a shudder went through the older man.

Then she stepped back and turned, and for a moment, the mask slipped and Maddie caught a glimpse of her face. It was over in a second and Jane adjusted her mask.

But it was enough.

Maddie knew why she recognized Jane.

Jane was the woman who met with Nolan. Jane worked for The Consortium.

She was about to whisper the revelation to MaeBe when Jane joined them, an oddly triumphant smile on her face. "I think we should find the men."

Maddie nodded. "Yes, we should do that."

A loud moan burst from the sub in the touch room. The Domme moved in. He howled and fought against his bonds. Maddie watched in horror as white foam rolled from his mouth.

"We need medical," MaeBe yelled.

Jane sighed and reached behind her, pulling a small gun from the back of her corset. "Well, that worked too fast. MaeBe, darling, shut your mouth before I kill you. I don't want to kill you. Yet. We have things to talk about. So let's you and I and Maddie walk out that back door right there."

Maddie glanced over but the mistress was trying desperately to save her sub. There was no help from that corner.

"Maddie, run," MaeBe began.

There was no sound, but suddenly MaeBe's left arm bloomed with blood and Jane had a hand on the back of her neck. "I wasn't joking. Madeline, run if you want your friend to die. Or you go over there and open that door for me."

She glanced over and sure enough, there was an emergency door.

"MaeBe, if you try that falling shit on me, I'll put a bullet in your head and your boyfriend will find you laying right here," Jane was saying. "And then I'll kill him, too."

MaeBe grimaced but remained standing.

Maddie took a deep breath and went to open the door. She prayed Deke would get to them in time.

* * * *

Deke walked through the main lounge, letting Josh Hunt do most of the work. He was the one who knew the club, after all.

"This is where most of the members begin and end their evenings," Josh explained. Byrne had been gamely following them for fifteen minutes, asking questions every now and then, but mostly listening. "The bar is fully stocked, but alcohol is limited to one drink before play. After, you're welcome to have as much as you like, though the bartender will take your keys if he thinks you've had too much."

"Well, I'll have a driver most of the time," Byrne replied. "Though I drove us here tonight. I didn't want to bring anyone else into it until you decide on my membership."

They moved further into the lounge, Josh introducing Byrne around.

Deke hung back.

"I think I'm going to go find MaeBe." Kyle had been by his side, despite the fact that he wanted to be velcroed to his girl.

"We're meeting up with them in ten minutes or so. Stay calm, man." The last thing he needed was a Kyle freak out. "We get through tonight so we can do the job tomorrow."

"Something's wrong with Jane," Kyle insisted.

Kyle hadn't even been there when they'd met Jane. He'd been in the office talking to Drake, who'd been glued to his computer for hours. Kyle had been holed up with him for much of the time, but both men were being quiet about what they were up to. He was going to have a long talk with Kyle tonight because he needed backup tomorrow—not a dude who looked like he was working with the Agency again. "What's wrong with Jane? Give me something I can work with."

Kyle huffed. "I don't know, but Drake's looking into it. He needs more time. Have we thought about the fact that she shouldn't be around MaeBe?"

"Jane checked out. MaeBe didn't find anything wrong with her background," Deke whispered, frustration welling. "She's got years of data, and MaeBe didn't think it's been faked. She checked it with her contacts at the actual platforms. Do you not believe that MaeBe is capable of doing her job?"

"Of course not. She's great, but there are people out there who can do terrible things and she won't even be able to conceive that it could happen," Kyle countered. "Have we considered that Jane could be The Consortium agent?"

"Maddie didn't…" He realized something he hadn't thought of before. "I never had her look at Jane's file. There didn't seem to be a reason since we were meeting her in person. But she didn't say anything tonight. Surely she would have seen her in the locker room."

"Unless she was already wearing that mask," Kyle pointed out. "We don't know how quickly she put it on. She was already wearing a wig when she and Byrne got here."

"All right." He hadn't thought to talk to Maddie about the background checks. He'd wanted to spend his time with her on other things. "I'll have Maddie take a look at the pictures we have of her. Is there something else that bothers you? Something new?"

Kyle hadn't liked Jane since he'd first taken a look at her picture.

Kyle's jaw tightened. "When she walked in tonight, I noticed something. She was wearing a pendant. It's the same pendant I gave to my partner, the one who died. I don't think it's a coincidence."

He'd noticed the necklace. It was a lot like one Charlotte wore. He knew it was expensive because Ian had moaned about it for weeks. "Because she's wearing a necklace?"

"Because she's wearing that necklace," Kyle insisted.

"A lot of women have similar necklaces," Deke replied. "Charlotte has one, though it's blue and not black. I think it's popular among wealthier women."

"Things have been happening lately, and I've started to wonder if they're all coincidences. My family has had a terrible run of luck. MaeBe's had some, too. What if Julia had friends in The Consortium and they're fucking with me? What if they're coming after my family? Wearing that necklace would be a way to taunt me. I bought that necklace for Julia. I put it around her throat when I thought we were meant to be, before I found out she was a psychotic narcissist. Julia could be charming. People liked Julia. What if one of her sisters in that group wants revenge on me?" Kyle asked.

Deke moved back, making sure Josh still had Byrne's attention. Another actor had joined them and was shaking Byrne's hand. Jared Johns. He'd played Dart on TV for years, and it looked like Byrne was a fan. Excellent.

He pulled out the cell phone he wasn't supposed to be carrying and quickly dialed Boomer.

"Hey," Boomer said.

"Have you seen anything weird tonight?" Deke asked, well aware that Kyle was giving him cover and likely listening in.

"I've seen a lot of weird shit," Boomer replied. "There's some kind of anime convention going on at the hotel two blocks over, and apparently their parking lot is full because they're starting to park close to the club. I've got a lot of traffic around right now. I wouldn't hate another set of eyes. Any way Drake could come out here with me? Tell him to pick up something from the kitchen. I already ate the sandwiches Kay gave me."

Shit. Boomer was across the street, watching the club from the roof of the building there. Normally this street was dead at night. All the shops closed and there weren't any residences. It should have been perfectly quiet, and Boomer should have been able to watch the front of the building.

Kyle was right. Too many things were starting to add up. He couldn't see what the pattern was, but the very fact that there might *be* a pattern got his instincts flaring.

"Are you nervous about it?" Deke trusted Boomer's instincts.

"There's a black SUV that's circling," Boomer said. "I can't tell if it's looking for a parking place or waiting for someone. It could be a ride share. But honestly, I don't like it. I know tonight's supposed to be low key, but I got a bad feeling. I'm going to head down and check out the SUV. I think it parked. It hasn't come back around. I want to make sure it's not sitting behind the club. It could be reporters. It could be something else. Are we sure Drake doesn't have friends hanging around?"

"I don't know." Deke looked up because Kyle was nudging him. "Check it out and get back to me." He hung up the phone and slipped it into his pocket as Josh and Byrne walked up.

"Everything okay?" Byrne looked oddly out of place in a set of leathers, like they didn't quite fit even though he'd had them tailor made.

Kyle nodded. "Yeah. I was thinking it might be time to find our subs and begin the night."

Deke agreed. It was definitely time to put eyes on Maddie. "I've heard there are some fun scenes about to play out. Josh, do you know where Kayla is?"

Hollywood's best-paid actor frowned his way. "She's in the women's locker room. Someone passed out in there. Jared's wife is a nurse. She's going to join her."

All the little things started to add up, and his gut took a deep dive. Something had gone wrong that needed Kay's attention just when Jane was alone with Maddie and MaeBe? He didn't like the sound of that. "Why don't we find the women?"

That was when he heard someone shout. It came from the back of the building, and he could barely hear it over the music. "We need medical!"

Kyle started running. "That's MaeBe."

Damn it. Maddie was with her, and Kayla had been waylaid. He looked to Josh. "Is there a back way out?"

"Of course," Josh replied, jogging beside him. "We have a fire exit, but the alarm will go off if someone…"

A loud, clanging alarm filled the space, making Deke's heart rate triple. He took off running, pure panic flooding his veins. It didn't make sense. What was happening? All that mattered was finding

Maddie.

He followed Kyle, who seemed to know where he was going. The Reef was a bit like a maze, and he ran through. He barely registered the half-naked subs, clinging to their tops, scenes ruined and chaos raining down on them.

Deke ran until there was nowhere else to run to, until he'd made it to the door, pushing through, the alarm going off again.

"Where are they?" Kyle looked around, his hands in fists at his sides. "MaeBe!"

Deke stood there, the parking lot completely empty, and realized he might never see Maddie again.

Chapter Fourteen

"**W**here the fuck are they? What are you hiding from me?" Kyle slammed his fists against the conference table, confronting Drake, who merely looked up from his computer.

"I'm not hiding anything, but I'm starting to see a pattern and I don't like it," Drake replied, as calm as Kyle was enraged.

Deke wasn't about to insert himself in that argument. It was obvious that the CIA agent had a lot on his hands. Deke had other things to do. "Kay, do you have anyone here who can hack into the traffic cams around the area? They absolutely didn't walk away from here. Boomer said there was a car circling the block. I need to know where that car went. I also need to know where Byrne is."

At some point in the last fifteen minutes, Byrne had disappeared. Deke knew he hadn't been with Jane, but they'd very likely reconnected now that Jane had taken Maddie. He needed to know where the man had gone if for no other reason than to question him. He would make Byrne talk if he had to pull the man's balls off his body.

"Call home base, Deke. I can't help you with this." Kayla had shucked her heels and paced, cell phone in hand. "Do you understand that I have a dead plastic surgeon tied up in a BDSM club, another woman who nearly died in the locker room, and if I'm not careful I'll have cops all over the place? The only reason I didn't have to call an ambulance is Sarah Johns is a hell of a nurse, but we still don't know what happened to the woman."

"The woman was obviously a distraction," Deke pointed out. "They wanted to get Madeline and MaeBe alone."

"Yes, for what appears to be an assassination," Kayla countered. "Who the fuck is this Jane Adams because she's not who that background check said she is. Corporate drones don't assassinate doctors in BDSM clubs."

"Hey, baby, it's going to be okay." Josh moved in behind his wife, putting his hands on her shoulders. "I've gathered the board members in the men's locker room and we're going to talk about how to handle this. The last thing Bernie would have wanted was a scandal. He has…had three grandkids he adores, and he wouldn't want them shoved into the middle of a true crime documentary. You know he always said if he died in this club, we were to find a way to move him."

"He meant if he had a heart attack, Josh," Kayla argued. "I don't even know what killed him. I don't know if moving the body might be dangerous."

"We'll figure it out," Josh promised. "He wasn't the only doctor in the club."

"I'll get the cameras for you, Deke." Drake seemed to be the only one of them who wasn't panicked. "As to what killed the good doctor, I suspect you'll find it's a fast-acting poison the Agency has been experimenting with. The poison is cyanide, but the delivery mechanism is what's new. It's a tiny needle the user wears on his or her hand, often hidden under a layer of foundation makeup so it's hard to see. One prick and the poison is delivered to the victim's system, often without the victim even feeling the pinch of the needle.

I suspect she microdosed the woman in the locker room with just enough to make her sick."

"He was completely vulnerable to her." Kayla's eyes shone with tears. "I'm going to kill that bitch, Josh. I know I promised…"

Josh wrapped his arms around her. "You're going to do whatever you need to do, and let me and the others handle Bernie. I'm going to go meet with them right now and discuss how to ensure none of this disrupts Bernie's family. You figure out why she wanted him dead."

It was clear to Deke. Drake wasn't the only one who could see a pattern. "She's a former patient. Look, she's clearly not the Jane Adams her background check shows. These Consortium operatives have to find ways to pass background checks. Even if all the paperwork is done perfectly, someone like MaeBe can figure out if it's likely faked. She can do it by checking social media footprints and looking at the code on the paperwork. So what's the best way to fake it?"

"To not fake it at all," Kyle said, his mouth a flat line. "You take over someone else's life. You find someone without much of a family, without many friends, and you become that person. The real Jane Adams is dead. Your doctor helped whoever the fuck is wearing her face."

"Bernie wasn't into anything criminal," Josh argued. "He was one of the best plastic surgeons in LA. He worked on celebrities and models, not criminals."

"He might not have known what he was doing." Deke's gut was in a knot. Maddie was at the mercy of this woman who seemed to have none.

"Did he specialize?" Drake asked.

"Nose jobs," Kayla replied. "He was known as one of the best in the world when it came to nose jobs."

"Jane has…had an interesting nose. It's thin and slightly tilted up," Drake remarked. "It would have taken a pro to get it right, and I would bet it was the first thing she had done. Your doctor was likely the last person to see her true face, and she had to get rid of him. This has been one long setup, and we didn't see it coming."

"Why take MaeBe and Maddie?" Kyle asked. "She killed the guy she wanted to kill. What's the point of taking them?"

Drake's eyes finally came up. "You know why."

Deke didn't have time to play Agency games. He'd put together a lot in his head in the last few moments. Sometimes dead didn't stay dead. "Is Jane the woman you worked with? Is this about getting revenge?"

He needed to understand what Maddie was up against.

Kyle had paled. "No. No. I killed her. She's dead."

"Did you bury her?" Deke asked.

"No. I had to leave very quickly. There was a fire." Kyle's eyes had gone blank as though he'd turned inward. "I fucked up. She didn't die. She's alive and she's going to kill MaeBe."

"Don't get ahead of yourself." Drake stood. "We can't be sure. And even if it is Julia, she's working. She took Madeline for a reason, and we need to figure it out. I've got Byrne's Ferrari turning out of the parking lot. I'm trying to track him."

Deke's cell buzzed. He pulled it out of his pocket because Kay had been right about one thing. He was going to have to call Ian. He looked down and Boomer's name flashed across the screen. "Hey, man. Come on inside. We need to talk."

"I can't, brother," Boomer said. "I'm following Byrne. I noticed him sneaking out the front and figured you would want me to follow. I took the car. We're on the freeway right now, but I think he might be heading back to his place."

He was going to buy Boomer all the hot dogs he wanted. "Hang back. Don't let him know you're there. His girlfriend turns out to potentially be Kyle's ex."

"The one he killed?" Boomer asked with a whistle.

"Yeah, she might not be as dead as he thought, and she's got MaeBe and Maddie. They're very likely in that same SUV you saw earlier." If Boomer had the car, then Boomer also had their provisions. "I need you to find a perch."

307

Boomer's sniper rifle was in the trunk.

"Tell him I'm going to send him schematics of Byrne's property," Drake said, moving back to his laptop.

"Drake's sending you an email. Open it before you get to Byrne's. It's a big property and it's got a lot of trees on it, but I need you to evade his security."

"No problem. I'll text you when I'm in place, and I'll let you know if I see the girls," Boomer promised. "I'm going to assume getting them out is our mission now."

"Absolutely," he replied. "You get them out if you can, and fuck the rest of the op. But be careful around Jane. She's not what she seems."

"Not if she's back from the dead she's not," Boomer replied. "I'll check in when I can."

The line went dead.

"She's going to kill MaeBe." Kyle looked like he was about to be sick. "If that woman is Julia, she's going to torture her and kill her. She'll do it to hurt me. She'll do it because she's been watching and she knows MaeBe is everything to me."

"The key word there is torture," Drake said. "She won't kill her right away. She'll take her time. Julia is a monster, and she likes to play with her prey. So the question now is what will they do with Madeline."

"He needs Maddie to integrate The Consortium's weapon with her AI." Deke could see how this would play out. "But he also wants to get rid of her. He'll have to because she's going to know what he's doing. They're counting on Kayla not bringing in the cops."

"You know why I can't," Kayla said. "They know it, too. And sending the cops out to Byrne's place could be risky, as well."

"I'm going to get a call soon," Deke explained, his panic starting to calm because he was right about this. The whole plan fell into place for him, and that meant he could counter it. "They'll tell me to come out to his place but to come alone or they'll kill Maddie and MaeBe. When I enter his house, he'll shoot me, but not until I'm securely

308

inside. He has to stage this properly. He'll then kill Maddie but make it look like I did it. Like I found out my girlfriend was cheating on me with him. It's a scandal but one the company can weather."

"If Julia is involved, then she knows exactly who you are and what we're all capable of," Kyle pointed out and then groaned. "Unless that's the whole fucking point. Byrne doesn't know. She hasn't told him. She's playing every single one of us. She wants us to take him out."

"I think so," Drake agreed. "She wants the tech, but she doesn't want Byrne. I'm going to assume he wanted a seat at the table, but he's a wild card. He's too much in the public eye to be involved. He's a risk for the whole group. She wants us to take him out for her. She might even be planning exactly the scenario Deke put forth but with Byrne dying as well. If she can set it up so Deke kills Byrne, she'll kill Deke and Maddie and make it look like Deke went insane with jealousy, killed them both, and then committed suicide. She walks away with everything, and no one is looking for her."

"I'm going to kill her again," Kyle said, a hard look in his eyes.

"You're not getting anywhere near her tonight." He couldn't trust Kyle to watch his back. The man was too emotional. Besides, he had other plans.

"She has MaeBe. I'm not leaving her there," Kyle insisted. "Have you heard anything I've said? She'll hurt MaeBe."

"Yes, and likely take her time doing it. She'll want you there," Deke explained. "She'll want you to watch."

"Or she'll throw her body on my doorstep. Or put her head in a box and ship it to me like a present," Kyle countered.

Drake stood, folding his laptop closed. "She's been playing this slow for a while now. You told me you've had trouble lately. Your whole family. Julia's probably behind most of it. She never does something quickly when she can do it slow. She'll want you to trade your life for MaeBe's."

"And then she'll kill her in front of me," Kyle spat. "Then she'll go after my brothers and sister and my mom and stepdad. Hell, she'll go after my friends. She won't stop until I understand she's taken everything from me. I have to kill her, and this time I'll make damn sure I see her body. I'll cremate her myself and keep her in a jar in my office so I never take my eyes off her again."

Deke's phone buzzed but when he looked down it wasn't a familiar number.

He'd been right. It was go time.

"Everyone keep quiet." He slid his finger across the screen. "This is Deke."

"Hello, Deke. I suppose you'd like to know what happened to your sub. She's with me." Nolan Byrne's voice was silky across the line. He obviously felt like he was totally in control. "Tell me. Have you already called the police in?"

"Of course not, and you know why I won't," Deke replied. "Your girl killed someone here tonight, and we have to protect his reputation. His family could be harmed if we call the police in, but I suspect you knew how we would react. That's precisely why she killed him here. Did Maddie see it happen?"

"None of that matters." Byrne was quiet for a moment and then his voice wasn't so silky. There was a fine edge of tension that caught Deke's interest. "I need Madeline to do a job for me. Once she's done, you can have her back. I need you to come to my house, but you have to come alone. If I get even a whiff that you've involved the authorities, I'll have to make sure no one can find her. Am I clear?"

He hadn't known about what his girlfriend was going to do. If he had, he would have explained the whole thing like the monologuing villain he was. Byrne liked to listen to himself talk, and the fact that he wasn't meant he'd been left out. He hadn't known she was planning an assassination. "Yes. I'll be there. I just want Maddie to be okay."

Byrne had no idea who he was. He didn't know about the team around him.

The woman who called herself Jane was leaving Byrne to be slaughtered.

"Be here in two hours. Not a moment sooner." The line went dead.

Deke turned to what was left of his team. "He wants me to pick her up in two hours, so that's how long he thinks the job will take. I'm supposed to go alone. He's going to have her do the work he can't and then he'll set me as the jealous boyfriend who killed her because she was cheating. Or Jane will simply kill us all and walk out with everything she wants."

"Including MaeBe." Kyle's tone had gone stark. "She'll take MaeBe with her and make her hurt until she's ready to bring me in. She won't stop until she's hurt everyone I love."

"Then we take her out first or find another solution." Deke felt ice start to flow in his veins because he was going to be ruthless when it came to getting Maddie back. "They gave us two hours. I think we can cause some chaos in two hours."

Kayla nodded. "Yeah, I think we can."

"I wonder who gets all that Byrne stock and all the tech intellectual property if Byrne dies," Deke mused.

"I assure you, Julia will make certain her group gets it all," Kyle explained. "They've likely maneuvered the situation to the point that they own some of the board members and a whole lot of stock. If Byrne dies and there's no police involvement, Julia's group could very quickly move to consolidate power. Perhaps they'll even make the timeline for the launch."

Drake sighed. "That's why she's moving now. She wants Byrne out of the way before the launch."

"Then we make sure the launch doesn't happen." A plan began to form in Deke's head, but he needed to talk to Ian before he started making things go boom. Deke pulled out his cell and made the call.

* * * *

Nolan Byrne hung up his phone and turned to the backstabbing bitch who'd lied to him. He shouldn't have found out that information from

311

one of their victims. "You killed someone at The Reef?"

Jane shrugged. "He was a loose end, and that was pretty much the only way I was going to get close to him without causing a scene. I had to kill him in the club otherwise the police would get involved, and none of us wants that. Since he died in the club in a very embarrassing position, I assume Mrs. Hunt is currently cleaning up the mess."

"Why the fuck did you need to kill a doctor?" He'd known Jane's work could get bloody, but he'd thought he had her under control.

She looked cool and competent. By the time he'd made it back to his place, she'd already changed into black pants and a black jacket, her hair in a neat bun on her head. She'd secured the prisoners—that had been a surprise, too, since their plans had only included kidnapping Madeline. He'd been informed that the plan had changed and that Jane had brought along an extra. Of course by the time he'd gotten here, Jane had also given the guards their instructions. When he'd demanded information from one of them, he'd been told to ask Jane.

She'd been the one to bring in the six burly and dangerous-looking men she'd assured him would be discreet and take care of any situation that might arise.

Now he was starting to wonder who they would be loyal to. Him or Jane.

"I have my reasons," she replied. "Is Madeline hard at work?"

Madeline was in his private office on his system. She had two hours to fully integrate the weapon with her AI. If she didn't get it done by then, he would use her boyfriend against her. He would cut Deke Murphy's fingers off one by one every fifteen minutes until she gave him a solution or he had to move on to the man's toes. "She's getting it done. Now explain why we have the extra body I'm going to have to deal with."

"MaeBe Vaughn?" Jane leaned against the sofa looking as casual as a person talking about the weather instead of kidnapping and murder.

"Yes. Why the hell would you bring her with you? Did she see something she shouldn't?" The plan had been to distract Kayla Summers-Hunt with a problem in the locker room and then sneak Madeline out the back. When Deke went to find her, Nolan would slip away.

He'd damn near had a heart attack when the alarms started going off. He'd almost gotten caught, and it was all Jane's fault.

Jane shrugged. "She saw me murder a guy, though I'm sure she couldn't tell you how I did it. MaeBe is a personal project of mine. Don't worry about her. All you have to do is ensure the weapon is functioning. My guys will handle everything else. It's imperative that the launch moves forward without a hitch."

"You don't think losing the AI expert is a hitch?" Somehow this whole thing had gone off the rails. He'd liked the idea the night before, but now all he could think about was how he was going to have to deal with the press. Jane would be long gone by then, and he would be left holding this particularly scandalous bag. "I think we should just kill them both and bury them where no one will find them."

"We have a plan, Nolan."

"No, you have a plan." He moved into her space, anger and frustration thrumming through his system. She'd put him in a terrible position. "You're manipulating me."

She didn't back down. "If I am, it's only because you need it."

He didn't think. He followed his instincts. She'd promised him a night of BDSM. Well, he was at least going to get the part where he disciplined her. He drew back his hand and slapped her right across her smug face. Her head snapped to the side, and he saw blood on her lips.

She slowly brought her head around, eyes on him. For a moment, he thought about taking a step away from her because he'd never seen that look in her eyes before, never seen such darkness in anyone's eyes. But then the moment passed, and she drew her hand over her mouth, wiping the blood away.

"I'm not trying to manipulate you, Nolan. I'm trying to deal with the situation the best way I can. You had two problem employees. I handled those situations for you, and it turned out fine. If you would like to take over, then please do so. How would you like to handle this situation? After all, you're the boss."

Now he did take a step back. It was good that she understood that none of this worked without him. "Don't you dare pull another stunt like that again. You want to kill someone, do it on your time."

She nodded. "Of course."

"I want you to tell these guards of yours that they answer to me." It was time to get things on the proper footing. "And I will be meeting the board before I give up anything else. Am I understood?"

"I'll make it happen," she promised. "But for now you should change. You don't want the police to find you in those leathers. They would ask questions you don't want to answer. I'll go check on Madeline and make sure she's got everything she needs to do the job at hand."

He didn't like how calm she was. He wanted her off-kilter, but there wasn't time to really hurt her. "You'll take the other one with you? I'm not going to keep some random girl here because you have an itch you need to scratch."

"I will absolutely take her with me," she agreed. "You don't have to worry about her at all. I'll go and talk to the guards and make sure they understand you're in charge, Nolan. I'm sorry this has been stressful for you."

Apparently slapping her around really did work for Jane. "Fix it for me and we'll be fine."

She nodded deferentially. "Of course."

She walked out, her feet not making a sound.

Nolan watched her disappear up the stairs.

She was right about changing. He didn't want to get caught in these leather pants. If he was going to deal with a scandal, he would do it in decent clothes.

And maybe he wouldn't leave everything to her. He had a gun of his own. It might be fun to see what it felt like to take that fucker's life. He'd never liked Deke.

And if Jane gave him more trouble, he'd shoot her, too.

He was the king of this castle, and it was time to let everyone know.

Chapter Fifteen

Madeline glanced over to where MaeBe was laid out on the couch. She was still and had been for a couple of hours. Had the bleeding stopped? There had been so much blood at first. The bullet had gone through her upper arm. Maddie had checked on it while they'd been in the back of the SUV that had taken them away from The Reef. MaeBe had already been out by then. Right before they'd been shoved into the car, Jane had taken a needle from her well-armed driver and shoved it into MaeBe's neck.

The driver turned out to also be an asshole guard who was standing at the door to the very office she'd meant to get into tomorrow night.

She was pretty sure the party was off.

The door came open and Jane strode in, but she'd changed out of her fet wear and into what looked like her version of tactical gear. And she had something new. The whole right side of her face was red and puffy, a bit of blood still on her cheek.

Had something gone wrong with Nolan? If there was a crack in their partnership, Maddie would try to find a way to use it.

"Uh, you okay?" The big guard's brows rose.

Jane looked up at him, one shoulder shrugging. "Cost of doing business sometimes. At least I never had to sleep with the fucker."

"You want me to deal with him?" the guard asked in a way that made Maddie wonder how close they were.

Jane sighed. "John, don't act like I need protection. If I was ready to deal with him, he would be dealt with. But I need him to verify our friend's work." The woman's focus shifted, gaze finding Maddie. "How is it coming, Madeline?"

Maddie sat back. She had to stay calm. As calm as she could when she was in the room with a couple of killers. "I think I understand where he went wrong. I can fix it but I'm going to need some time, and in order to test it, I'll need to be in my lab."

What she needed was to give Deke as much time as possible.

Jane glanced down at her watch. "Well, what you have is about forty minutes, and no one's taking you to the office, honey."

"I can't do it." She wasn't sure how to prove the integration was complete without going to the lab.

Jane nodded as though it was no big deal, but that gun was suddenly in her hand again and she stood over MaeBe's body, the threat made clear.

"Wait!" Damn it. She couldn't watch MaeBe die knowing she could have stopped it. "I'm almost done. Okay? I'm almost done. He was being sloppy. That's why it wasn't working. I've had to recode some of Clarke's base, but I can make it work."

Jane stared down at MaeBe, her lips curling up slightly. "She's awake, you know. She's surprisingly good."

MaeBe didn't move a muscle.

"Are you lying there trying to figure a way out, honey?" Jane asked. "Because there isn't one. There hasn't been for you since the moment you got involved with Kyle Hawthorne." Jane put the barrel against MaeBe's head. "He's the problem, you know. Not really you. He's the one who kills everything he touches. It's odd that I feel some sympathy for you. I didn't expect that. It might be kinder of me to end you here and now."

Maddie stood. "Then I won't fix anything for you. You kill her and I won't do another thing to solve this problem."

Jane's eyes rolled and she started to back away. "So much drama."

That was the moment MaeBe's eyes came open and she reached up, gripping Jane's wrist.

Maddie's heart rate tripled as she watched MaeBe bend Jane's hand, the gun coming out of it and hitting the ground.

Jane flattened the palm of her free hand and brought it down on MaeBe's arm, the cracking sound sickening to Maddie's ears.

MaeBe gasped and fell back, her arm bent at an impossible angle.

Jane calmly picked up the gun and holstered it. "Don't try that with me, honey. I know Taggart trains you all, but not the way I was trained. Trust me. Taggart is a preschool teacher compared to my handlers. And I bet Kyle protects you so you don't ever have to fight for your life. That's your fault. Don't ever expect a man to protect you. When he says he will, he's lying, and what he really wants is for you to be weaker than him." She looked back at John. "Now we have to fix her fucking arm. You remember any of your medic training?"

"She's a long-term project then?" John asked.

"As long as I can keep her. She's going to be fun to play with," Jane replied. "And she's also how I'll control Kyle and Drake when I need to. Madeline, do your job and I'll give you a shot at getting out of this alive."

Deke was her best shot at both of them getting out of this alive, but now she worried. "You know he works for Ian Taggart. You know who Kyle is."

"Of course, I do, but Nolan has no clue and that's the way I like it. I'm playing chess and everyone else is playing checkers," Jane announced. "Except for Nolan. He's not smart enough to even play the game. He actually thinks he's in charge. He slapped me. Like full-on, telenovela, girl-fight slap. I hope Deke kills him slow."

She expected Deke to kill him? "I thought you were working with him."

"I was and now I'm not. That's what I meant by giving you a fighting chance," Jane explained. "I'm not unfair. I like a love story just as much as the next person. But you're not going to get it if you don't finish that integration."

"But if I live, I can tell people about you." She wasn't following Jane's logic, and that meant Jane was probably lying. She wasn't about to give up the work if this woman was going to kill her anyway.

"And no one will believe you because I don't exist. You can talk all you like but no one will listen. Everything you'll say will sound like a conspiracy," Jane continued. "You'll tell them I walked out of here with a dangerous weapon, but you're not absolutely sure what it does or how I'll use it."

"You're going to use it to assassinate heads of state while they're flying." The longer she kept Jane talking, the longer she gave Deke.

"Well, no one said she was a dummy," the guard said under his breath.

Jane simply sighed. "It can be used for many things, especially once I take the schematics for the satellite. If you wouldn't mind downloading those, I would appreciate it. Believe it or not, I haven't been able to get on that system until tonight."

"Sure, I'll get right on that," Maddie replied.

Jane moved to stand in front of her, a frown on her face. "I'm not joking, Madeline. Do this for me and I'll pull my guards out. Deke can walk in here and take all his frustrations out on Nolan. I never meant for the weapon to go on this satellite. I simply needed the integration to work. I'll be taking all of it back to my bosses and then if you really want, you can tell the world and we'll start another game, you and I."

Well, that felt like a threat. It might be time to stop asking questions and play along. All that mattered at this point was ensuring Deke had his best shot at saving her. "I'll have it done soon."

"You know what you're doing?" the guard asked, the question

319

directed at Jane.

"Calculating risk is part of this job," Jane replied as she backed away, moving toward MaeBe. "And for what I'm doing next, it's necessary to clean up old messes."

Maddie's gut twisted. She looked back down at the laptop and started working on the problem. She hadn't lied about what the issues were. She could see where Justin had tried. He hadn't understood how to connect the systems, probably hadn't even understood what he'd been trying to do, and he'd died for asking questions. Pam had died for this, too. She had to make sure she and MaeBe weren't the next to go.

"You have to admit, though, the guy has a nice view." Jane stood in front of the floor-to-ceiling windows. This high in the canyon, a person could look out over the grounds of the estate all the way to the ocean. The grounds were meticulously kept, with trees on either side offering an unobstructed view if one stood in the right place. "This house was designed to be as luxurious as possible. Nolan made sure he had excellent views, but there are other features. Did you know he has an eleven-car garage on the other side of the property?"

Maddie wasn't sure if the woman was talking to her or the guard. "Yes. He brags about it often."

"I'm sure you haven't gotten the full tour I have. The man has a couple of secrets he likes to keep." Jane looked back at the guard. "He's got a Maserati in the garage. One that's not for sale. We should try it sometime."

The guard nodded. "Yes, that sounds like fun."

Jane moved away from the window and looked down at MaeBe. "I feel sorry for you. He doesn't love you, you know. I'm afraid he's with you because you're not me. You're pretty much the opposite of me, and that's what attracted him to you. You're a reaction, not an actual relationship. Kyle needs a strong woman, one who can set him on his ass from time to time, and that's just not you. I would bet you don't even know the real Kyle Hawthorne."

"I know him better than you," MaeBe managed to reply, tears

streaming down her face.

"Did he talk about me, then?" Jane asked.

"I know he thinks he killed you, Julia. I know you were the biggest mistake of his life," MaeBe said between gritted teeth. She cradled her broken arm as she tried to sit up.

"The biggest mistake he made was thinking he really could kill me." Jane, who turned out to be Julia, stepped back, watching MaeBe. "I don't think he tried his hardest. Believe me, that man knows how to kill, and he's excellent at it. If he truly wanted me dead, I would be. He's had time to think about it, and I'll give him a little more. I've been playing with him for a while now. His whole family, actually, but it's time to stop playing. I'm ready to deal with our problems. A love like ours isn't something you simply walk away from."

The door slammed open and Nolan strode in, a wild look on his face and a pistol in his hand. "There's a fire at the building where the satellite is being built."

Jane/Julia turned his way. "A fire?"

"Yes." Nolan ran a hand across his head. "Someone fucking firebombed my satellite five weeks from fucking launch. This is a disaster. You have to do something."

Julia shrugged. "What do you want me to do? Go grab a firehose? Is it salvageable?"

"I have no fucking idea," Nolan shot back. "But the fucking police want to talk to me. They want me to come down to the site."

Julia's eyes closed. "Fuck him."

"You know who did this?" Nolan asked.

Julia ignored him, looking her guard's way. "Where's her cell?"

The guard pulled it out of his pocket, tossing it Julia's way. Julia turned the front toward MaeBe's face and unlocked it, quickly looking through the screens to find what she wanted.

Nolan had moved in behind Maddie, his hand gripping her neck and squeezing to the point of pain. "I want that integration done now, Madeline. You think you can stop this from happening, but I'll just rebuild. You can't stop me."

"I wasn't trying to," she hissed, attempting to pull away.

"She can't work if you strangle her," Julia said, putting the phone to her ear. "Hello, lover. You've been busy. If you want to see this pathetic attempt to make me jealous again, you'll back off. Tell me something, is little brother with you?"

Nolan's hand had come off Maddie's neck. He stared down at the computer screen. "Yes. That's it. That's exactly what I need."

He put the gun to Maddie's head, and she nearly stopped breathing.

She wanted Deke. In this moment, her thought was of him, of the life they could have had, of the one they could have if she just survived. The past didn't matter in that moment when everything else was stripped away and she was left with the raw truth. She loved him. She loved him with every cell of her being.

It was all that mattered. Not her job. Not her work. If she lost all her progress, she could start again. She wouldn't ever get another Deke. There was only one of him, and she was never giving him up.

Julia dropped the phone and pulled her own gun. "John, try to get the other guards on the line."

Maddie noticed a red light. It pointed straight at Julia.

That was the moment the glass shattered and the whole world seemed to explode.

* * * *

"Do you have the security cameras?" Deke touched the earpiece he was using to communicate with the CIA operative. Drake wasn't actually nearby. He had his own job to do, but he could handle Byrne's security cameras remotely.

Deke stood in the midst of a bunch of tall bushes that offered concealment from prying eyes. He was sure Byrne thought of them as some sort of added security, but they worked against him tonight, the same way all the trees were going to.

"I'm shutting them down now," Drake said over the line. "You won't have long before Byrne gets them back up, though he might be distracted. He should be getting the news about his precious satellite right about now."

"The plan went off?" They'd decided to attack Byrne on two fronts, making damn sure that even if everything went to hell tonight, they would set Byrne back for months. He couldn't launch a satellite he didn't have.

"Kayla hasn't lost a step. She got us in and blew the thing all to hell without even breaking a sweat," Drake replied. "So now it's all on you guys. Does Boomer have a perch?"

"Yes, he's got a clear line of sight into Byrne's office. MaeBe and Maddie are both still alive," Deke explained. He nodded Kyle's way.

Kyle was wearing all black. Even the backpack he carried was black and contained two of the cakes of C-4 Deke had hoped he wouldn't have to use. But he was always prepared.

"All right. I'm coming your way," Drake said. "You know what to do if she gets away?"

Deke's gut tightened because he didn't like this part of the plan. He actively hated it, but no one could make Kyle change his mind. Not even Ian, who was likely already in the air.

He wished Ian was here, watching his back, taking some of the burden of what was about to happen.

All that mattered was Maddie was alive at the end of the night.

"I know what to do," Deke promised. "We're a go. Get here as soon as you can. Someone's going to have to deal with the authorities."

"I'm already on it. And I'll make sure everything goes smoothly. I've got a line on what we need," Drake said before the line went dead.

Deke looked to Kyle. "Boomer's on the west side. You ready?"

"I am." Kyle's whole body was tight. "I know where to plant the explosives so we don't risk starting a fire in the canyon."

Byrne's personal grounds wouldn't burn the way the natural

brush around them might. He was a selfish shit who kept everything green while a drought was going on. Deke had been an expert in explosives during his time in the military. He knew how to blow some shit up. There wasn't a wind this evening. The charges would be set inside the house and were calculated to bring the place down, not explode outward. Deke would rather be the one to do the setup, but he had to concentrate on Maddie.

Besides, bringing the house down was Kyle's drama, not his, though it might provide enough shock and awe that he could get Maddie and MaeBe out.

Deke had to switch to his cell, calling Boomer since his favorite sniper didn't have an earpiece. He quickly connected the cell line to his comms application, forwarding the audio into Deke's earpiece. He would be able to stay in touch with Boomer and still have his hands free.

"Yes." Boomer's hushed voice came over the line.

"We're on the ground. Do you still have eyes on the women?"

"Yeah, and we need to do something soon. I didn't see what that woman did to MaeBe, but she's hurt bad," Boomer said. "Can I take the shot?"

"Tell him if he's got a shot at Julia to take it," Kyle insisted.

He was so fucking glad Kyle couldn't hear Boomer's part of the conversation. He'd likely go mad at the thought of MaeBe being injured.

"Only if she's alone and there's no one else who can possibly hurt the women." He wasn't taking chances until he had to. "How many guards do we have to deal with?"

"Six," Boomer replied. "You've got two on the front door, two on the back, one is in the room with the women, and the other is circling. He should be coming near your position in less than two minutes. I do not have eyes on Byrne."

"I'll handle Byrne. Stay on the line and I'll update you as we move through the house." He nodded Kyle's way and pulled his Smith & Wesson. He'd attached the suppressors to his and Kyle's weapons while making their way here. Quiet was his friend at this point.

And so was time. He still had thirty minutes before Byrne's deadline. If Kyle was right and Julia hadn't told Byrne who he really was, Byrne would be expecting him to show up like the good boy he was supposed to be.

"We've got incoming," Kyle said.

Deke nodded and stepped out from the bushes, lifting the gun and firing. One to the throat and the man went down without a sound. Kyle stepped out behind him.

"You take the front and I'll take the back," Kyle said, settling the backpack over his shoulder.

Deke nodded. "Don't take chances."

"Get MaeBe out." In the moonlight Kyle's eyes seemed darker than usual. He pulled up the bottom of the balaclava he wore, concealing his face, with the exception of his eyes. "I'll handle the rest. And, Deke, tell her…fuck. Don't tell her anything at all. Just help her move on."

"Or you could have a little faith." Deke knew Kyle wouldn't listen, but he had to try.

"All my faith died when Julia came back to life. She's my personal hell, and I have to deal with her," Kyle said. "Remember your promise, brother. See you on the other side."

But he wouldn't. Not if this stupid plan of his worked out, and Deke would be left with a secret he couldn't share with anyone.

Deke shoved aside all those dark thoughts.

"Byrne's in the room with the women now," Boomer said over the connection. "He's armed, but I would bet he doesn't know how to use it. I've got Kyle's ex and a guard in the same room."

"I'm about to come in the main door." Deke flattened his back against the side of the house, inching toward the front. He would have seconds to take out the guards before they started firing, and then all hell would break loose. He needed hell to stay fully intact for another few minutes. Then chaos would be his friend.

He stepped out as one of the guards turned his back. He fired quickly, taking out the first and getting the second as he turned again, felling the man before he could even pull his gun.

It had been a while since he'd killed a man, but he hadn't forgotten how to do it.

Deke eased into the house. Kyle would handle the two on the back door and then get his own work done.

The stairs were to his left and would take him to the private office where Maddie was being kept. He took a deep breath. He'd fixed the charges so Kyle would have very little to do beyond place them and then blow everything to shit when the time came, but he needed a minute or two to place them properly.

It would be the longest fucking minute of Deke's life.

He stood outside the door, his heart pounding in his chest. She was right there. He saw the scene play out in his head.

"Deke, when you come through the door, Byrne will be right in front of you. He's standing over Maddie, who's sitting down. You'll have a clear head shot," Boomer explained, his calm tone coming over the line. "The guard will be to your right. He's got a pistol in his hand. Kyle's ex is standing in front of the window. Her weapon is holstered, but she'll be able to get it out very quickly. I'm worried about her shooting MaeBe."

"Take her out first." He whispered the command.

"Kyle's done," Boomer said. "He texted me he's ready. I'm lining up my shot."

"John, try to get the other guards on the line." The shouted command had come from inside the office, almost certainly from the woman formerly known as Julia.

It was go time.

"Take the shot, Boomer."

He kicked in the door as he heard glass shatter.

Time seemed to slow as he took in the scene before him. Byrne was exactly where Boomer had said he would be, his eyes wide with shock. Maddie sat behind the desk, Byrne standing over her.

Then Byrne wasn't standing at all because Deke put a bullet between his eyes.

The guard who should have been to his right had obviously moved when Boomer had taken his shot. He'd pulled Julia out from Boomer's line of sight. Julia was leaning on the man, a bullet wound in her left shoulder. She'd managed to evade a heart shot, but Deke would bet it hurt like fuck.

Unfortunately, they were at an impasse.

The guard had his weapon pointed straight at Deke while Julia had hers pointed at MaeBe's head. The former CIA agent might have been shot, but she held the gun steady, and there was no doubt in Deke's mind she could still pull the trigger. She straightened up and stood on her own.

MaeBe was on the floor. Her skin was covered in blood and her arm was obviously broken, but she sat patiently.

"Madeline, I'll take that computer now," Julia ordered between gritted teeth. "Or I'll put a bullet in her head."

"I'm bringing it." Maddie was on her feet, pulling the laptop up with her.

"There's nowhere to go, Julia." Deke didn't move an inch as Maddie started to make her way across the office. "My backup will be here any minute. Let MaeBe go and we'll talk about taking you in."

He was lying. If Kyle came up here, he would shoot the woman in front of him in a heartbeat. Especially if he saw how fucked up MaeBe was.

"I'll worry about that," Julia replied.

"Just kill her, Deke," MaeBe said. "She'll do anything to hurt Kyle. Take her out."

Maddie had made her way across the big office and handed the laptop to Julia.

Any minute Boomer would be up here, and it would be two on two. He liked those odds. The minute he realized Julia and her guard wouldn't be stupid enough to get in front of the window again, he would come running.

"Maddie, get behind me," Deke ordered.

"I can't leave MaeBe," Maddie said, her voice shaking.

"Deke, Byrne has a panic room. The door is right behind me." Despite the bullet in her shoulder, Julia's voice was steady as a rock. "John and I are going to get in it and then you can call anyone you would like."

If she was right, they would be trapped. They wouldn't have to go through with Kyle's insane plan. "Move slowly. I swear I think for a second you're going to pull that trigger, I'll take you out myself."

Julia nodded and started to back up. "MaeBe, you need to think about the fact that you're willing to give your life for a man who doesn't even care enough about you to show up. Deke's here but Kyle is far more concerned with pulling some shady shit to get me than he is about taking care of you. Grow a backbone, sister, because we're not done yet."

She put her palm against the wood of the wall and a panel opened, showing him a hint of the panic room inside.

Except it wasn't a fucking panic room. It was an elevator.

"Stop right there," he shouted and then pain flared through him because the guard had taken a shot as he'd closed the door behind them.

"Deke!" Maddie ran across the room as it registered what had happened.

He'd taken a bullet and Julia was getting away.

He touched his earpiece. "Kyle, we're moving out right fucking now. Julia is in an elevator that wasn't in the schematics Drake sent. It likely goes to a basement. I don't know. If you're going to blow this place, give us one minute and then do it."

Boomer rushed in, checking around the room for threats. "She moved at the last minute. I had her. Where did she go?"

"Byrne had a secret elevator. She and that guard of hers went down it." His left arm was going blissfully numb. "Kyle's going to blow the place. We have to get out of here. Carry Mae out."

"What the hell did she do to you?" Boomer easily lifted MaeBe into his arms. "I'm sorry, honey. This is going to hurt, but we have to move."

Boomer jogged out with Mae.

Maddie ran back to the desk.

"We have to move," Deke commanded.

Maddie pulled a small metal box from under the desk, holding it up triumphantly. "She doesn't have shit. I erased everything I'd done the minute you shot Byrne. I probably got rid of most of my own work. There's a backup hard drive that we now have, but there's nothing on that laptop."

She'd always been the smartest person he knew. "Baby, you just saved the day. Let's go."

She nodded and ran back.

"Kyle, she's got nothing," Deke explained. "Stand down. We'll get her later."

"You've got forty-five seconds, Deke. I already set the timer."

"Then unset it. We don't have to do this. You don't have to do this," Deke pleaded.

"I do." Kyle's voice sounded hard over the line. "I have to do it. She's going to get away. You think she's trapped but she's not. She always wins. I have to stop her. I'm sorry, Deke. It's done."

Fuck. "We have to go, Maddie. We have to run. This whole place is about to explode."

"What?" Maddie hustled to his side.

He took her hand and ran for the stairs. "We have to get away from the house. We're going for the trees. When we get out, you jump for cover, understood? Boomer will take care of Mae. If I fall, you keep running."

"I'm not leaving you."

He stumbled on the stairs, but Maddie held him up. He forced himself to move, feet pounding on Byrne's hardwood floors and then the marbled entryway. The door was open, the bodies of the guards he'd killed still lying on the gorgeous porch.

He ignored them, the only thought in his head, getting as far away as possible.

"Where's Kyle?" MaeBe was shouting. "He can't go after her."

Boomer kept moving.

"Where's Kyle?" Maddie asked.

Deke simply ran, holding her hand.

He was still holding it when the world exploded around them.

Chapter Sixteen

"You know I'm usually the one who gets hit on the head," Boomer remarked, sitting back in the chair that Maddie had slept in the night before. She'd been with Deke through everything, holding his hand when the ambulance had come, sitting by his bed after surgery had fixed the bullet wound in his shoulder, calling his parents to let them know what had happened.

They'd barely escaped that blast, and she wasn't taking anything for granted.

She wouldn't leave him. Not ever again. Especially since she'd thought he was dead. It had been a terrible moment and it passed the second he'd opened his eyes, but she was still way too close to it.

"Well, you were faster than him this time, buddy." Ian Taggart was a massive presence in the small room. "And you were carrying a girl. You get the best rescuer trophy at this year's awards."

Big Tag had shown up a few hours after Deke had come out of surgery and immediately gone to work. He'd had a lot of cleanup to do. She'd been in the middle of an interview with the police right outside this hospital room when Ian had shown up with Drake in tow.

The interview had stopped and ten minutes later the police had walked out with nothing more than a *thank you for your time, ma'am.*

She wasn't sure what sort of magic they'd worked, but even the news was now reporting the incidents as Nolan Byrne's final fuck you to the world.

And amidst all of it, Taggart had been forced to identify his nephew's body.

She squeezed Deke's hand and blinked back a tear. She hadn't known Kyle well, but finding out he'd still been in the house when it exploded had rocked her world. She could still remember how MaeBe had gone quiet as though she hadn't cared about anything else that happened around her. MaeBe was in the room across the hall, recuperating from her own surgery. Maddie had tried to help the other woman out, but Mae just stared at the window, not saying a word.

"I should have been faster," Deke said. "Hell, if I'd been faster, I would have caught that door before it closed. I thought it was a panic room. I thought she would be locked in and we could deal with her when Drake got there. I thought we had her cornered."

"Well, what we've figured out is that the elevator she used went down to an underground tunnel that led to Byrne's garage. The douchebag had eleven different cars," Ian explained. "Although now he's down to ten, or rather his estate is."

"So she's in the wind." Deke sighed, a weary sound. "And it was all for nothing."

"Well, I have to hope that Kyle's death means this Julia Ennis person will ease up on Mae," Ian replied. "She won't have any reason to come after her. From where they found his body, I think he was trying to find the elevator so he could follow her. He wanted to kill her, and it cost him his life."

"He's not dead," a hollow voice said.

"Mae, you should be in bed." Ian Taggart crossed to the open door, a deep frown on his face.

"You all think I'm a moron, but I know what he's doing. Whose body did you use? One of the guards? There were a bunch of them, but no one's mentioned a single one on the news. The only dead bodies they mentioned were Nolan Byrne and Kyle. I thought that was interesting, don't you?" Mae was pale, her vibrant hair pulled back. Her right arm was in a cast, and without makeup or jewelry, she looked so young and vulnerable.

Maddie didn't understand any of it. "I saw a lot of dead bodies as we were running out of there. I assumed Deke and Boomer killed them. How would the press not know about them? I assume the police worked the scene."

"They worked the scene until the CIA took over," MaeBe countered. "We all know that. Let's not pretend that every piece of information isn't coming straight out of Drake Radcliffe's mouth."

"But how could they just lie?" Maddie asked, knowing the question sounded incredibly naïve.

"There are things that they do to protect the public," Deke began. "If it got out that there's a rogue group working and it's made up of corporations who don't mind killing each other, the conspiracy theories would never end. Drake needs to be able to work in the shadows. If he can't, everything he knows up until this point changes and he has to start over again. Everything Kyle worked for. Years of investigation and making contacts that he's going to use to take the organization down would be lost because the minute the light turns on, the rats will run."

Yeah, she still wasn't sure she got it, but some things were above her paygrade.

"I'm sure Julia won't mention it to anyone," Mae said under her breath.

"A fuck-up like this?" Deke straightened up, his back against the pillow. "If she does admit that she showed herself to Kyle and Drake, they'll kill her. She'll keep her mouth shut because what we have is mutually assured destruction. Right now, they think Byrne's the one who went insane. If they know what she did, they'll decide she's not worth the trouble and they'll cut her."

"She won't talk," Boomer said. "I don't like the dirty stuff, but

Drake and Ian are doing the only thing they can."

"By pretending Kyle's dead?" MaeBe asked, some of her fire back.

There was a little hitch to Deke's breath that made Maddie wonder.

"Mae, would I lie to you?" Ian asked, sounding infinitely weary.

"Yes. You would lie to anyone if you thought it was for the good. This is not for the good, Ian." Mae walked into the room, her feet in hospital slippers and a robe around her body. Maddie had brought her the robe. The cast on her arm peeked out of the too-long sleeves.

"I know you've been through a lot," Ian began.

"Show me the body," MaeBe countered, her chin tilting up stubbornly. "Is it in the morgue downstairs?"

Ian's jaw went tight. "You know I'm not going to show you the body. I assure you I can identify my own nephew. I'm not going to make the woman he loved do it any more than I would put Sean through that trauma."

"Don't say that. He didn't love me. He left me behind. He lied to me and forced all of you to lie to me, too, and I won't ever forgive him for it." MaeBe's head turned up, locking eyes with her boss. "She *will* come after me. She won't be fooled by this insane ruse of his. All he's doing is leaving me completely vulnerable to her. But then she's the important one, isn't she? That's been made plain to me."

"Mae, you need to rest." Ian's tone was patient. "And you need to accept that Kyle is gone and he's not coming back."

"Oh, I accept that he's gone," MaeBe replied. "I one hundred percent accept that he's not coming back. He's going to follow her."

Was it possible Kyle was alive? She glanced down at Deke who watched MaeBe, his eyes haunted.

If Kyle was alive, he would need everyone to believe he wasn't. He would have put that on Deke. But now that she thought about it, Deke had been trying to talk Kyle out of doing something in those final moments before the world had exploded.

"I quit, by the way," MaeBe said quietly. "I already sent Hutch my resignation letter."

"Oh, you should have done that after you got a ride home." Ian's voice had gone cold. "You going to hoof it back to Dallas?"

"Yeah, well, maybe Dallas shouldn't be my home," MaeBe replied.

"Come on, Mae. You can't leave." Boomer stood up, his expression turning worried. "You have a family in Dallas."

"I don't have a family," Mae replied tightly, her head shaking. "I have coworkers. I had a guy I liked who it turns out I didn't even know. My blood family doesn't want to have anything to do with me, so I have no family."

"Don't say that." Boomer moved into her space, reaching for her hand. "Because if you don't have a family, then neither do I, and I can't stand the thought of that. Blood doesn't have to make a family. God, I hope not. All I have in this world is you guys. Don't make it less than it is because you're mad. Losing Kyle is going to devastate all of us. We can't lose you, too."

"We didn't lose him. He left us," MaeBe insisted.

"Whatever you believe, we lost him," Boomer said, a hitch in the big guy's voice.

"She's not going anywhere," Ian announced, his shoulders squaring. "I mean it, Mae. I'm not about to let you go out into the world alone. You can hate me all you like, but I'll lock you in a fucking room if I have to. If that psycho is going to come after you, she'll have to get through me."

"She'll have to get through all of us," Boomer agreed.

MaeBe took a step back and shook her head. "No. I'm not going to be the girl who hopes someone stronger protects me. If I come home, I want training. Real training, Ian. Not the little bit of self-defense you give non-operatives. I come back and you make me a badass."

"Done. I'll have a training schedule for you Monday morning. We can work around the cast. You want to be a badass, you learn to work through the pain," Ian announced. "You'll train with me and

335

Erin on weapons and self-defense, and you'll join the bodyguards in their daily workouts. You'll do everything they do, and you'll be accountable for the same goals they are."

MaeBe nodded, her eyes shining with unshed tears. "Then I'll come home."

Boomer put a hand on her shoulder. "Come on. I'll take you back to your room. There's a nurse who's sweet on me. I can get us pudding or Jell-O. Anything you want."

They walked out and Ian's head fell forward on a low groan. "I hate everything and everybody."

"I'm sorry," Deke said.

Ian sighed, a long-suffering sound. "You have nothing to be sorry about. Kyle made his decisions, and we have to live with them. You did what you needed to do, and Madeline made sure The Consortium didn't get the intel they needed. You should know the Agency is working to clean everything up. There shouldn't be any blowback. They're saying it was a gas leak. Kyle had recently applied to work security for the company, but Byrne hired him as a private bodyguard. Both he and Byrne were killed in the accident."

The CIA guy had worked very quickly. "And they're saying Byrne sabotaged his own satellite?"

"It didn't work, and he couldn't make it work. The story is he lied to his employees and his board members," Ian said with a shake of his head. "Yeah, the conspiracy theories are already swirling, but the Agency is going to keep a lid on this because they believe Madeline. It looks like that weapon was going to be used on high-value targets while in the air. Some things are more important to the Agency than investments, and that's power."

"Well, my investment portfolio is currently taking a major hit." She didn't want to think about how much money she'd lost. "But the good news is my boyfriend has an excellent job, and I hear Texas is cheaper than California."

"Maddie, no," Deke said, bringing her hand to his chest. "I go where you go. Ian, I'm so sorry, but I'm going to have to…"

She wasn't going to let that happen. "He's going to go home and go back to work because like Boomer said, his family needs him. Though we would like a little time off. We need to go to see his parents or they will swoop in on us, and his condo isn't big enough for that."

Deke stared up at her. "Maddie, I will not…"

She stared right back at him, hoping that the look she gave him had her full will in it. "What? You will not what, Deke?"

"Uh, he will not make the same mistake again?" Ian offered. "He will not prove he learned nothing."

"Fuck." Deke brought her hand up to his lips. "I need you to know, I will be there for you. I will sacrifice anything but you. I love you, Maddie. You're my life now, and I won't make a decision for you. If you want to come with me, I'm happy, but if your career takes you somewhere else, I'll go with you."

Ian nodded. "Then something good came from this. The doctors said you could go home in a couple of days. Head to your parents and heal a little more. Let me know when you're ready to come back to Dallas and I'll send the plane for you. I'll be taking MaeBe and Boomer home with me. She doesn't know it yet, but she's going to have a bodyguard twenty-four seven. MaeBe has a point about Julia still wanting to hurt her. If MaeBe doesn't believe Kyle is truly dead, who knows if Julia will. My nephew played some deep games, and Drake has a lot to answer for."

"You didn't know he worked for Drake?" Deke asked.

"I've known for a while, but Kyle asked me to stay out of it. I only know what Kyle's been willing to tell me so far. I know he was involved with a woman named Julia Ennis since her mother actually hired Adam's company to look for her last year. She's officially missing, and from what I can tell the mom knows nothing about her involvement with the CIA. I'm glad I can tell Adam why he couldn't use his software to ID her. She has a new face." Ian had his hand on the door. "Now I have to go and talk to my brother and… Well, it's a conversation I never dreamed I'd have to have with him. Get better soon, Deke. We need you at home. And Madeline, I think you'll find you can choose again."

He walked out, the door closing behind him.

"What does that mean?" Maddie had many choices she would make again, starting with being way more stubborn back in her teen years.

"No idea, but Ian works in mysterious ways." Deke squeezed her hand. "I meant what I said. Anywhere you go, I go, too. From now on we make those decisions together. And that means I should tell you something."

She shook her head because she thought she knew what he was about to confess, and she didn't need it. "Unless it directly affects you and me, you keep your secrets. Things you promised to your friends, it's okay to keep those. I trust you."

He tugged on her hand, bringing her close. "Thank you."

"Always." She kissed him and rested her forehead against his.

They were together, and they would get through anything.

* * * *

"Sylvester, stop climbing on the dog. He's not a horse," Deke's mother yelled from the back porch.

Deke chuckled because that dog was pretty much as big as a horse and way more patient than any he'd known. Sylvester, though, took a step back from the gigantic mutt and started looking around for his next adventure.

Deke's next adventure began tonight.

"How you holding up, son?" His father stepped up beside him. "You ready for tonight?"

Tonight, he was going to ask the love of his life to become his wife. Tonight, their future began.

He just wished his friends were here to see it. He'd made the decision to ask Maddie to marry him here in Calhoun where their journey had begun for sentimental and practical reasons. He wanted to be surrounded by his sisters and nieces and nephews, but he would miss the family he'd made in Dallas.

But they were in mourning.

"I am. I know it seems too soon," he began.

His father shook his head. "Absolutely not. You're years behind. It's time to catch up with your sisters."

"Don't expect more grandchildren any time soon." Not that he and Maddie weren't already talking about starting a family.

He glanced out over the big backyard where both their families were gathered. Maddie stood by the oak tree they used to sit under on hot summer days and drink his mom's lemonade and make out when no one was looking.

"Take your time, but not too long," his dad said with a chuckle. "Your mom's making a cake. I figure it's a celebration cake if Maddie says yes, and if she doesn't, you can drown your sorrows in it."

Maddie's head turned slightly. She caught him staring at her, and she gave him the most brilliant smile.

Deke winked her way. "She'll say yes."

"I suspect she will," his dad agreed. "How's your shoulder doing?"

The spot where he'd been hit by the guard's bullet had healed nicely over the last few weeks. He'd been in the hospital for a couple of days and then back at Maddie's before coming up here to spend time with the family. In two days Big Tag was sending that airplane for him, and he would go home.

"It's good. I'm ready to get back to work." He was ready to show Maddie all around Dallas, and they would start looking for a new place while she began her job hunt. Byrne Corp was in legal shambles, but she'd managed to get much of her work out. She would have to start over, but not from scratch.

He rather thought she was looking forward to the challenge.

"I was real sorry to hear about your friends." His father's expression turned solemn.

"Me, too, but we'll make it through." They would. They would huddle close and mourn their losses and when the inevitable happened, they would get through that, too.

"Is his girlfriend doing all right?" his father asked. "You said something about her getting out of the hospital, too."

MaeBe had been shot and her arm broken, but it was her heart he was worried about. Big Tag wasn't letting her stay at her own place. She was currently holed up at Hutch and Noelle's condo, but he was planning to move her around while he assessed the danger.

"She's healing, but it's going to take a while for her to get over what happened here." He hated his involvement in breaking MaeBe's heart. Especially when he'd gotten his heart's desire back in his arms.

"Of course it will." His dad stepped back. "You're a good man, son, and you're going to make a wonderful husband. I'm going to make sure the champagne is chilling properly because the truth is we both know there's going to be a celebration tonight." His dad pointed to his left. "Ruthie, do not throw that at your sister."

And his dad was off, trying to hold back the chaos every family gathering brought.

"Deke, I think I know what your boss meant." Maddie walked up the porch steps, her cell phone in hand and her eyes wide.

He reached for her free hand, taking it in his and threading their fingers together. "What happened?"

She held up her phone. "I have a meeting with Drew Lawless. He was the other big offer. I took Byrne's because of the stock, but Mr. Lawless is certain we can come to terms with that this time around. Apparently he's got some kind of think tank going and he wants me to join. And it's in Dallas, not Austin. How crazy is that?"

It wasn't crazy at all. Ian Taggart was at work doing what he could to make his friends' lives better in his quiet way. "One of Tag's brothers is married to Lawless's sister. I'm sure he mentioned you could use a new gig. But you don't take a job until you're ready. You don't have to take one because it's in Dallas."

She went on her toes and kissed him. "I know, but I think this one is going to work out. I've got a good feeling about it. So if you want

340

to…you know…ask me anything, I'll probably say yes." She winked his way. "Or maybe not. I don't know. Sylvester told me he thought I was pretty. I might want to go younger."

She made him smile. "Don't you even think about it." He tugged on her hand. "I think I need to show you what I can bring to this relationship."

He drew her close and kissed her, ready to begin the evening early.

* * * *

Drake Radcliffe turned into the gravel parking lot, the neon light of the bar illuminating the pitch black all around. It got incredibly dark here in Wyoming.

"I just want to make sure you're back in DC in time for the party." His mother's voice came over the speakers of his rented SUV. "Your father is only going to turn seventy once, you know."

"I promise I'll be there. This trip I'm on right now won't take long," he replied, putting the SUV in park in the second row of the makeshift lot. There were no neatly marked off rows to show the patrons where to park, so it was a bit haphazard, and that played hell on his desperate need for organization. He parked away from the other vehicles, in a place where a person would have to be drunk to hit him.

Of course he was in front of a bar, so there was that.

"They're working you too hard." There was a motherly *tsk* to her tone. "I don't understand why an analyst has to travel so much. If I'd known how much time you would spend away from home, I never would have let you take that Defense Department job."

On paper, Drake Radcliffe worked for the Department of Defense as a midlevel analyst. Of course he wouldn't travel so much, but his mother didn't know that despite the fact that she'd worked for the government for most of her adult life, first as a young congresswoman and later serving in the Senate.

341

Yet the woman still didn't know that two of her children had been CIA operatives.

"All right, sweetheart. I'll let you go. I don't suppose there's been any news," she said without much hope in her voice.

Oh, there was so much fucking news, but none he would tell his mother. "No. I'm sorry."

A sniffle came over the line. "I know she's gone, but not having a body…well, it's killing me. I had such high hopes when I hired that firm."

Miles-Dean, Weston, and Murdoch hadn't been able to find anything because the Agency had cleaned the world that day.

Julia Ennis was missing, and it was presumed she'd been killed. At the time, he'd thought Julia's death was the worst secret he would have to keep from his mother.

If only that had been true.

"Well, I'll see you when you get home. I love you, honey," his mom said.

"Love you, too." He was a thirty-one-year-old man, and keeping secrets was his life.

So was lying. He lied to everyone, especially his family.

The line went dead, and Drake eased out of the SUV and made his way across the lot, gravel crunching beneath his feet. The whole place was practically rocking, thudding with raucous country music being played inside. He pushed through the doors and realized exactly how out of place he was.

Every person in the building had on boots and jeans and hats. Including the proprietor, who looked up from her seat at the bar and flashed him a smile that damn near made his heart melt.

Sandra Croft.

She could be his grandmother but once she'd been his lover. His first lover, and there was still such a soft spot in his heart for her. One of the only soft spots he had left.

"Drake." She approached him with open arms.

He hugged her tight. "How are you? I heard the wedding was

342

lovely. I'm sorry I missed it."

She grinned up at him. "Never thought I would get hitched again, but she's my soul mate. I'll show you some pictures when we have a chance to catch up. The grandkids all look adorable."

He would bet they had. Sandra had made a wonderful life for herself out here in Wyoming. "I would love to see them, and thank you so much for helping me out. I know I didn't have a right to ask you..."

"You hush," Sandra replied with a shake of her head. "I will always help you and I will always help Tag. But you should know you owe me. The kid's annoying. I put him in the back washing dishes so he didn't keep getting into fights with my customers."

"I'm sorry about that." Drake looked around and saw no sign of either of the people he'd come out here to pick up. "Is she here?"

"Your operative?" Sandra asked, one brow raised. "She's upstairs. She's not what I expected. I can definitely understand how she flies under the radar. I wouldn't view that woman as dangerous at all."

Sandra had been out of the game for too long. Constance Tyne was the most dangerous operative the CIA had produced. She was also the quietest. Almost no one had seen her face, which would make her perfect for the job she was going to do.

She would be his way into the lion's den. She would be how he took down The Consortium.

"Excellent, then we should get started."

Sandra nodded. "Go on back and see him. He'll show you up to your rooms, and I'll meet you for a debrief."

He should have known Sandra could handle anything he threw at her. He nodded and made his way past cowboys drinking longnecks and line dancing, toward the kitchen, where the music seemed to fade slightly. He walked past the grill and fry stations, past the waitresses and cooks. Back to the station where the lowliest of the workers toiled.

Kyle Hawthorne turned and frowned his way. "I fucking hate

343

you."

The feeling was often mutual. "It's time."

Kyle wiped his hands on the towel at his waist. "Then let's go kill her."

It wasn't going to be that easy.

But it was time to take down the most ruthless villain he'd ever met.

His sister, Julia.

Drake followed Kyle upstairs, ready to begin.

Drake and the whole Masters and Mercenaries team will return in *No Time to Lie.*

Author's Note

I'm often asked by generous readers how they can help get the word out about a book they enjoyed. There are so many ways to help an author you like. Leave a review. If your e-reader allows you to lend a book to a friend, please share it. Go to Goodreads and connect with others. Recommend the books you love because stories are meant to be shared. Thank you so much for reading this book and for supporting all the authors you love!

No Time to Lie
Masters and Mercenaries: Reloaded, Book 4
By Lexi Blake
Coming September 13, 2022

A grandmaster of lies and deception

Drake Radcliffe has spent half his life in the shadows. Recruited by the CIA when he was barely out of high school, Drake doesn't know how to have a normal life. While most people his age were playing sports or video games, he was playing spy games with the world's most dangerous adversaries. It has been a life filled with thrills and adrenaline, but it's also been lonely. All that might change when a mistake from Drake's past rears its ugly head and he's forced to face the only woman he ever loved—the one he pushed away.

A beacon of love and compassion

Taylor Cline committed the cardinal sin for an analyst—she fell for the operative she was working for. Drake was everything she wanted in a man, until he broke her heart. She had one unforgettable night with him and then he never looked back. Her career threatened, she shut down and moved on, hoping to never see him again. Just as she is beginning to put it all behind her, a critical assignment puts her under his authority and right back in his arms.

A deadly mission that brings them together

From the wilds of Wyoming to the glittering cities of Europe, Drake and Taylor must race against time to uncover the truth and expose an evil organization. The stakes couldn't be higher. If they fail, the world could crumble. If they succeed, they could finally have everything their hearts desire.

Delighted

Masters and Mercenaries, Book 24.5
By Lexi Blake
Coming June 7, 2022

Brian "Boomer" Ward believes in sheltering strays. After all, the men and women of McKay-Taggart made him family when he had none. So when the kid next door needs help one night, he thinks nothing of protecting her until her mom gets home. But when he meets Daphne Carlton, the thoughts hit him hard. She's stunning and hardworking and obviously in need of someone to put her first. It doesn't hurt that she's as sweet as the cupcakes she bakes.

Daphne Carlton's life revolves around two things—her kid and her business. Daphne's Delights is her dream—to take the recipes of her childhood and share them with the world. Her daughter, Lula, is the best kid she could have hoped for. Lula's got a genius-level intelligence and a heart of gold. But she also has two grandparents who control her access to private school and the fortune her father left behind. They're impossible to please, and Daphne worries that one wrong move on her part could cost her daughter the life she deserves.

As Daphne and Boomer find themselves getting closer, outside forces put pressure on the new couple. But if they make it through the storm, love will just be the icing on the cake because family is the real prize.

About Lexi Blake

New York Times bestselling author Lexi Blake lives in North Texas with her husband and three kids. Since starting her publishing journey in 2010, she's sold over three million copies of her books. She began writing at a young age, concentrating on plays and journalism. It wasn't until she started writing romance that she found success. She likes to find humor in the strangest places and believes in happy endings.

Connect with Lexi online:

Facebook: Lexi Blake
Twitter: authorlexiblake
Website: www.LexiBlake.net
Instagram: authorlexiblake/

Lightning Source UK Ltd.
Milton Keynes UK
UKHW012356060622
404005UK00001B/72